SHOCK WAVE

SHOCK WAVE

JOHN SANDFORD

DOUBLEDAY LARGE PRINT HOME LIBRARY EDITION

G. P. PUTNAM'S SONS, NEW YORK

This Large Print Edition, prepared especially for
Doubleday Large Print Home Library, contains
the complete, unabridged text of the original
Publisher's Edition.

PUTNAM

G. P. Putnam's Sons
Publishers Since 1838
Published by the Penguin Group
Penguin Group (USA) Inc., 375 Hudson Street,
New York, New York 10014, USA

Penguin Books Ltd, Registered Offices: 80 Strand,
London WC2R 0RL, England

ISBN 978-1-61793-025-6

Printed in the United States of America

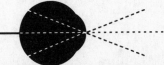

This Large Print Book carries the
Seal of Approval of N.A.V.H.

I wrote this book in cooperation with my friend David Cronk, a schoolteacher, golf professional, politician, Catholic catechism instructor, sometime actor—the Nazi in *The Sound of Music*—and longtime thriller-novel enthusiast. Dave and I have played several hundred rounds of golf, mostly at the Clifton Hollow golf course outside River Falls, Wisconsin. Soon after we began playing together, I noticed his talent for fiction: scores, stories of golf-course heroics, his attractiveness to women, etc. Dave, in fact, gave me my most valuable golf tip, one that will lower the score of even the worst duffer; that is, always carry an extra ball in your pants pocket. He is NOT the model for the golf-pro schoolteacher in this novel; any passing resemblance is purely coincidence.

—JOHN SANDFORD

SHOCK WAVE

1

From the boardroom windows, high atop the Pye Pinnacle, you could see almost nothing for a very long way. A white farmhouse, surrounded by a scattering of metal sheds, huddled in a fir-tree windbreak a half mile out and thirty degrees to the right. Another farmhouse, with a red barn, sat three-quarters of a mile away and thirty degrees to the left. Straight north it was corn, beans, and alfalfa, and after that, more corn, beans, and alfalfa.

Somebody once claimed to have spotted a cow, but that had never been confirmed. The top floor was so high that the board members rarely even saw birds, though every September, a couple of dozen turkey vultures, at the far northern limit of their range, would gather above Pye Plaza and circle through the thermals rising off the concrete and glass.

There were rumors that the vultures so pissed off Willard Pye that he would go up to the roof, hide in a blind disguised as an air-conditioner vent, and try to blast them out of the sky with a twelve-gauge shotgun.

Angela "Jelly" Brown, Pye's executive assistant, didn't believe that rumor, though she admitted to her husband it *sounded* like something Pye would do. She knew he hated the buzzards and the saucer-sized buzzard droppings that spotted the emerald-green glass of the Pinnacle.

But that was in the autumn.

On a sunny Wednesday morning in the middle of May, Jelly Brown got to the boardroom early, pulled the drapes to let the light in, and opened four small vent windows for the fresh air. That done, she went around the board table and at each chair put out three yellow #2 pencils, all finely sharpened and equipped with unused rubber erasers; a yellow legal pad; and a water glass on a PyeMart coaster. She checked the circuit breakers at the end of the table to make sure that the laptop plug-ins were live.

As she did that, Sally Humboldt from food services brought in a tray covered with cookies, bagels, and jelly doughnuts; two tanks of hot coffee, one each of regular and decaf; and a pitcher of orange juice and one of cranberry juice.

The first board members began trickling in at eight forty-five. Instead of going to the boardroom, they stopped at the hospitality suite, where they could get something a little stronger than coffee and orange juice: V-8 Bloody Marys were a favorite, and screwdrivers—both excellent sources of vodka. The meeting itself would start around nine-thirty.

Jelly Brown had checked the consumables before the board members arrived. She'd put an extra bottle of Reyka in the hospitality suite, because the heavy drinkers from Texas and California were scheduled to show up.

A few minutes after nine o'clock, she went back to the boardroom to close the windows and turn on the air-conditioning. Sally Humboldt had come back with a tray of miniature pumpkin pies, each with a little pigtailed squirt of whipped cream and a birthday candle. They always had pie at a Pye board meeting, but these were special: Willard Pye would be seventy in three days, and the board members, who'd all grown either rich or richer because of Pye's entrepreneurial magic, would sing a hearty "Happy Birthday."

Jelly Brown had closed the last window when she noticed that somebody had switched chairs. Pye was a man of less than average height, dealing with men and even a couple of women on the tall side, so he liked his chair six inches higher than standard, even if his feet dangled a bit.

She said, "Oh, shit," to herself. Almost a bad mistake. Pye would have been mightily pissed if he'd had to trade chairs with somebody—no graceful way to do that. She then made a much worse mistake: she pulled his chair out from the spot at the corner of the table and started dragging it around to the head of the table.

The bomb was in a cardboard box on the bottom shelf of a credenza on the side wall opposite the windows. When it detonated, Jelly Brown had just pulled the chair out away from the table, and that put her right next to the credenza. She never felt the explosion: never felt the blizzard of steel and wooden splinters that tore her body to pieces.

Sally Humboldt was bent over a serving table, at the far end of the room. Between her and the bomb were several heavy chairs, the four-inch-thick tabletop, and the four-foot-wide leg at the end of the table. All those barriers protected her from the blast wave that killed Jelly Brown and blew out the windows.

The blast did flatten her, and broken glass rained on her stunned, upturned face. She didn't actually hear the bomb go off—had no sense of that—and remembered Pye screaming orders, but she really wasn't herself until she woke up in the hospital in Grand Rapids, and found her face and upper body wrapped in bandages.

The bandages covered her eyes, so she couldn't see anything, and she couldn't hear anything except the drone of words, and a persistent, loud, high-pitched ringing. For a moment she thought she might be dead and buried, except that she found she could move her hands, and when she did, she felt the bandages.

And she blurted, "God help me, where am I? Am I blind?"

There were some word-like noises, but she couldn't make out the individual words, and then, after a confusing few seconds, somebody took a bandage pad off her left eye. She could see okay, with that eye, anyway, and found herself looking at a nurse, and then what she assumed was a doctor.

The doctor spoke to her, and she said, "I can't hear," and he nodded, and held up a finger, meaning, "One moment," and then he came back with a yellow legal pad and a wide-tipped marker and wrote in oversized block letters: *You were injured in an explosion. Do you understand?*

She said, "Yes, I do."

He held up a finger again and wrote: *You have temporarily lost your hearing because of the blast.* Another page: *You have many little cuts from glass fragments.* Turned the page: *Your other eyelid is badly cut, but not the eye itself.* Another page: *Your vision should be fine.* Another: *You also suffered a minor concussion and perhaps other impact injuries.* Finally: *Your vital signs are excellent.*

"What time is it?" she asked. The light in the room looked odd.

5 o'clock. You've been coming and going for almost 8 hours. That's the concussion.

There was some more back-and-forth, and finally she asked, "Was it a gas leak?"

The doctor wrote: *The police believe it was a bomb. They want to talk to you as soon as you are able.*

"What about Jelly? She was in the room with me."

The doctor, his expression grim, wrote: *I'm sorry. She wasn't as lucky as you.*

More or less the same thing happened all over again, three weeks later and four hundred and fifty miles to the west, in Butternut Falls, Minnesota. Gilbert Kingsley, the construction superintendent, and Mike Sullivan, a civil engineer, arrived early Monday morning at the construction trailer at a new PyeMart site just inside the Butternut Falls city limits.

Kingsley, unfortunately for him, had the key, and walked up the metal steps to the trailer door, while Sullivan yawned into the back of his hand three steps below. Kingsley turned and said, "If we can get the grade—"

He was rudely interrupted by the bomb. Parts of the top half of Kingsley's body were blown right back over Sullivan's head, while the lower half, and what was left of the top, plastered itself to Sullivan and knocked him flat.

Sullivan sat up, then rolled onto his hands and knees, and then pushed up to his knees and scraped blood and flesh from his eyes. He saw a man running toward him from the crew's parking area, and off to his left, a round thing that he realized had Kingsley's face on it, and he started retching, and turned and saw more people running. . . .

He couldn't hear a thing, and never again could hear very well.

But like Sally Humboldt, he was alive to tell the tale.

The ATF—its full name, seldom used, was the Bureau of Alcohol, Tobacco, Firearms and Explosives—instantly got involved. An ATF supervisor in Washington called the Minnesota Bureau of Criminal Apprehension and asked for a local liaison in Butternut Falls.

The request got booted around, and at an afternoon meeting at BCA headquarters in St. Paul, Lucas Davenport, a senior agent, said, "Let's send that fuckin' Flowers up there. He hasn't done anything for us lately."

"He's off today," somebody said.

Davenport said, "So what?"

2

Virgil Flowers was sitting on a bale of hay on a jacked-up snowmobile trailer behind Bob's Bad Boy Barbeque & Bar in North Mankato, Minnesota, watching four Minnesota farm girls duke it out in the semifinals of the 5B's Third International Beach Volleyball Tournament.

The contestants were not the skinny, sun-blasted beach-blanket-bingo chicks who played in places like Venice Beach, or down below the bluffs at Laguna and La Jolla. Not at all. These women were white as paper in January, six-three and six-four, and ran close to two hundred pounds

each, in their plus-sized bikinis. They'd
spent the early parts of their lives carrying
heifers around barnyards, and jumping up
and down from haylofts; they could get up
in the *air*.

Well, somewhat.

And when they spiked the ball, the ball
didn't just amble across the net like a bal-
loon; the ball *shrieked*. And the guys
watching, with their beers, didn't call out
sissy stuff like, *Good one!* or *No way!* They
moaned: *Whoa, doggy!* and "Let that ball
live. Have *mercy*!"

Of course, they were mostly dead drunk.

Sitting there in the mixed odors of saw-
dust and wet sand, sweaty female flesh
and beer, Virgil thought the world felt perfect. If it needed anything at all, nose-wise,
it'd be a whiff of two-stroke oil-and-gas
mixture from a twenty-five-horse outboard. That'd be heaven.

Johnson Johnson, sitting on the next
bale over, leaned toward Virgil, his forehead damp with beer sweat, and said,
"I'm going for it. She wants me."

"She *does* want you," Virgil agreed.

They both looked at one of the bigger women on the sand; she'd been sneaking glances at Johnson. "But you're gonna be helpless putty in her hands, man. Whatever she wants to do, you're gonna have to do, or she'll pull your arms off."

"I'll take the chance of that," Johnson said. "I can handle it." He was a dark-complected man, heavily muscled, like a guy who moved timber around—which he did. Johnson ran a custom sawmill in the hardwood hills of southeast Minnesota. He'd taken his T-shirt off so the girls could see his tattoos: a screaming eagle on one arm, its mouth open, carrying a ribbon that said not *E Pluribus Unum*, but *Bite Me*; and on the other arm, an outboard motor schematic, with the name "Johnson Johnson" proudly scrawled on its cowling.

"Personally, I'd say your chances of handling it are slim and none, and slim is outa town," Virgil said. "She's gonna eat you alive. But you got no choice. The honor of the Johnsons is at stake. The *honor* of the Johnsons."

Virgil was thinner, taller, and fairer, with blond surfer-boy hair curling down over his ears and falling onto the back of his neck. He was wearing aviator sunglasses, a pink Freelance Whales T-shirt, faded jeans, and sandals.

They were just coming up to game point when his cell phone rang, playing the opening bars of Nouvelle Vague's "Ever Fallen in Love." He took the phone out of his pocket, looked at it, and carefully slipped it back in his pocket. It stopped after four bars, then started again a minute later.

"Work?" Johnson asked.

"Looks like," Virgil said.

"But you're off."

"That's true," Virgil said. "Hang on here, while I go lock the thing in the truck."

Johnson tipped the beer bottle toward him: "Good thinkin'," he said. And "Man, that's a lotta woman, right there."

The woman hit the volleyball with a smack that sounded like a short-track race-car collision, and Virgil flinched. "Be right back," he said.

As he walked down the side road to his truck, carefully stepping around the patches of sandburs, he was tempted to call Davenport. That would have been the right thing to do, he thought. But the day was hot, and the women, too, and the beer was cold and the world smelled so damn good on a great summer day. . . . And he was off.

The fact was, the only reason that Davenport would call was that somebody had gotten his or her ass murdered somewhere. Virgil was already late getting there—he was always the last to know—so another few hours wouldn't make any difference. The powers that be in St. Paul would want him to go anyway, because it'd look good.

He popped the door on the truck, dropped the phone on the front seat, locked the door, and went back to the 5B.

Virgil was based in Mankato, Minnesota, two hours southwest of St. Paul, depending on road conditions and the thickness of the highway patrol. He routinely covered the southern part of the state. On non-routine cases, he'd be picked up by Davenport's team and moved to wherever Davenport thought he should go.

A couple of hours after Davenport first

called, Virgil left Johnson at the 5B, romancing the volleyball player. Their attachment was such that Virgil would not be required to drive Johnson back to his truck, so he headed home, across the river into Mankato.

Once on the road, he picked up his phone and pushed the "call" button, and two seconds later, was talking to Davenport.

"We got a bomb early this morning," Davenport said. "One killed, one injured, in Butternut Falls. We need you to get up there."

"What's the deal?"

Davenport told him about the explosion and the casualties, and said that the ATF would be on the scene now, or shortly.

"I'll be on my way in an hour," Virgil said. "Wasn't there another PyeMart bomb, killed somebody in Michigan a couple weeks back?"

"Yeah. Killed one, injured one. If it'd gone off twenty minutes later, it would have taken out the board of directors along with Pye himself," Davenport said. "This guy is serious, whoever he is."

"But if he started in Michigan, he could

be a traveler. Unless we've got finger-prints or DNA."

"We've got two things on that," Daven-port said. "The first thing is, the explosives are tagged by the manufacturer. The ATF has already identified the tags in the Mich-igan bomb as Pelex, which is TNT mixed with some other stuff, and is mostly used in quarries. In April, somebody cracked a quarry shed up by Cold Spring—that's about an hour northeast of Butternut Falls—and two boxes of Pelex were taken. Other than the theft in Cold Spring, the ATF doesn't have any other reports of Pelex theft in the last couple of years. So, the bomber's probably local."

"Okay," Virgil said. "What's the other thing?"

"Butternut is having a civil war over the PyeMart. People are saying the mayor and city council were bought, and the Department of Natural Resources is being sued by a trout-fishing group that says some trout stream is going to be hurt by the runoff. Lot of angry stuff going on. Over-the-top stuff. Threats."

"There's runoff going into the Butternut? Man, that's not just a crime, that's a mortal sin," Virgil said.

"Whatever," Davenport said. "In any case, the DNR okayed their environmental impact statement. I guess they're already building the store."

"What else?"

"That's all I got," Davenport said. "Interesting case, though. I didn't want to take you away from your sheriff. . . ."

"Ah, she's out in LA, being a consultant," Virgil said. "Having dinner with producers. Guys with suits like yours."

"Sounds like the bloom has gone off the rose," Davenport said.

"Maybe," Virgil conceded.

"I can hear your heart breaking from here," Davenport said. "Have a good time in Butternut."

Virgil lived in a small white house in Mankato, two bedrooms, one and a half baths, not far from the state university. He traveled a lot, and so was almost always ready to go. He told the old lady who lived next door that he'd be leaving again, asked her to keep an eye on the place, and gave her a six-pack of Leinie's for her trouble. He packed a week's clothes into his travel bag, mostly T-shirts and jeans, put a cased shotgun on the floor of his 4Runner, along with a couple boxes of 00 shells, and stuck his pistol in a custom gun safe under the passenger seat, along with two spare magazines and a box of 9-millimeter.

A quick Google check said that Butternut Falls would be two hours away. He printed out a map of the town, and while it was printing, turned the air-conditioning off, checked the doors to make sure they were locked, and turned on the alarm system. On the way out, he thought, with his last look, that the house looked lonely; too quiet, with dust motes floating in the sunlight over the kitchen sink. Nothing to disturb them. He needed . . . what? A wife? Kids? More insurance policies? Maybe a dog?

When the truck was loaded and the house secure, Virgil pulled out of the driveway into the street, reversed, and backed up in front of his boat, which had been parked on the other side of the driveway. His fishing gear was already aboard. But then, it was always aboard. After a quick look at the tires, he hitched up the trailer, folded up the trailer jack, and took off.

He got fifty feet, pulled over, jogged back to the garage, opened a locker, took out a pile of fly-fishing gear, including a vest, chest waders, rod case, and tackle box, and carried them back to the truck.

Better to have a fly rod and not need it, than to need a fly rod and not have it. He climbed back in the truck and took off again.

Packing up and getting out of town took an hour, just as he had told Davenport it would. The sun was still high in the sky, and he'd be in Butternut well before sundown, he thought. The longest day of the year was just around the corner, and those days, in Minnesota, were long.

And he thought a little about the sheriff out in LA, Lee Coakley. She was still warm enough on the telephone, but she'd been infected by show business. She'd gone out as a consultant on a made-for-TV movie, based on one of her cases, and had been asked to consult on another.

And then another. Women cops were hot in the movies and on TV, and there was work to be had. Her kids liked it out there, the whole surfer thing. Just yesterday, she'd had lunch in Malibu . . .

Once you'd seen Malibu, would you come back to Minnesota? To the Butternut Falls of the world? To Butternut cops?

"Ah, poop," Virgil said out loud, his heart cracked, if not yet broken.

Virgil took U.S. 14 out of town, back through North Mankato and past the 5B, resisting the temptation to stop and see if Johnson Johnson was still alive. He went through the town of New Ulm, which once was—and maybe still was—the most ethnically homogeneous town in the nation, being 99 percent German; then took State 15 north to U.S. 212, and 212 west past Buffalo Lake, Hector, Bird Island, and Olivia, then U.S. 71 north into Butternut Falls.

Butternut was built at the point where the Butternut River, formerly Butternut Creek, ran into a big depression and filled it up, to form the southernmost lake in a

chain that stretched off to the north. Butternut's lake was called Dance Lake, after
a man named Frederick Dance, who ran
the first railroad depot in town, back in
the 1800s.

The railroad was still big in town, and
included a switching yard. The tracks ran
parallel to U.S. 12, which ran through the
town east to west, crossing U.S. 71 right
downtown. Butternut, with about eighteen
thousand people, was the county seat of
Kandiyohi County, which was pronounced
Candy-Oh-Hi.

Virgil knew some of that—and would
get the rest out of Google—because he
had, at one time or another, been in and
out of most of the county seats in the
state, also because he'd played Legion
ball against the Butternut Woodpeckers,
more commonly referred to, outside Butternut, and sometimes inside, as the
wooden peckers.

Virgil drove into Butternut at half past six
o'clock in the evening, in full daylight, and
checked into the Holiday Inn. He got directions out to the PyeMart site from a

notably insouciant desk clerk, a blond kid, and drove west on U.S. 12 to the edge of town. He passed what looked like an industrial area on the south side of the highway, crossed the Butternut River—a small, cold stream no more than fifty feet wide where it ran into the lake on the north side of the highway—then past a transmission shop. After the transmission shop, there were fields, corn, beans, oats, and alfalfa.

Most people, he thought, didn't know that alfalfa was a word of Arabic derivation. . . .

He was beginning to think that he'd missed the PyeMart site when he rolled over a low hill and saw the plot of raw earth on the south side of the highway, along with some concrete pilings sticking out of the ground. When he got closer, he saw the pilings were on the edges and down the middle of two huge concrete pads.

Everything else, including the soon-to-be parking lot, was raw dirt. A couple of bulldozers were parked at one edge of the site, and to the left, as he went in, he saw the construction trailer. There was a ring of yellow crime-scene tape around it, tied to rebar poles stuck upright in the dirt, to make a fence. Two sheriff's deputies, one of each sex, sat on metal chairs just outside the tape, in the sun, and watched Virgil's truck bouncing across the site.

Trailers on the plains are sometimes called "tornado bait," and this one looked like it'd taken a direct hit. Virgil had seen a lot of tornado damage and several trailer fires; one thing he realized before he'd gotten out of the truck was that as hard as this trailer had been hit, there'd been no fire. In another minute, he was picking out the difference between a bomb blast and a tornado hit.

A tornado would shred a trailer, twisting it like an empty beer can in the hands of a redneck. This trailer looked like a full beer can that had been left outside in a blizzard to freeze: everything about it looked swollen. A door had been mostly blown off and was hanging from a twisted hinge.

He climbed out of the truck and walked up to the trailer, and as he did that, the female deputy, who wore sergeant's stripes, asked, "Where do you think you're going?"

"Well, right here," Virgil said. He was

still in the pink T-shirt and jeans, although he'd traded his sandals for cowboy boots. He had a sport coat in the car, but the day was too warm to put it on. "I'm Virgil Flowers, with the BCA, up here to arrest your bomber."

Both deputies frowned, as though they suspected they were being put on. "You got an ID?" the woman asked. She was a redhead, with freckles, and a narrow, almost-cute diastema between her two front teeth. One eyelid twitched every few seconds, as though she were over-caffeinated.

"I do, in my truck, if you want to see it," Virgil said. "Though to tell you the truth, I thought I was so famous I didn't need it."

"It was a Virgil Flowers killed those Vietnamese up north," the male deputy said.

"I didn't kill anybody, but I was there," Virgil said. "The sheriff around? I thought this place would be crawling with feds."

"There're two crime-scene guys in the trailer," the female deputy said, poking a thumb back over her shoulder. "The rest of them are at the courthouse—they should be back out here any minute. The chief left us out here to keep an eye on things. I should have been off three hours ago."

"I was having a beer when they called me," Virgil said. "Watching some young women playing beach volleyball."

"That's better'n what I was going to do," the male said. "I was just gonna mow my yard."

They still seemed a little standoffish, so Virgil said, "Let me get you that ID."

He went back to the truck, got his ID case, came over, and flipped it open to show the woman, who seemed to be the senior cop. She nodded and said her name was something O'Hara, and that the other deputy was Tom Mack. Virgil stuck the case in his back pocket and asked, "So where'd this guy get killed? Right here?"

Mack nodded, and faced off to his left, pointed behind the yellow tape. "Right over there. You can still see a little blood. That's where most of him was. His head was over there—popped right off, like they do. There were other pieces around. The guy who was wounded, he soaked up quite a bit of the body."

"He still in the hospital?" Virgil asked.

"Yeah, he was crazy hysterical, I guess," O'Hara said. "He's not right yet. They gave him a bunch of drugs, trying to straighten him out. Not hurt bad. Can't *hear* anything, but there're no holes in him."

At that moment, a business jet flew overhead, low, and Mack said, "That must be Pye. Willard T. Pye. They said he was coming in."

"Good, that'll help," Virgil said.

O'Hara showed a hint of a smile and said, "Nothing like a multibillionaire looking over your shoulder, when you're trying to work."

"So, you said the guy's head popped off, *like they do*," Virgil said to Mack. "You know about bombs or something? I don't know anything."

Mack shrugged. "I did two tours in Iraq with the Guard. That's what you always heard about suicide bombers—they'd pull the trigger, and their heads would go straight up, like basketballs. Think if there's a big blast, and you're close to it, well, your skull is a pretty solid unit, and it hangs together, but it comes loose of your neck. So . . . that's what I heard. But I don't really know." He looked at O'Hara. "You hear that?"

"Yeah, I think everybody did. But maybe it was from some movie. I don't know that it's a fact."

"You in the Guard, too?" Virgil asked.

She nodded. "Yeah, I did a tour with a Black Hawk unit. I was a crew chief and door gunner."

"I did some time in the army, but I was a cop, and never had much to do with bombs," Virgil said. They traded a few war stories, and then Mack nodded toward the road. "Here comes the VIP convoy. That'd be the sheriff in front, and that big black Tahoe is the ATF, and I don't know who-all behind that. They've been having a meeting at the courthouse."

"Good thing I'm late," Virgil said. "I might've had to go to it. . . . You got media?"

"Yeah, and there they are," O'Hara said. "Right behind the convoy. Tell you what, and don't mention I said it, but you don't want to be standing between the sheriff and a TV camera, unless you want cleat marks up your ass."

Virgil saw a white truck, followed by another white truck, and then a third one. "Ah, man. I forgot to wash my hair this morning."

"Forgot to bring your gun, too," Mack said.

"Oh, I *got* a gun," Virgil said. "I just forgot where it is."

The Kandiyohi County sheriff was a tall beefy Swede named Earl Ahlquist, a known imperialist. Four years past, he'd pointed out to a money-desperate city council that there was a lot of police-work duplication in Kandiyohi County, and they could cut their policing costs in half by firing their own department and hiring him to do the city's police work. There was some jumping up and down, but when the dust settled, the two departments had merged and Ahlquist was king.

Ahlquist climbed out of his car, nodded at Virgil, and said, "I hate that shirt."

"It's what I wear on my day off," Virgil said. "How you doing, Earl?"

"Other than the fact that a guy got murdered this morning, and we got a mad bomber roaming around loose, and I missed both lunch and dinner, and I'm running on three Snickers bars and some Ding Dongs, I'm just fine."

"I had some pretty good barbeque and a few beers this afternoon, before I was called on my day off," Virgil said. "I was watching some good-looking women play beach volleyball."

"Yeah, yeah, I got it. This is your day off. Tough titty," Ahlquist said. He turned to the crowd coming up behind him. "You know Jack LeCourt? He's our top man here in the city. Jack, this is Virgil Flowers from the BCA, and, Virgil, this is Jim Barlow, he's with the ATF outa the Grand Rapids field office, he's been working the first bomb up in Michigan. . . . This is Geraldine Gore, the mayor."

The sheriff made all the introductions and they all shook hands and had something to say about Virgil's pink shirt, and then O'Hara said, "We got a jet just landed at the airport, Chief. I think Pye's here."

"Aw, man," Barlow said. He was a tall

dark man, with hooded dark brown eyes, salt-and-pepper hair, and a neatly trimmed black mustache. He was wearing khaki slacks, a blue button-down shirt, and a dark blue blazer.

"He hasn't been that much help?" Virgil asked.

"First thing he did was offer a one-million-dollar reward leading to the arrest and conviction," Barlow said. "Then he gave his secretary's family a two-million-dollar gift from the company, and gave the food-service lady, who was cut up, a quarter-million-dollar bonus. All the millions flying around meant he got wall-to-wall TV, and every time he went on, he bitched about progress. When we told him what we were doing, he leaked it. When I heard about this bomb, I thought, *Now we're getting somewhere. At least we know where the guy's from.* But you watch: it'll be wall-to-wall TV here, too, in about fifteen minutes."

"I can handle that. No need for you to get involved," Ahlquist said, and from behind his back, O'Hara winked at Virgil.

Virgil said, "So, as the humblest of the

investigators here . . . can somebody tell me what happened?"

The mayor unself-consciously scratched her ass and said, "I'd like to know that myself."

3

Barlow knew his bombs.

The explosive, he said, had the same characteristics as the first one, so he was assuming that it was again the stuff called Pelex, as in the Michigan bomb. "That's basically TNT, which is 2,4,6-trinitrotoluene. To make Pelex, they mixed in about fifteen percent aluminum powder, which makes the TNT faster—increases the speed with which it develops its maximum pressure."

"To give you a bigger pop," Virgil said.

"Exactly. The bomber put this stuff, I think, inside a good-sized galvanized steel plumbing pipe," Barlow said. "The pipe was sitting on the floor, just inside the door. The trigger could have been something as simple as a string down from the handle to a mousetrap."

"Mousetrap?"

"Yes." Barlow gestured at the techs working inside the trailer. "We found a wire spring that looks like it came from an ordinary mousetrap. We don't know if there were mousetraps set inside the trailer to catch mice, but it would have been an effective way to fire the switch on the bomb. You get a battery, an electric blasting cap, a switch worked through the mousetrap, and there you go. Move the door, fire the mousetrap, and boom."

"That sounds dangerous . . . to the bomber," Ahlquist said.

"You'd need good hands," Barlow agreed. "The bomb in Michigan used a cheap mechanical clock as a switch, and was a lot safer. But that was a time bomb, and this was a trigger-set. Of course, we haven't found all the pieces of the switch here. . . . It might not have been all that dangerous. For example, there could be a safety switch in the circuit that wasn't as touchy as the mousetrap. So he'd set the trap, and then only close the safety switch when he was sure the mousetrap was solid and he was on his way out."

"So is that sophisticated, or unsophisticated?" Virgil asked.

"Interesting question," Barlow said. "We occasionally run into guys who are bomb hobbyists and take a lot of pride in building clever detonation circuits. Using cell phones, and so on. They're nuts, basically, but their engineering can be pretty clever. These bombs look as if they're made by a guy working from first principles. That is, he doesn't know the sophisticated ways of wiring up a weapon like this, but he's smart enough to figure out some very effective ways of doing it. That means—this is just my opinion—that he's a guy who learned how to build bombs for this single mission. He's not bombing things to hear the boom and make his weenie hard, he's bombing PyeMart because he's got a grudge against PyeMart."

"How much of this Pelex stuff did he steal?" asked LeCourt, the chief of police. "Is he done now, or has he got more?"

"If he took it from the Cold Spring

quarry, which we think he did, he's got enough to make maybe fifty or sixty of these," Barlow said.

"Oh my Lord," said Ahlquist. He looked at Virgil. "You better get him in a hurry."

"What are the chances that he'll find out he likes it?" Virgil asked. "That he'll go from grudges, to getting his weenie hard?"

"That happens," Barlow said. "The thing is, he's nuts. Whether he's killing because he likes to kill, or because he's got a grudge, either way, he's nuts. And nuts tend to evolve toward greater violence."

Barlow had more to say about the bomb and the technique, and from what he said, Virgil came to two conclusions: (a) building an effective bomb was not rocket science, once you had the explosive and some blasting caps, and (b) the killer was smart.

They continued to talk for fifteen minutes or so, and stuck their heads inside the trailer, which looked as though somebody had attacked it with a sledgehammer and a lot of time. When Barlow began to run out of new information, Virgil drifted over to Ahlquist and said, "I'll buy you dinner if you're hungry."

"I'm starving to death. Let's go up to Mable Bunson's—today's Fish Monday."

Virgil got directions to the restaurant, and they were all about to get back in their trucks, leaving the trailer to the ATF technicians, when a white stretch limo eased out of the street and onto the beaten-down dirt track to the trailer.

"That's the prom limo," Ahlquist said.

"Gotta be Pye," said Gore. She added, "I've never seen that limousine in the daylight."

The limo bumped nervously over the last few feet, and then a short heavyset man popped out of the second door behind the driver. He was wearing a blue chalk-striped suit over a golf shirt, a Michigan Wolverines ball cap, and an angry look. One second later, the second door opened on the other side, and a tall, thin woman climbed out. She had honey-blond hair worn loose to her shoulders, eyes that were either green or brown, wore a tweed suit and a tired look, and carried a note-book.

"That's Mr. Pye," Barlow said, and he went that way and said, "Mr. Pye—I didn't realize you were planning to come out."

"Of course I came, you damn fool. One of my people's dead," Pye snapped, as he walked up. His face appeared to be per-manently red and frustrated. "When the hell are you gonna get this nut? It's been two weeks and we've seen nothing."

Barlow said, "We're focused on it, and this new bomb tells us a lot. We now be-lieve we're dealing with a man from here in the Butternut Falls area. We're coordi-nating with the Kandiyohi sheriff's depart-ment and the state Bureau of Criminal Investigation."

"Apprehension," Virgil said.

"Sounds like more bullshit to me," Pye interrupted. "Is this the trailer? Holy crap, it looks like the Nazis bombed it." He said gnat-zees. "Where's the hospital here? Is this boy Sullivan still there? Has Mrs. Kingsley got here yet? I hear she got hung up in Detroit, plane was delayed or she got bumped or some crap like that. I'm talking to the CEO of Delta, he's seeing what he can do, but it don't seem like much."

Barlow and Ahlquist took turns answering questions, and introduced LeCourt and Virgil. As they were doing that, Virgil noticed that the tall woman was taking notes, in what looked like shorthand; O'Hara was watching her with one eye closed, like a housewife in a butcher shop, inspecting a suspect pork chop. Pye looked at Virgil's shirt and asked, "What the hell's these Freelance Whales?"

Ahlquist jumped in: "It's a band. Virgil rushed up here on his day off, didn't have time to change."

Pye turned back to Barlow and LeCourt, and the sheriff caught Virgil's eye and tipped his head toward the trucks. They started drifting that way, until Pye said, "Whoa, whoa, where're you going? We've got some planning to do."

"We're going to go investigate," Virgil said. "If I need to talk to you, I'll let you know."

"Hey: this is my goddamn building going up here, and my people got hurt and killed," Pye said. "I want to know what the crap is going on here, and you're gonna tell me or I'll call somebody up and tell them I need a new investigator."

Virgil nodded, slipped his ID case out from his pocket, took out a business card, and scrawled Davenport's office number on it. "This is my boss. Call him up and tell him you need a new investigator."

"That don't worry you, huh?" Pye cocked an eye at him.

"Not much," Virgil said. "Davenport will either tell you to kiss his ass, or, if you're important enough, he'll pass you on to the governor, who'll tell you to kiss his ass. So either way, somebody'll tell you to kiss his ass, and I'll keep investigating."

Pye frowned. "Huh. Your goldanged governor's got almost as much money as I do, and it's older." He scratched his head, then asked, "How long will it take you to catch this nut?"

He and Virgil were now almost toe to toe, and the woman was still taking notes, writing at such a pace that it had to be verbatim.

Virgil looked at his watch, scratched his cheek, then said, "I can't see it going much more than a week."

Pye nodded. "All right. You get me this guy in a week, and I *will* kiss your ass." To the woman, he said, "You got that? One week and I kiss his ass."

"I got it," she said. Her eyes flicked to Virgil: "Good luck, Mr. Flowers. I'll prepare an appropriate ceremony."

Virgil thought, *Hmm.* But then, his sheriff had been in Hollywood for a while.

Ahlquist and Virgil went on to their trucks, and Virgil followed the sheriff out of the parking lot. Virgil had worked with Ahlquist a couple of times, to their mutual satisfaction. A former highway patrolman turned to politics, Ahlquist probably knew half the people in the county on sight, and, since the sheriff's department ran the jail, all of the bad ones. As a politician, he'd know all about any local pissing matches over the PyeMart site.

Mable Bunson's Restaurant and Cheesery was on the other side of the Butternut downtown from the highway, all the way through the business district to the lake, and then a couple blocks down the waterfront. A solid brick building with a peaked roof and small windows, it looked as though it might have been a rehabbed train station; it turned out, when Virgil asked the hostess, that it was a rehabbed bank.

Ahlquist got a booth in the back, a couple places away from the nearest other customers. Ahlquist ordered a bourbon and water, Virgil got a Leinie's, and as they started through the menu, Virgil said, "I hear you're still fighting over the PyeMart."

"*I'm* not fighting over it," Ahlquist said. "But there's sure as shit some questions floating around. The mayor was against it, but then she says she saw the youth unemployment figures, and she does an about-face and now she's all for it. We got seven city councilmen, six against and one in favor, and somehow, time passes, and four are in favor and only three against."

"You're saying that they might have been encouraged to change their positions."

"*I'm* not saying that, but some people are. And not in private. One of the councilmen, Arnold Martin, lived here all his life, doesn't have a pot to piss in. Never has had. He's worked retail since he got out of high school, he's now a stock manager out at a car-parts place. Him and his wife took a winter vacation last February, took off in their car and went to Florida, Arnold says. The Redneck Riviera. But the rumor is, they went to Tortola and took sailing lessons, and this spring they've got a nice little sailboat out on the lake. Not a big one, and it was used, but, it's a sailboat."

"You look into it?"

"Not the Tortola part. But I was chatting with a guy over at Eddie's Marine, and he said the former owner wanted fourteen grand for the boat. It's called a Flying Scot, it's two years old, and I'm told it's got a high-end racing rig. I had one of my deputies, who can keep his mouth shut, talk to the former owner, and he said Arnold financed it through the Wells Fargo. I got a friend *there*, and I found out Arnold *did* finance half of it, over three years, and he's been making regular cash payments on the deal."

"So what does that make you think?" Virgil asked.

"What it made me think was, Arnold got some money from somewhere, but wasn't dumb enough to just go plop it down on a boat," Ahlquist said. "He financed the boat, and is making payments out of the stash."

"That's not very charitable of you," Virgil said. "Maybe he saved the money."

"And maybe the mold on my basement door will turn out to be a miracle image of Jesus Christ, but I doubt it," Ahlquist said.

A waitress dropped a basket of bread on the table, took their orders, and Ahlquist got another bourbon.

Virgil said, "So there might be a little informal economic assistance going on . . . but the bombs wouldn't be coming from those guys. The bombs would be coming from somebody who *doesn't like* those guys. So who would that be?"

"If I knew, I'd be on them like lips on a chicken—but I don't know," Ahlquist said. "There's always been rumors that this-or-that councilman or county commissioner took a little money under the table, for doing this-or-that. Who knows if it's true? Impossible to prove."

"But this is different."

Ahlquist nodded. "It is. See, Virgil, you know about these big-box stores all over the place. You get a bunch of them in a small town, and it can wreck the place. Drive out half the merchants, and their families, who always made decent livings, and the downtown dies. In exchange you get a bunch of minimum-wage jobs. You hollow out the town. Well, we're big enough that we could take a Walmart and a Home Depot. It hurt, but we took it. People adjusted. You throw in a Pye-Mart, which is a little more upscale, and it doesn't leave people with anywhere to adjust."

He shook his head. "A lot of these folks are going to lose their businesses. Going to lose their livelihoods. Some of them have been here a hundred years, their grandfathers and great-grandfathers started their companies. They're bitter, they're angry, they've said some crazy things."

"Crazy enough that there might be a bomber amongst them?"

"Yeah, that's one place he could be

coming from," Ahlquist said. "Then, there's the trout-fishing cranks."

"Careful," Virgil said.

Ahlquist grinned at him. "I know. I see you're dragging your boat. Anyway, the Butternut runs a half mile or so behind the PyeMart site, and then makes a big loop down to the south, and then comes back north and runs into town. Some people think that the runoff from the Pye-Mart parking lot is going to pollute their precious crick. If it does, it'd be the whole bottom two miles, before it runs into the lake. That's the best part, I'm told. Some of the trout guys, they were screaming at the council meetings. They were completely out of control."

"Could I get some names?" Virgil asked.

"Sure. I can get you a list. People you can go around and talk to."

"If I'm gonna handle this fast enough to get my ass kissed, I'll need the list pretty quick."

Ahlquist nodded, fished in his over-sized uniform shirt pocket, and pulled out a black Moleskine reporter's notebook. "I can give you a good part of it right now.

I'll think about it overnight, and give you the rest tomorrow."

"Works for me," Virgil said. He slid down in the booth a bit, yawned, and asked, "So how's your old lady?"

"Pretty damn unhappy right now, since the housing bust," Ahlquist said. He wrote a couple names in his notebook. "She can find people who want to buy, and people who want to sell, but the buyers are having a hell of a time getting loans. Goddamn banks."

"Maybe she could just find a place to sit down and chill out for a while," Virgil suggested. He'd eaten several partial dinners with Ahlquist's wife; she was eternally on her way to somewhere else.

Ahlquist snorted: "Like that's going to happen. Woman hasn't sat down for fifteen minutes since she got her real estate license. Five years ago, it was glory days. You could sell a shack on the lake for the price of a castle. Now you can't sell a castle on the lake for the price of a shack."

"Somebody's going to make money out of that situation," Virgil said.

"You're right," Ahlquist said. "Just not none of us."

They spent the rest of the meal chatting about life, speculating about the bomber and the nuts Ahlquist knew, and which of them had both the brains and the motive to get into, and then blow up, the board-room at the Pye Pinnacle. "That there's a tough question," Ahlquist said. "I was talk-ing to Barlow about that, and he said that penetrating that building took time, plan-ning, and maybe an insider."

"You give a list like this to Barlow?" Vir-gil asked.

"No, and he hasn't actually asked for one. He's more of a technical guy, going at it from the computer end. He cross-references stuff. That could work; and maybe not. He's not so much of a social investigator, like you," Ahlquist said.

"I didn't even know that's what I was," Virgil said.

Virgil got back to the Holiday Inn after dark. He unloaded the loose stuff in his boat, locked it in the back of the truck, dug his pistol out of his gun safe, and carried both the pistol and the shotgun into the motel room. A pistol was as good

as money on the street; he was deter-
mined not to contribute.

When he was settled in, he looked at
the clock—nearly ten—and called Lee
Coakley, in Los Angeles. He and Coakley
had been conducting a romance for six
months or so, until a production company
began making a TV movie about Coakley's part in breaking up a huge, multi-
generational child-abuse ring in southern
Minnesota. Coakley, as the local sheriff,
had been the media face on the whole
episode.

The production company had rented
an apartment for her in West Hollywood,
for the duration of the shoot. The duration had recently lengthened, and Coakley had grown evasive on the exact time
of her return.

So Virgil called, and her oldest son,
David, answered the phone. "Uh, hi, Virg,
Mom's, uh, at a meeting of some kind. I
don't know when she's getting home."

He was lying through his teeth, Virgil
thought; he was not a good liar. Mom
was somewhere with somebody, and you
probably wouldn't go too far wrong if you
called it a date. "Okay. I've got a deal I'm

working on, out of town—a bomb thing. I'm going to bed. Tell her I'll try to give her a call tomorrow."

"Yeah, uh, okay."

Virgil hung up. Little rat. Of course, she *was* his mother. If you wouldn't lie for your mom, who would you lie for?

Virgil took off his boots, shut off all the lights except the one in the bathroom, lay on his bed, and thought about his conversation with Ahlquist. The bomber almost certainly had a direct tie to some of the protesters—either the people whose livelihoods were threatened by the PyeMart, or the trout freaks.

Of the two, he thought the businessmen were more likely to produce a killer. Some of the people who'd lose out to PyeMart would move from prosperity to poverty, and virtually overnight. Businesses, homes, college plans, comfortable retirements, all gone. How far would somebody go to protect his family? Most people wouldn't even shoplift, much less kill. But to protect his family . . . and all you needed was one.

And then the environmentalists . . .

Virgil had a degree in ecological science, and was a committed green. But he'd met quite a few people over the years who'd come into the green movement from other, more ideologically violent movements—people who'd started as anti-globalization protesters, or tree-spikers as opposed to tree sitters, who thought that trashing a McDonald's was a good day's work, people who talked about Marx and Greenpeace in the same sentence.

The greenest people Virgil knew were hunters and fishermen, with Ducks Unlimited and Trout Unlimited and Pheasants Forever and the Ruffed Grouse Society, and the Conservancy and the National Wildlife Federation and all the rest, people who put their money and their time where their mouths were; but these others . . .

There could be a radical somewhere in the mix, somebody who had twisted a bunch of ideologies all together and decided that bombs were an ethical statement.

A guy sitting home alone, the blue glow of the Internet on his face, getting all tangled up with the other nuts out there, honing himself . . .

Again, all it took was one.

Before he went to sleep, Virgil spent a few minutes thinking about God, and why he'd let a bomber run around killing people, although he was afraid that he knew the reason: because the small affairs of man were of not much concern to the All-Seeing, All-Knowing. Everybody on earth would die, sooner or later, there was no question about that: the only question was the timing, and what would time mean to a timeless Being?

But a bomb brought misery. A nice quiet death at age eighty-eight, with the family gathered around, not so much.

He'd have to read Job again, he thought; not that Job seemed to have many answers.

Then he got up, peed, dropped on the bed, and was gone.

4

The bomber sat in his basement—it had to be a basement—looking at the stack of bombs. He'd already packed the Pelex, which had a rather nice tang about it: like aftershave for *seriously* macho dudes. He'd packed in the last of the blasting caps, which looked a bit like fat, metallic ballpoint pen refills, and he'd already wired up all the batteries except the last one, because he was afraid of that one: afraid he'd blow himself up.

He'd given himself two missions this night: the first would be to take out the water and sewer pipe the city was planning to run out to the PyeMart, as well as the heavy equipment that'd be used to lay the pipe.

The second one . . .

For the second attack, he needed a bomb that would blow with motion—and since he didn't have access to sophisticated detonators, he'd made do with an old mercury switch. To use it, he'd have to do the final wiring on-site, in awkward conditions, wearing gloves, with a flashlight in his mouth. Possible, but tricky.

The trickiness gave him a little buzz. If anything went wrong, of course, he'd never know it, with his face a foot from the bomb. When they identified him, wouldn't they be surprised? Wouldn't they wonder?

Made him smile to think about it.

The bomber was slender and tough and smart. He worked out daily, ninety minutes at a time. He had a sense of humor, he often looked in a mirror and thought, *Pretty damn good.*

But pretty damn good wasn't enough.

Time was passing; he wasn't old, but age would come, and then what? Twenty years on Social Security? There were very limited opportunities ahead, and he had to seize the ones that presented themselves.

And there was the competitive aspect to the challenge: Could he beat the cops and the federal government? He knew they'd all come piling in when the bombs started going off.

He shook off the intrusive thought, and picked up the latest bomb, and turned it in his hands. Very, very simple; and deadly as a land mine.

Not particularly delicate, though. He'd read that he could mold the Pelex into a ball and whack it with a golf club, with no effect. The blasting caps were a little more sensitive, but no more so than ordinary shotgun primers, which tens of thousands of people had sitting around in their houses—there were whole racks of them at sporting goods stores.

No, the pieces were essentially inert, until they got put together. Then, watch out.

He'd taken hours to make each of the first few bombs, until he got some traction. He'd done his research on the Internet, and figured out his materials. He'd cracked the supply shed at Segen Sand & Gravel in the middle of the night and removed the cases of Pelex and the boxes of blasting caps. He'd been sweating blood when he did that, his first real crime, creeping around the countryside in camo and a mask. After all the planning and preparation, and after an aborted approach when a couple kids parked in the quarry entrance to neck, the break-in had been routine. The explosives shed had been secured with nothing more than a big padlock.

He'd found the bomb pipe under a cabin at a lakeside resort, where it had been dumped years before, when the owner put in plastic pipe. He got that at night, too, and had taken it down to the college for the cut. *That* had taken a little gall, but he hadn't committed himself to anything at that point, and when the cutting went off without a hitch, he was good. If he'd been caught, he would have said he was making fence posts, and then started over. . . .

His first bombs were small. He didn't need a big bang to know that they worked. When he finished building them, he'd taken them out in the country, deep in the woods, buried them, and fired them from fifty feet away, with a variety of triggers. There'd been a thump, which he'd felt more than heard, but the thump had proved the pudding: he could do it.

The bombs worked.

After that, the bomb-making was the least of it. Everything he needed to know about switches he could find on the Internet, with parts and supplies at Home Depot.

Getting into the Pye Pinnacle had been simple enough; in fact, he'd done it twice, once, in rehearsal, and the second time, for real.

Having the bomb go off too early . . .

He'd made the assumption that a ferociously efficient major corporation would have run their board meetings with the same efficiency. When he learned that the board members had been in the next room drinking—the Detroit newspaper hadn't said they were drinking, but had implied it clearly enough—he'd been more disgusted than anything, even more disgusted than disappointed. What was the world coming to? Cocktails at nine o'clock in the morning? All of them?

The second bomb, planted at the construction site, had been much, much better. Everything had gone strictly according to plan. He'd come in from the back of the site, carrying the bolt cutters, the pry bar, a flashlight, and the bomb. In his bow-hunting camo, he was virtually invisible.

The trailer had two doors: a screen door, not locked, and an inner wooden door, which was locked. He'd forced the inner door, cracking the wood at the lock. Inside, he'd set up the bomb in the light of the flashlight. When he was ready to go, he'd flashed the light once around the inside of the trailer, and caught the reflection off the lens of a security camera.

There had been no effort to hide it. If it worked in the infrared . . .

He was wearing a face mask, another standard bow-hunting accessory, but he disliked the idea of leaving the camera. He walked back to it, got behind it, and pried it off the wall. A wire led out of the bottom of it, and he traced it to a closet, and inside, found a computer server, which didn't seem to have any connection going out.

The server was screwed to the floor, but the floor was weak, and he pried it up and carried both the server and the camera outside.

The rest of it had taken two minutes: he placed the bomb on the floor next to the door, reaching around the door, and then led the wires from the blasting cap under the door, and then closed the door.

The switch was a mousetrap, a method he'd read about on the Net. One wire was attached to the spring, the other to the top of the trap's wooden base. A piece of fish line led from the trap's trigger to the inside doorknob on the screen door. When the door was opened, the trap would snap, the two ends of the copper wire would slam together, completing the circuit, and *boom*.

Which was exactly what happened.

He remembered walking away from the

trailer, thinking about the lottery aspect of it: Who would it be, who would open the door? Some minimum-wage asshole hired to pour the concrete? Or maybe the building architect?

He'd tracked through the night, enjoying himself, until he got to the river. The camera and server were awkward, carrying them with all the tools he'd brought for the break-in, pushing through the brush along the track. He listened for a minute, then threw the server and the camera out into the middle of the river, a nice deep pool, and continued through the dark to his car.

He had the technique, he had the equipment, he had the balls.

Thinking about the earlier missions, he smiled again.

This night would take perhaps even more balls, and he looked forward to it. Creeping through the dark, wiring it up . . .

One thing: if a single dog barked, he was out of there. The first target was on the edge of town, not many people around. He'd spotted a parking place, at the side of a low-end used-car lot, a block away from the target. There were no cameras at the lot; he'd scouted it carefully. He could park the car, making it look like one of the used cars, cross the road into a copse of trees, and sit there for a bit and watch. Then he'd walk through the trees and across a weedy vacant lot, right up to the target car.

And that's what he did, at two o'clock in the morning, dressed in camo, with a bomb in a backpack, a gun in his pocket. He'd already killed, and if the owner of the house caught him planting the bomb, he'd shoot him and run for it. Nothing to lose.

The night was warm, for early June, when it could still get cold; but not this night. He left the car, as planned, sat in the trees and listened and watched: a small town, trucks braking on the highway, or speeding up as they headed out; the stars bright overhead; no sirens or dogs to break the silence.

He could see the target car, sitting across the vacant lot like Moby-Dick:

there'd been no sign of activity from the house next to it. He gave it the full half hour, then began a slow stalk across the lot.

He was a deer hunter, a stalker rather than a sitter, and he knew how to move slowly. He took ten minutes to cross the hundred-foot lot. He was satisfied that even if there'd been a dog, it wouldn't have heard him.

At the car, he sat and listened, one full minute, letting his senses extend into the night, and then he slid beneath it, next to the axle. He'd taped the end of a deer hunter's LED flashlight, so only a single LED could shine through: a red one.

After looking the situation over, he decided the most reasonable thing would be to tape the bomb to the hydraulic line that led toward the back of the car. He did that, fumbling with the tape in the dark, until it was solid. He made sure that the thermostat bulb was hanging straight down, checked it twice—if he got it wrong, he'd be a rapidly expanding sphere of bloody cellular matter. When everything was right, he pulled the circuit wires down the car for a couple feet, looped them

around another fluid line, then twisted together the wires that would complete the
circuit.

The bomb was live.

He eased out from under the car and,
once clear, looked up into the night sky at
the billions and billions . . .

Felt comfortable there, in the smell of
the night, the odor of gas and oil, the
presence of death.

Like, he thought, *Ka-boom.*

Time to move.

The second site wasn't quite as big a
deal, in terms of risk, though it was a lot
more work. The site was in a warehouse
district on the backside of town, and there
was a spot where he could park his car,
off the road, where it wouldn't be seen.
There was a fence, but he had the cutters
with him. In his scouting trips, he'd seen
no cameras.

He timed the traffic until he was alone,
made the turnoff, pushed back into the
trees. Got out and listened again. Nothing.

The construction yard was a two-minute walk through the brush to the back fence, but he had twenty-two bombs to move, and they were heavy. He took them five at a time, in a Duluth pack. He cut through the fence with the bolt cutters, and was in.

His target was the water and sewer pipe that would be used to feed the PyeMart.

The water pipe was stacked across the construction yard, in bundles, five pipes high, five pipes wide, made out of some kind of blue plastic stuff. The sewer pipe was reddish brown, and seemed to be of some kind of ceramic, though he could be wrong. He had the bombs in place after four trips, then made a fifth trip for the firing harness, the batteries, and the two bombs he'd use on the shovel and the pipe-layer. He used lantern batteries for the heavy-equipment bombs, and an old car battery for the pipes. Three mechanical alarm clocks would serve as switches. The clocks were ready to go.

It took almost an hour before he was finished wiring up the bombs—longer than he'd expected, but within his planned limits: and he was very, very careful, tracing and retracing his work.

When he was done, he carefully, carefully set the three clocks to trip in two hours, which would be a little after five-thirty in the morning. Two of them would take out the heavy equipment, the third would wreck most of the pipe, he thought. He was a little unsure about that, so he made the bombs bigger than he might otherwise have. He would have liked to watch the handiwork, but that would be too risky.

When he was finished, he squatted next to the fence and thought about it for a minute, scanning the yard. Had he left anything behind? He inventoried his gear: everything was there. He'd probably have left footprints, but there were footprints all over the yard, and the area around the fence was covered with heavy weeds, so there wouldn't be much for the police to work with.

Don't go yet, he thought. *What are you forgetting?*

Thirty seconds later, satisfied that he

was good, he walked out of the construction yard and back to his car. He took off the camo jacket and mask, threw them on the floor of the backseat. A minute after that, satisfied that no traffic was coming, he was back on the road.

He didn't drive home—he worried that the neighbors might hear him come in. Instead, he drove down toward the Twin Cities, to an all-night diner off I-494, and had breakfast.

At five thirty-five, halfway through a stack of pancakes and sausage, he looked at his watch, smiled, and closed his eyes, and said to himself, for the second time that night,

Ka-boom.

5

The bombs in the two pieces of heavy equipment went off first, in quick sequence, *boom . . . boom*. A few seconds later, the pipes went, the whole bunch fired with a single impulse from the car battery: *BOOM*.

Virgil heard the motel windows flex and rattle, but barely woke up; from his bed, it might have been a motel door slamming. Instead, he rolled over, facedown, and fell deeper into sleep.

The bombs were heard by most of the people awake at that hour, but because there was nobody in the equipment yard, and the yard was away from any main streets, and no businesses were really open yet, nobody knew quite where the blasts had come from, until they saw the dust.

There was no fire, but there was a lot of dirt in the air. A cop drove down the street toward the dust cloud, which had formed a mushroom, not quite certain of where he was going until he got there. When he got there, he was not quite certain of what he was seeing. There was still a lot of dust in the air, but the corrugated-iron equipment building was still standing, and looked fine.

Not until he walked down the length of chain-link fence to peer into the yard, and saw the pipe strewn around like jackstraws, did he understand what had happened—and even then, he didn't realize that the two large pieces of heavy equipment had been turned into a pile of scrap, frames bent, engines dismounted, transmissions ruined. He did see that two windows had been blown out on the back of the building, and when he looked across a narrow street, more seemed to be missing from a sign-company building.

The deputy called back to the city station. The duty officer woke up the sheriff, who said he'd be along, and said to call Virgil. A minute later, the sheriff called back and told the duty officer to call Barlow, as well.

A phone doesn't ring before six in the morning unless there's trouble. Virgil woke, checked the clock, said, "Man . . ." and picked up the phone. The duty officer said, "We've got a bomb out at the city equipment yard. Blew up some pipe. Agent Barlow is on his way out."

"Anybody hurt?"

"Don't know for sure, but I don't think so. I don't think anybody was out there."

"How do you get there?" Virgil asked.

The duty officer gave him instructions, and he rolled out of bed, put on yesterday's clothes, and then headed out. The morning was crisp, the sky was a flawless blue: a good day, not counting the bombing.

A bunch of patrol cars and a few civilian vehicles were lined up on the road beside the equipment yard when Virgil got there. He ID'd himself to the deputy standing by the entrance, then walked through the equipment building and out the back door, where he found the sheriff, Barlow, a couple of civilians, and two or three other deputies looking at the wreckage.

Virgil asked Barlow, "Anybody hurt?"

Barlow shook his head. One of the civilians, who apparently was with the public works department, said, "Our budget took a hit. I gotta look at our insurance. We'll get most of the money back, but not all of it. He blew up our shovel and the pipe-layer, along with the pipe. I don't think the pipe can be saved; it's all screwed up."

Virgil stepped over to a pile of the blue pipe: some kind of plastic, he thought. Most of the pipes had been blown in half and had split lengthwise. Somebody said to his back, "I was outside and heard it. It sounded like an atom bomb."

"At least he wasn't going after people," Ahlquist said.

Barlow said to Virgil, "This is something new, though. We've counted at least sixteen separate explosions, and there are probably more than that. They went off more or less simultaneously, so he was working a seriously complicated firing apparatus. He's getting more sophisticated."

"The practical effect is . . . what?" Virgil asked the civilian. "If you guys got insurance, he delays you for a week or two?"

"Longer than that. More like a couple of months," the civilian said. "Even if we go with emergency bid procedures, there's a lot of bureaucracy to go through. Then, we've got to get the stuff shipped in from Ohio, and we've got to retrain the operators on the new equipment. . . . It'll be a while."

"But it won't stop the building."

The civilian shook his head. "No. Not unless everybody gets too scared to work. I've got to tell you, I'm getting a little nervous, and so are the other guys."

They stood around and talked about it for a while, and Barlow said that he was going to ask for another technician.

"How's it going at the trailer?" Virgil asked. "Find anything?"

"Finding all kinds of things, just nothing that'll get us to the bomber," the ATF agent said. "Not so far, anyway. There supposedly was some kind of security system, but it either got torn apart in the explosion, or the bomber took it with him."

"Huh. If he took it with him, he'd have had to spend some time inside."

Barlow nodded. "Be pretty bold. And you'd have to ask, why? If you're sneaking around with a big goddamned bomb under your arm, it's not like you'd be more noticeable if you wore a mask. So why not wear a mask?"

"You think there might have been something else that was identifiable?"

"Could be," Barlow said. "Maybe something about his size, like he's really fat, or maybe he's got a disability, a limp or a missing arm, or maybe he's six-eight or something. But if we don't find that camera, and we haven't found anything like it, then we sort of wonder why."

"How about a camera mount?"

"Should be one, can't find it," Barlow said. "We were hoping the video was cycled out to the Internet, but it wasn't that sophisticated. It apparently was fed through a wire to a digital server, which cycled every twenty-four hours. The recorder might still be there, somewhere, but we haven't found it yet. Now we got this one to work. . . ."

Virgil looked around at the mess, shook his head. "Good luck with that."

Barlow gestured toward the metal building, and they stepped away from the group looking at the blown shovel. Barlow said, quietly, "Listen . . . I spent some time talking to the sheriff last night, and he says you're pretty much the BCA's golden boy. That's fine with me. I've got no connections with the locals. I can do all the technical stuff, but nobody's gonna sit around and eat macaroni and cheese with me and tell me what's what. So I gotta lean on you."

"I can work with that," Virgil said. "If you could get me what you find . . ."

"You'll know in ten minutes," Barlow said.

"Good. I've already got some people I need to talk to—I'm going to do that now."

"Keep me up," Barlow said. "The trailer bomb was a big break, though that sounds awful, with the dead guy and all. If the bomber had kept trying up in Michigan, we'd have never figured out where he was from. Hell, an hour after the bomb went off, we were ankle-deep in Homeland Security and FBI guys. They wanted to investigate every Arab in the state, and there are something like a half million of them. This is a little more manageable."

Virgil nodded. "Yeah. Not a hell of a lot of Arabs around here. Maybe a few, but a lot more Latinos."

"I'll tell you something else, Virgil. These guys do one or two bombs, and it gives them a serious sense of importance," Barlow said. "We see it when we catch them and debrief them. They're usually people who feel like they should be important, but they aren't. When the bomb goes off, they get all kinds of attention, and they're all kinds of important . . . and they don't want to quit. It's like cocaine:

the high goes away after a while, and they want another hit."

"You're telling me he's going to do it again," Virgil said.

"He made a whole batch of bombs for this attack. I wouldn't be surprised if we got another one tonight. Something else: he's got enough material to blow up a building. If he decides to go big, he could turn the city hall into a pile of brick dust."

"That's not good," Virgil said.

They exchanged cell-phone numbers, and e-mails, and then Virgil headed back downtown to the motel.

Virgil had heard of the ticking-time-bomb theory of building up stress in the movies—Bruce Willis rushing around New York to keep the schools from blowing up—but this was ridiculous. Now *he* had a ticking time bomb, and the biggest expert around said that more were on the way.

At the motel, he got cleaned up, put on clean clothes, and headed to Bunson's, the restaurant.

At Bunson's, the hostess said, "I'll buy that shirt if you want to sell it."

Virgil was wearing his most conservative musical T-shirt, a vintage Rolling Stones "Tongue" that he'd found on America's Fence. "I'm sorry, I have an emotional attachment to it," Virgil told her. "I was wearing it when my third wife told me she wanted a divorce."

"Oh, well, in that case . . ." She smiled, and led him back to a booth overlooking the lake.

He had the sweet-butter pancakes with bacon and maple syrup; at eight-thirty, which was still way too early, he called Davenport at home. "I hope this is a goddamn emergency," Davenport said, when he picked up the phone.

"The guy just set off at least sixteen bombs at once, and wrecked God-only-knows how much stuff," Virgil said. "I'm told it was like an atomic bomb going off."

"Ah, jeez. Tell me."

Virgil filled him in, and when he was done, Davenport asked, "You got media?"

"We had media, and now we're gonna

get a lot more," Virgil said. "This thing is really blowing up, if you'll excuse the rapier-like wit."

"So talk to the sheriff, have a press conference, emphasize that you're making progress, that you expect arrests. That you've got some kind of forensic evidence. Say that because of the interstate aspect, the killer can be tried in federal court and get the death penalty. Give the bomber a reason to hunker down, to be careful, to think about it. Try to buy some time."

"A pageant. Good idea," Virgil said. "The sheriff likes the whole television routine. I'll get him to organize it."

"I never had much to do with bombers, but this Barlow sounds like he knows what he's talking about—and it sounds like a lot of the other freaks we've seen. They like it. You better catch this guy, Virgil."

"I'll catch him. I just can't guarantee that the city hall will still be standing up," Virgil said. "Talk to you tomorrow."

Virgil called Ahlquist—the sheriff was still out at the equipment yard—and told him about Davenport's idea for a press conference. Ahlquist jumped on the idea and said he'd set it up. "I've been working on the rest of your list, all morning. I'll give it to you at the press conference," Ahlquist said. "Or you can stop by anytime."

"It's a mess out there, isn't it?" Virgil asked.

"Oh, yeah. Is it gonna get worse?"

"Barlow thinks so," Virgil said.

Virgil dug out the list of contacts that Ahlquist had given him the night before. Ahlquist had suggested that he talk first to Edwin Kline, one of the three city councilmen who voted against PyeMart, and a pharmacist. Ahlquist said that Kline had been on the city council for twenty years, and had been mayor for twelve, and knew all the personalities. "Since he's a pill-pusher, people talk to him, like they would a doctor. He knows what's going on in their heads."

Virgil found Kline in his drugstore on Main Street, introduced himself, waited for two minutes until he'd finished rolling some pills for a single customer, and then followed him to a backroom office.

Kline was an older, balding man in his late fifties or early sixties, with glittering rimless glasses and a soft oval face. He wore a white jacket like a doctor, and pointed Virgil into a wooden swivel chair that might have been taken from a nineteenth-century newspaper office, while he sat on a similar chair behind his desk.

"There's some pretty damn mad people in town, and I know all of them—heck, I'm one of them—but I don't know which one is crazy enough to do this," he said.

"I don't know exactly how to ask this," Virgil said, "or where the ethics come in . . . but of all those angry people, do you know which ones might be using anti-psychotics? Or who should be?"

"Mmm." Long hesitation. "You know, it probably *would* be unethical to give you that information, though I don't doubt you could get a subpoena. Just between you, me, and the doorpost, I'd tell you if I thought one of them was the bomber. But the people I know of, who are getting that kind of medication, are not really involved in this whole thing. I suppose they could be picking up some reflected anger. . . . If you want to come back this afternoon, and if you don't let on where you got it, I could get together a list."

"If you'd prefer, I could get Sheriff Ahlquist to give you a subpoena, just to cover your butt, if there were any questions," Virgil said.

"That might be best—but I'll get started on the list," Kline said. "You ought to go out to Walmart and check with them, too. They roll a lot more pills than I do, now."

Virgil asked him who he'd have been most worried about, of the angry people. Kline thought for a moment, then said, "Well, there are about three of them. And goddamnit, now, I have to live in this town, so this has to be between you and me."

"That's fine," Virgil said. "Nobody needs to know where the names came from."

Kline slid open a desk drawer, pulled out a pack of Marlboros, and said, "I can't have people seeing me smoking. I only smoke a couple a day. . . . Come on this way." He led Virgil out of the office, through a stockroom, up an internal stair to the roof, where four chairs, an umbrella, and a two-foot-tall office refrigerator were sitting on a deck.

Kline took a chair, lit up, blew a lungful of smoke, and said, "First up would be Ernie Stanton. Ernie's a redneck, a hard worker. Doesn't show it, but he's smart. He started out with nothing, and now he owns two fast oil-change places. Ernie's Oil. He got hurt when Walmart came in. They've got that Lube Express thing. But Ernie's faster and just as cheap, so he got hurt, but he hung on. I don't think he'll get past PyeMart. He's a guy with a temper, he's a hunter, he's got guns and all that, and he's spent thirty years scratching his way up. Done a lot of roughneck work—might know about dynamite. He's gonna lose his livelihood. He's gonna lose it all."

Virgil made a note of the name. Kline had two others, both businesspeople. Don Banning, who ran a clothing store selling work clothes; he'd also been hurt by Walmart, but he'd moved to somewhat higher-end stuff, brand names that Walmart didn't carry. "As I understand it, PyeMart carries the same brands he does. He won't be able to match the prices," Kline said.

The least likely one, in Kline's opinion, was a woman named Beth Robertson, who ran the Book Nook. "She says she's gone. She's gonna try to make it through Christmas—PyeMart won't open until spring—but then she's getting out. But she's crazy mad about it. The bookstore is her life. She swings back and forth between this cold acceptance, planning to sell out, and this red-hot screaming anger. It's like watching somebody who just found out they got terminal cancer. The thing is, she's mad enough, but I don't think she could work a hammer, much less make a bomb. She's the kind who doesn't understand how a nut and bolt go together."

"Any more?" Virgil asked.

"Well, there's me," Kline said. "I'm done. I'm gonna retire, sell out the store while I can still get some money for it. Got a good location, maybe somebody'll think of something they can do here."

"Sorry to hear that," Virgil said.

"Nothing lasts forever," Kline said. "I

can't match the big boys when it comes to peddling pills, and I'm not even sure that's a bad thing. People already pay too much for medicine. And, my kids are gone, they're not interested in the store, and I've got some money. I think my wife and I might move up to the Cities. Buy a condo, go to some plays, that kind of thing. Be useless old farts for a while. Then die."

Virgil said, "As a city councilman . . . you might have noticed that there were some unusual vote changes on the PyeMart zoning."

Kline snorted, and smoke came out of his nose. "No kidding? Where'd you hear that?"

"You know . . . around."

"Those boys got bought, is what happened," Kline said. "Three of them, anyway. The fourth one, he thinks PyeMart's a good idea: jobs for kids and low prices. They didn't have to buy him. Those other three, Pat Shepard, Arnold Martin, Burt Block . . . well, they're not exactly friends of mine, but I've known them for a long time. And I've got to say, they'd take the money. That's my bottom line on them.

They'd take the money. I doubt that you could prove it."

"I'm gonna have to talk to them," Virgil said. "They could be targets."

"You haven't asked about the mayor. Geraldine."

"What about her?"

"Geraldine was probably the bag man on the whole deal. Bag woman. She's the one who talked the others into it. She is the personification of greed," Kline said. "As mayor, she had a veto, and then it would have taken five votes to override her. But that's not what happened."

"She buy a new house?" Virgil asked.

"No, nothing like that. She's not dumb. I can tell you what I suspect—my theory. Her husband has a seasonal business, renting out golf carts, and selling some."

"That's not an everyday business," Virgil said.

"Well, it's not uncommon, either," Kline said. "Probably a couple of them in every big city, the cart rental businesses. You get these golf courses, they have week-end tournaments, and they don't have enough carts of their own—so, they rent from Dave Gore. He pretty much services a tournament every weekend, is the way I hear it. It's a legitimate business."

"So what's your theory?" Virgil asked.

"This could just be bs. But: I was up in the Cities two weeks ago, and stopped in a Goodwill store to drop off an old chest of drawers," Kline said. "There's a PyeMart right there, and as I was pulling out, here comes a PyeMart employee, driving across the parking lot in what looked like a brand-new golf cart."

"Hmm."

"That's what I said: Hmm. Wikipedia says there are two thousand four hundred PyeMart stores in the U.S., and about one thousand one hundred in other countries. If you bought a new golf cart for only one store in ten, and bought them through Dave . . . that'd be a nice little chunk of change. Just about invisible. Not only that, if you're PyeMart, you'd have the golf carts, and even a business write-off."

"You got any proof?" Virgil asked.

"Proof? Hell, all I got is an idea, from driving past a PyeMart store." Kline snubbed out his cigarette, and snapped it off the roof into the alley behind the store. "I gotta get back. Who knows, a customer might wander in."

They stood up and Virgil looked across the top of the building, out onto the lake. A single sailboat cruised a few hundred feet off the waterfront, and Virgil asked, "That's not, uh . . ." He dug in his memory, found the name. ". . . Arnold Martin, is it?"

Kline looked out at the sailboat and said, "Nope. I'd say Arnold's boat is about half that big."

Back downstairs, Virgil thanked Kline for his time, and Kline asked, "Was I any help?"

"Well, you know, the possibility of municipal corruption is always interesting, if you're a cop," Virgil said. "But it's not the PyeMart supporters who are blowing stuff up. Not the crooks on the city council. I'll probably go around and talk to some of these people you told me about."

"Let me add a name to your list: Larry Butz. He's one of the trout guys. He said publicly that we had to stop the PyeMart any way we could. This was in a city council meeting, and Geraldine jumped right on him and said something like, 'You don't mean that; we're civilized people here.' And Butz said, 'I did mean it. We got to do anything we can.'"

"Good guy? Bad guy?"

"Not a bad guy. But I happen to know that he's taken a pretty wide variety of anti-depression and anti-anxiety pills. He has some problems."

"Thanks for that," Virgil said. "I'll stop by later and get the rest of the list."

"Get me a subpoena and get one for Walmart, too," Kline said. "I don't want people thinking I'm a rat."

Virgil's next stop was at city hall, where he talked to Geraldine Gore, who had an office the size of the smallest legal bedroom. With just enough space for a desk, four file cabinets, two visitor chairs, and an American flag, she pointed him at one of the two chairs, but didn't seem all that excited to see him.

Gore was a short woman, but wide, the kind who might have stopped a hockey puck without moving too much. She had stiff magenta hair over mousy brown eyebrows, and suspicious blue eyes.

She said, "I have to tell you, I have no idea what this is about."

Virgil pushed his eyebrows up: "Well, it seems simple enough. You guys approved PyeMart, a lot of people think it'll damage the town and its environment."

"That's nonsense," she snapped.

"So what?"

She frowned: "What do you mean, so what? We had environmental impact statements, we had economic studies—"

Virgil interrupted what threatened to become a PowerPoint presentation. "I mean, it may be nonsense, what people think—but they think it anyway. One of them apparently is so mad about it that he's killing people. As a potential target, I'd think you'd be pretty anxious to get this straightened out."

"I'm not a target—"

"Tell that to the bomber," Virgil said. "You're the one single person who could have stopped the PyeMart, if you'd vetoed the city council's approval of the zoning change. You didn't. The feds think the bomber is probably already building his next bomb, and thinking about a target. Between you and me, they say that if he put all the explosive he's got into one bomb, he could reduce the city hall to flinders."

"Flinders?"

"You know. Bits and pieces."

"That's nonsense." She looked around her office, suddenly nervous. "This building . . . this building . . ."

"Mrs. Gore, this Pelex explosive is used in quarries," Virgil said. "It turns solid rock into *gravel*."

She looked at him for a moment, then said, "The two people you should talk to are Ernie Stanton and Larry Butz. They are completely irrational about this. I can get you their addresses."

"I've already got them," Virgil said. "Who else?"

Virgil came away with four names that he hadn't had before: eight names altogether; but she'd named all the people mentioned by Kline.

He'd decided to start with Stanton, and was walking down to his truck, when another bomb went off.

6

Virgil had heard bomb-like devices explode in the past. In the army's Officer Candidate School, he'd thrown four hand grenades at a wooden post, while standing inside a concrete trench, and later watched from behind a thick Plexiglas screen while other members of his training unit threw more. He'd also had the opportunity to pop off a few rounds from an M203 grenade launcher.

When the bomb went off—it was somewhere close by, and behind him—he had no doubt what it was. He turned and saw people running along a street two blocks away, got in his truck, and went that way, in a hurry.

The first thing he saw when he turned the corner was a wrecked white stretch limo, half of it a smoking ruin. The limo was sitting sideways in the street, and a man in what looked like a doorman's uniform was crawling away from it on his hands and knees.

Virgil got as close as he could, outside the blast zone, parked, and ran over to the limo and looked inside. It was empty; finding it empty was like having a boulder lifted off his chest. The man in the dark uniform had reached the curb, and he rolled over and sat down, his hands covering his ears.

Virgil hurried over to him—there were sirens now, and they were coming his way—squatted and asked the man, "You the driver?"

"Look what they done to my car," the man moaned.

"Where's Pye and his assistant?"

"Down at the AmericInn. I was just going to get them," the driver said. He was looking at the car. "No way that can be fixed."

Virgil looked at the car: the bomb, he thought, had been in the vehicle's small trunk, and had blown off most of the back third of it. The middle third was still there, but was a shambles, with all the glass blown out, the seats uprooted and thrown against the back of the driver's compartment. Anyone seated behind the driver would have been killed, or badly injured.

"I think you're right," Virgil said. "Hope you got insurance."

"That was my baby," the driver said.

"You'll get another one," Virgil said. "It coulda been a hell of a lot worse."

The driver said, "Yeah, and you know how? Oh my God, I stopped down the street, two blocks back, to let the kids go by on a field trip. Little kids from the elementary school, looked like they were going to the library. If that'd gone off . . . there must've been fifteen of them."

A thin young man in a dress shirt and a necktie ran up, stopped a few steps away, peered at them over a weedy mustache, whipped out a camera and took a picture of the driver and Virgil sitting together, with the wrecked limo in the background.

"I'm with the *Clarion Call*," he said, running the last few steps up. "Harvey, what'd you think when the bomb went off?"

"Hey, you're walking all over the goddamned crime scene," Virgil said. "Back off."

"Who the hell are you?" the reporter asked.

"With the BCA," Virgil said.

"Ah, Flowers. Have you made any progress?"

A deputy came running up, glanced in the car, then said to the reporter, "Larry, get the fuck outa here."

The reporter backed away, brought the camera out again. The deputy asked Virgil and the driver if they were hurt, and Virgil said, "I just got here—I'm with the BCA."

The cop was impressed: "Boy, you got here in a hurry, huh?" He stood up as another car came up and shouted, "Block off the street. Route the traffic around. Keep those people away from here."

Virgil took a break from the driver to call Barlow. "You hear the bomb go?"

"What?"

Virgil told him about it, and Barlow

said, "Have them freeze the site. I'll be there in five minutes."

Virgil passed the word to the first deputy, then a fire truck arrived, and another one, and an ambulance, and two or three more cop cars. The whole area smelled of burned tar and leaking oil—there didn't seem to be any gasoline. Virgil went back to the driver, who said his name was Harvey Greene. Greene kept the limo at his house. "I park it right beside the house."

"Are you the only white limo in town?"

"I'm the only white limo in the county," Greene said. "Some more come in for the prom and so on, but I'm the only one that's right here."

"How hard would it have been to get in your trunk?" Virgil asked.

"I don't think it was in my trunk," Greene said.

"You don't? It looks to me like—"

Greene shook his head. "Number one, nobody touches my car that I don't know about it. If I'm not in it, it's locked. If he'd jimmied my trunk, I would have heard. I park that baby right outside my bedroom. Number two, when I go out, the first thing I do is, I walk around the car with a spray bottle and a rag, and wipe it down. There was no sign anybody had been in the trunk."

"If he had a key—"

"There're two keys. One's still in the ignition, and one's in the console. I saw it this morning: I always check to make sure I've got the spare, so I don't hang nobody up if I do something stupid and lose the one in my pocket. Whoever it is, he had to put the bomb in last night: I didn't know but yesterday afternoon that Mr. Pye was coming in."

The red-haired woman deputy, O'Hara, walked around the car, looking at it, then ambled over to Virgil and Greene and put her hand on Greene's knee: "You okay, Harvey?"

"Yeah, I'm okay."

"So what do you think?" Virgil asked. "How'd this happen?"

"I think somebody snuck up to my house with a bomb and some duct tape, and taped it to the rear axle, or something else down there. I never look *under* the car. Maybe I should," Greene said.

Virgil patted him on the back. "You're a pretty smart guy, Harvey. I think you're probably right. We'll see what the feds have to say about it."

Virgil stood up and O'Hara said, "The bomber knows his way around. Harvey lives out on the edge of town, and there's not much out there. If he was seen, people out there will remember."

"Makes me think he probably wasn't seen."

O'Hara nodded. "Why'd he blow up those pipes? That won't stop anything."

"If you come up with an answer, let me know," Virgil said.

Barlow arrived, looked at the car, and agreed that Greene was probably right— the bomb had been under the car, rather than in the trunk. If anyone had been sitting in the rearmost seat, he would have vaporized.

Barlow had left one of the crime-scene techs at the construction trailer, while the other one worked the city maintenance yard. When the sheriff arrived, he asked for, and got, two deputies to guard the bombed-out trailer, and ordered that tech into town to work the limo.

To Greene, he said, "As soon as I've got this place settled down, we'll go over to your house and take a look at where you parked the car. That'll be another crime-scene site. Is there anybody out there now? Your wife . . . ?"

"Not married anymore," Greene said. He added, "And now, I'm unemployed."

The perimeter of the bomb scene had turned into a circus: a hundred people had gathered to watch and more were coming in. There was a pizza place across the street, and slices were beginning to circulate. Then Pye showed up with his assistant, and when Barlow saw them arguing with a deputy, he said to Virgil, "You handle Pye better than I do. Be a good guy, and go over and talk to him."

Virgil walked over and said to the deputy, "Let them through, will you? My responsibility."

Pye came through and said, curtly, "Thank you. And thank the good Lord that I wasn't in that car. That would have really screwed up my whole happy hour."

Virgil told him what he knew, which wasn't much. "Barlow can probably tell you about a detonator, but you can see . . . they were trying to kill you, man."

"No kidding." Pye raked his lower lip with his upper teeth a few times, looking thoughtfully out at the blast zone, then said to his assistant, "Pye spoke to Flowers for a minute, getting the lay of the land, then resolved to hunt down this monster no matter what it took."

She took it down in shorthand, and Virgil asked, "Are you writing a book?"

"I take down everything Mr. Pye says," the woman answered.

"Is that possible?" Virgil asked.

"Barely," she said.

"She damned well better get it all," Pye said. "I pay her enough."

"Barely," she said.

When Barlow saw that Pye had calmed down, he came over, nodded, and said, "No sign of the detonator, but the guy's getting more sophisticated. He must've used a mercury switch, or a roll ball, or maybe even an accelerometer of some kind. Something that would set it off with movement. Not a mousetrap or a timer."

"Could you track it?" Pye asked.

Barlow shook his head: "It's pretty common stuff. The thing is, you could take a mercury switch out of a fifty-year-old thermostat, wire it up on a pipe bomb, and when the car hits a big enough bump, the mercury gets thrown up on the contacts and boom!"

Virgil said, "That would assume that the guy knew that Mr. Pye would be in Greene's limo today, which he couldn't have known before yesterday afternoon at the earliest. He had to manufacture the bomb and get it in place before dawn. So he had what, less than twelve hours? And, he had to know where Greene lives, and how to approach the car."

"Local guy for sure," Barlow said. "A smart guy, with good intel."

"Maybe there's more than one," Pye suggested.

"I don't think so," Virgil said. "Nuts don't come in bunches. Only grapes do."

Pye said to his assistant, "Put in your

notebook that I said that. The grape-nuts thing."

Pye wanted a closer look at the car, and Barlow said, "I'll take you over there, but I'd rather your assistant didn't come along. I'll talk to you as a courtesy, but I don't want anything written down. It'll wind up in court, with me being cross-examined because I used the wrong adjective or something."

Pye agreed, and they walked over to the car, and the woman said to Virgil, "You are a tall drink of water."

"You're pretty much of an ice cream cone your own self," Virgil said. "What're you doing working for Pye?"

"Oh, I do it for the money," she said. "It's not uninteresting."

"Huh. I notice you say 'uninteresting,' rather than 'disinteresting,'" Virgil said.

"That's because I have at least an eighth-grade education," she said. "And Willard pays me for my grammar."

"I wouldn't do it for a million bucks a year," Virgil said.

"Neither would I," she said.

Virgil: "Are you serious?"

"Yes. I'm selling him three years of my life," she said. "He pays me one-point-two, which is about point-seven-two per year, after state and federal, plus all expenses. For that, I follow him around everywhere, take down everything he says, verbatim, and provide him with both the original text and a polished narrative. In another year, I'll have a bundle tucked away. Then I'll write a tell-all book about him, and make another bundle."

"I guess it's a plan, though I'm not sure that many people would read a tell-all book about a short fat guy," Virgil said.

"How about a short fat guy with thirty-two billion dollars?"

"Maybe," Virgil said. "I personally wouldn't buy it."

"Since you're not going to buy my book, why don't you buy me a margarita tonight?"

"Who should I ask for?"

"Marie Chapman. Room one-nineteen at the AmericInn." She got off around seven o'clock, right after Pye finished dinner, she said. "Give me until eight."

"Are your eyes green or brown?" Virgil asked.

"Depends on my body temperature," she said. "As I get hotter, they turn greener."

They chatted for another two minutes, trying out movie lines on each other—"I'm outa here like a cool desert breeze," she said, when Pye walked back toward them—and then Virgil wandered off into the crowd. He knew nothing about bombs, so standing around looking at a bent wheel didn't seem likely to produce either a clue or a bomber. The crowd, he thought, might be a different story. There was some chance that the bomber might be there, checking out the results.

So he sidled through the rubberneckers, looking at faces, looking for signs of furtiveness, guilt, the wrong kind of excitement. A tall stout man with a shiny red face asked, "You Flowers?"

"I am," Virgil said.

"Saw your name in the paper this morning. You got any ideas about who's doing this?"

"Must be somebody who's trying to stop the PyeMart," Virgil said. "Either for financial reasons, or it's somebody upset about the runoff into the river."

"Or somebody who just hates Pye," the man said. "He's that little short fat fella, right?"

"That's him."

"He don't look like twenty billion dollars to me," the guy said.

"Thirty-two billion. I got it on good authority," Virgil said.

A guy in a post office uniform said, "You could have fun with that kinda money. Go to Vegas."

"Go to Vegas in your own jet airplane, and then buy it, the whole town," the stout man said. "Hookers'n all."

A woman in running shorts and a cutoff sweatshirt said, "It's not just the runoff in the river. The river goes into the lake, and if you fouled up the lake . . . there goes the reason for the town."

The stout man said, "They're talking about a little gasoline, a little oil. Probably leak more gas and oil into the lake from the marinas than you'd ever get off that parking lot."

"You're not buying the pollution, huh?" Virgil asked.

The stout man shrugged. "I'm not saying yes, I'm not saying no. I'm just saying, that parking lot is probably a half mile from the river. I don't see how that could equal all the trucks backing down into the lake to dump off boats, and the boats starting up. . . . I'm just sayin'."

"He sure is a little fat guy," the woman said, looking at Pye.

The stout man asked Virgil, "How do you know it's not just somebody who follows him around, and tries to kill him? Tried in Michigan, set off the bomb here, sucked him in, and then went for him again this morning?"

"Well, for one thing, the explosive came from a quarry up around Cold Spring," Virgil said.

The stout man's eyebrows went up. "Okay, give me the pointy hat. I'll go sit in the corner."

"No, no. I think you asked an interesting question," the woman said to the stout man. "It's something to think about. Is the bomber person trying to stop this store? Or trying to stop Pye?"

"Bomber person," Virgil said with a smile. "You think it might be a woman?"

"Why not?" she asked. "I've got a degree in mechanical engineering from Purdue. I could go down in my workshop and build a bomb in about fifteen minutes, if I had the explosive."

"Don't let me catch you in a quarry," Virgil said.

The stout man asked, "You take a close look at postal workers? They're supposed to be crazier than an outhouse mouse."

The mailman said, "That's real funny." And to Virgil: "What's your profiler say about this guy? Age, socioeconomic status, all that?"

"I wish you hadn't asked that," Virgil said. "We're trying to keep that a little close to the vest, for a while."

"Why? The bomber knows who he is, so it won't be anything new to him," the mailman said. "If you put out a profile, maybe you'd get some ideas from the people who live here."

"I'll think about that," Virgil said. He nodded at the three of them, and drifted away, looking at the crowd, and eventually made his way back through the crime-scene tape to Barlow.

"Listen," Virgil said. "You got a profiler I could talk to? Somebody who could give me some idea of what I might be looking for? Age, socioeconomic status, and all that?"

Barlow shook his head. "We don't do that so much. We found out most profiles are ninety percent bullshit. If you just look at what this guy's done, and where he's done it, you'll get a better idea than anything you'll get from some shrink."

"Really?"

"Really," Barlow said.

"Okay. Then I'm gonna take off, I got more people to talk to," Virgil said. "Call me if you find anything."

"Will do," Barlow said.

Virgil stopped at a SuperAmerica, bought the *Star Tribune*, the *Butternut Falls Clarion Call*, and a Diet Coke, then sat in the convenience store parking lot and read the papers' stories on the store bombing. Pye had announced a two-million-dollar gift to the dead man's family, more money to the injured man, and reiterated his million-dollar reward for information leading to the arrest and conviction of the bomber. Virgil was identified as "one of the BCA's top investigators."

Virgil was uncertain how the reward would work. If he (Virgil) spoke to two hundred people in town, and from among that information fished out the strands of an identification, would all two hundred of them wind up suing Pye—or somebody— for a piece of the million-dollar action? Seemed like a truckload of trouble coming down the road.

But, that was Pye's problem.

He tossed the papers over the seat and into the back, and took another hit on the Diet Coke. The Purdue engineer woman had given him an idea. The bomber should have a workshop of some kind, shouldn't he?

He got on the phone to Barlow, and when the ATF man answered, he asked,

"You find any pieces of the bomb casing? The pipe, or whatever?"

"Yeah, a few pieces from the trailer," Barlow said. "It's galvanized steel pipe, probably salvaged from an older house, used for interior plumbing. Same as was used in Michigan. Might have got it from a dump. Hell, sometimes it's used for outdoor railings . . . used to be all over the place."

"Did you ever find a piece of a cut end?" Virgil asked.

"Yeah, we did. We found both ends in Michigan," Barlow said. "We're not talking about it, because if we find the guy, we can match the pipe. We don't want him to get rid of it."

"Was it cut with a power saw, or a hacksaw?"

"Power saw, definitely. . . . Hmm, I think I see where you're going with this."

"The guy has some tools," Virgil said. "He has a power saw that cuts pipe. That's not something you see in everybody's workshop. He can get parts. He knows about electrical wiring . . . at least something. How to use batteries . . ."

"See? You're profiling him," Barlow

said. "This town has eighteen thousand people? You probably got it down to a few hundred. Maybe less."

"Yeah, but I don't know which few hundred," Virgil said.

Butternut Falls had a half-dozen hardware stores, but only a couple that might sell something as specialized as a pipe cutter. Virgil didn't know much about metal-cutting tools, but even if the bomber was simply able to buy a metal-cutting blade for a table saw, there were only a few places that sold table saws: a Home Depot, a Menards, a Fleet Farm, a Hardware Hank.

He'd seen the Home Depot when he came into town, so he headed that way, a five-minute trip, parked, went inside to the "Tools" section, found a woman in an orange apron, identified himself, and asked, "You got anybody here who's like a woodworking hobbyist, a guy who knows about workshops and so on?"

"That would be Lawrence," she said. "Let me find him for you."

While she did that, Virgil went down the aisle and looked at all the power saws—table saws, band saws, miter saws. He'd always been handy enough with simple tools, but like a lot of men, always felt guilty about not knowing more. Like, exactly how did a router work? Shouldn't all males know that?

The store clerk came back with a mustachioed older man in another orange apron, and introduced him as Lawrence, who had a home workshop and gave woodworking lessons. Virgil explained the problem, and concluded with: ". . . so we'd like to know who'd have a workshop well-enough equipped to cut a three-inch galvanized steel pipe."

"Well, hell, you could do that with a Sawzall. You wouldn't need a workshop. If you didn't want to buy the Sawzall, you could rent one from us," Lawrence said.

"Really?"

"Sure. You'd have to buy a bi-metal blade, but I mean, you really don't need a workshop," Lawrence said. "Who told you you'd need a workshop?"

Virgil didn't want to say, "I did," because he'd sound ignorant, so he said, "This federal guy. Hang on, I'm going to give him a ring."

He stepped away and got Barlow on the phone and relayed what Lawrence had said. "Sawzall's are a dime a dozen, man."

Barlow said, "Well, your Lawrence guy is absolutely right, you could cut the pipe with a Sawzall. But our guy didn't. Our tool-marks specialist says it was cut with some kind of chop saw, *not* with a Sawzall."

"I'll get back to you," Virgil said.

Virgil relayed what Barlow had said, and Lawrence scratched his thinning yellow hair and said, "They can tell that? Huh. Must be, heck, I don't know—I probably know forty guys who have chop saws, miter saws, in their workshops, and there are probably two hundred floating around town. Of course, we sell almost no metal-cutting blades here. Most people use their saws for woodworking."

"You sell any of the metal-cutting blades recently?" Virgil asked.

"I didn't. But the guy probably wouldn't

ask, he'd probably just come in and find it himself. There's probably some way to look at the inventory . . . that'd be one of the computer guys who could tell you that," Lawrence said. "They sell them over at Fleet Farm and Menards, too. And if you were going to do something illegal, and didn't want to buy one locally, you might run into the Cities, and they probably sell hundreds of blades over there."

"Damn it: I thought I was onto something," Virgil said.

"Let me ask around, the boys," Lawrence said. "Maybe somebody'll have an idea."

Virgil thanked him, gave him a card, and told him to call if he learned anything.

Back in the truck, he made a note to check with the BCA researcher to see if there was a way to check with Home Depot, Menards, and Fleet Farm to see if any metal-cutting chop-saw blades had been sold recently, and if so, if there'd been a credit card attached to the sale. He had little hope that anything would come of it.

Sitting there in the sun, looking at Ahlquist's list of possible interviews, and Kline the pharmacist's list of names, he sighed and shook his head. He'd have to do the legwork, but if the guy was clever, the legwork wouldn't turn up much.

What, the guy was going to confess when Virgil dropped by?

If he got anything, it'd come at an angle—he'd get it as a result of looking at something else. Looking at Kline's list, he called Ahlquist and asked him to get subpoenas for people who used anti-psychotic medications.

"I'll have O'Hara do it, and have her serve them," the sheriff said. "We'll have them tonight."

"How about the press conference?"

"We're gonna have one whether we want to or not, with two separate incidents, now. I got a TV truck right now, taking pictures of the limo, and talking to Harvey, and more are coming in. What time should I make the conference?"

"Later this afternoon . . . give us some space, and time to think. Maybe . . . three o'clock?"

"See you then. Unless another bomb goes off. Then I'll see you sooner."

With that taken care of, he dug out his iPad, turned it on, and got a map with directions to the hospital. He stopped at a local coffee shop and got a skinny hot chocolate, and then went off to the hospital.

Michael Sullivan was in a bed in the critical care ward, not because he was badly hurt, but because he was confused, and the confusion could be the result of some continuing head injury.

"We want to protect against the possibility of a trauma-induced seizure, or stroke," a doctor told Virgil.

Sullivan's confusion seemed to be diminishing, the doc said, but at times he flashed back to the moment after the explosion, when he wiped the gore from his face and eyes and saw Kingsley's head on the ground, and saw the dead man's eyes open and looking at him.

"A pure psychological thing, but real enough," the doc said. "It should get better over time, but he'll never escape it completely. The effects will always be there, the changes in his life and career and prospects."

"Could those be better, instead of worse?" Virgil asked.

The doc grinned and said, "Nobody ever asked me that. Okay, they could be better, but how would you know? Say he goes on to be a millionaire, and he thinks, *If I hadn't been blown up, I'd be a billionaire.* So what do you say about that?"

Virgil shrugged. "You say, 'Well, that's life. Suck it up, cowboy.'"

"That's why you're not getting paid two hundred dollars an hour, like me," the doc said.

Sullivan was propped up on a couple of pillows, and except for what looked like a wind-burned face, seemed okay. A handsome young woman sat on a chair to one side, flipping through an *Elle* magazine, while a guy in a suit had his butt propped against a windowsill, taking notes on a yellow pad inside a leather folder.

When Virgil came in and introduced

himself, the woman said, "He's been really good. He still has a ringing in his ears, but I think he'll be just fine."

And the man said, "Whoa, whoa, whoa, we don't know anything of the sort, Mary, and you have to stop telling people that."

Virgil understood that the man with the folder was a lawyer and the woman was Sullivan's wife. Virgil turned to the injured man and said, "I don't really, uh, want to question your condition, Mr. Sullivan. I'm more interested in what happened before the explosion. People you may have seen around the site. . . ."

The lawyer said, "No matter who he may or may not have seen around the site, I don't think we can say he really had any responsibility—"

Virgil said, "Look, I'm here to interview Mr. Sullivan. He is not suspected of a crime and I'm not investigating him. He's a witness and he has no right of silence. So, I'm happy enough to let you sit there, but if you interrupt, I'll have to ask you to leave. Okay?"

The lawyer said four or five hundred words, which Virgil waved off. "Fine, fine. But if you interrupt, I'll ask you to leave. If you don't, I'll arrest you for interfering with a police officer, even though doing that would be a pain in the ass, and hand-cuff you out in the hallway until I'm done here, and then we'll both go down to the jail. Okay? Just shut up, and let me do my job."

The woman said, "I don't think you can talk to a lawyer like that."

"Of course I can," Virgil said. "I just did. Now, Mr. Sullivan . . ."

Sullivan had one thing.

He couldn't remember the explosion, though he could remember seeing King-sley's head. He didn't see anything sus-picious around the work site, except the one thing.

"The one thing was, there was a guy who was watching us through binoculars. We all saw him, once or twice. We joked about it. He was off behind the site, be-tween the site and the river. I only actually saw him once. He was pretty far away, and I saw more movement than I did his body. He was wearing camo, I think, which seemed weird to me, because I don't think there are any hunting seasons going on. It made me wonder if he'd been watching us regular-like. The way I saw him was that it was in the evening, and the sun was going down to the northwest, and he was south of us, and I saw the flash off the binocular lenses. I saw the flash two different days, but the second day, I never saw the man, just a flash from down in the bush."

"Down in the bush," Virgil said. "He was below you?"

"Yeah. There's heavy brush back there, but the land generally falls away from the store, toward the river," Sullivan said. "That's why these people think the parking lot will drain into the Butternut, because the land falls away. We've got retention systems and everything else and I was telling—"

Suddenly his eyes went wide, the blood drained from his face, and he turned his face to the woman and groaned, "Mary, my God . . ."

The woman dropped the magazine and stood and then bent over him and said, "It's okay, Mike, you're just fine, Mike."

"Oh, Jesus Christ, his eyes are looking right at me but they're all white, looking right at me . . ."

The flashback lasted only a few seconds, but there was no question of its reality: Sullivan appeared to be slipping into shock, and Virgil sent the lawyer to find a doctor.

"I don't think we should talk about this anymore," Sullivan's wife said.

Virgil nodded: "I think you're right."

Back outside, Virgil thought about what Sullivan had said, and decided to go look in the brush behind the PyeMart site. Maybe he'd find a matchbook from the café where the bomber hung out.

Or not.

7

Before driving out to the PyeMart site, Virgil stopped at the scene of the limo bombing. The twisted vehicle was still in the middle of the street, and Barlow was working on it with one of the ATF technicians. Virgil ducked under the crime-scene tape and asked Barlow, "Anything?"

"The usual. Did find pieces of the pipe, that galvanized plumbing stuff, but finding a fingerprint . . ." He shook his head.

"A pipe dream," Virgil said.

"Yeah."

Virgil filled him in on his morning, and Barlow said that Sullivan's symptoms weren't unusual. "People see other people shot to death, and it affects them, but not the way a nearby bomb does. The Israelis have all kinds of studies on it—there's actually a physical impact, from the shock wave, and then the psychological aftereffects. Any of it can kill you. Bombing victims have an elevated rate of suicide . . . they can't deal with it, a bomb."

Willard Pye and his assistant were still on the scene, and Pye came over and asked Virgil for a minute of his time. They stepped away from Barlow, who went back to work, digging out the inside of the limousine, scrap by scrap.

Pye said, "I've decided to stick around for a couple more days, but I've had my assistant researching you, and what she found out, it's pretty interesting. You might be my guy."

"Mr. Pye—"

Pye made a shushing hand gesture and said, "Just listen for a minute. I'm gonna stay out here and watch them work this. In the meantime, my jet airplane is sitting out there at the airport, doing nothing, for a couple thousand dollars a day. I'm wondering if you'd be interested in flying back to Grand Rapids, to take a look at the Pinnacle. See if you can figure out how this butthead got inside, for one thing. Maybe you'll learn something. Barlow's a smart guy, but he's not somebody who can . . . put himself in a criminal's place, so to speak."

Virgil said, "Well, that's not a bad idea, if I come up dry here. But I've got more stuff to do here."

"We're two hours from the airport at Grand Rapids. When you finish up tonight—you can't be working it much after dark—you could get on the plane, have a nice little meal, a couple of beers, check out the building, bed down in the Pinnacle's guest quarters, good as any hotel, get up early and be back here for breakfast."

"How many people are going in and out of the building?" Virgil asked.

"A lot," Pye admitted. "There's right around twenty-five hundred employees, and we have another big administrative site over in Grand Rapids, and those people are coming and going all the time. But we have security. We have a card check at the door, we have cameras, we have guards all over the first couple of floors."

"Did the feds go through the photography?"

"Yeah, they had a couple of guys working it, but it didn't come to anything."

"Let me think about it," Virgil said.

"You got the plane if you want it," Pye said. "I hope you take it."

Virgil went out to the PyeMart site and found two deputies sitting on the same two folding chairs, and a patrol car, but no crime-scene technician. The senior cop told Virgil, "The one guy is helping Barlow at the car-bombing scene, and the other went out to the limo driver's house, to see if there's anything around where the car was parked. So, we're just sitting here."

"Nice day for it, anyway," Virgil said. And it was. He went back to his truck, put on hiking boots, got a hat and his Nikon, and headed across the construction pad. Given the location of the trailer, and with the binocular flash coming from the southeast, the watcher, whoever he was, must have been in a fairly narrow piece of real estate to the left of the main building pad.

Virgil walked to the edge of the construction site—nobody working, construction had been halted until the ATF gave the go-ahead—and plunged into the brush. He hadn't gone far, quartering back and forth through the scrub, before he found a game trail that led away to the south. Fifty yards south, a gopher mound that overlapped the trail showed the edge of a human footprint. Virgil stepped carefully around it, then took a photo, using a dollar bill for scale, and moved on south.

He'd looked at the site on a Google satellite photo: a loop of the Butternut cut a channel in the rising land to a point that the Google measuring tape said was about six hundred and fifty yards from the highway, and directly south of the PyeMart site. The game trail went that way, and Virgil followed it, looking for more prints. He found a couple of indentations, but nothing that would help identify a shoe.

He'd been walking for fifteen minutes or so, brush and weeds up higher than his head, following the game trail, slowly, when he broke into an open grassy slope that went down to the Butternut.

The river—creek—wasn't much more than thirty or forty feet wide at that point, and shallow, with riffles showing where the water was running over stone. Both above and below the riffles, broad pools cut into the banks. A hundred yards upstream, a man in a weird-looking white suit, broad-brimmed white hat, and waders was working deeper water with a fly-casting rod. Virgil went that way, and when he'd covered about half the ground, the man snapped the rod up, and Virgil saw that he had a fish on the line, and stopped to watch.

The man's rod was long and slender and caramel-colored, and he played the fish with great delicacy. At some point, Virgil realized that the rod was made of bamboo—something you didn't see much of—and the pale gold fishing line was probably silk.

The man brought in the trout, landing it with a small net that he unclipped from an equipment belt. He looked around, as if for witnesses, spotted Virgil, and held up the trout—it was perhaps a foot long, not a bad fish, for a trout, in the Butternut— and then slipped it back in the water.

Virgil continued toward him, and the man clambered out of the water and said, "Be nice if the water were about ten degrees warmer. Nice for me, if not the trout."

Virgil said, "That was a nice little fish. I'll have to bring my rod down."

"I haven't seen you around," the man said. "Are you working over at the Py-eMart?"

"Sort of," Virgil said. "I'm with the Bureau of Criminal Apprehension. I'm looking for this bomber."

"Good luck with that," the fisherman said.

As they were talking, Virgil was looking the guy over. He was tall and thin and large-nosed, his face weathered from sun exposure, like a golfer . . . or a fisherman. He was perhaps forty-five. Virgil had never seen a fishing outfit like the man was wearing: not quite white, more of a muslin color, and fitted like a suit coat, with lapels, and matching pleated pants.

The man said, "What? You've never seen a nineteenth-century fly-fishing outfit?"

"Uh, no," Virgil said. "Can't say that I have."

"Not a lot of us traditionalists around," the man said. "But a few." He pulled out a gold pocket watch, looked at it, and said, "Mmm. I've overstayed, I'm afraid."

Virgil said, "Listen, have you seen a guy in camo hanging around here? A local guy? Maybe carrying a pair of binoculars?"

"Camouflage? No, no, I haven't, but then, I don't usually fish this low," the man said. "I'm usually upstream, but things weren't going so well up there, so I persisted, and here I am."

"You know anybody who fishes down here?"

"I do," the man said. "Cameron Smith. He likes these two pools, and two more down below. There's an old mill dam, fallen down now, but there's still a good deep pool behind it. He's more of a wet-fly man. I'm dry."

"Cameron Smith . . . he's in town here?"

"Yes. He's the president of the Cold

Stream Fishers, which is a local fly-fishing club. I'm also a member."

"The club members pretty pissed about the PyeMart?"

"Shouldn't they be? I'll tell you what, this river is one of the western outposts of the trout in Minnesota. Everything south and west of here is too warm and too muddy. Too many farms, too much plowing, too much fertilizer. There's a river fifteen miles south of here. In the middle of the summer it gets an algae bloom you could almost walk across, from the fertilizer runoff. Looks like a goddamned golf fairway. This creek is a jewel; it should have been a state park long ago. Nothing good can happen with this PyeMart. Nothing. Maybe nothing terrible will happen, but then, maybe something terrible *will* happen. That's the way we look at it. There's no upside, but there could be a huge downside. There are damn few things worth blowing up people for, but this creek might be one of them."

"But you wouldn't do that," Virgil said.

"Of course not. I'd be chicken, for one thing. For another, I'm not that certain of the moralities involved. We do know one thing about the world, though, and that's that we've got way too many people, and way too few trout. Ask almost anyone, and they'll say, 'That's right.' We're not talking about trout *qua* trout, but trout as a symbol of everything that's good for the environment."

They talked for a few more minutes, as the man pulled off his waders and packed up his fishing gear, and Virgil learned that his name was George Peck. "Of course people are angry about this silly damn PyeMart. We don't need that store. It won't do anything good for anybody, except maybe Pye. And he's got enough money that he doesn't need any more, so what the heck is he doing?"

As he talked, he was stripping the line out of the rod, pulled the reel and dropped it in one of his pockets. That done, he pulled the rod apart, in three sections, and slipped each one into a separate section of a long cloth sleeve, which he bound up neatly with cloth ties sewn onto the edges of the sleeve.

"You think anybody in the club is crazy enough to try to blow up Pye?" Virgil asked.

Peck didn't answer, but said, instead, "You police officers are investigating this whole thing in the wrong way. You're old-fashioned, stuck in the past. You know what you ought to be doing? Two words?"

"Tell me," Virgil said.

"Market research."

"Market research?"

"Do an interview with the newspaper. Tell the paper that you're setting up a Facebook page, and you want everybody in town to sign on as your friends and tell you confidentially who is most likely to be the bomber. You set up some rules: tell people they aren't to name old enemies, or people of color or other victims of prejudice. Then give them the clues you have, so far, tell them to think really hard: Who is he? If you put this in the paper, you'd have five thousand replies by tonight. You go through the replies, and you'd find probably ten suspects, coming up over and over. One of them will be the bomber."

"You think?"

"I'd bet you a thousand American dollars," Peck said. He finished putting the last fly in a fly case, put it in another pocket.

"You got a thousand dollars?" Virgil asked.

"I do."

Virgil said, "I like the concept, but it'd be pretty unorthodox. My boss would have a hernia."

Peck said, "Because he's stuck in the past." He nodded to Virgil and said, "Don't fall in," and went on his way, back upstream.

Virgil went downstream, for a quarter mile, then back up, ambling along the bank, looking for anything, not finding much. The riverbanks saw quite a bit of foot traffic, Virgil thought, judging from the beaten-down brush. He got back to the spot where he'd met Peck, and continued upstream after him, but never saw him again.

Fifty yards above the place where they'd talked, he saw another trail cutting into the brush toward the PyeMart, and he followed it. Toward the end of it, fifteen yards from the edge of the raw earth of the construction zone, he found a nest beaten down in the weeds—a spot were somebody, or something, had spent some time. It could have been a deer bed, he thought, although it might be a little short for that, and he'd seen none of the liver-colored deer poop he would have expected around a bedding area.

On the other hand, even if it wasn't a deer bed, there wasn't anything about it that would point toward a particular human being. He walked along the edge of the construction line, back to the point where he'd first stepped into the brush, but saw nothing else that looked like a bed, or a nest.

If somebody were still watching the Py-eMart, would he be coming back? Might it be worthwhile to ask the sheriff to have a deputy camp out here for a while? Get a sleeping bag and a book or two, and simply lie back in the weeds and see who came along?

He'd think about that.

He'd also think about market research; and about the man who suggested profiling. Wouldn't market research just be a mass profiling? Didn't the FBI believe in profiling, even if the ATF didn't?

In the meantime, he had people to interview.

Ernie Stanton was working in his office behind Ernie's Oil #1—the office was one of the modest, prefab brick-and-corrugated-metal buildings that could be thrown up in a couple of weeks, and that dotted the back streets of small working towns. His secretary, with a plaque that said "Office Manager," sat next to the door, a delicate, slightly fleshy prairie flower with honey-blond hair and pink cheeks. Stanton, a squarish man with deep lines cutting his wind-burned face on either side of his prominent nose, sat at a desk in the back. Virgil introduced himself and Stanton said, "I wondered when you'd be around, me being the town radical and all."

He smiled, but there was nothing funny or happy about his face, which was getting redder by the second.

Virgil said, "Well, you said it. I mean, everybody I talk to says, 'Ernie Stanton.' They say that not only do you want to stop PyeMart, any way you can, but you've got the brains and the background to do it."

"You mean I'm a shitkicker," Stanton said.

"Hell, I'm a shitkicker," Virgil said. He dropped in a chair in front of Stanton's desk. "But I don't go around blowing people up with pipe bombs."

"Neither do I," Stanton said. "Though, if somebody's got to get blown up, Pye would be a good place to start. That damn store is going to tear this town up. Hell, it already has. Everybody knows that Pye bought the city council and the mayor. They'll be leaving town right after the next election."

"So you didn't blow anybody up, and you don't know who's doing it?"

"If I knew, I'd tell the cops," Stanton said. He hesitated, then added, "Maybe."

"Maybe?"

"Pye's killing me. I won't even be able to *sell* my businesses when he gets through. Probably won't even be able to sell the buildings—what'd you use them for? Art studios? If he got killed and they pulled the plug on this store, it'd be like I got a reprieve from the death penalty."

Virgil looked at him for a moment, and from behind him, the secretary said, "I second everything Ernie just said."

"Where were you last night?" Virgil asked.

"At home. Ate dinner down at Bunson's with my wife and my youngest kid, got home about seven, watched a ball game until about nine o'clock or so. Put the kids to bed, watched TV with my wife until eleven, went to bed. Of course, that alibi's no good, because it's only my wife and kids, and this whole deal will drag them down, just as much as me."

"You been out of town in the last month?"

"No, sir. I been here every day," Stanton said.

"And you've got people who aren't in your family . . . aren't your secretary . . . who'll say that?"

"Well, hell, I don't know," Stanton said. "Probably. I use my credit card for most everything I buy, and I usually buy something every day. Groceries, or something. But, how'd I know I'd have to prove I was here every day? If I'd known that, I could have set something up."

"Good answer," Virgil said.

He saw Stanton relax just a notch, his shoulders folding back and down into his office chair. From behind Virgil, the secretary said, "I also have a calendar which gives you his appointments every day. Like he went to the dentist twice last week."

Virgil swiveled around and said, "Don't throw it away."

Going back to Stanton, he asked, "You know about the car bombing this morning?"

Stanton nodded. "Yeah, I went out and looked at it. It's still sitting there. Didn't hear the boom, but my wife was down at County Market, shopping, and she heard it, and saw it, and called me."

Virgil said, "The bomb was probably triggered when the limo went over a bump or something. Something that jarred the car. About a minute before it went off, the driver went past a bunch of elementary school kids on a field trip. If it had gone off next to them, you'd be missing a few kids."

Stanton leaned forward and said, "That's why I wouldn't be a bomber. If I was going to kill Pye, I'd figure out a way to shoot the sonofabitch. But a bomb . . . this bomb in Michigan, killed that gal, the secretary. Why would you take a chance of doing that? Then our first bomb, he killed the construction super. That won't stop the store—they'll just get another supervisor. I mean, what the guy is doing is nuts."

"But shooting him with a gun wouldn't be?"

"Be a hell of a lot less nuts," Stanton said. "Wouldn't it?"

"I wouldn't make that kind of judgment," Virgil said.

"You would if you were a real shitkicker, and not some phonied-up city cowboy in crocodile boots and a Rolling Stones tongue shirt."

"Listen—"

"Come on, admit it," Stanton said. "You got a guy like Pye, wrecking a town, and you might not like him getting shot, but it's a hell of a lot less nuts than taking a chance of blowing up some schoolkids. Isn't it?"

"Well . . ."

"C'mon, say it," Stanton said.

"All right. It's less nuts," Virgil said. "I still don't hardly approve of it."

"Neither do I," Stanton said. "That's one reason I didn't do it. Shoot him, I mean."

Stanton said he'd thought about the bomber, but the more he thought, the more bewildered he became. "I know guys around town who could do it, but they wouldn't. I mean, they've got the skills. Hell, I could probably do it. Me and my friends, we sit around talking about it—we're asking each other, who's nuts enough? We really don't know anybody like that."

With that, Virgil left.

As he was going out the door, the prairie flower said, "If you see that cocksucker Pye, tell him I hope he roasts in hell."

"I'll try to remember," Virgil said.

Out in the sunshine, Virgil looked at his watch. Time was passing, and he wasn't getting anywhere. And, he thought, the bomber was probably already at work on another bomb. He took a call from Ahlquist. "The TV's already here, taking pictures of the limo and the blown-up pipes, interviewing everybody in sight. They're asking if you're gonna make a statement for the BCA?"

"No, no, apologize if anybody asks for me. Tell them that I'm tracking down leads, or something," Virgil said. "But I'll sneak in the back and watch."

"Are you? Tracking down leads?"

"Not so much. I just finished talking to Ernie Stanton. I'm gonna go find this Don Banning guy, that runs the clothing store, and then Beth Robertson over at the Book Nook."

"I think Don is too much of a sissy to pull this off. Beth isn't a sissy, but she's not crazy, and I really can't see her crawling around under a car, with a bomb. Or breaking into a quarry shed and stealing explosive. She's too . . . ladylike."

Ahlquist was right about Banning, Virgil decided: he was a basic clothing salesman, deferential, eager to please. Soft and slender, he seemed unlike a man who'd have enough executive grit to travel to Michigan with a bomb, and then crack a skyscraper to plant it. Like Stanton, he confessed that he would not be unhappy to see Pye drop dead.

"But you know, I'm not really all that angry with Mr. Pye himself. He's just doing what he does. I'm more angry with the city council, who let him come in here and set up a store in an area that was supposed to remain open space, or, at least, not to have city facilities, for at least another fifty years. Instead, they completely subvert the city plan, and run water and sewer out there, specifically for the Pye-eMart. They were bought, and that's what you should be investigating."

Virgil said, "I've been told that by a couple of people. Of course, if I find any evidence of it, I'll act on it. Right now, I'm more focused on stopping this bomber."

"And when you do that, you'll never come back to look at the city council," Banning said. "That's just too much trouble for the BCA, and they've all got political friends, and it wouldn't be an important enough case for somebody like you anyway."

"After I stop the bomber, we'll see about that," Virgil said.

Banning showed a little grit: "I'm sorry. I don't believe you."

Virgil was back in his truck, mentally scratching Banning off his list of suspects, when Lawrence, the clerk at Home Depot, called on Virgil's cell phone. "I put out a message on our woodworker phone tree. I got a call back from Jesse Card at BTC. You better get over there and talk to him."

Butternut Technical College was a collection of a half-dozen yellow-brick buildings surrounding a group of tennis and basketball courts on the far south side of town. A two-year college, it functioned as an extension of high school, and focused on a variety of building trades.

Jesse Card was the lead instructor in the metal shop, and had a small paper- and manual-clogged office down the hall from the shop itself. The office smelled pleasantly of tobacco and oil, as Virgil thought such places should, though the tobacco was illegal. Card was talking with another instructor when Virgil arrived, and Card broke away to take him down to the shop.

Card was excited: "The thing is, our number one rule here is, you clean up. You get these kids in here, and if you didn't make them clean up, spotlessly, every time they use a tool, it'd be chaos. So, about a month ago, I came in and was walking through, when I see this mess behind the pipe cutter. This is the pipe cutter."

Card pointed at a power saw with a circular blade, that was bolted on a black steel table. The saw looked like an ordinary miter saw, except for a vise-like tool on the front, designed to hold a pipe in place while it was being cut.

"I'm pretty sure that there was no mess when I went home the night before—my eye catches that kind of stuff. So I see all these metal filings behind the saw and on the floor, and I'm asking, What the heck? I got the kids and asked who did it: they all swore that they hadn't. I believed them, because, for one thing, they would have had to come in at night, and for that they'd need a key. There was a night class for adults going on, but the instructor there said they hadn't been doing any pipe-cutting at all. Anyway, I let it go until I got the call from Lawrence."

"So whoever came in, had a key," Virgil said.

"Unless they were in the night class," Card said. "Or maybe somebody forgot to lock up. There are lots of keys around, and sometimes the doors don't get locked."

"Do you know what kind of filings? Was there much of it?" Virgil asked.

"Yeah, there was quite a bit. Whoever used it cut quite a bit of material. It was steel, was what it was. It was magnetic, and it was bright, so it was steel."

Virgil said, "Hmm. There weren't any bits and pieces left over?"

"There were, unless somebody took them. Come over this way."

Virgil followed him across the shop to a metal bin, which was half full of pieces of steel and iron. An adjacent bin contained a bucketful of copper pieces.

"This is where we throw metal debris,"

Card said. "A guy from the local junkyard picks it up when it gets full, and we get a few bucks for it. So after this incident with the mess by the saw, I was throwing some stuff in here—the bin was almost empty—and I noticed this piece of three-inch galvanized pipe in there. We don't use anything like that, we're not a plumbing shop. It occurred to me right then that this might be where the filings came from. I didn't do anything about it, I just noticed it, and it popped right up in my mind when Lawrence called."

Virgil peered into the bin: "You think it's still in there?"

"I believe so. Unless, like I said, somebody took it."

Virgil said, "Okay, this is good. I'm bringing the ATF in."

He got on the phone to Barlow and told him about it. "I'll be there in ten minutes," Barlow said. "Don't go anywhere. Keep an eye on the saw, too."

While they waited for Barlow to show up, Virgil and Card sat on a couple of stools and talked about who'd have a key, or access to the shop. Card said the shop was unlocked from about seven o'clock in the morning, when he got there, until about ten o'clock at night, when the night adult class ended and the instructor locked up.

Sometimes, he said, the door didn't get locked—"I run into that a few times every year. Then, there are quite a few keys around, janitors and administrators. The local firefighters have a master set. . . . What I think happened was, it was a guy with a key. He came in late . . . The pipe would be heavy, so he'd have to park right outside and carry the pipe in. Wouldn't have to worry about turning on the lights, because there are no windows. He cuts his pipe and gets out. He doesn't take the time to clean up, because he's in a hurry, but he does know enough to throw the waste piece in the bin."

"So then . . . It'd have to be a guy who works here," Virgil said.

"Well, a guy who has a key for here. Could be a firefighter. And then, this place has been here since the fifties. I bet there are a hundred keys for these doors.

Maybe more. We don't know where most of them are at. If you had somebody come through here as a student . . ."

"Okay."

They thought about it together, and then Virgil asked, "Why wouldn't he just buy a saw? He could do it in his basement with a ten-dollar hacksaw. Buy the hacksaw in the Cities, nobody would remember."

"It's a hell of a lot of work, that's why. This is *steel* we're talking about, and it's pretty thick," Card said. "If he wanted to make a lot of cuts, he could wear himself out doing it. And maybe he doesn't think that way. Maybe he gets the pipe and thinks, *How do I cut this stuff?* And he thinks, *Hmm, there's my old shop. . . .*"

"That could happen," Virgil said.

"One more thing," Card said. "This is a tech school. When people who work here upgrade their homes, they tend to do it themselves. Put in a new bathroom or finish a basement, most of us would think nothing of it. A lot of guys here look at the school as a resource. Need to cut some pipe, go on down to the shop and

do it. Technically, you're not supposed
to, but almost everybody does. And why
not?"

"So it could be an instructor."

"It could be. It's a logical possibility,"
Card said. "We got a lot of instructors—a
couple hundred, when you include out-
siders."

"You've given me something to think
about, Jesse," Virgil said.

Barlow arrived, bringing one of the techs
with him. Card ran through the whole ex-
planation again, and they went over and
peered in the metal debris bin, and after
taking a photograph, the tech started
digging through it, throwing non-relevant
bits and pieces into a trash can that Card
wheeled over. After two or three minutes,
he said, "There it is."

He was wearing yellow plastic evidence
gloves, and he stripped them off, pulled
on a fresh one, then reached down and
slipped two fingers inside a three-inch
length of pipe and lifted it out. The pipe
had been crushed at one end; the other

end showed bright steel where the blade had gone through it.

Card said, "That's it."

They all looked at it for a moment, then Barlow asked the tech, "What do you think?"

"I'd be really surprised if this isn't a piece of the bomb pipe," the tech said. "It's exactly the right size, the cut looks the same as in the end we found, the material looks exactly the same—we can check that in the lab—and it looks like it was used as a piece of old plumbing pipe, a water pipe, same as the bombs. I'd say he cut it off to get rid of the crushed part. He wanted access to both ends."

Barlow turned to Virgil and said, "Good catch."

"Not me," Virgil said. "It was Jesse and his gang."

Card said, "Man, this is something else. This is a *story*."

Barlow would send the pipe end to the ATF lab to see if any fingerprints or DNA could be recovered.

As Virgil was leaving, he asked Card if he knew the fly fisherman George Peck. "Oh, sure, I know George. Why?"

"Is he an instructor here?"

"No, no. He's the town photographer," Card said. "He does portraits and high school yearbooks and so on. He's a blowhard, in my opinion. Harmless, though."

"I met him up on the Butternut, fly-fishing."

"Was he wearing that white suit?" Card asked.

"Yeah. I'd never seen anything quite like it," Virgil said.

"That's George. He can't just be a fly fisherman, he has to be an antique fly fisherman. He's also a member of a tommy-gun club over in Wisconsin. They get together and shoot tommy guns. He collects pocket watches. He's got an enormous camera, a hundred years old, the size of a Volkswagen. He uses it to go around and document authentic people. He used to be a glider pilot. A regular airplane wasn't exotic enough—he had to go up without an engine."

"Authentic people?"

"You know. Poor people, I guess," Card

said. "I've known him a long time. Since we were kids. Wouldn't hurt a fly. You don't seriously suspect him?"

"No, no. Just doing market research," Virgil said.

Before going back to his truck, Virgil walked down to the college admissions department and got a copy of the current class catalog, which also listed instructors. The woman behind the admissions desk told him that all instructors, both full-time and part-time, were listed on the college's website, and most had e-mail addresses.

He sat in the 4Runner for a few minutes, flipping through the catalog. There were dozens of courses, more dozens of instructors. Browsing through the list of courses, he realized that the level of technical sophistication meant that not only the instructors, but the students, could almost certainly build any kind of bomb you wanted.

Including, he thought, atomic. Even if they couldn't provide the plutonium, they almost certainly could build the mechanism of an atomic bomb, with their computer-assisted design programs: *Electronics technology, engineering CAD technology, machine-tool technology, manufacturing engineering technology, mechanical design tech (CAD), research-and-development technology, welding and metal fabrication technology . . .*

A pipe bomb would be child's play.

In fact, the bombs so far had perhaps been too unsophisticated for the college . . . but then, there was that pipe debris. Virgil bought the idea that the pipe had been cut in a machine shop, that the bomber had been there.

Ahlquist called: "Everybody's here for the press conference. You coming?"

Virgil looked at his watch. The time was sneaking past him. "See you in five minutes," he said. "You know what you're going to say?"

"Well, it'll be just like we decided. That we're making progress, that we're expecting arrests. It'd be nice if we had *made* some progress. I'd feel less like a dirty rotten liar, but I guess I can live with it."

"We did find the bomb factory," Virgil said. "You could mention that."

"What?"

"And I'd like to talk to you about market research."

8

The parking lot was full of white television vans, with camera guys in jeans and golf shirts lolling about the courthouse doors, the talent in dresses and sport coats. Three or four newspaper reporters mixed in, along with a radio guy from Minnesota Public Radio and an online reporter from *MinnPost*.

Ahlquist bustled about, glad-handing the television people, joking with the reporters. Pye was there, with Chapman, his assistant; the redheaded cop, O'Hara, sat in a chair by herself at the back of the press conference, arms folded across her chest, watching. Barlow came in, wearing a suit and tie, a few minutes after Virgil got there. Barlow said he was mostly a prop. "I'll just say that we're making progress, and confirm the find up at BTC. What's this thing about market research?"

Virgil told him about George Peck's suggestion, and Barlow scratched an ear and said, "I dunno. I never heard of anything like that."

Virgil said, "Can't hurt. I mean, everybody in town knows we're looking for the bomber, and most of them have some opinions. The sheriff already has a reserved website for natural disaster information and so on. We could use that. . . . Be kind of interesting, I think."

"But it's not based on evidence—it's just based on . . . nothing. A vote," Barlow said.

"No, it's based on collective judgment," said Virgil. "It doesn't mean that we don't have to have proof. We'd still have to prove that the bomber did it."

"Let me suggest something—think about it for a couple of days," Barlow said. "It sounds goofy to me and it'll sound goofy to the media. In fact, let me make an executive decision here: I'm gonna stay as far away from it as I can."

"So I'll think about it," Virgil said. "No big rush."

"What? Of course there's a big rush," Barlow said. "We can't get this guy too soon, no matter how we do it."

The press conference was held in a courtroom at the new county courthouse, a space that did its best to translate justice into laminated wood. A *Minneapolis Star Tribune* reporter stopped to chat, and when he drifted away in pursuit of Barlow, Pye walked over, trailed by Chapman and her steno pad, and asked, "You still thinking about the plane?"

"I started thinking about it again," Virgil said. "If I don't come up with anything the rest of the day, I might go."

"If you can figure out how the bomber got in the building, I think you'll know who he is," Chapman said, over Pye's head.

"Why's that?"

She tipped her head toward the back of the courtroom, and the three of them found a pew and sat side by side, Pye in the middle, and Chapman spoke around him. "This all comes from my stenography, my reporting in following Willard around, talking to ATF guys."

The Pinnacle, she said, was deep in the countryside, all by itself, surrounded by a wide plaza that sat fifteen feet above the surrounding parking lots. The parking lots were a hundred and fifty feet across, and were, in turn, surrounded by farm fields.

"You can't see the bottom floor of the building from the fields, because the plaza is set up too high. That means you can't do long-term surveillance from the cornfields, because you can't see up on top of the plaza. And you can't get close to the plaza without being in the open, where the security cameras would pick you up. The cameras never found anybody. Everybody who comes through, front and back, twenty-four hours a day, is on multiple cameras, and there are no gaps in the videos."

"Barlow said that the bomb had to be in there less than a day," Virgil said.

"The ATF found fragments of the clock used as a timer. The technicians say that it didn't have a running time of more than twenty-three hours and fifty-nine minutes. So the bomber had to be in the building less than twenty-four hours before the bomb went off. They checked everybody coming through the front and back—the loading dock is around back— and checked them off. Found them all. No obvious suspects," Chapman said.

Pye bobbed his head, and Chapman continued: "So then they thought that the bomb had been placed by an insider. They'd tracked down the probable origin of the explosives, up at that quarry— around here someplace, Cold Spring?— and decided that an insider had simply known about that quarry for some reason, and had come here to get the explosives. They also checked out people, insiders, who'd been out here for this construction project. There were about a dozen of them, and they were all eliminated by the ATF."

Pye jumped in: "So that was it: had to be an insider, who came out here by chance. Then the bomb went off here, and they were . . . confused. Because that made it seem like it might be an outsider again, and they didn't think it *could* be an outsider. Now this second bomb—"

"It wasn't an insider," Virgil said. "At least, it seems unlikely. We've located the place where the pipe was cut for the bombs." He told them about the tech college, and the metal shop.

Pye clouded up: "How come nobody told me about this? This is a big deal."

"Just happened, a few minutes ago," Virgil said. "They got a piece of pipe. Maybe it'll have a fingerprint, or DNA."

"Not the way that our luck has been running," Pye said. "But it sounds like you've been making progress. I don't want you to go running off to Grand Rapids if it'll slow you down."

"If you can turn me around in a hurry, I won't lose much time here," Virgil said. "But I'd want to work tonight, and get back on the plane first thing tomorrow morning."

Chapman said to Pye, "If you want, I could go along with him. That way, I could cut through any bureaucratic bullshit."

Pye squeezed his lower lip, thinking about it, then said, "If you got out of here at seven o'clock, you'd be in the building by eleven. You lose an hour in the time zones. I could have everybody waiting for you. You talk to them, look around, see what you think, get a few hours' sleep, get back on the plane at eight—the pilots need an eight-hour turnaround. You could get another couple hours of sleep on the plane, and still be back here by nine o'clock in the morning, because you get the hour back. Eat breakfast on the plane, you'd lose no working time at all."

Virgil said, "Set it up. I'll be at the airport at seven o'clock, if nothing else blows up."

The press conference almost went off as planned, with Ahlquist as an upbeat master of ceremonies. He told the gathered reporters that substantial progress had been made toward finding the bomber, that arrests were expected in the next few days, that the ATF lab was processing DNA evidence found on pieces of the bomb.

And he announced that they'd found the saw where the pipes had been cut, but refused to say where that was. "We have to hold some of this tight, for investigative reasons."

One of the reporters said, "We heard it was out at Butternut Tech."

Ahlquist said, "I can't confirm anything—"

"Everybody already knows," the reporter said.

"Ah, shit," Ahlquist said, then, "Excuse me."

Barlow, in his turn, conceded that the lab work would take a few days, and that "nothing was certain." The media people detected the tap dancing and went after him, asking for a timetable on which they could decide whether or not the investigation was looking like a failure. Barlow slipped that punch and turned the pageant back to the sheriff.

Ahlquist recovered some ground by lying about the amount of progress made, including references to additional information that couldn't be disclosed.

Then things turned ugly.

A middle-aged dark-haired woman stood up and shouted, "How come you spend all this time investigating this bomber, and you don't investigate that little fat man for killing this whole town?" She turned around and poked an index finger at Pye, who was still sitting next to Virgil. "That one! The people who elected you to office would like to know that."

"This ain't good," Pye muttered, and Chapman wrote it down.

Ahlquist tried to dodge the bullet by saying, "Now, Beth, goldarnit, you know I'm not a city official and I had nothing to do with the PyeMart deal."

Beth Robertson, the bookstore woman, Virgil thought. She shouted, "Everybody knows that Pye bought the city council and the mayor, and you sure got the right to investigate that. If you investigated that—"

At that point, the mayor, who'd been sitting in the front row, half-stood and turned, and shouted, "Robertson, you shut your mouth or I'll sue your butt off. I never did anything I didn't think was for the good of this town. I work sixty hours a week—"

"YOU shut up, bitch-face," Robertson shouted. She stepped into the aisle and took a couple steps toward the mayor. Virgil wondered why none of the sheriff's deputies were trying to get between them; it seemed like the responsible thing to do. Chapman leaned around Pye and said, "Maybe you ought to stop them."

Virgil: "Me?"

Robertson screamed at the mayor, "You and that goddamned crook you're married to would sell your children for ten dollars and a rubber tire. . . ."

Her voice reached toward a screech and Virgil thought, Hmm, and, at the same time, decided he liked her turn of phrase. Pye had lowered himself in his seat, but nobody was much looking at him anyway, because the mayor squeezed out of her pew into the aisle, the same aisle that Robertson had just gotten to.

The cops were moving now, nearly too late, and though Robertson was the smaller of the two women, probably giving up twenty pounds, she went for the mayor like a lion after a zebra, teeth and claws. The mayor was right there, ready to take her on, but one of the cops got to Robertson just two feet short of the mayor, grabbed her around the waist and horsed her toward the back of the room, kicking and screaming.

As the cop wrestled with Robertson, a tall bearded man in a plaid shirt stood up and shouted, "Beth is right, Ahlquist, and you know it. Those sonsofbitches were paid off big-time. Now that parking lot is going to bleed all over the Butternut and we're gonna leave our children a polluted swamp. A *polluted swamp*."

A television reporter called, "What do you have to say to that, Sheriff?"

Ahlquist ignored her and said, "We're all done here, we're all finished. Let's have a little peace and quiet, folks. . . ."

Robertson started screaming from the crowd in the back, as a deputy cuffed her, and the man in the plaid shirt shouted, "No! We deserve some answers. Who's investigating the city council, is what we want to know."

The mayor shouted, "Shut up, Butz. Just shut up."

Chapman leaned over to Virgil and said, "Fistfight in Butternut. Film at eleven."

"I better get the fuck out of here," Pye said. He stood up, and behind him, Chapman wrote it down. Pye said to Virgil as he was leaving, "I'll tell the pilots you're flying at seven o'clock. Marie'll come with you."

Out in the hall, Virgil bumped into Ahlquist, who had a shiny patina of sweat on his forehead. The sheriff said, "That worked out real well."

"Am I gonna be able to talk to Robertson?" Virgil asked.

"Sure. Why not?"

"Well, she was being cuffed."

"Aw, shit, she just scratched one of my guys," Ahlquist said. "We all agreed that nothing serious happened, and she's on the way back to her store."

Beth Robertson was one of those bookstore women who wore her hair in a bun, who was a little overweight, but not too, who dressed in shades of brown but referred to them as earth colors, and who always tried to sell you an Annie Dillard when you were looking for a Stephen King. Nice enough, and sometimes a pain in the ass, Virgil thought. She was peering out the front window of the bookstore when Virgil went in; he was the only other person in the place.

"Virgil Flowers," she said, turning away from the window. "You were pointed out to me. You seem to be pretty close to Pye."

Virgil shrugged. "I'm not, no. But he's a target of this bomber, and I need to talk with him from time to time."

"So, what do you want with me?"

"I need to scratch you off my list of people who might be making these bombs," Virgil said.

She suddenly sat down on a metal folding chair and began to weep. Virgil let her go for a minute, then said, "Is there anything . . . ?"

"I am completely humiliated," she said. "I completely lost control back there. They handcuffed me."

"That was to keep you from scratching any more deputies," Virgil said. "You have a lot of sympathizers, from what I can tell."

"Ah, God," she said, wiping her eyes with the heels of her hands.

"So, about the bombs . . ."

Robertson said she'd never do anything to hurt a living creature; she neither
ate meat, nor wore leather. "I sure wouldn't
make a bomb. Though I could."

"Make a bomb?"

"Sure. All these idiot rednecks run
around making bombs, why couldn't I?"
she asked.

"Well, a lot of rednecks aren't idiots,"
Virgil said. "A lot of them have experience
with tools and so on."

She waved him off. "I could do it. I just
wouldn't. No: we need to stop the PyeMart, and we could, if anyone would just
pay attention to the simple fact that the
mayor and the city council were bribed
to approve the zoning change. Once
that was established, PyeMart would be
stopped cold."

"If you have any evidence of that . . ."

"There's the problem. We all *know* it,
but we can't prove it."

They spent ten minutes talking, and
two minutes in, Virgil scratched her off the
list. She really wouldn't hurt a flea, he
thought. She told him that she had no
idea of who'd done the bombings, but
there were a lot of people who were angry

enough to be suspects. She wouldn't name them, because there were too many of them, and because she didn't want to point at a lot of innocent people—"And all but one of them is innocent."

He asked about the college and she shook her head. "None of the people who seem the angriest are from the college, as far as I know. But if I were so angry that I'd start setting off bombs, I'd pretend that I wasn't angry at all. Wouldn't you? Just keep my mouth shut and build my bombs."

Virgil scratched his chin and said, "Yeah. You may be right. I should be looking for somebody who *isn't* angry."

She showed the smallest of smiles: "Doesn't sound like you have an easy job."

Virgil found Larry Butz, who'd joined Robertson in shouting at the sheriff at the press conference, working in the back of Butz Downtown Jewelers. "I figured you'd be showing up," he said, after a sales clerk ushered Virgil into the back office. "I'm not blowing anybody up."

"You know anybody who might be?" Virgil asked.

"I probably know him, if he's local, but I couldn't identify him as the bomber, if you see what I mean," Butz said. He hesitated, and then said, "Aren't you pulling a fishing boat around? Somebody told me that you write for *Gray's* and a couple other magazines."

"I do from time to time," Virgil said.

Butz leaned forward: "Then you should be on our side, man. These drainage things are insidious. We've got them all over the state—gas and oil and brake fluid getting into the groundwater, and then into the lakes. It's a disgrace."

"I *am* on your side, from that angle," Virgil said. "But I wouldn't be murdering people to stop it."

"Probably won't help me to say it, but killing off a few of these assholes would probably be a good thing," Butz said. "Trouble is, this bomb guy is blowing up the wrong people. He killed two innocent people, just doing their jobs, and he missed Pye. He missed the board of directors. If murdering people was going to help, he's managed to murder all the wrong ones, and turn Pye into a hero, giving away all those millions of dollars. How in the hell did that happen? Is he really on our side? What I want to know is, how did one of us Butternuts get up on top of Pye's skyscraper? He's got all kinds of security, is what I hear. I think we're being set up."

"Huh," Virgil said.

They talked for a few more minutes, and then Virgil left: he did not scratch Butz off the list. Butz did get him thinking about the Pye Pinnacle again, and he called Barlow.

"Are you sure that bomb at the Pinnacle was set off with a clock?"

"Pretty sure. We found the clock. Pieces of it, anyway."

"What if the bomber is bullshitting you? What if he had the bomb wired through a cheap plastic cell phone or walkie-talkie, and he put it right on top of the Pelex, or molded the Pelex around it, with the clock off to one side. Then, when it went off, the cell phone vanishes and you find pieces of the clock . . . which means you look for somebody who was in the building twenty-four hours before the explosion, and maybe he was there a week before."

Barlow said, "Well, the reason is, our lab is really good at this stuff, and our techs are really good at picking up evidence. That's why we're still out there in that trailer, two days later. If there'd been a cell phone involved, we'd have picked it up."

"For sure? One hundred percent?"

"Nothing's one hundred percent," Barlow said.

"How fast can you get to your lab guy?" Virgil asked.

"Got him on my speed dial."

"Call him up and ask him what percent," Virgil said.

"Get back to you in three minutes," Barlow said.

Five minutes later, Barlow called back: "He said seventy-five to eighty percent. I was kinda surprised it was that low."

"So there's one chance in four or five that you wouldn't find a cell phone," Virgil said.

"Yes, under certain conditions, but the guy would have to know a lot about what he was doing. We're not seeing that level of sophistication."

"We're talking about a tech college," Virgil said.

"Yeah . . . gives us something more to think about. I'll get the ATF guys to look at that video as far back as it goes. There's a terabyte of memory for every one of the cameras, so that'd cover a lot of time."

"Keep talking to me," Virgil said.

By the time he finished with Butz, it was five o'clock and people were going to dinner. He hadn't gotten any closer to identifying the bomber, but he was getting the lay of the land, Virgil thought. He went back to the Holiday Inn, set his clock for six, and took a nap.

At two minutes to six, he rolled out, turned the alarm off before it had a chance to start beeping at him, went in the bathroom and brushed his teeth. Then he sat on the bed and called Davenport, told him about the trip to Michigan, and also about the market research idea.

Davenport approved of the trip and was interested in the market research concept. "Let me run it by a couple of computer people. I think it's worth a try, if we're confident that people would try to tell the truth. Probably every high school kid would nominate one of his teachers."

"It could get messy, but if you got enough people to participate . . . Lots of smart people around, and they all know each other."

"You know what would be even better?" Davenport asked. "If you charged ten dollars per person to make a suggestion, and then the winners divide up the pot. Give them some incentive to be right."

"Jeez, I dunno. Would that be legal?"

"Why should I care? I'm not planning to do it," Davenport said. "Anyway . . . I'd give it some more thought before you do anything. It's interesting, but in a funky way. Maybe too funky."

Virgil said he'd call if anything broke, rang off, put a couple of clean shirts, a fresh pair of jeans, and some socks in a duffel bag, along with his dopp kit, sunglasses, laptop, and pistol, threw it all in the truck, and drove out to the airport.

A black SUV was arriving just as he did, and Marie Chapman got out, carrying nothing but an oversized purse.

"An adventure," she said.

"Adventures are what you have when you screw up," Virgil said.

"Been there," she said, "and done that."

9

Pye's pilot was a reassuringly square-chinned, gray-haired man wearing a military-style olive-drab nylon flight jacket over a blue canvas shirt, jeans, with brown leather boots and a long-billed blue hat that said "Pye" in white script. The copilot was a square-chinned man with salt-and-pepper hair, also reassuringly aviator-like, in the same flight jacket, canvas shirt, jeans, boots, and hat, which Virgil took as a uniform dreamed up by a designer with delusions of manhood.

The plane itself was larger than Virgil expected, a blue Gulfstream 550 with the same white "Pye" script as the pilots' hats. A cabin attendant, an Asian woman in a jade business dress, was putting together a meal in a forward galley when Virgil climbed aboard; she asked, "Something to drink after takeoff?"

"Diet Coke?" Virgil asked.

Chapman said, "The usual."

Chapman said that the interior of the plane had been customized for long-distance trips; that Pye was expanding in Latin America and Asia, and that they traveled twenty weeks of the year. "He's pushing really hard, because he's got nothing else to do. Willard's wife died six years ago. He's never gotten over it. He told me that he still talks to her at night, when he goes to bed."

"That's tough," Virgil said; though he really had no idea.

Chapman showed him two private sleeper cabins in the back, with fold-down beds; the center of the plane was taken up with six seats that could be swiveled into a meeting formation, with a folding desk that could be swiveled in front of each. The plane had Wi-Fi and electrical plug-ins for laptops.

Forward of the cabin door, but behind the pilot's cockpit, was the galley, and a long folding chair for the cabin attendant.

The pilot called back to suggest that they take their seats, and Chapman said, "Come on, I want to show you something." She led him back to the bedroom suites, leaving the door open behind her, then opened a smaller, shorter door that Virgil thought probably went back to the baggage compartment. Instead, he found himself on his knees in a four-foot-high, four-foot-long compartment.

Chapman, kneeling beside him, said, "Pull on your side," and Virgil helped peel back a thick plastic cover over two body-length windows set in the fuselage floor.

"This is always a trip," she said. "The idea is to lie down and look straight down while we take off. . . . It's like flying."

And it was. Ten minutes later, they were off the ground, Virgil and Chapman lying side by side with their noses right on the window glass, and Chapman started laughing in delight as the plane banked in a tight turn to the east. They climbed quickly over the summer-green landscape, the trees below throwing long shadows like dark hands over the farm fields, the lakes as dark and hard as granite tiles set in a glowing green carpet.

When they'd finished climbing out, Chapman said, "That's the show," and Virgil said, "You were right—it was like flying." They went back to their seats, and the cabin attendant brought Virgil his Diet Coke, a martini with three olives for Chapman, and a paper menu.

Virgil ordered a cheeseburger with fries and a chopped salad, and Chapman a salmon steak.

"Hell, this is better than what we'd get in Butternut," Virgil said, when the food came. "We ought to eat here every night."

As they ate, they chatted about the bombings, and Chapman got out a sketchbook and drew cartoon-like pictures of the Pye Pinnacle, to illustrate the problems a bomber would have getting in. "I'm not an expert on security, but we've had all kinds of experts there in the past two weeks. They all talked to Willard, and I took notes," she said. "It's almost like a locked-room mystery, but the problem is, how did the guy get in?"

"I was an MP captain in the army, and a lot of MPs wind up guarding prisons," Virgil told her. "I never did, but I took the course work, and we looked at a lot of prison escapes. The ways people get out of prison are amazing—and they mostly depend on sleight of hand, just like with magicians."

"Like what?"

"Like guys disguising themselves as guards and walking out. Make the guard uniforms right in their cells. Another guy . . . See, when trucks come and go, the guards roll mirrors under them to make sure nobody has tied themselves onto the bottom. One guy made a folding papier-mâché box and spray-painted it brown and gray that looked like the underside of a Sysco truck. He tied himself on, with the box facing down. The guards looked at it, not expecting to see anything, and they didn't, and waved the truck through. What the guy hadn't figured out, though, was that the truck was traveling a long way, and by the time he got to where he was going, he was almost dead from carbon monoxide poisoning. They found him lying on the ground under the truck. He'd managed to cut himself down before he passed out. But, he got out."

"But they've got all these cameras at the Pinnacle."

"The point is, they *see* what happened, but they don't understand it," Virgil said.

"The guys who were looking seemed smart," Chapman said. "I think they would have made allowance for that."

"Maybe," Virgil said. "But everybody knows magicians do tricks, and they still don't see it. If you're good enough . . . but who knows? Maybe it *was* an insider, who was cooperating with somebody from Butternut Falls. Did anybody look at the insiders and ask about relatives from Minnesota?"

"That's something I don't know," she said. "You'd have to ask Barlow."

They spent the rest of the flight talking about how they'd gotten where they were—she'd worked as a reporter for a while, hadn't liked the money, wrote for a couple of magazines as a freelancer, then caught on doing research for a Washington, D.C., public relations company, and worked for a Michigan congressman for a while. After a couple years with the congressman, she ghostwrote, for the congressman, a moderately successful book about Washington lobbying. The congressman introduced her to Pye, after Pye mentioned to him that he was looking for an unusual kind of assistant.

She said, "When I was researching *you*, I found a lot of stuff about shoot-outs you'd been in, and then I found out you were a writer. You've even written for the *New York Times Magazine*."

"I have," Virgil admitted. "I don't like to talk about it, for fear of offending my straight friends."

"I read the articles," she said. "You're really good. Why would you continue to do . . . this?"

"Because I like it. It's extremely interesting," Virgil said. "I like writing, too, but in small doses. Sitting in a room, alone, for six hours a day, like a full-time pro writer . . . that's no way to go through life."

She was attractive, articulate, and liked to talk about writing: she made Virgil nervous. His sheriff was still out there, somewhere, and she was heavily armed.

They arrived at Gerald R. Ford International Airport outside of Grand Rapids at ten o'clock at night, eastern time. As they turned, just before they started down, Virgil could see the faint orange glow of sunlight to the west. On the ground, it was full dark. They were met by a man in a large blue Chevy Tahoe, with the Pye script on the doors.

"Fast as you can get there, Harry," Chapman told the driver, and he said, "Yes, ma'am."

A few minutes later, they were headed east on I-96, and Harry put the speedometer on eighty. Virgil sat in front, and Chapman dozed in the back. Thirty minutes later, Harry said, "There she is."

The Pye Pinnacle came up as a shaft of shimmering light that, a few miles later, had resolved itself into hundreds of brightly lit windows climbing up into the sky. The highway ran just to the south of the building; but all around the building was a puddle of pitch darkness.

Harry took an off-ramp that seemed to go nowhere but the Pinnacle; and then a couple of right turns got them on an approach road, and they drove through a parking lot, stopped at a railroad-style guard arm, which Harry opened with a key card, and then they rolled up a gentle ramp to an entrance door on the side of the building. Chapman, yawning, said, "VIP entrance. Thanks, Harry."

As they pulled up, three men in suits stepped out through the glass doors, and Virgil and Chapman got out and Chapman said, "Hey, guys," and they said, "Marie," and Chapman said, "This is Virgil Flowers," and then, "Virgil, this is Bob Brown, head of security, David McCullough, he's with the ATF, and Barrett Newman runs the building systems."

They all shook hands and Virgil said, "You know what I'd like to do? Right now, I'd just like to walk around the outside of the building and look at stuff. You mind?"

They didn't and Virgil said, "Just a minute," and walked over to the door, and pulled on it, and it opened. "The door isn't locked," he said.

"The inside one is," said Brown. "You can wave at the cameras while you wait for the guard to unlock it."

"Okay," Virgil said.

"So the idea is," Brown said, "that a guy with a skateboard, which can be quiet, is waiting at the bottom of the ramp, under a car. A VIP truck comes up, and he rolls out and grabs the bumper, and they tow him up the hill, right to the glass. He's got a key card, which he stole off a careless employee. . . . But how does he get past the guard? And why didn't we see him on the cameras?"

"I didn't think of the skateboard idea," Virgil said. "Hadn't gotten that far."

"We did," Brown said.

"Any of the regular employees check in, who should have been on vacation?" Virgil asked.

"Two did. Both had reasons," Brown said. "We checked the reasons. Neither one went above the fiftieth floor. To go higher than that, you have to have a specially authorized key card, which they didn't."

"So you checked."

"Yes, we did."

"Anybody's houses get broken into? When the key cards might have been compromised?"

"Not in the last month," Brown said.

Virgil asked, "Did you check all the board members?"

"We did," Brown said.

"Are there cameras inside the stairwells above the fiftieth floor?"

"No, nothing like that, though the access doors are locked at the fiftieth. But if you had a key card to get through those doors, you could go all the way to the top."

Newman, the building systems man, said, "There's another crack in the security, too. Years ago, there was a deck up on the top floor, and the employees were allowed to go to sixty, on the elevator, without a key card, and then out the doors to the deck. But not many people went, and maintenance got expensive, so that was eventually ended. But if you had one of those old key cards, you could still get to sixty. Then, you could go outside, and down the interior stairs to the fifty-to-fifty-nine levels without anybody seeing you. But you'd have to have that old key card . . . and we don't know that anybody does."

"Custodians?"

Brown said, "When everything is said and done, there are at least two hundred and fifty-one insiders who could get up to fifty-five and place the bomb. We've talked to every one of them. That's pretty much gotta be how it happened, but boy, it's tough. We've found anger, and grudges, and resentment, and whatever—but nothing like what you'd need to plant a bomb. At least, not that we've been able to detect."

McCullough, of the ATF, said, "We are, by the way, looking at all the video for the last month, after Barlow called us. He told us about the pipe, about finding that piece of pipe at the college, and the possibility that the bomb might have been detonated by cell phone."

"Huh," Virgil said. "Let's take that walk."

_____

They walked around the building, looking at exterior doors, at the loading dock, at the outlets for a package sewage-treatment plant, at storm-water drains; all of it was lit by heavy exterior lighting, which, though designed to enhance the building's aesthetics, also made it impossible to get close to the building unseen. When they were done, Virgil was ready to concede that the building would have been difficult to penetrate from the outside—as difficult as it would be to penetrate a prison. Even if it had been possible to penetrate the building because of some regular security lapse discovered by an intruder, he'd still be on the comprehensive video, and he wasn't.

"So you're now where we're at," Brown said. "It's an insider."

"Who must have some connection to a bomb maker in Butternut Falls," Virgil said. "Has to be a tight relationship. Probably not a relative, now that I think about it. Probably an ideological connection."

Done with the inspection of the building's perimeter, the group took Virgil inside, through the front doors, past a guard desk with two guards, and through an electronic gate operated with a key card. Brown pointed out an array of cameras that covered the doors and the reception area, showed him how the elevators worked, and finally took him up to the fifty-fifth floor, where the bomb had been set off.

The boardroom was still a mess, though sheets of Plexiglas had been fitted into the gaps left by blown-out windows, and the furniture pushed into a corner. "What about the woman who was killed?" Virgil asked.

"Angela 'Jelly' Brown, Mr. Pye's secretary," Brown said. "What about her?"

"Have you checked her out?"

After a moment of silence, McCullough said, "Yeah, to a certain extent. Not much to check. Quiet, routine life. Husband works as a driver at a data-services place. No politics that we could find—registered Republicans, but not active. They live in

Grand Rapids. We didn't, uh, go through her apartment or anything."

Virgil said, "Huh."

McCullough said, "I suppose we could have done that, but to tell the truth, I'd bet my job on the idea that she's innocent. That she had no connection with the bombing. She liked Pye, a lot, and she liked her coworkers, and they liked her . . . and if she placed the bomb, why in God's name would she have been standing one foot away when it blew?"

"Could she have been moving it?"

"No. We've established that it was inside the credenza, on the upper shelf, above four reams of paper, when it blew. The credenza door was closed."

"Okay," Virgil said. The room still stank of death, though the carpet had been taken away. A bunch of thin waxy pink and blue birthday candles were scattered along the base of one wall. Virgil asked about that, and Brown said, "They were going to have a birthday party for Mr. Pye. The board was. Almost died at his own birthday party."

There were no security cameras on the fiftieth floor, the barrier floor, Brown said, because there were cameras at every access point.

"Except the elevator . . . going up the elevator to sixty, and then coming down the stairs," Chapman said.

"And just climbing the stairs if you had a key card," Virgil said. "If you had a card for the door at the fiftieth floor . . . right?"

"Yeah, that's right," Brown said. "It's like we said—we can see the possibility that an insider could have planted the bomb. The complication is, we don't see any way an outsider could have done it, and everything you guys developed in Minnesota suggests that there's an outsider involved. Whoever planted that bomb in Willard's limo out there . . . he wasn't from here. Whoever cut the pipe at the college, he wasn't from here, either. We started checking as soon as we heard about it—where everybody was, who worked here. So it's either a conspiracy, or we just don't know what happened."

"Is there any possibility that the bomb

was there a long time?" Virgil asked. "If it had a cell phone as a detonator . . ."

McCullough said, "Not really. The cabinet was used to store office supplies—notebooks, file folders, reports, that kind of thing. You couldn't tell when it was going to be opened, but it was opened often enough. I know it's possible, but I really don't think there was a cell phone. I think it was set off by the clock, and it was placed inside the twenty-four-hour period before it went off."

"Another thing," said Newman, the building systems guy, "is that whoever planted the bomb had to know exactly when and where the board meeting was, and had to know something about the building layout, and how to get into the room." He turned to Brown: "*Has* to be an insider. *Has* to be a conspiracy."

After leaving the boardroom, Virgil was shown what McCullough called Pye's inner sanctum, a small but comfortable office behind a large outer office, with a big desk, "in" and "out" boxes, a computer, and a view of the interstate.

"We've wondered why the bomber didn't put it in here, but it's possible that Jelly Brown locked the outer office doors at night. We don't know that she did, but we can't ask her."

Virgil looked through the office suite, which included a conference room, a small bedroom with a bathroom, and a sitting area with a wide-screen television. When he was finished looking, he asked to be taken up the stairwell to the roof. He noticed that the doors into and out of the stairwell were not locked—"Because of nine-eleven," Brown said. "Willard considered us something of a target out here, and we did a review of what we could do to get people out in case we were hit by a plane. One thing we could do is allow people to go down one stairwell or the other—there are four of them, one on each side of the building—and then cross over and go down another one. So you could zigzag down through the building if you needed to. If you're below fifty, you can't go up, but if you're above fifty, you can go out."

The roof was big and flat and had the usual ventilation equipment and a big shed for window-washing equipment. Virgil asked about that, and Brown said, "Nobody used the window-washing grooves. They begin thirty feet above ground level, and even if you managed to get at them, unseen, it'd take you hours to climb the building. You'd be in plain sight all the time."

There wasn't much of a view from the top. Virgil could see the glow of Grand Rapids on the horizon to the west, another glow to the southeast—Lansing? Virgil thought—and headlights and taillights on the highway to the south. To the north there was nothing but darkness.

Chapman looked up into the night sky and said, "If you parachuted onto the roof . . ."

Brown said, "Right. You get a pilot and a skydiving plane to fly you over the building in the middle of the night with a bomb in your arms, and then you base-dive off the building when you're done. . . . I don't think so. If you're gonna have a conspiracy, it's a thousand times more likely that it's an insider."

McCullough said, "I bet Ford International has a radar track tape for that night. . . . Maybe we ought to check."

Brown said, "Sure, check."

They came off the roof and took the elevator down to the third floor, where the company had set up overnight suites for visitors, and a lounge. They sat in the lounge, and the three men detailed the investigation, and again, Virgil had a hard time faulting it. When they were done, Brown asked, "What do you think?"

"I'm glad I saw it, so it wasn't a total waste of time coming out," Virgil said. "I gotta say, the place seems pretty tight. I mean, maybe, *maybe* there's some way a guy could have ridden in, inside a UPS truck or something, with a key card, and gotten up there . . . but I don't see it. He'd have to know too much. Too much small detail. He'd have to have done a lot of surveillance."

"It's an insider," McCullough said.

"And a conspiracy," Brown said. "But that's weird. How did they hook up? What's the relationship?"

"I don't know, but that's what we're

going to focus on," McCullough said. "There has to be a link between here and Butternut Falls. We have to push until we find it."

Virgil was shown into a room a little before two in the morning. He lay awake for a few minutes, thinking about this and that, and for a while about God, and then almost went to sleep. But not quite asleep. Eventually, he crawled out from under the sheet and got out his laptop and linked into the Pinnacle's Wi-Fi system, and went out on the Net, researching "Pye Pinnacle."

It took a while, but he eventually found a PyeMart promotional video about the building that included a shot of a much younger Willard Pye greeting board members as they got off the elevators. When the doors opened, Virgil could see a metal "55" set in the edges of the elevator doors.

He said, "Huh."

In twenty minutes, he had the information he needed to plant a bomb in the boardroom; he even knew he could plant it in the credenza.

But he still had no way in, or up.

He checked his e-mail before he went to sleep and found a message from Lee Coakley, his sheriff in Malibu, or West Hollywood, or wherever it was. The note said: *I tried to call you several times on your cell, but got no service. Talk to you soon.*

He checked his phone: she'd called while he was in the air, with the phone turned off.

He got to sleep a little after three, and the alarm woke him at seven. At seven-twenty, he was in the Pye truck with a sleepy Chapman, who said, "We'll have breakfast on the plane, and then I'm gonna crash again. I feel like somebody put a Vulcan nerve pinch on me."

"Sounds right," Virgil said, yawning.

"You figure anything out?" she asked.

"I spent some time online. There's enough information about the Pinnacle that you could figure out where the board-room is, and you can also figure out when the board meetings are, and where. The last board meeting, before the bomb, was in Dallas. I don't know where the next one will be, but I could probably find out a few days before it happens. . . . It's deep in the business news, but it's in there."

"Hmm," she said. "I'll mention that to Willard."

Virgil shook his head. "It looks like a conspiracy, but it doesn't feel that way. Everything is too clockwork-like, too precise. If it's a conspiracy, that would mean that we have two nuts—one here and one in Butternut—who are both absolutely murderous, and who were willing to trust each other, and both intelligent. How did they find each other? How did they get together?"

"Well, maybe on the Internet," she said. "There are anti-PyeMart and anti-Walmart and anti-Target websites. What if a couple of people cooked up a conspiracy . . . I mean, one was from Butternut, but the other one could have been from anywhere. He or she moves to Grand Rapids or Lansing and gets a job out at the Pinnacle—gets a job for the sole purpose of blowing up the board."

Virgil thought about that for a moment,

then said, "I've got a researcher at the BCA who is really good at the Net. I'll have her troll those PyeMart sites, see what she comes up with."

"But we don't know when they would have met."

"In the last two years, if there were two of them. PyeMart didn't start making noises about building in Butternut until two years ago," Virgil said. "Took them a year to get the permits, and another year to get under way."

"Have to check," she said.

"Yeah, but I still . . . don't think it's a conspiracy. We're missing something. I think it's one guy, pretty smart, who figured out a way to get into the Pinnacle. Are there tours of the building? If there are, did anyone go missing for a few minutes? That kind of thing."

"There are tours, but not often—and not one recently," she said. "McCullough checked that. The ATF guys are really good."

They speculated, but came up with nothing solid; got to Ford International a few minutes after eight, were off the ground at eight-fifteen. After a quick breakfast of Cheerios and sweet rolls, the cabin attendant folded out beds for Virgil and Chapman, and Virgil was asleep in two minutes; he woke again when the wheels touched down in Butternut.

The trip, he thought, might have been time wasted.

But it didn't feel wasted; it felt, instead, like he'd learned something about the mind of the bomber. He was clever, and had a streak of boldness, even recklessness. He'd somehow gotten into the Pinnacle, and back out, and had never touched any of the trip lines set up by a very professional security system.

Interesting.

10

The bomber got a little drunk, and he did it deliberately.

He'd been trained as a straight-line thinker, which was good, most of the time, but he was smart enough to recognize the weaknesses of straight-line thinking. Sometimes, you had to get out of the box, out of the geometry. In his experience, nothing loosened up the mind like a pitcher of martinis, drunk alone. He had the pitcher, he had the gin, he had the vermouth. And he certainly was alone.

He mixed up the booze, got a tumbler,

and carried it out to his tiny backyard deck, where he sat in a wooden deck chair with plastic cushions, looked up at the stars, and let his mind roam free.

How had he landed here, in Butternut Falls? He should be in New York, Chicago, Los Angeles. At Columbia, the University of Chicago, UCLA. He had this recurring image of himself, pushing through some gilded revolving doors somewhere—a big city, probably New York, because he's wearing a New York kind of hat—and a newsman pushes a microphone in his face and asks, "What do you think of the president's plan?"

"The president's a fool, a lightweight," he'd say, his face sharply outlined, almost like one of those yellow-suited superheroes in the comics.

Like that was going to happen. Every time he'd been ready to make a move, something had jumped up to thwart him. Everything from an ill-timed job recession, to an ill-planned marriage. Barbara had been the worst of it. She'd dragged him out to Butternut and used her family's influence to get him a job, and the job had nailed his feet to the ground. All so she could be near her mother; though he couldn't imagine anybody would want to stay close to that witch.

Barbara had dragged him, pushed him. Hectored him.

The power of pussy, he thought. The power of pussy.

And time kept passing. He was hardly aware of it, the days passing so quickly and seamlessly; every time he turned around, it seemed like he was shaving in the morning to go out and waste another day of his life. He *felt* like he was in his twenties, still a young guy, on the move, with a great future—but somehow, nearly twenty years had slipped away. He was nearly as old as that fool, the president.

Oh, he'd made plans. One of them involved dumping Barbara, but, surprise, surprise, she'd moved first, and he'd found himself with no house and only half an eventual pension. She'd nailed him down with pussy, and then, when she left, nailed him down with economics and legal decrees. She was followed by a couple more mistakes, and finally, he would sit on this patio and he could see the future stretching out in front of him, ending in penury . . . ending with dog food and a hot plate.

That made him smile: the alcohol talking.

He was in no serious danger of dog food, but he *was* in danger of something that was probably worse: irrelevance, in his own eyes. He looked at the people around him, at their trivial lives, and he sneered at them, but then he came home to look in the mirror and ask, "How am I different?"

The truth was, he wasn't. If a Martian landed tomorrow, and was told to sort people into piles of the relevant and the irrelevant, judging by what they did, by what they *were*, he'd wind up in the same pile as those he sneered at.

Then came PyeMart, and everything that rained down from that.

Loosen up, he thought, *loosen up.* He poured another martini, and thought about bombs.

Jesus God, he was becoming fond of his bombs. Nobody—*nobody*—would say that his bombs were irrelevant. He was already the most important element in the lives of two people, in that he'd ended those lives.

Where should the next one go? Where would it do the most good?

There'd been a rumor that the state cops were protecting the city council and the city hall. That there were snipers in town. He wasn't sure he believed it, but it had to be considered. He considered it, more than a little drunk after the third martini . . . and there were still two martinis left. He giggled: whoa, boy, he was really gonna be pounded when he finished the last one.

So what about the city council? He went back and forth on them. Could they hurt him more than they could help? If they all went up in an instant of smoke and flame, would that be the beginning of everything? Or the end?

He thought about the council all through the fourth martini, and decided that while he had no objection, in principle, to killing them all, the fallout from such an event was too unpredictable.

No. He'd started out to intimidate PyeMart, to slow them down, and also to lay a trail of bombs that had a seeming purpose. He was not stupid, so the trail was a crooked one, but it would eventually lead the authorities, by the nose, to one certain conclusion. And that still seemed the best way to go.

He'd never had a full set plan for his campaign; a set plan could crack. He'd known from the start that he had to remain flexible, and improvise from time to time. This was one of those times.

If the city council was actually found to be corrupt, if a city councilman could be terrorized into confessing, or if the cops could be pressured into looking at them seriously, then the whole PyeMart deal would go down like the *Titanic*.

That was a compelling thought.

But PyeMart's deal couldn't go down too soon, or too late. Like Baby Bear's porridge, it had to be just right.

He considered the thought, and drunk as he was, it was a slippery thing to hang onto. The problem was, the local cops couldn't be counted on to cooperate with the city council. Basically, they couldn't find their own balls with both hands and a radar unit. A serious investigation was unlikely.

The ideal thing would be to bring in the state cops, or the FBI. The ATF was in town, but the ATF wouldn't be much interested in doing a political corruption investigation.

Stray thought: somebody had been distributing a bumper sticker in town—he'd seen three or four of them—that said: "Alcohol, Tobacco, Firearms . . . What's not to like?"

Anyhoo . . .

Whoa, really drunk now. He struggled to stay on track.

The state cops were in town; state *cop*, that is. One guy, and all he apparently was thinking about was finding the bomber.

What you really needed, the bomber thought, was a whole bunch of cops, pulling the whole town apart. If that happened, they'd eventually get around to the city council.

The bomber sat on his deck, drunk and plotting, and at some point well into his last martini, too drunk to even consider getting up and making more, an out-of-the-box plan began to form.

Take brass balls, but he *had* brass balls. No question about that. Not anymore.

He needed to think about it sober; couldn't do it tonight, anyway. There was too much action right now, too many people with an eye out. Paranoia was a good thing, in the bombing business. So tonight he'd sleep it off, and tomorrow, he'd make the bomb. Make the bomb, and plant it tomorrow night.

Bring in a whole *swarm* of cops.

Guaranteed.

Or was that just the alcohol talking?

Billions and billions of stars shone down at him, twinkling their asses off, but they didn't say shit.

The bomber fell asleep in his deck chair, and slept the sleep of the innocent.

11

Virgil dropped Chapman at her motel and called Davenport to report on the trip out to Michigan. He was sitting in the truck, talking to Davenport, when he saw George Peck, the traditionalist fly fisherman, walking along the street, looking into store windows.

"I just saw a clue," Virgil said. "I gotta go."

He hung up and waited until Peck got even with him, then rolled down the passenger-side window and yelled, "Hey, George."

Peck turned, a frown on his face, saw

Virgil in the truck, and walked over. "You shouted?"

"Yeah. I need to talk to you. Come on, get in."

Peck paused for a moment, as if thinking about it, then nodded and popped the door and climbed in. He pulled the door shut, tilted his head up, sniffed, and said, "This truck smells like McDonald's french fries."

"It should—french fries are about eighty-five percent of my diet when I'm traveling," Virgil said. "Listen, I've talked to a few guys about your whole market research idea. They don't like it. I kinda do—but then, I might not be as smart as they are. There's talk of lynch mobs."

"I doubt you'd get a lynch mob," Peck said.

"That's not real reassuring—if you only doubt that I'd get one."

"Not my problem," Peck said. "But, consensus-seeking research seems to work with problems like yours. Of course, they're usually asking about stock market moves, or some such. There's usually no lynching involved. Or bombs."

Virgil said, "What if instead of putting up a website, I got twenty very knowledgeable people . . ."

Peck was shaking his head. "That might not be enough. You need lots and lots of people. You could ask twenty people and just out of coincidence, because of social-class acquaintance problems, maybe none of them know the bomber . . . so they can't nominate him. You need not just one set of smart people, but a whole spectrum of people."

"But the bomber has to come from a class of people who object to PyeMart. So if I come up with a long list of people who don't like PyeMart, they'd almost certainly know him."

Peck thought about it for a minute, then said, "Unless . . . hmmm." And he thought some more.

"Say it," Virgil said.

"I was going to say, 'Unless he was acting on an impulse.' I was thinking, what if it's, say, a college kid, and these opinions are new and he got swept up in them, but doesn't have a history in town politics or issues arguments. He's simply crazy, and looking for an outlet. Then, you might never see him, if you only surveyed people who were familiar with PyeMart opponents. But . . . on second thought . . . from what I know, that doesn't seem likely. It seems more likely to be the work of a mature man. A planner. Somebody who thinks things through. Somebody more like me. So I'd probably know him. So . . ."

"So . . . ?"

"So if you made a list based on your investigation, and on the federal investigation, of the bomber's characteristics, and if you gave that list to me and, say, ten other people I might suggest . . . I think those ten people might be able to come up with a second list of a couple hundred people you could survey. Then, I think you would get your man."

Virgil turned and pulled his briefcase out of the backseat. "Let's make a list of characteristics right now. Then you can give me your list of names, and I'll get the list around."

Peck said, "Why don't we go down to McDonald's and work through this. It's right around the corner."

"Good with me. I could use some fries," Virgil said.

They got a booth at McDonald's, and soft drinks and fries, and Virgil laid out what he'd found to that point. Peck listened carefully, and they began their list.

The bomber, they thought:

- was almost certainly male (because bombers almost always were).
- was willing to take serious, but calculated, risks, both in building bombs and in planting them.
- was intelligent. Was building bombs and detonators from first principles. Knew something about switches and electricity.
- had hard opinions and was willing to act on them, even to the point of killing people. A streak of fanaticism. The bomber is crazy.
- was acting out of an economic or environmentalist impulse.
- probably had some close connection with Butternut Tech.

- was intimately familiar with Butternut environs and personalities, down to limousine drivers.
- could have close relatives or friends in the Grand Rapids, Michigan, area.

"In the letter you write to the survey people, you have to say that they need to consider all the points," Peck said. "But in the end, you're also looking for gut feelings."

Virgil wrote *gut feelings* at the bottom of the list.

"And you'll have to say that nobody will see the answers except you, and that you'll destroy the lists. Or, better yet, that it'll all be anonymous, and nobody will know who answered what, not even you. Or even, who answered. Because not everybody will."

"George, you're a big help," Virgil said. "Give me the list of ten names that'll get me the list of two hundred."

Getting Peck to produce ten names took a while, but when he got them, Virgil drove over to the county courthouse and began putting together a letter to the ten people recommended by Peck. The sheriff came by to see what he was up to, and Virgil showed him Peck's list.

The sheriff agreed that the ten names had been well chosen, added two more names, plus his own and his wife's, for a total of fourteen. He had a deputy get together a list of home and business addresses.

In his letter to the first, smaller group, Virgil asked that their lists be returned to the sheriff's department that afternoon or evening.

Time is of the essence, he wrote. *We hope to begin distributing the survey tomorrow morning.*

The sheriff got two deputies and told them to chase down the twelve people on Virgil's list; he would take his own letter and his wife's. "This is gonna be weird," Ahlquist said. "Never heard anything like it being done. Could freak people out."

"With any luck, it'll keep the bomber laying low," Virgil said.

"Speaking of which, you oughta lay low yourself," Ahlquist said. "You're the most obvious threat to him. You could wind up with a bomb in your boat."

"I don't think he's that kind of a monster," Virgil said. "Bombing a man's boat."

"I'm serious," Ahlquist said. "I'd ask the people at the Holiday to move you to another room, one that opens to the inside, over the pool, where he'd be seen if he went to your door."

Virgil said, "I'll do that. I'll be back at eight o'clock or so, to pick up the responses. If I can collate the list we get back tonight, and get the second letter out to however many people we have— Peck thinks a couple hundred would be good—we could start getting a list together tomorrow night."

"Be interesting," Ahlquist said. "What're you doing for the rest of the day?"

"I got a couple of guys I want to talk to, and, uh . . . you got any fish in that lake?"

Virgil found Cameron Smith, president of the local trout-fishing club, at work at the

Butternut Outdoor Patio Design Center. Smith was busy with a female customer when Virgil walked in, so he spent fifteen minutes chatting with a nice-looking blond bookkeeper who worked in the back office. When Virgil introduced himself, she called Smith, who was thirty feet away, on the other side of a door, on her cell phone. Smith said he'd be there as soon as he could get away.

"That's a big order out there," the woman said. Her name, according to a desk plaque, was Kiki Bjornsen. "She's looking at spending over nine thousand on patioware and a spa."

"Is that PyeMart gonna sell patio stuff?"

"Not like ours," Bjornsen said. "I mean, they might sell some rickety old aluminum chairs, but they won't be selling any Sunbrella products."

"Good for you."

"And I can tell you for sure that Cam didn't blow anything up," she said. "He just got back from Canada last night. He was up there with about six college friends. He was up there for a week."

"Well, shoot, there goes my day," Virgil

said. "I was planning to drag him kicking and screaming down to the county jail."

"That'd be something to see," she said.

Smith was a chunky, sunburned man who said he'd just spent five days getting blown off Lake of the Woods, and Virgil told him that he'd been blown off Lake of the Woods himself, on several occasions.

"Fishing out of Kenora?" Smith asked.

"Yeah, most of the time. I really like that town," Virgil said.

"Got the most vicious, impolite, asshole game wardens I ever met," Smith said. "We were out five days, got stopped three times. Hell, we're fishing on a conservation tag, not keeping anything, and they're tearing our boats apart."

"They do that," Virgil said. "But the fishing is good."

"And they got some good pizza," Smith said. "So, what can I do for you?"

"Is there anybody in your trout club that might be setting off these bombs?"

"I been thinking about that ever since I heard about the bomb, the first one," Smith said. "I call my wife every night to tell her I didn't drown, and she told me about it, about that poor bastard getting blown to pieces. I mean, jeez, nobody deserves that. . . . Anyway, no. I don't think any of our guys would do that. We've got some rednecks, but you know, they're all . . . fishermen. Fishermen don't kill people."

"Well, maybe muskie fishermen," Virgil said.

"Okay, I'll give you that," Smith said. "But not us trout guys. Crappie guys might be bombers, but I don't think walleye guys, or bass or bluegill guys. Bullhead guys . . . well, we don't talk about bullhead guys. I don't think they'd go violent, but they're not quite right in the head, if you know what I mean."

Virgil nodded: he tended to agree with Smith's characterizations.

"You know Larry Butz," Virgil said.

"Yeah, and he's the one everybody would point at, because he's got a loud mouth. But he's really a good guy," Smith said. "The paper this morning said that a group of kids were crossing the street just before Harvey's limo blew up, and that's the kind of thing that Larry would

have thought of. About other people getting hurt. He's got five kids, and there's
no way he'd ever take a chance like that.
That he'd hurt a kid. I mean, I don't think
he'd hurt anybody."

"I'm getting a lot of that," Virgil said.
"Nobody knows anybody who'd do something like this."

"Well, do you know anybody who'd
do it? A bomb guy, he's gotta be a rare
creature."

"That was my opinion, before I got tangled up in this, but the ATF guy tells me
they're not as rare as you'd think," Virgil
said. Then, "Have you ever been fishing
any of those lower pools and seen a guy
around there in camo? Maybe with a camera or a pair of binoculars?"

Smith said, "Noooo . . . not exactly. I
mean, if you mean sneaking around the
PyeMart site. I mean, in the fall we get a
couple of bow hunters back there."

"I was thinking, sneaking around looking at PyeMart, specifically," Virgil said.

"Haven't seen anything like that, but
then, I'm only back there once a week.
Maybe not that often. Hardly ever see any

cars parked up by the bridge, either. Those are usually guys that I know, and could vouch for."

"The bridge?"

"Yeah, there's a bridge upstream a half mile or so above the Walmart site, off County Road Y. There's a parking area down beside the bridge."

"Could you ask around, among your friends, about any unusual cars?"

"I can do that," Smith said.

Virgil pushed himself out of his chair, gave Smith a business card, and said, "Just mostly wanted to check with you. Think about it. If anything occurs to you, give me a ring, or if somebody saw a strange car out there in the last month."

Half an hour later, Virgil was backing his boat into Dance Lake. The lake had two basins, a shallow upper basin with lots of weed, and a deeper lower basin. After parking his rig, he took his boat north out of the landing, under a bridge and into the upper basin, picked out a weed bed on the flattest part of the lake, dropped his trolling motor. The depth finder said he was in four feet of water. He wasn't expecting much, just a short afternoon of messing with small pike.

He got his fly rod going, throwing a Bigeye Baitfish, and zenned out, letting the problem of the bomber percolate through the back of his brain. Talking with Peck had been useful; he had some hope for the survey. The connection with the tech school should help winnow suspects.

Critical question: What should he do to keep pressure on the bomber? What would make him keep his head down? He was thinking about that when a small pike hit the Bigeye and, feeling the resistance of the line, tried to make a run into the weed bank. Virgil turned his head, got him running sideways, turned him toward the boat, played him, eventually brought him alongside—maybe twenty-three or twenty-four inches, he thought—grabbed the eye of the hook and shook it loose.

He'd gotten some pike slime on his hand and rinsed it off, then sat in the boat and let the sunshine sink into his shoulders; nothing like it. After a few minutes, he sighed, took the cell phone out of his pocket and called a reporter, Ruffe Ignace, at the *Star Tribune*.

"Ruffe? Virgil Flowers here."

"Virgil—I heard you were up in Nutcup, trying to find that bomber."

"Yeah, I am, still," Virgil said. "Some of the media are spreading a rumor that I'd like to squelch."

"A rumor? In the media? No, you gotta be joking," Ignace said.

"As far as I know, there are no plans whatever to secretly deploy seventy-five to a hundred BCA infrared cameras around Butternut Falls, to monitor the coming and going of cars to sensitive sites," Virgil said.

"Wait-wait-wait, let me get the last part of that . . . 'to monitor the coming and going of cars to sensitive sites.' Is that right?"

"That's right. I have no information about any such plans."

"By sensitive sites, you mean like the city hall, the county courthouse, the city councilmen's houses, Willard Pye's cars, the PyeMart site, and so on?"

"Those would be sensitive sites," Virgil agreed.

"You're not saying that there aren't any plans, you're saying that you don't have any information about such plans."

"That's correct."

"I'm not writing the story, but I'll pass it on," Ignace said.

"God bless you," Virgil said. "And any children you may have spawned."

Done with Ignace, he called Barlow to see if the ATF had come up with anything at the tech school. They had not. "It's not a dead end, it's a rats' nest," Barlow said. "There're hundreds of people coming and going all the time, and they have adult evening classes, enrichment classes, and most of the adults in Butternut have been through there, at one time or another."

"I have a feeling that it's not a casual acquaintance, it's somebody who goes through there on a regular basis. Somebody who's familiar with the working of the place. A staff member, a full-time student."

"Well, we're still looking," Barlow said.

Another possibility occurred to him: What if there were more than one thing going on? What if the first bomb was aimed at Pye himself, as the third one had been— and had been brought in by some desperate board member? Desperate, why? Virgil didn't know, but he was sure that board members must get desperate from time to time. Pye was an older man, and there must be some kind of succession waiting in the wings. If you knew when the bomb was going to go off, then you could absent yourself. . . . Of course, if you knew when it was going to go off, you would have set it for later, after the board meeting was sure to be under way.

Still, there might be something in it— someone desperate, or greedy, in Grand Rapids, hooking up with somebody desperate in Butternut Falls.

As weird as it seemed, there was a history of crazy bombers getting together—9/11 of course, but also the Oklahoma City bombing. There'd been cases of serial killers finding each other, or recruiting accomplices.

How would you do that? The Internet.

He remembered Marie Chapman talking about anti-PyeMart sites. He'd forgotten to do anything about that. . . . Virgil got back on the phone and called the BCA researcher. "Sandy? This is Virgil. You got time to do some Internet research?"

She said, "If Lucas approves it."

He outlined what he wanted: for her to go back in the archives of any anti-PyeMart sites she could find and see if it looked like a couple of the crazier posters seemed to be getting together . . . and then tracking down where they were from.

"I can do all of that from home, so that'll make it cheaper," she said. Sandy worked on a part-time basis, and sometimes as a consultant. "I'll talk to Lucas and get back to you."

Another idea popped up. Would the bomber have taken all of the risks associated with building a bomb, and smuggling it into the Pinnacle, if he wasn't sure it would work? Most likely, he'd rehearsed somewhere. That "somewhere" was most likely around Butternut. While the town *was* out in the countryside, it wasn't a wilderness—if a bomb had gone off within a hundred miles of Butternut, somebody had heard it.

How to find those people?

Virgil went back to the fly rod, but his heart wasn't in it, and after another ten minutes and one strike-and-miss, he motored back to the landing and yanked the boat out of the water. On the way back into the downtown, he called the sheriff, asked for the name and number of the local paper, which he couldn't remember— the *Clarion Call*, as it turned out. He got the editor on the line and asked about the possibility of a public request-for-help on the next day's front page.

"Well, what do you need?"

"I need a story that says the bomber probably rehearsed his bombings—he probably touched off a couple explosions within the last month or so. Probably not too far from Butternut—it'd be someplace familiar to him. You can attribute all those thoughts to me. I'd like to ask your readers if any of them heard an unexplained explosion. If they have, call the sheriff's department."

"Sure, we can do that. Give it a good spot, too."

"I appreciate it," Virgil said.

The day was still hot, but the afternoon was wearing on, and he'd been up early. Nap time? If he could get an hour or two, he'd be good until midnight. Back at the Holiday Inn, he was headed for his room when the desk clerk came running out to the parking lot and called, "Hey, Virgil."

Virgil stopped. "Yeah?"

The kid was waving a piece of paper. "You got a call. It's important."

"A confession, I hope?"

"Well, yeah, something like that." He handed a piece of paper to Virgil. "It was kind of anonymous. I took it down word for word."

Virgil unfolded it. In the clerk's neat handwriting, the note said: *For Virgil Flowers of the Bureau of Criminal Apprehension. Important. Pat Shepard's wife Jeanne knows he took $25,000 from Pye but* *doesn't know what he did with it. She thinks he used it to pay back taxes. He didn't. He hid it so he could spend it on his girlfriend Marilyn Oaks (sp?). Jeanne doesn't know about Marilyn.*

Pat Shepard was one of the city councilmen who voted for the PyeMart. Virgil took a minute to digest the note. A cricket started chirping from the flower bed around the parking lot, an annoyance that brought him back. He asked the desk clerk what he thought. "I think Jeanne Shepard is the second-hottest woman in town."

Virgil checked him out: a fairly good-looking blond jock-like kid of seventeen or eighteen, with big shiny white teeth; a kid who reminded him somewhat of himself, when he was that age. "How old is she?"

The kid shrugged: "I don't know. Thirty-five?"

"What are you doing, thinking a thirty-five-year-old woman is hot?"

"Hey. If you're hot, you're hot," the kid said. He was wearing a name tag that said *Thor*.

"Did you take the message?" Virgil asked.

"Yup. It was a man," Thor said. "He refused to give his name, but it was Doug Mackey. Mr. Mackey."

"Mr. Mackey?"

"He's a teacher at the high school," Thor said. "He was my golf coach for three years, and I took driver's ed from him. I recognized his voice, but he didn't recognize mine. Mr. and Mrs. Shepard are teachers, too. You want to know what I think?"

"Sure," Virgil said.

"Mr. Mackey and Mr. Shepard are friends and they play a lot of golf together, at least once or twice a week. I think Mr. Shepard told Mr. Mackey that he's nailing Marilyn Oaks. I don't know Marilyn Oaks, but she must be the first-hottest in town, if Mr. Shepard is chasing her, instead of staying home. I'm telling you, Mrs. Shepard has got an ass like a couple of slow-pitch softballs. If it was me, I'd be—"

"Stick to the story," Virgil said.

"Hey. I'm trying to get you fully informed. Anyway, I figure Mr. Mackey wants to nail Mrs. Shepard, or already is, and he's trying to get Mr. Shepard out of the picture. He thinks you'll go over there and tell her about Marilyn Oaks, and one way or another, Mr. Shepard is outa here and Mr. Mackey moves into Mrs. Shepard's thong."

"Mrs. Shepard wears a thong?"

"Better believe it," Thor said. "Black in color, and just about the size of a pirate's eye patch."

"Eye patch?"

"She once wore a pair of tight white pants out to the country club—I was caddying at the time—and you could see it, right through the pants, when she started to sweat a little," Thor said. "I want to tell you, I had a woody she could have putted with, and I was only fourteen. Another time, I was supposed to take some stuff for a school play over to her house, and she came out wearing a T-shirt and no bra, and she had nipples like the end of my little finger, and hard as marbles. Honest to God, I wish—"

"Stick to the story," Virgil said. "How did Mackey find out that Shepard took the money?"

"Either Mr. Shepard told him, because they're pals, just like he told Mr. Mackey about nailing Marilyn Oaks. Or, Mr. Mackey already nailed Mrs. Shepard, and she told him. Or, he's lying about it, and he doesn't know anything."

"How old are you, Thor?" Virgil asked.

"Eighteen. Just graduated."

"You have a very suspicious mind," Virgil said. "And not entirely unsullied."

"I've been told that," Thor said.

"You know what unsullied means?"

"Sure."

Virgil closed one eye and peered at the kid. "I actually have a gun in the car," he said. "If you tell anybody about this note, I'll kill you."

"Whatever," the kid said.

"I don't want a *whatever*, I want your mouth shut," Virgil said. "This is important stuff."

"Make you a deal," Thor said. "I'll keep my mouth shut and you tell me if Mrs. Shepard finds out about Marilyn Oaks. From you, or anybody else."

"If I made that deal, what would you get out of it?" Virgil asked.

"Mrs. Shepard always liked my looks. I could tell," Thor said. "I had her for tenth-grade American literature and senior English. Soon as she throws her old man out, I'd run over to Pizza Hut, get an anchovy pizza, and go over to her house for a chat. Get there before Mackey."

"Ah, man. Anchovies. Just like a ninth-grader," Virgil said. "You get a woman like that, you buy a meat lovers' and nothing else."

"A meat lovers'?"

"Take it from me. The hormones in the meat gets them hot."

"Nasty, but I believe you," Thor said. "So, we got a deal?"

"Maybe."

"Maybe?"

"I want to get a look at Mrs. Shepard first," Virgil said. "A youth like yourself might not be qualified to handle her."

"That is *not right*," Thor said. "That is *wrong*."

Up in his hotel room, Virgil called Davenport, who was about to leave the office, and told him about the note.

"Can you do both? Get the bomber and the city council?"

"If this note is real, I might," Virgil said.

"The thing is, half the people in town believe the council sold out, and they may be right. And they're looking for somebody to help. They deserve at least a look."

"Fine. But keep the bomber on the front burner," Davenport said. "If you can do the other . . . I hate that kind of corruption shit. It drags us all down. But they're not killing anybody. Not yet, anyway."

"Okay. I thought I'd check," Virgil said.

"I okayed Sandy for some research time on anti-PyeMart sites," Davenport said. "She'll be getting back to you."

"Good. Hell, I'm gonna push everything," Virgil said. "I think I can crack the whole town open. The fact is, moving on the city council might get me closer to the bomber, too."

"Good luck with that," Davenport said. "Stay in touch. And stay out of the boat, goddamnit."

"What boat?"

12

That evening, Virgil called the AmericInn and got transferred to Marie Chapman's room. She'd just come through the door, she said, when she picked up. "Willard's got his computer out, and he's looking at spreadsheets, so I'm done."

"Good. Can I buy you dinner?"

"Yes. Is there anywhere besides Bunson's? I'm about Bunsoned out."

"There's an exceptional Applebee's in Butternut," Virgil said. "Mmm-mm."

"Bunson's it is," she said. "Give me a half hour. I'll meet you in the lobby."

———

Virgil did a quick run through the bathroom, showered, brushed his teeth, slapped a little Old Spice behind his ears, went outside, dropped the boat trailer, cleaned out the truck, and still had five minutes to get to the AmericInn.

On the way over, he questioned his motives: he was still attached to Lee Coakley, but had the feeling that Lee was drifting away, if not already gone. Should he push on Chapman a little, to see what would happen? With her rootless type of job, he didn't doubt that she would be a little lonely, and sophisticated enough not to put too much importance on . . . what? What exactly was he doing here? And if he should hustle her into bed, or vice versa, what would that do for, or to, his soul?

Anyway, he got to her motel in three minutes, and precisely a half hour after he'd spoken to her on the phone, she walked into the lobby and said, "Right on the minute."

She was wearing a turquoise blouse and black pants, with a Hopi silver necklace and earrings. "You look terrific," Virgil said.

"You're getting off on the right foot," she said. "I require large amounts of flattery."

"You came to the right guy," he said.

On the way to Bunson's, they chitchatted, and at the restaurant, got a quiet table. Virgil ordered a Leinie's and Chapman got a margarita, and Virgil started filling her in on the lack of any new developments in the search for the bomber.

"The sheriff said something about doing a survey . . ."

"Yeah, I gotta go back there tonight and print up a bunch of letters and stuff them in envelopes and get them addressed," Virgil said. "Gonna get the sheriff's deputies to deliver them tomorrow . . . and then tomorrow night, I'm going to put it all together."

He explained the survey idea, and she said, "I'm familiar with the market concept, but usually, you need the players to bet on the outcome with some kind of pot they can win. Money. I could probably get Willard to put up some cash."

Virgil was shaking his head: "No, no. The kind of thing you're talking about, there's got to be a payoff to get people to play, and be serious about it. With this one, the payoff is catching the bomber and keeping yourself from getting blown up."

She said, "Maybe. You're gonna have to sort thousands of different names."

"I'm hoping not. I'm hoping there'll be hundreds, or maybe only dozens. That everybody knows who the potential crazies are," Virgil said. "The guy who gave me this idea thinks the bomber will be in the top ten."

They talked about that, ordered dinner, steaks and potatoes, and talked some more about it, and then Virgil said, "You know, a lot of people think Willard bribed the mayor and city council to approve the zoning change for the store."

"I know." She said nothing more.

Virgil waited for a minute, then asked, "What do you think about that?"

"I don't know," she said. She stopped talking as the food arrived, and when the waiter went away, she continued: "There was a situation in Indiana where a PyeMart construction expediter was charged with bribing members of a city council. This was four or five years ago. He was convicted and was sentenced to a year in jail. Willard said he didn't know anything about it. I believe him, but . . ."

"What's an expediter?" Virgil asked.

"PyeMart only goes into a town after a lot of market research—especially if there's already a Walmart," she explained. "Their target markets overlap somewhat. Margins are pretty low, and they want to make sure the store will make a profit. After the market research is done, if they decide that the market will handle the store, then an expediter is appointed. He fronts the company to the town—finds out what will be needed to get the store built. Local regulations, zoning, makes contacts with city officials and building-supply places. PyeMart tries to get the actual construction work done locally, and supplied locally, because that's an economic point that the town will have to consider."

"This guy expedited the store by bribing the city council?"

"Apparently. There was a slush fund in the construction department, and some of the slush got transferred to the councilmen," Chapman said. "Willard said he never knew. I believe him on that exact point, but I also know that expediters are paid a lot of money—a lot more than somebody normally would be at that level. I expect some of that is risk money. Expediters are not expected to come back and say they can't get the permits to build the store. They *get* the permits. Period."

"So Willard doesn't know of any specific case of bribery, but at some level, has to know that it goes on," Virgil said.

"Willard can be a very sweet man and he's tremendously loyal to his employees—but he is a ferocious businessman. He does what he thinks he needs to do." She hesitated, and rolled the bottom of her margarita glass on the tabletop, making a tracery out of a couple drops of water. "We're now getting into an area that I want to reserve for my book."

"So he knows."

"I can't say that. I can tell you that the man, the expediter, who went to jail in Indiana, served eight months of the one-year sentence. When he got out, he landed on his feet: he got a great job with a major paper company, a maker of all kinds of paper products, everything from notebooks to paper plates."

"Yeah?"

"A major supplier to PyeMart," she said.

"So the guy got taken care of."

"That would be for somebody else to say," she said. Then, "Are you investigating Willard?"

"I'm trying to find the bomber," Virgil said. "But you know there've been accusations of bribery . . . you were at the press conference, almost a fistfight there."

"Well, I'll tell you, Virgil, I've said about as much as I'm going to say," Chapman said. "I won't betray Willard, or go sneaking around to find information for you. If you're going to investigate him, you'll have to do it on your own."

"Be a good thing for your book," Virgil said. "You know, if Pye got pitched into some kind of crisis."

She looked at him for a long moment,

then laughed, a short, choppy sound, and said, "The snake crawls out from behind the surfer-boy smile."

"Hey . . . I'm just telling you what's going on," Virgil said.

"We ought to talk about something else," she said.

So they did.

They had a pleasant meal, talked about writing, and about police work, about where they grew up, and about Virgil's cases—Chapman had access to an excellent news clipping service, and knew about Virgil's major busts. She was, Virgil thought, an interesting woman, but something had fundamentally changed between them when the word "snake" came out of her mouth. He dropped her at the AmericInn at nine o'clock and, feeling a little melancholy, went on to the sheriff's department.

Of the fourteen letters sent out, they'd gotten back eleven—three people declined to participate. Virgil took two hours to work through the mass of names, entering them on his laptop, with addresses.

After eliminating duplicates, he had a list of a hundred and seventy-eight people who'd be asked to nominate possible bombers.

Ahlquist had come through several times while Virgil was working out the list, and finally he said, "You sure you want to go through with this? It's gonna cause a stink."

"Yeah, it will, but it's a whole new way of looking at an investigative problem," Virgil said. "I'm almost as curious to see how it comes out as I am anxious to catch the bomber."

When he had the list, and the addresses, he wrote a carefully worded cover letter, explaining the idea behind the nominations, asking that the lists be returned to the sheriff's department no later than the next evening. He left space at the bottom, with ten blank underlines, for the bomber nominees, and noted that the letter's recipients didn't need to sign the letter or identify themselves in making their nominations.

He was working through the letter, revising, when he took a call from Lee

Coakley. He perked up as soon as he saw the incoming number, and heard her voice: "Virgil, how are you?"

"Aw, I'm in a mess of a case. I'm up in Butternut Falls."

"David told me, I looked it up on the *Star Tribune*'s website. Are you getting anywhere with it?"

"Well, I'm trying something new. . . ." He explained about the letters. When he finished explaining, she started laughing, and after a minute, said, "Virgil, you have a different kind of mind."

"*I* didn't think of it."

"But *you're* doing it. I hope Earl knows what you're getting him into."

"Earl's gonna do just fine, if I pull this off. Anyway, what have *you* been up to?"

So she told him, a bunch of stuff he didn't entirely understand about working through a gunfight on a TV show. "It's about half real, and half movie. I tell them what'd really happen, they tell me what they need to have happen, for the movie. Then, we try to work something out that feels sorta real, but gets done what they need done."

She went on for five minutes and

sounded so enthusiastic about it that Virgil felt the melancholy coming back. Because, he thought, Lee probably wouldn't be. When she said, "I gotta go, the boys are raising hell," it was a notably friendly, and non-intimate, good-bye. A kind of good-bye he recognized, a good-bye from a friend, not from a lover. He wondered if she recognized it, and thought she probably did, since women were always a few steps ahead in such matters.

Which, when he thought about it, was how he lost his Tim Kaihatsu–signed Gibson guitar when his second wife moved out.

He went back to the letters, editing them, then printing them. Before stuffing them in envelopes, he numbered each of the one hundred and seventy-eight names on his list, and on each letter, carefully, with black ink, put a small dot in a word that corresponded, in number, to the number of each name on the list.

In other words, the letter began with the phrase, *As you undoubtedly know . . .* and the first name on the list, Andrew

Lane, got a small black dot between the legs of the capital *A* in *As*. The second name on the list got a tiny dot in the *o* in *you*. The third name got a dot in the *o* of *undoubtedly*.

Because the letters had said the responses would be anonymous, it felt dishonest, but, he thought, it might be useful to know who nominated whom. He couldn't think of a reason *why* it might be useful, but then, he'd never done anything like this.

He finished after one o'clock in the morning, left a stack of letters with the duty officer, for delivery the next day, and headed back to the hotel.

He spent a restless night in the over-soft bed; too much to think about. He didn't have many new ideas about chasing the bomber, at least, not until the letters came back. That would give him as much work as he could handle.

In the meantime, he could look into the question of whether the city council had been bribed. That would not be fun—he would need to extort the necessary information, using marital infidelity as a wedge. He'd had a checkered past himself when it came to women—three divorces in three years, before he at least temporarily quit getting married. So you had some schoolteachers engaging in some bed-hopping—so what? Except, unfortunately for them, it might be tangled up with bribery.

He could also stay in bed, the pillow hard as a pumpkin, and spend the night brooding about Lee Coakley. Had she already been unfaithful? What about himself; was thinking about the honey-haired Marie Chapman actually unfaithful? Taking her out to dinner? Jimmy Carter would have said . . . But, you know, fuck Jimmy Carter.

In the morning, he cleaned up and decided to head out to Country Kitchen for French toast and link sausage; and, he thought, since he didn't know exactly what he'd be doing all day, he might as well take the boat, just in case.

He backed around, hooked up, and took off. At the street, he took the curb-cut too short and he felt the trailer's right wheel bounce over the curb.

In an infinitesimally short space of time, the bomb in the trailer blew up and the world lurched and Virgil found himself on the street, crawling away from the truck, with the sense of blood in his nose and mouth, though when he wiped his face with his hand, there wasn't any. He rolled onto his butt and looked back. The boat had been cut in half, but the truck itself seemed untouched; gasoline was pouring onto the street, and he thought, *Fire.*

He turned and continued crawling, then got to his feet and staggered away. He thought, *How did I get in the street . . . ?*

He could hear sirens, then, and two people ran out of the Holiday Inn's front door; he saw a window had blown out. The smell of gasoline was intense. . . . He pulled himself together and realized that when the bomb went off, he'd instinctively jammed the truck's gear shift into park, and had rolled out the door. . . . Hadn't thought about it—nothing had gone through his mind at all—he'd just done it.

More people were running toward him, and the truck and trailer, and he pointed at the two closest, the ones who'd come out of the Holiday Inn, and said, "Keep everybody away. Keep everybody back. There's gasoline all over the place. One of you, get inside and call nine-one-one and tell them we need a fire truck here now. Go."

A minute later, when the first deputy arrived, Virgil was already on the phone to Barlow: "The guy came after me. He blew up my boat."

"I'm coming," Barlow said.

The deputy ran up and asked, "You okay?"

"Well, I'm scared shitless," Virgil said.

"Man: you're lucky to be alive. Anybody hurt inside?" He went running into the Holiday Inn.

Virgil let him go: he was feeling a little distant from events.

Gas had stopped pouring out of the boat, but was still trickling out. He had a twenty-gallon tank that ran under the floor, and it had been a miracle, he thought, that the gas hadn't started burning. Staying well back, Virgil made a wide circle, checking the damage. The boat was gone: totaled. The blast had ripped the boat in half, right at the midsection. The bomb must have been in one of the rod-storage lockers down the right side of the boat, he thought.

He worked through it. The bomb would have been more certainly deadly, he thought, if it had been placed under the driver's door of the truck. That would have done him for sure. But he'd parked the truck right out front, where it could be seen from both the Holiday Inn and the highway. Too much traffic to take the risk . . .

The boat, on the other hand, had been in the overflow lot, where Virgil had parked it to get it out of the way. There were lights, but it'd still be dim back there; and depending on how the bomb was rigged, it wouldn't have taken more than a few seconds to put it down inside the rod locker.

At least, he thought—still feeling a little distant—they hadn't gotten his muskie rods. He hadn't had them out yet. He'd lost a couple walleye rigs, and a nice little ultralight bass rod and reel. . . .

More deputies came in, and rubber-neckers, and then the fire truck, and Virgil stood on a curb and watched them foam the gasoline. Barlow arrived, and came trotting over, followed by one of the crime-scene technicians. He put a hand on Virgil's shoulder and asked, "You okay?"

"More or less," Virgil said. "I'd like to get the truck away from there, so I can stay mobile. I didn't want to do anything until you got here."

"Give us a few minutes to look at it," Barlow said. Then, "I wonder why he didn't put it under the truck . . . ?"

Virgil told him his theory on that, and the ATF man nodded and said, "You're probably right." They'd been drifting down the line of the wrecked boat, still well away, as the firemen finished up. Barlow said, "I bet it was another mousetrap and it was set to go off when you opened that locker. It would have taken you apart. It would have been like somebody stuffed a hand grenade down your shirt. You were lucky."

Ahlquist showed up, red-faced and angry: "Man, he's going after us now. He's completely off the goldarned rails. You okay? Man . . ."

Virgil wandered off and took his cell phone out of his pocket and called Davenport. "Did I mention to you that I brought my boat along, you know, in case an after-hours fishing opportunity came up?"

"Tell me something surprising," Davenport said.

"Okay. This fuckin' bomber just blew it up."

"What?"

"It's gone, man. Cut in half. Truck's okay."

"Are *you* okay?"

"I'm a little freaked. He set it to kill me, no question. Goddamnit, Lucas, I'm shakin' like a shaved Chihuahua."

"You want some guys? I could get Shrake and Jenkins and be up there in a couple hours, help you tear the ass off the place."

"Nothing to tear up right now. Maybe tomorrow—I'll let you know. I just gotta get organized here, I gotta get the truck and get going."

"Hey, Virg—go get a beer, or a cheese-burger, or something. Sit down for a while. That's what I do when some shit happens. Man . . ."

Virgil rang off and walked back to where Ahlquist was standing, talking to Barlow, and asked, "Anybody hurt inside?"

"Two windows got knocked out, that big one on the front, and then there's a small one, upstairs, in an empty room," Ahlquist said. "So . . . no. Nobody hurt."

"But he was trying his best," Barlow said. "When he put the bomb in that rod locker, he did you a favor—there are about six aluminum walls between the bomb and the truck, and they soaked up the blast going forward. Didn't even knock the windows out of the truck. But if somebody had been standing on the sidewalk when it went, they'd be dead."

"It's been sheer luck that he hasn't killed a whole bunch of people," Ahlquist said.

"We can move the truck, if you want it," Barlow said. "We're not going to get much out of this bomb—all that gasoline and foam would have taken out most of the evidence."

Ahlquist: "I wonder why the gas didn't blow?"

"Not much fire involved," Barlow said. "That's why most cars don't burn when they're hit."

"I'll take the truck," Virgil said. "I gotta get some breakfast. I'm just, uh . . . I gotta get some food."

"Sure you're okay?" Ahlquist asked. "You're sorta mumbling at us."

"I was scared," Virgil said. "But now, I'm getting pissed. Really, really, royally . . . I gotta get some food."

He ate what he thought was about a three-thousand-calorie breakfast at Country Kitchen: French toast with hash browns, eggs over easy, regular toast, and two or-ders of link sausage, gobbling it down like somebody was going to take it away from him. When he was done, he felt a little sick from the grease, but his head was clearing out.

The bomb wasn't the first time somebody had tried to kill him, but this one had shaken him. He hadn't been kept alive by skill, or by reflexes, or by fast thinking; he was alive because he got lucky. If he hadn't driven over a curb, he'd have died sometime during the day.

Simple as that. The coldness of the fact shook him. He was finishing the third of his three Diet Cokes when Davenport called him.

"You sure you're okay?"

"Except for the fact that I just swallowed about a pint of grease, I'm okay."

"'Cause I just talked to Hendrix, and he said if you're too close to an explosion, the atmospheric pressure overload can screw you up, all by itself. Even if you don't get hit by any of the shrapnel. They're seeing that with guys coming back from Afghanistan."

"I'll take my pulse three times a day," Virgil said.

"Seriously, keep it in mind," Davenport

said. "They say that what happens is, the next time you're under a lot of stress, a vein pops in your brain. Usually, when you're having sex. You get really worked up, and your blood pressure goes up, and just when you're, you know, *getting there*, pop, there goes the vein, and you're dead."

"Now you're lying," Virgil said.

"I did make up that last part, about the sex," Davenport said. "But seriously, if you start getting funky, talk to someone. It's called 'blast-related traumatic brain injury' or 'blast syndrome.' You can look it up on the Net. They see it even in people with no obvious physical injury."

"Lucas . . . thanks. I'm more pissed off than hurt. I'm so *mad*, I . . . Now it's personal."

"Glad to hear it," Davenport said. "Things move quicker that way."

13

Virgil went back to the scene of destruction: because of the mess caused by fire suppression, preservation of the crime scene wasn't as important as it otherwise might have been, and the boat and trailer had been towed out of the street and parked at the far end of the Holiday Inn lot, where one of the ATF crime-scene techs was working through it.

"The guy's giving us a lot of business," he said, when Virgil walked up.

"You find anything good?"

"Got one end of the pipe. It blew right

through the front sidewall on that locker, and the wall of the next locker, but then the hull stopped it. Same pipe as before. The guy went into that college and cut it up, and he's using it one piece at a time. If we can find him, we can hang him with the rest of it."

"We'll find him," Virgil said.

"Sorry about your boat. I thought maybe you could salvage the engine, but some shrapnel went right through the cowling. The electronics are toast."

"Wonderful." Made him want to cry.

The boat was an older Alumacraft Classic single-console model with a fifty-horse Yamaha hung off the back; a decent boat, usable on big water only on calmer days, but fine for most smaller Minnesota lakes. Virgil had bought it used, with a state credit union loan, and had only just finished paying it off. He wasn't sure, but if he remembered correctly his insurance policy had some kind of caveat about payment in case of "war or civil insurrection."

Was a bomb the same as war?

He was still looking at the boat when he
got a call from Ahlquist: "The paper got a
crazy note, supposedly from the bomber.
You need to come take a look at it. We've
got it down at my office."

"Are they sure it's from the bomber?"

"Yeah. They're sure. It mentions, I quote,
'state Gestapo agents.' The state Gestapo
agents would be you," Ahlquist said.

"I'll be over," Virgil said. "Listen, have
you had anybody checking the motel and
the other buildings around here for witnesses?"

"I got O'Hara organizing that," Ahlquist
said. "She and her crew are talking to everybody for a couple blocks around."

"What about the letters?"

"We're delivering them right now. We
should be done by noon."

Before he went to the sheriff's office, he
walked around the block and found
O'Hara.

She jogged up, smiling, squeezed him

on the upper arm, and said, "Man, you got bigger balls than anybody I ever heard of."

"Huh?"

She stepped back and said, "I heard all about it. Your boat got blown up right behind you, and you got knocked out of your truck, and then, then, *you went out and got breakfast*. That is *cold*, dude."

Virgil said, "That's not exactly . . . hmmm . . . Anybody see anything?"

She shook her head. "Nobody saw nuthin'. The thing is, this guy is very smart, and he's careful. I'm really interested to see who it's going to be."

"If you find out, call me," Virgil said.

Virgil left her and drove to the sheriff's department, and looked at a Xerox copy of the note sent to the newspaper. It was couched in a faintly ridiculous faux-lefty cant:

The bombing campaign against PyeMart, Willard T. Pye, city officials who support the PyeMart's oppressive action against our people, and state and federal Gestapo agents will con-

tinue until PyeMart steps back from its current plans and the Butternut City Council withdraws permits to build the PyeMart store.

To ensure this gets done, we demand:

-A public statement from Willard T. Pye that store construction will be abandoned.

-Destruction of the footings already laid for the store.

-Reversal of the zoning changes made to allow the store to be built.

-Elimination of the sewer and water lines to the store site.

-Resignation of those members of the city council who voted to allow the changes.

-Resignation of Mayor Geraldine Gore.

-Withdrawal of federal and state Gestapo agents investigating the case on behalf of PyeMart.

Until this is done, we will continue to deliver our bombs to those who support PyeMart. To prove that this note is legitimate, we will reveal that another attack will take place today, and another boot will be removed from our necks.

"I'm saying that 'another boot will be removed from our necks' hooks up with 'Gestapo agents.' He didn't want to say that you specifically were going to be attacked, in case you hadn't been by the time the note got here," Ahlquist said. "But the hint is strong enough, after the fact, for us to know what he was talking about."

"I see that," Virgil said. "I'd say you're right. That's clever—a clever guy. Do we know where it was mailed from?"

"Here in town. It went through the post office, but there are lots of places where it could have been dropped."

"Fingerprints . . . ?"

"We sent the original letter and envelope down to St. Paul, to your lab, to see if they can get anything off it. It looked pretty clean, just eyeballing it. No watermark on the paper, or anything—it looked like standard copy paper."

The note was interesting, in a way, helping to build a better mental image of the bomber, but there wasn't much real information in it. The scariest thing, Virgil thought, was that the guy was picking targets and turning out the bombs so quickly. He told Ahlquist, "If I were you, I'd have a serious talk with the city council people, and tell them they're at risk. I told Gore, but she didn't want to hear it."

"All right. Are you just waiting for your letters to come back?"

"I got another thing I'm working on," Virgil said. "I'm going to spend a little time with that. I'll see you again this evening. I want to get going on those letters as soon as we start getting them back."

"Already got two," Ahlquist said. "I'm looking at the names, and I'm thinking, Yeah, this might work. Some people I didn't think of, but you see their name, and you think, You know . . . that might be right."

"All right. Maybe it'll be something," Virgil said. Then, "Do you know a woman named Marilyn Oaks?"

"Marilyn Oaks . . . that seems . . . Just a minute." He stuck his head out in the hall and called, "Hey, Helen? Could you step in here?"

A clerk came in, an older woman with silvery hair: "Yes?"

"Marilyn Oaks. I'm thinking, the country club. Like the . . . dining lady, the caterer . . ."

Helen bobbed her head at her boss: "That's right. Thin woman. Dark hair."

"Got her," Ahlquist said. "Thanks, Helen." When Helen was gone, he said to Virgil, "Now you know everything I know about her."

"Is she hot?"

Ahlquist's eyes narrowed, then he said, "Nooo . . . I guess I wouldn't call her *hot*, exactly. She does have a look about her. Like, you know, she'd fuck back at you. Is that sexist?"

"No, I don't think so, but I'm not totally up on my feminist theory."

Five minutes later, after getting directions from Ahlquist, Virgil was on his way to Doug Mackey's house, the schoolteacher who'd phoned the tip to Thor, the desk clerk. Mackey wasn't home, but a neighbor said, "He's probably out at Cottonwood. He's the pro there, in the summers."

Cottonwood was a privately owned public golf course five minutes south of town. After inquiring in the pro shop, Virgil found Mackey by himself, on the driving range, working on a half-swing pitch out to a fifty-yard can.

He turned to Virgil with a golf pro's inquiring smile, which faded when Virgil introduced himself and said, "I need to talk to you about how you know that Pat Shepard took twenty-five thousand dollars from Pye—and how you know he's nailing Marilyn Oaks."

Mackey's mouth dropped open: "You were . . . Did you . . . Was there a tap on my phone?"

"No, nothing like that. But you know how word gets around, especially in a small town," Virgil said.

"What?"

"You know how word gets around," Virgil repeated. "Anyway, we do know, and lying to me is a crime, called obstruction of justice, but knowing what you know isn't a crime, so it'd be best if you just told me the truth. If you tell the truth, you don't get arrested, get to keep your job, and so on."

Mackey stared at him for a second, did a baton twirl with his sand wedge, stuck it back in his bag, and then said, "I gotta have a beer."

The club had a porch overlooking the eighteenth green, and they got a Bud Light for Mackey and Virgil got a Diet Coke, and they sat down at the far end, away from a foursome that had just come off the course.

"This is pretty awful," Mackey said, after a couple of swallows. "They're friends of mine. I feel like I'm betraying them."

"Things were going to get awful the minute you picked up that phone," Virgil said. "The other way to look at it is that you're an honest citizen, doing your duty."

"Doesn't feel that way," Mackey said. They sat looking at each other for a moment, then he asked, "Do they have to know that I'm the one who turned them in?"

"I don't know," Virgil said, though he thought it would probably all come out, if the case ever got to court. "It depends what happens. I was talking to a psychologist about all of this, and explained that you were all teachers in the same school. He suggested that this might involve some personal relationship between you and Jeanne Shepard."

Mackey didn't say anything, but took another hit on his beer. Virgil took one, and finally Mackey said, "Pat's a golfer. Not very good, but he works at it. He asked me to give Jeanne some lessons, so they could play together."

"Something happened there?"

Mackey shook his head. "Jeez. You know? It didn't take long. A little kissy-squeezy stuff. Then one day she came out for a lesson, and we saw Pat teeing off with his regular foursome, knew he'd be gone for at least five hours. We dropped my car off at Walmart, and took her car over to her place."

"Is she the one who told you about Pat taking the money?"

"Yeah . . . I'm not sure why. I kind of think she wouldn't mind if somebody spilled the beans and Pat went away," Mackey said. "She could get a divorce, probably get the house. They've got a fifteen-year mortgage, almost paid off.

Start over, maybe have another kid. She'd like to focus on her art."

"She a good painter?"

"If you like sunsets," Mackey said. "I never cared that much for them, myself."

"You think she'd talk to me?"

Mackey said, "If you came onto her, like you came onto me—like you already knew about it, and like lying would get her in trouble, too . . . Yeah, she'd tell you about it. Things haven't been good between her and Pat for quite a while."

"Does she know about Marilyn Oaks?" Virgil asked.

"No. Pat told me about that. I think he might be lining her up as the next Mrs. Shepard."

His affair with Jeanne Shepard, Mackey said, had begun right after golf season started, the second week of April. It had been going hot and heavy through May, but in the last couple of weeks Jeanne Shepard seemed to be cooling off. Then, he said, he found out that "she'd blabbed to her friend Bernice, who's got the biggest mouth in Butternut Falls. No way she was going to keep the secret, and we got in an argument over that."

Bernice, he said, had already outed one affair at the school, which had ended with resignations and divorces.

"Huh. Sounds like you've got a little rats' nest over at the high school."

"Nah. You know, it's just pretty human," Mackey said. "People getting to be middle-aged, and rearranging their lives. Pat and Jeanne have a ten-year-old daughter. Pat doesn't care much for her, and I do, and we'd make a nice little family."

"Well . . . might still happen," Virgil said.

"I don't think so, really," Mackey said. "It all looks pretty bleak, with you figuring me out. I would never have made the call if it hadn't seemed to be slipping away."

Jeanne Shepard, Mackey said, was at home. Pat Shepard, he said, was out on the golf course, "probably on number three. He and his friends aren't fast, they'll be out there for another three hours."

Virgil called Davenport, to tell him about the political break, but Davenport was out of touch. He called Ahlquist and said, "I need an honest prosecutor to come talk to a woman with me. Like right now."

"You got a break?"

"Not on the bomber; something else. I need a prosecutor who can keep his mouth shut, and isn't much interested in politics."

"I'd have to think about that for a couple days," Ahlquist said.

"C'mon, man—it's something I don't want to talk about yet. I could do it on my own, but it'd be better if I had a guy."

"Let me talk to Theodore Wills. He's the county attorney. Get back to you in five."

More like ten. In the meantime, Virgil took a call from a blocked number.

"Lucas told me about the bomb. You okay?"

"I'm good," Virgil said. "My boat is a smoking ruin."

"But you've got insurance."

"Yeah, with State Farm," Virgil said. "I'm a little worried about that clause that says they won't pay if there's a war or civil insurrection."

"Who's your agent?"

"A woman named Mary Trail, down in Mankato," Virgil said.

"I'll give her a call. Tell her I'm worried about it."

"I'm not sure that would be appropriate," Virgil said, but he couldn't keep the hope out of his voice.

"Sure it is. I'm just a friend making an inquiry for you, since you're busy with this investigation."

"Well . . ."

"Relax, Virgil," said the governor of Minnesota. "It's just fine. You take care of yourself, hear? I mean, goddamnit, you're my third-most-favorite troublemaker."

"I got you a prosecutor," Ahlquist said, when he called back. "We're all curious about what you've got going."

"I'll tell you this evening," Virgil said. "What's the guy's name, and where do I find him?"

"Her name is Shirley Good Thunder, and she's at the courthouse. Let me give you her number."

Good Thunder was a Sioux—a Dakota, for sticklers—a good-looking, dark-eyed woman about Virgil's age, with long legs and a large briefcase. When she climbed into the truck, she asked, "Are you okay? I mean, after the bomb."

"Yeah, I'm fine," Virgil said. He was a little tired of the question; it wasn't like he was bleeding from the ears. "Are you any relation to Larry Good Thunder, from Marshall? I played basketball with him."

"Probably, somehow, like a great-uncle-fifth-cousin or something," she said. "Quite a few Good Thunders running around."

"Terrific ball player, but he didn't shoot enough," Virgil said. "He was too good not to put it up more often."

"Tell me more about basketball," she said. "I find it almost as fascinating as soil management." But she said it with a smile.

"I'm happy to hear you're interested in soil management, 'cause we're out to dig up some dirt," Virgil said.

The Shepards lived all the way across town, on a wide, well-treed peninsula that stuck out into the lake. On the way over, Virgil told her about the tip from the kid at the Holiday Inn, and about his conversation with Mackey. When he finished, she said, "All right. I'm now officially nervous."

"About what?"

"Oh. Let me think," she said, putting an index finger at the corner of her mouth and cocking her head. "Okay, uh, how about, if you're right, we're about to set Butternut Falls on fire, and I have to live here, and my boss is the most political guy in the county."

"One good thing about it," Virgil said.

"What's that?"

"I live in Mankato," Virgil said. "I won't have to listen to it."

That didn't make her laugh. Instead, she got busy with her briefcase, pulled out a yellow pad, and said: "All right: give me the names, and tell me the story again. I gotta say, I hate the idea of people taking money under the table. Especially when a whole bunch of people are going to get hurt by it."

"That's my attitude," Virgil said. "Though, I feel kind of sleazy, getting it this way."

"I feel a whole bunch sleazy, and we're not even at the Shepards' place yet."

When they got to the Shepards' place, a minivan was sitting in the driveway, with the side doors open. A young blond girl was pulling out a bag of groceries, and Virgil said, "Damnit. That's their kid, I think. I hate to hit her with the kid around."

"Go on past," Good Thunder said. She took her phone out of her pocket, asked Virgil if he had the Shepards' phone number, and he said he didn't. She pushed a single button on the phone, then said into it, "This is Shirley. I need a phone number for a Mrs. Pat Shepard, a Jeanne Shepard, on Bayview."

She got the number, punched it into her phone, got an answer, identified herself, asked if she was speaking to Mrs. Shepard, got a "yes," and said, "We have to talk to you about a legal matter. We just went by and saw your daughter in the driveway. We'd prefer to talk to you alone—we don't want to upset your child."

After a minute of back-and-forth, in which Good Thunder refused to say why they wanted to talk, she listened, and then said, "That would be best. We'll see you in ten minutes."

She hung up and said, "She can leave the kid with a sister, but has to take her over there. Her sister lives south of the highway, less than a mile. She said she'll be back in five minutes."

"Good enough," Virgil said. They sat at the end of the block and watched Shepard, in sunglasses, a short-sleeved shirt and slacks, usher her daughter into the van and take off. She was too far away for Virgil to tell for sure, but he thought Thor, the desk clerk, might have been right: she did look fairly hot.

"What? Did you say something?" Good Thunder asked.

"I said, it's gonna be hot out."

She laughed. "Oh, jeez. I thought you were looking at her ass, and said, 'hot.'"

"Hey, c'mon," Virgil said.

She was gone not five minutes, but twenty, and Virgil and Good Thunder were getting a little itchy before she showed up. They were still sitting down the block, and after

Shepard had parked, and had gone inside, Virgil started the truck and pulled into the driveway behind the minivan.

The front door was open, and they could hear Shepard inside. Virgil rang the doorbell and Shepard called, "Come in." They went in, and found her dragging a second suitcase into the living room. The first one lay open on the couch.

Virgil asked, "Are you, uh . . ."

"Going over to my sister's," Shepard said. She was a tall, busty blonde with a narrow waist and a slender, foxy face, with down-slanting eyebrows. No makeup; she didn't need any, with a face as smooth as a peach, and gray-green eyes. She said, "I need to get out of here before Pat gets back."

Virgil introduced Good Thunder, and then himself, and asked, "You know why we're here?"

"I think so. I'm going to need a lawyer before I talk to you," Shepard said.

"That might not be a bad idea," Good Thunder said. "I would want to get that going as quickly as possible. If you don't have a lawyer of your own, I can recommend one, and I can get you a public defender if you can't afford one—"

"Tom LaRouche," Shepard said. "He's over in the Lakeside Center."

"Okay, good, I know him," Good Thunder said. And, "We basically have hard information that you know about your husband's taking a bribe from PyeMart Corporation, in exchange for his vote on the zoning. We are willing to offer you immunity from prosecution on the basis of your providing us that information. Do you think you will have something to discuss? I'm not asking you to commit yourself, but just to tell me whether we're wasting our time."

"If you give me immunity, we've got something to talk about," Shepard said, blowing a hank of blond hair away from her eyes. "When I found out about what Pat had done, I felt terrible. So many people are getting hurt. I felt even more terrible when I found out he was having an affair."

"You know about the affair?" Virgil asked.

She stopped, looked at him: "*You* know about it?"

Virgil said, "Yeah . . . I guess, our source . . ."

She shook her head and said to Good Thunder. "Carol Anne Moore? You know her? She works for the county, in the license office. I couldn't believe it. . . ."

Virgil thought, *Oh, boy.*

Shepard called her attorney, explained the situation to him. He told her to stop talking to Virgil and Good Thunder, and said that he could see her that afternoon, and Virgil and Good Thunder immediately afterward.

She hung up, made a hand-dusting slap, and said, "Finally. Something is getting done. But he says I shouldn't talk to you again until I speak to him."

"Well, we'll see you this afternoon, then," Good Thunder said.

Back in the truck, Good Thunder said, "So Pat Shepard tells his pal that he's having an affair with Marilyn Oaks, but Pat's wife thinks he's having an affair with Carol Anne Moore."

Virgil said, "I feel bad about myself for saying this, but if the lawyer tells her that she might not want to talk to us . . . I bet Marilyn Oaks could change her mind."

"I've got to go talk to the boss," she said. "This is going to get ugly, on a lot of levels."

Virgil dropped her at the courthouse and drove back to look at his boat. It was still blown up. The crime-scene tech had finished, and had thrown a blue plastic tarp over the hulk, like pulling a sheet over the face of a dead man.

He left it that way, and walked into the motel. Thor was behind the desk, saw him coming, and asked, "Did you talk to Mrs. Shepard?"

"I can't really talk about that," Virgil said.

"So, was she as hot as I said?"

"She was . . . yes, she was," Virgil said. "Did some deputies come around and talk to you about people prowling your back lot?"

"Yeah, they talked to everybody, but nobody saw anything," Thor said. "You think I got a chance to get Mrs. Shepard before Mr. Mackey?"

"I gotta go," Virgil said.

From behind him, Thor said, "Sonofagun, he already got there, didn't he?"

Virgil turned around and Thor said, "I'll tell you what's got me scratching my head."

Virgil turned back. "Yeah?"

"Why'd they try to kill *you*?" he asked.

Virgil said, "Well, see, I'm a cop, and I've been assigned to find the bomber—"

"Yeah, and what happens if you get killed? About, what, a hundred more cops come in?" Thor asked. "Right now, we got the sheriff's department, and Sheriff Ahlquist is a nice guy, but to be honest, his deputies couldn't find a stolen bike unless it was parked between the cheeks of their ass. So we got two real cops here, one state and one federal. If he kills a real cop, what happens? We get a *hundred* real cops, and they're all pissed off. So, what's the percentage? Is the guy stupid? He doesn't seem stupid."

Virgil had no answer for that. He said, "You need to lie down and take a nap before your brains burn up."

So, Virgil asked himself, back in his truck, *why'd he try to kill me?*

14

Virgil intended to spend some time thinking—stretch out on the bed and have at it. As a backup, and just to make sure he didn't fall asleep, he set the alarm, and the alarm woke him a half hour before he was to meet Good Thunder at Shepard's lawyer's office.

He got up, checked his vital signs—he had an after-nap erection, which was always good—brushed his teeth and took a quick shower.

Good Thunder had given him directions to the lawyer's office, and wearing his most conservative T-shirt—an unauthorized souvenir from My Chemical Romance, with the band's name only on the back, and with a black sport coat covering it—he set off for the lawyer's office.

The office was in a low, low, rustic strip mall—fake log cabins—with Butternut's most complete collection of upscale boutiques, including one called Mairzy Doats with a window full of stuffed velvet moose dolls. Good Thunder was sitting on the hood of her car, a new fire-engine-red Chevy Camaro, waiting. When Virgil got out of the truck, she said, in a phony baritone, "Johnny Cash, the 'Man in Black.'"

"You seem to be in a pretty good mood," Virgil said.

She hopped off the hood. "My boss put a thumb in the wind—that's not where he usually keeps it—and decided that if we can bag the city council, if they really did it, then he'll be a lock for reelection. What he really doesn't want, though, is for us to screw it up. He's gonna be really unhappy if we just wound them."

Virgil nodded. "I know how it is. You get a wounded city councilman out in the brush, they'll charge at the drop of the hat."

"Whatever," she said. "Let's not have any show of wit in here. Let's just play it straight."

"This lawyer's pretty smart?"

"As a matter of fact, he is."

The lawyer was an extremely white man named Thomas LaRouche. His secretary ushered them into his office, where Jeanne Shepard sat in a corner chair, looking apprehensive. LaRouche was tall, courtly, and silver-haired, wearing a blue suit and a white shirt, open at the throat; a burgundy necktie was curled on a corner of his desk. He was maybe sixty, Virgil thought.

When they came in, he stood up, smiling, said, "Shirley," and came around the desk and kissed Good Thunder on the cheek, and shook hands with Virgil and pointed them at two leather visitor's chairs.

"I heard your boat was blown up this morning," he said to Virgil, as he settled behind his desk. "That qualifies as a war crime."

"You're right," Virgil said. "People keep asking me if I'm all right, but I keep thinking about the boat. I took that thing all over the place."

LaRouche asked him what kind of boat it was, and when Virgil told him, he lit up, a bit, and said, "I used to have one like that—but it was years ago. I had a 40 Merc tiller off the back. One time up on Mille Lacs . . ."

By the time he got finished, he had Virgil liking him; that had happened before with lawyers, usually the kind who won in court. "So," he said finally, "we have a situation here. I've agreed to represent Jeanne, and I have to say that I was a little disturbed when I heard about your conversation this morning."

Then he and Good Thunder went back and forth for a while, on the propriety of having spoken to Jeanne Shepard without a lawyer being present, and while he scored a point or two, when they were done, Virgil had Good Thunder four points up and standing on the free-throw line with two seconds left in the game. It was over, and LaRouche knew it.

"The point being," Good Thunder said for emphasis, "we do not necessarily have an issue with Mrs. Shepard, although, of course, she should have spoken to police immediately after learning that Mr. Shepard had taken a bribe."

"We should be able to handle that," LaRouche said.

"Oh, I think so. I've spoken to Theodore"—Theodore was her boss— "and he is totally on board with immunity for Mrs. Shepard, contingent only on her complete cooperation."

"I should put in here," Virgil said, "if Ms. Good Thunder doesn't mind, I'd like to say that we're coming from several different directions on this investigation. If Mrs. Shepard declines to cooperate, then, of course, there will be no immunity, and no second chance."

"Aw, c'mon, Virgil, you don't have to bring the knives out," LaRouche said. "We're all friends here, trying to do what's right."

When he was finished, and everybody agreed they were friends, Good Thunder produced a file of papers—a contract, more or less—that defined the terms of the immunity and the scope of her cooperation. LaRouche said he would look at them overnight, brief his client in the morning, and, if everything was properly done, return them signed that afternoon.

"The terms are all standard stuff, they shouldn't give you any trouble," Good Thunder told LaRouche. "But time is a major problem. It'd help a lot if we could get them back this afternoon, and talk with Mrs. Shepard tonight. We understand that she's left her husband, and that could signal to him, and to the other people involved in this conspiracy, that there could be trouble. Evidence could be lost, if there's a delay; or the conspirators could have a chance to talk about a common defense, before we can get to them."

LaRouche: "I'm afraid we'll need a little more time than that."

Good Thunder: "Agent Flowers is planning to continue his investigation—time is of the essence. I have to warn you, that if there's another development, with another suspect, the same deal might not be available tomorrow."

LaRouche: "Shirley, gosh darn it, we need a *little* time."

Good Thunder: "I'm not trying to be harsh, Tommy, I'm just saying that we have a serious time problem. Things are moving fast. If something else breaks . . . it breaks. We'll have to jump at it. We have to take the bird in the hand, we can't count on the one in the bush."

There was more back-and-forth, and LaRouche asked them to step out of the office for a moment, so he could talk privately with Shepard. Virgil and Good Thunder sat outside for twenty minutes, talking about nothing, for the benefit of LaRouche's secretary, who listened carefully while pretending to type, and finally LaRouche called them back.

"Shirley, I'm about ninety percent that your stance here was an effort to stampede us."

"Tom, I'd never—"

"If so, you've succeeded. I've canceled my plans for the evening, and if you can get back here at six o'clock, we can at least start the conversation."

"That will be fine," Good Thunder said, with a smile. "I think this will be best for all of us."

Back outside, she showed some excitement: "Damnit, Virgil, I'm actually gonna do some of that stuff we talked about in law school. Clean up the town. So far, it's mostly been plea bargains to small amounts of marijuana. Tire theft and public urination."

"Will you go after Shepard, or try to turn him?"

"I gotta talk to my people," she said. "Jeanne Shepard might get us only her husband. If we can nail him down before anybody finds out, we might be able to make a deal with him. Put a wire on him, even. Get the whole bunch."

"Up to you," Virgil said. "I'd go for the whole banana stand, if I were you."

"That's what I'd do, too, but the boss might see one of those bird-in-the-hand deals."

"So: see you at six," Virgil said. "If you don't mind, I want to tip Ahlquist off: I don't want it to catch him with his pants down. He's already been in the paper standing next to Pye."

She was hesitant: "He's gotta keep his mouth shut."

"He can do that," Virgil said. "We've worked together in the past, and he's good at that, when he needs to be."

Virgil followed her toward the courthouse, but swung into a McDonald's drive-through for a shot of calories, talked to Davenport about the Shepards, while he waited for the food, then went on to the courthouse. Ahlquist had just left, going home for dinner. Virgil got one of the deputies to call him, and Ahlquist said he'd come back.

When he arrived, Virgil was finishing his cheeseburger while looking at the hundred and seven letters that they'd already gotten back from the survey group. Twenty-two had declined to participate, for reasons ranging from a lack of time to concerns about civil rights, leaving eighty-five lists of names. More were arriving every few minutes. They'd asked for ten names, and had gotten back as few as four, on a few lists, to as many as twenty-one on the longest list. Most were ten.

Virgil had opened his laptop, set up an

Excel spreadsheet, and started entering names. In the first five letters, he'd had three duplicates, a Lyle McLachlan.

Ahlquist came in, looked over his shoulder, stole a couple of Virgil's french fries.

"McLachlan isn't smart enough to pull this off," he said. "He's crazy enough, and violent enough, but he's not the guy."

"Bummer."

"So what's up?" Ahlquist asked. He took a couple more fries.

"These rumors about the city council being bribed," Virgil said. "Uh, they're true."

"You say that like a cop," Ahlquist said.

"Yeah."

"Ah, shit." Ahlquist dropped in a chair. "How bad?"

"We got at least one, Pat Shepard. He's gone, unless Good Thunder decides to flip him."

"Ah, man. He teaches civics up at the high school. How to be a good citizen."

"Yeah, well . . . I got Good Thunder to agree that I could tell you about this, on the basis that you not mention it to a single person," Virgil said. "We don't want

Pye shoveling dirt on it, we don't want people hiding cash in coffee cans out in the woods. When we move on it, we want it all raw."

"I can keep my mouth shut," Ahlquist said.

"That's what I told her," Virgil said. "I just thought you oughta know, so you don't wind up standing too close to Pye."

"I appreciate that, Virgil. You're a good egg," Ahlquist said. "So how'd you bag him? Shepard?"

Virgil filled him in on the details—the affairs, the probable divorce, the money, and the immunity agreement with Jeanne Shepard.

"Ah, Jesus. I dread all of this, what's going to happen," Ahlquist said, when Virgil finished. "We'll be busting old friends. Or acquaintances, anyway."

"It won't be pretty," Virgil said. "If you want, I can talk to my boss, bring in a BCA crew. Keep you out of it."

"That'd make it look like you guys thought I couldn't handle it," Ahlquist said. "Or maybe was involved."

"You can handle it, Earl, but the question is, do you want to?" Virgil asked.

"I gotta think."

Virgil said, "We could fix it for you to make the announcement, along with the county attorney. You could say something like, 'I've recused myself and the sheriff's department to avoid any appearance of a conflict of interest.'"

He bobbed his head: "That might be the way to go. Once you say I can talk, I'll tell Mary Alice about it, ask her what she thinks. She's my brain trust." Mary Alice was his wife.

"We'll probably move in the next day or two, so you gotta decide what you're gonna do, and pretty fast. You think Mary Alice can keep her mouth shut?"

"When she needs to," Ahlquist said.

"Then talk to her," Virgil said. "Let me know tomorrow morning what you're gonna do."

"I'll tell you tonight," Ahlquist said. "I want to see your final list, so I'll be back anyway."

Virgil went back to work on the list, pushing hard. Lyle McLachlan, he thought, must be an enormous asshole, because he was on about every other list. George Peck was on one list. Virgil checked the number of the letter that nominated Peck, against the secret numbered list, and found that Peck had nominated himself.

Interesting.

The desk officer came in and handed him more letters. He put them in the pile, and went back to sorting names.

Time went by. He was fifteen minutes from finishing when he glanced at his watch and realized he didn't have fifteen minutes: it was time to get back to La-Rouche's office.

He went out past the front desk, and found he had sixteen more letters. "Hang onto these, will you?" he asked the desk officer. "I'll be back in a couple hours to finish up."

When he got to LaRouche's, the office window was dark, and the door locked, but Good Thunder's Camaro was parked outside. He knocked, and pushed a door-bell, and a minute later, a clerk-like woman came to the door and asked, "Are you Agent Flowers?"

"Yes, ma'am."

She let him in, said, "I'm Coral Schmidt, I'm the reporter," and he followed her down a hall past LaRouche's office, to a conference room, where LaRouche and Good Thunder were chatting, while Shepard sat next to LaRouche, listening and toying with her purse. Schmidt sat down next to a black steno machine and, as Virgil took a chair, nodded to Good Thunder and said, "Anytime."

Good Thunder dictated some time and date stuff to the reporter, the identities and offices of those present, then she and LaRouche agreed that they would abide by the terms of an agreement reached earlier that day, with copies to everyone, etc. With the bureaucratic bullshit out of the way, they started.

Good Thunder said to Shepard, "Mrs. Shepard, you've asserted that your husband, Patrick Shepard, a member of the Butternut Falls City Council, received a bribe of twenty-five thousand dollars to change his vote on a zoning application from PyeMart Corporation, in regard to a PyeMart store to be built on Highway 12 West in Butternut Falls. When did you become aware of the offer from PyeMart?"

Shepard unrolled the story: the first contact with a PyeMart expediter named John Dunn, a series of discussions between Dunn and other members of the council. The discussions had the effect of softening up the council members, she said, and when an offer came to "help" Shepard with some credit card and income tax debt, it was not unexpected.

The offer, she said, had not come directly from Dunn, but from Mayor Geraldine Gore, who had also delivered the money. Pat Shepard, she said, had come home and told her excitedly that their problems were over: they might even have enough left to buy a home theater system.

"Did he buy one of those?" Good Thunder asked.

Shepard bit her lip, looked away: "No. I have reason to believe that he'd begun a relationship with another woman, Carol Anne Moore, who works for the county clerk, and that he spent a good deal of money on her."

Virgil: "Was this a serious relationship? Was this a fling, or did you consider your marriage endangered or over?"

"The marriage was over. I was just picking a time to leave," she said. "I don't know how serious the relationship was. Is. I don't know if it's still going on; I assume it is. Why would it make any difference?"

Virgil asked, "I wonder if he would confide in Miz Moore."

She shook her head: "I don't know."

Good Thunder: "In regards to your own personal life, I would suggest that you act with discretion. If it comes to a jury trial, it will be . . . less difficult."

"You mean, 'Don't fuck anyone new'?" Then, with a quick glance at the stenographer, "Oh my God, I'm sorry I said that, I just . . ."

"A lot of stress," Good Thunder said.

"It's completely understandable," said LaRouche.

Shepard said that her husband had laundered much of the money by giving it to his brother, who owned an autobody shop in St. Cloud. The brother ran it through his bank, then returned it to Shepard as a "temporary employee."

"I don't know if Bob knew where the money was coming from, but Pat told me it was no skin off Bob's butt. The money came in, he paid it to Pat, deducted Pat's wages as a temporary employee, and it all came out even, tax-wise."

After they'd wrung her out, Virgil said, "Mrs. Shepard . . . your husband will likely be looking at a jail sentence here. Do you think that if he were offered a deal, a reduction in the sentence, that he would be willing to implicate some of the other members of this conspiracy?"

"If you said that you could keep him out of prison if he ran over our daughter with the car, he'd do it," she said. "He is a coward and a rat. And he cheats at golf."

Good Thunder: "Do you know a woman named Marilyn Oaks?"

Shepard stared at her for a moment, then closed her eyes and leaned back: "I knew it. That sonofabitch."

When they were all done, and the stenographer had folded up her machine, Shepard said, "The thing that defeats me is, Pat is a jerk, and his hair is falling out, and he's got a little potbelly. . . . How does he have *two* mistresses? That we know of?"

"Lonely people," Virgil said.

"I'm lonely," she said.

"Yeah, but Pat apparently can't fix that for you."

She shook her head, then looked at Good Thunder and said, "I'm not sure I can act with discretion."

Out in the parking lot, Good Thunder asked Virgil, "Can you guys give us some technical support? Now that we've got Mrs. Shepard nailed down, I'm going to pull in Pat Shepard. You won't have to be there for that—I can handle it with an investigator—but if Shepard agrees to flip, I'll need a wire and support."

"Count on it," Virgil said. "I'll talk to my boss tonight, and he'll call you tomorrow."

"Deal," she said.

At the courthouse, the duty officer had another stack of letters for him, and Virgil asked the officer to find George Peck's phone number. He waited, got the number, and dialed. Peck picked up, saying, "Peck."

Virgil suppressed the urge to tell him he sounded like a chicken, and instead, said, "George? Virgil. Listen, I'm over at the courthouse, compiling those names. If you've got time, you could come over and take a look."

"As a matter of fact, I do have time," Peck said. "I was just about to get in the bathtub. I'll be an hour or so, if that's okay."

"See you then."

Virgil had set up the spreadsheet to rank the names by the number of entries in each name-cell; McLachlan had one hundred and eight nominations. The second most, a man named Greg Sawyer, had seventy-four. After that, the numbers dropped sharply. There were four ties with eight, five with seven, eight with six nominations, lots of names with five, four, three, or two nominations, and the rest were scattered, with one each; a total of more than five hundred names.

When he finished, he went out and found two more letters, entered those, with no change in the standings; he was just finishing when Peck showed up.

Virgil asked, "Why the hell did you nominate yourself, George?"

"IQ test," Peck said. "I wondered if you were smart enough to keep a secret list of which letter went to who. What'd you use, something that shows up under ultraviolet?"

"Nope. Just added a dot in one of the letters on the right-numbered word in the letter."

Peck was pleased. "Excellent. So even if somebody sent back a non-original copy, a Xerox, you'd still know who it was."

"Yeah, I guess, but I didn't think of that," Virgil said. "Hey—here's the list. Take a look."

Peck settled in front of Virgil's laptop. Looked at the list, his lower lip stuck out, stroked his left cheek with an index finger, then muttered, "What a fascinating list. McLachlan is a moron, there's no way he did these bombings. Throw him out, and you've got eighty people with two or more nominations. I know most of them, and I wouldn't have nominated several of them, but I'd still say, 'Yes, I can see that.' Fascinating."

"You think the bomber's on the list?"

"I'll bet you a thousand dollars he is— that he's among those eighty, for sure. He's probably among the top ten or twelve, once you throw out McLachlan and a couple more."

"You know this Greg Sawyer?"

"Yeah, he's another semi-professional criminal. I mean, he's a big rough redneck bully who steals stuff when he can, usually pigs and calves, and usually gets caught. He's not the guy."

Ahlquist came in, saw Peck, frowned, but then said to Virgil, "On that other thing. We're going to let you guys handle it. You want me to call Davenport?"

"You can do it, if you want," Virgil said. He said to Peck, "George, keep thinking. I've got to go talk to Earl in secret, where you can't hear."

Peck waved them off: "Go ahead. Ignore my feelings."

Down in Ahlquist's office, Virgil called
Davenport at home. "I've got the sheriff
here, and he's got a request. We're cracking the city council, big-time. Here, talk
to him."

Ahlquist took the phone, explained the
situation—that he worried about the appearance of a conflict of interest—nodded
a few times, and said, "We'll be in touch,
then. Virgil or me."

He handed the phone back to Virgil,
who told Davenport, "We're also going
to need some tech support, if we man-
age to flip Pat Shepard. I got a name and
number for you, a Shirley Good Thunder."

"Not a problem," Davenport said, and
took down the information. He was too
cheerful about it, and Virgil said so.

"What you're doing, is proving that
we're worth the money the taxpayers give
us," Davenport said. "That's always good.
Anyway, I'll call Good Thunder, and send
Jack Thompson down with the equipment.
When you're ready to move, I can have
Shrake and Jenkins down there in two

hours. I'll call everybody and get them cocked and locked."

Virgil said, "Ten-four. Say hello to your old lady for me."

Back with Peck, Ahlquist took his turn looking at Virgil's list. "Heck of a list. You got some serious people on there, important people, and every one of them is a sociopath," Ahlquist said. "But don't quote me."

"Are any of them instructors at the college?"

"Mmm . . . no. Not regular instructors, anyway, not that I know of," Peck said. "Somebody might be a part-timer. There's all kinds of guys teach a class from time to time. I do myself, photography and Photoshop."

"This guy here . . . he's pretty far down, John Haden, he teaches there," Ahlquist said, tapping the screen. "He's on the staff. And this guy, Bill Wyatt."

Haden had been nominated twice, Wyatt, three times.

"Gotta look at them. And the top eighteen," Virgil said.

"Tonight?"

"Tomorrow," Virgil said. "And pray to God that there's not another bomb."

"You're wasting your time," Peck said. "There is no God, and why an intelligent person would think so, I cannot fathom."

As they broke up for the evening, Virgil said, "Listen, guys, do me a favor. Ask yourself, 'Why would the bomber try to blow up Virgil Flowers?' Because it's a lot more interesting question than you might expect. If we could figure that out, it might help."

They said they'd think about it, and Virgil went back to the Holiday Inn, where he carefully parked his truck in a no-parking zone directly in front of the front window, where the desk clerk would be looking straight out at it.

He went in the lobby, to explain, and Thor came out of the back room.

He said, "Hey, Virg."

"I parked my truck there so nobody would put a bomb in it. Keep an eye on it, would you?"

"No problem. I'm going off in an hour,

I'll tell the night girl." Then, "So, you talk to Mrs. Shepard?"

Virgil said, "Thor . . ." He sighed, shook his head, and said, "I need some sleep."

"Hot damn, you did! I'm going over there."

"She's not over there," Virgil said. "She moved out."

Thor thought for one second, or less, then said, "She's at her sister's. I'm going over *there*."

"If you mention my name in any way . . ."

"You'll kill me. Got it."

"She's in pretty delicate shape," Virgil began.

"So am I," Thor said. "You wouldn't believe how delicate a shape I'm in. And don't worry about it, dude. I'm not gonna go in there and jump her. I'm gonna offer her my friendship."

"And a pizza."

"Well, yeah. A meat lover's."

Virgil went up to bed, undressed, lay in the dark, and asked God, "Why did the bomber try to kill me? And how did he sneak into the Pye building? You can answer this question either as a sudden revelation, or you could write it up in the sky, or whisper it to Thor, your namesake. Okay? Deal? I'm going to sleep now, God. Please answer before anybody else gets hurt. Oh—and keep an eye on Mrs. Shepard. She seems like a nice-enough lady. And Thor. Keep an eye on Thor."

Satisfied, he went to sleep, and slept well, for a man who'd almost been blown up.

The last thing he thought of, as he drifted off, was that Lee Coakley hadn't called.

15

The bomber was worried. He'd missed twice in a row, once with Pye, once with the cop. The misses weren't really the problem. His intention with the cop was to pull more cops into town, to bring more pressure, to tear the place up. That would now surely happen, would it not?

What worried him was not the misses, but his own reaction to them. When he heard about the miss with Pye, he'd been angry about it, but accepted it as just a matter of chance and inexperience. He'd taken a shot—a good shot, a creative one—and it had gone sour. The cop was no different, though he'd taken some extra risks there, in placing the bomb so close to a busy street; but again the reflexive anger came, stronger this time, almost despair.

He controlled it, but . . . where did that come from? The despair?

He'd started out thinking of the bombs as tools. But now, he thought, it was like he *needed* them. Almost like he was addicted to them.

The bomber had been addicted to cigarettes earlier in life, and kicking the habit had been a struggle. He could remember the gravitational pull of the cigarette packs, sitting on their shelves in the gas stations and the convenience stores, calling to him. For years after he'd quit, he would wake up in the night, having dreamed that he'd fallen off the wagon, that he'd taken a cigarette . . . and when he woke, he could taste the nicotine and tar, and feel the buzz.

The bomb thing was almost like that. When he heard that he'd missed the cop, he felt a powerful impulse to get in his car, drive up in the hills, to the box of explosives, and get what he needed for another bomb. To do it right now.

To hit them again.

To kill somebody.

That was the problem.

His whole campaign had been a rational effort to solve a serious problem—serious from his point of view, anyway—and the killing was just a by-product of that effort.

If he just let himself go . . . it seemed like the killing could become the *point*. If that should happen, if he should need to kill, then sooner or later he'd be caught, and he'd spend the rest of his life in a hole in the ground.

He had to be coldly rational about it: he would need another bomb or two, simply to complete the campaign as he'd planned it. He *didn't* need to start building bombs willy-nilly, and hitting everything in sight.

He hadn't thought of all of this at once, but in bits and pieces as he worked through his day, did the mail, wrote some checks. Late that night, he saw the delivery guy unloading the next morning's paper at County Market. He no longer got the paper, but glanced at this one because of all the tumult around the bombings, and found an end-of-the-world headline, which said:

STATE POLICE ASK TOWN: WHO'S GUILTY?

Beneath that was a secondary head that said:

PIPE BOMB FACTORY FOUND.

And below that, the stub of a story, which jumped inside for a much longer spread. The headline on the third story said: POLICE BAFFLED BY PYE TOWER ATTACK.

He stuffed the paper in his basket with the vanilla-flavored rice drink, the fat-free Rice Krispies, the tofu wieners, the Greek yogurt, the salads, waited impatiently at the cash register for an old woman to write a check for three dollars and fifty-three cents, and finally paid and got out of the place.

He couldn't wait to get back to the house, so he sat in the parking lot, under a streetlamp, and read the two stories. Flowers, he read, had sent out a letter asking a selected group of people in the town to nominate suspects in the bomb-ings. Some of the people objected to the idea, and a couple of them had sent the letters along to the newspaper, which had reproduced them.

The idea was outrageous. Flowers would get dozens of nominations, and if the very best thing happened, for Flow-ers, they'd all but one be innocent. Was the cop that stupid? Maybe it was a good thing that he hadn't killed him.

The second story reported that police had discovered the pipe-bomb factory where the pipes had been cut, and that "factory" was Butternut Tech. The story said that Flowers refused to comment, which suggested that Flowers was the one who had found the place.

How had he done that? Maybe not so stupid after all.

He closed his eyes and thought about it. Really, how outrageous, he wondered, was this survey the cop was doing? The more he thought about it, the more complicated it seemed, the more intricate the possible outcomes.

Finally, he concluded, it wasn't crazy at all. It was even . . . interesting. If he weren't the object of the hunt, he wouldn't mind participating in it.

The third story was a long Associated Press piece out of Minneapolis, wrapping up all the bombings so far. One of the most baffling aspects of the case, according to the story, was how the first bomb got into the Pye Pinnacle. "If we could figure that out, we'd know who the bomber is," an ATF agent said.

On the drive home, the bomber began to wonder: Had anyone suggested his name, in Flowers's survey? He did have a temper, which flashed from time to time. Would the cops be looking at him? If they did, they would quickly discover his relationship to Butternut Tech.

Not good, not good at all.

He felt the first hot finger of panic. That damn pipe thing . . . what had he been thinking of? Pure laziness, that's all it was.

The pipe cutter was there, he knew about it, he could get in and out. But he *could* have cut the pipe the way he first intended, with a hacksaw. He even tried it. The first cut took nearly an hour, and nearly wore out his arm. Still, he could have done one a day, and it would have been time well spent: the hacksaw would now be in the bottom of the river. . . .

He smacked his hands against the steering wheel as he looked up at the red light on a traffic signal. Damnit. Damnit.

One thing he had to do: go over the house and the car with a fine-tooth comb and make sure there wasn't the slightest evidence of bomb-making activity. He'd stashed the explosives out in the hills, but had actually assembled the bombs in his basement. If there were any chemical remnants about, much less any mechanical stuff, and if it came to a search by the ATF, they might well have the equipment to detect the residue.

He had, he thought, thrown the bodies of three old thermostats in the trash, their mercury switches torn out. In the same trash, probably, were such things as junk mail with his address on it.

That had to stop. In fact . . .

He was halfway home, but he turned the car around and headed back toward County Market, where he planned to buy a few bottles of the harshest chemical house cleaner he could find, along with new sponges, a pail, and a mop. When he was done with them, they'd all go in the trash.

Somebody else's trash, he thought. Things were coming to a head: he was almost there, and he had to be extra careful.

Which brought up a new thought: he needed to end this, but there was more to be done. He'd not yet finished. If he quit now, it'd all have been for nothing.

So he had to go on, but the quicker he finished, the sooner he could pull back into the weeds, and lay low.

He pulled back into the County Market parking lot and thought of something he'd once seen in an all-night Home Depot: a man who'd bought some chain, an axe, and a large black plastic tub.

All right, the ax and the chain could be used to cut down and drag a tree. But the tub? The tub made you think of bodies being cut up with the ax, and sunk with the chain . . . or something.

If he went into County Market and bought six bottles of assorted detergents, would the cops . . .

Ah, fuck it: that *was* paranoid.

Had to watch himself. Had to be careful. Had to walk between the over-recklessness generated by the pleasure of the bombs, and the paranoia caused by the fear of prison.

He had to walk between the raindrops of pleasure and paranoia, but he still had to move.

A new thought popped into his head, full and complete, like a religious vision: a way out.

He needed to build another bomb, and *right now*.

16

The next morning, quote, the shit hit the fan, unquote.

Virgil had expected that there might be some reaction, but he hadn't expected the intensity of it. The phone rang the first time a few minutes after seven o'clock, and the *Star Tribune* reporter Ruffe Ignace asked, "Why are you asleep? I'm not. I just had a fourteen-year-old assistant city editor snatch my ass out of bed because you did some kind of cockamamy survey. What the hell are you doing, Virgil?"

Virgil told him in a few brief sentences,

and Ignace said, "That would almost make sense, if we didn't have a Constitution."

"What part of the Constitution does this violate?" Virgil asked.

"It must violate some part," Ignace said. "I'll look it up on Wikipedia later."

"Call me back when you find the violation," Virgil said. "Right now, I'm going back to bed."

"Not for long. They got morning news cycles on TV, and they are gonna be on you like Holy on the Pope. The shit has hit the fan."

"You think?"

"Of course I think. I'm about to call up the governor and ask him what the hell you're doing," Ignace said. "You know, with the Constitution and all."

"Can we go off the record for a moment?" Virgil asked.

"Just for a minute."

"Good. Fuck you, Ruffe. I'm going back to bed."

The sheriff called eight minutes later and said, "Virgil? Man, you gotta get up. The shit has hit the fan. They're saying we're running a witch hunt."

"Earl, could we go off the record for a minute?"

When Virgil got down to the courthouse, there were three TV vans in the parking lot. He went in a side entrance, through the jail, and down to Ahlquist's office. Ahlquist said, "We've got a lot to talk about, but let me say, the goddamn Fox reporter is not believable."

"Why?"

"Because everything jiggles," he said, astonished by the thought. "*Everything.* I'm afraid to go on with her, because I'd forget how to speak in English. To say nothing of having a boner like a hammer handle."

"You gotta model yourself on me, Earl," Virgil said. "Mind like moon. Mind like water."

"I don't know what that means, but it sounds like more hippie shit, and I don't think it has anything to do with the Fox reporter."

"I'll handle it," Virgil said.

The news people were stacked up in the open lobby. Virgil went out, trailed by Ahlquist, and stood on the second step of a stairway and asked for everybody's attention. He introduced himself, and a bunch of lights clicked on, and a triangle of on-camera reporters moved to the front. At the very tip of the spearhead was the Fox reporter, whom Virgil had seen on television, but had not experienced in person.

As Ahlquist had said, she jiggled even when she was standing still. She had a flawless, pale complexion with just a hint of rose in her cheeks, and green eyes, and real blond hair. She got along with just a touch of lipstick. She did not, Virgil thought, appear to be from this planet.

She asked the first question, and her teeth were perfectly regular, and a brilliant white, and her voice a husky paean to sex: "Agent Flowers, isn't this questionnaire a violation of the Constitution?"

Virgil wanted to say, "What the fuck are you talking about?" but, for a few seconds, he forgot how to speak English.

His pause was taken for either guilt or stupidity, or she was simply familiar with the reaction, and she enlarged on her question: "The American Constitution?"

Virgil leaned toward her and said, "I'm glad you specified 'American.' No, it's not. I'd suggest you read that document. Nowhere does it mention either surveys or questionnaires."

"You don't have to get snippy about it," she said.

A guy from public radio, edging into the camera's line of sight, and maybe going for a little frottage on the Fox reporter, along with the validation of TV time, asked, "But aren't you essentially establishing a state-sponsored witch hunt?"

"No. I looked up 'witch hunt' in the Merriam-Webster dictionary, before I came over here," Virgil said. "I believe I'm quoting verbatim when I say that a witch hunt is defined as, one, a searching out for persecution of persons accused of witchcraft, and two, the searching out and deliberate harassment of those (as political opponents) with unpopular views. Are you suggesting that we are doing one of those things?"

"Not exactly," he conceded.

"Not at all," Virgil said. "All we're doing is surveying responsible citizens to see if they have any ideas who might have been involved in murdering two people, injuring two more, and barely missing several more. The surveys can't be made public because they are anonymous, and it wouldn't be ethical to make anonymous accusations public; and since a number of people refused to participate, by not returning letters, even we don't know whether a particular individual participated or not. We won't be making public the names of any of those mentioned in the survey."

The public radio guy: "But somehow . . . it feels like a witch hunt."

"That's because we'll be looking at people against whom we have no evidence at all," Virgil said. "But, if you'll excuse me for making the point, that's what a detective always does, in any kind of complicated case. You go around and ask people who they think did it, whatever it was. Often, just walk up and down the street, knocking on doors. This is just like that, except that we have to move faster. This bomber is now turning out a bomb a day. Another thing: a witch hunt operates on fear and emotion and rumor. *We* have to have definitive proof before we can accuse somebody. We're not going to indict somebody on somebody else's say-so. We need to find explosives, blasting caps, bomb parts, and motive. We're asking people where we should look. In a small city like this, where most people know most other people, we have hopes that we'll pinpoint some good suspects."

They went on for a while, and Virgil outlined what he thought about the bomber, and the TV people finally went away, apparently satisfied. Back in Ahlquist's office, the sheriff said, "You see? She never stopped jiggling." And, he added, "You're goldarned near as good on TV as I am."

Virgil got Ahlquist to assign him an assistant, Dick Pruess, and between them, they began running the list of names through the National Crime Information Center. Lyle McLachlan, the leading candidate in the survey, had thirty NCIC returns, varying from resisting arrest without violence at the bottom end, to felony theft and aggravated assault at the high end. He was thirty-eight, and had spent fourteen years in prison.

"Not him," Pruess said. "Be nice if it was, but the guy can barely make a sandwich. He could never figure this out."

They had seven more hits among the twenty names they checked, fewer than Virgil expected, given that all those named were, in the mind of some sober citizen, capable of multiple murder.

Ahlquist came by and looked at the list, and the hits, and said, "The problem I see with most of the hits is that they involve guys right at the bottom of things— they've hardly got a stake in the town, so why would they do something as weird as attack a PyeMart? If anything, these guys would want to take revenge on the town, not defend it."

Of the two people with direct ties to Butternut Tech, one came back clean, the other had a drunk driving conviction. The first one had served in the army, and Virgil called a BCA researcher and asked her to get in touch with the army and see if he'd had any training in explosives.

They were still looking for returns when Davenport called and said, "Your press conference made all the news shows. You looked pretty straight, with that black-on-black coat and shirt."

"Pain in the ass," Virgil said.

"I've got a bet for you—and I'll take either side," Davenport said. "Do you think only one, or both, of the major papers will use the phrase 'witch hunt' in an editorial tomorrow?"

"Both," Virgil said.

"Damnit, I was hoping you'd pick 'one.'"

"I can't help it, Lucas. I'm doing the best I can," Virgil said.

"I know it, but everybody's watching now. It'd be best if you wrapped this up in the next couple of days."

"Did Ruffe call the governor and ask him about the Constitution?"

"Everybody called the governor," Davenport said. "I think this is what us liberals call 'a teaching moment.'"

Good Thunder called: "I took down Pat Shepard this morning, early, because he had a summer school class. He freaked.

He cried. You know what? This isn't going to be any fun."

"It never is, when you go after people who think of themselves as honest, upright citizens," Virgil said. "Because down in their heart, they feel the guilt."

"And because he's going to lose both his wife and his job."

"Yeah, it *is* brutal," Virgil said.

"I'm waiting for you to do the 'Don't do the crime if you can't do the time.'"

"Be a long wait," Virgil said. "Will he flip?"

"Yeah, I think so. He wasn't as enthusiastic about it as his wife suggested he'd be," Good Thunder said. "In fact, I'm a little worried. I don't want to find him at the end of a rope, or with his head in the oven."

"Where is he?" Virgil asked.

"Last time I saw him, he was with his lawyer. I've told him that he'll be arrested, but I haven't arrested him yet. I've laid out the deal. They're talking, and if he's not crazy, he'll go for it. We're going to need the wire, and the monitoring gear."

"I'll talk to Davenport," Virgil said.

"Boy, that survey thing . . . the shit really hit the fan, huh? Pardon my French."

Virgil and Good Thunder were talking about who they'd go after first, if Shepard cooperated, to see if they could triangulate on the mayor, when Ahlquist ran in the door and blurted, "We've got another one, another bomb."

Virgil said into the phone, "Shirley, I gotta go. Earl says we've got another bomb."

"Talk to you later," she said. "Be careful."

Ahlquist was in a hurry. "Follow me out of the lot. You got lights?"

"Yeah."

They trotted out of the courthouse and into the parking lot, and Virgil saw a TV truck moving fast. The TV already knew. "Okay, stick close, we're going west and south," Ahlquist said.

"What's the deal?"

"Something different—could even be a break," Ahlquist said. "The bomb blew in a guy's garage. Henry Erikson. Big trout guy, one of the loudmouths. Not a bad guy, but pretty hard-core. Car salesman out at the Chevy dealer."

"I'll follow you," Virgil said, and jogged to the truck.

They got across town in a hurry, but never did catch the TV truck, which, when they arrived, was already unloading behind a couple of wooden barricades that said "Butternut Public Works." Ahlquist didn't slow much for the barricades, just put two wheels of his truck up on the curb and went around, and Virgil did the same. The Erikson house was a long half-block down from the barricades, where three deputies, including O'Hara, were standing in the yard talking, and looking into a wrecked garage, with a twisted SUV sitting inside. Two fire trucks were parked in the street, but there was no fire.

A scent of explosive and shattered pine and drywall lingered in the air, as Virgil climbed out of the truck. He and Ahlquist headed across the lawn.

O'Hara said, as they came up, "We got

a situation here. Henry was hurt bad. He could die. It looks like the bomb was under his car seat, and blew when he sat down."

"No fire?"

"No fire, the scene is still pretty much intact," O'Hara said.

Ahlquist: "When was this?"

"Fifteen minutes ago," O'Hara said, looking at her watch. "The first guys were mostly interested in getting Henry out of here, getting the ambulance, but one of them . . ." She turned, looking for the right deputy, spotted him and yelled, "Hey, Jim. Jimmy. Come over here."

The deputy was a young, fleshy guy wearing mirrored sunglasses, with a white sidewall haircut, and he hurried over.

O'Hara said, "Tell them what you saw in there."

The deputy said, "Erikson was a mess, he was lying on the ground by the wall over there. We did what we could, got the ambulance going. Don't think he's going to make it, though, looked like both legs are gone, looked like his balls . . . looked like stuff blew up into his stomach. . . ."

"Anyway," O'Hara said, prompting him.

"Anyway, when he was gone, I was looking around the mess in there, and noticed over there by his workbench, it's all blown up, but there's a pipe over there. It looks like the pipes that were used in the bombs."

Ahlquist: "You mean . . . from the bomb? Or another pipe?"

"It looks like an unused pipe from these bombs. I saw the piece of pipe that the feds had, and it looks like the same pipe."

"Let's see it," Virgil said, and, as they stepped toward the wrecked garage, "Did you touch it?"

"Absolutely not. We knew you'd want prints or DNA. As soon as I saw it, I cleared everybody away."

Virgil nodded. "You did good."

The deputy took them into the garage, close to the front fender of the wrecked truck, and pointed out the pipe: it was lying against one wall of a cabinet, where the cabinet intersected with a workbench. A trashed table saw was overturned on the other side of the bench, along with a toolbox and a bunch of tools. The place smelled of blood—a lot of blood, a nasty, cutting odor, like sticking your head in the beef case at a butcher shop.

The pipe looked right.

The deputy said, "We're trying to find his wife, but a neighbor said she's in the Cities, buying some fabric. She's a decorator. We haven't been able to get in touch."

Ahlquist said, "Speaking of the feds, here they are."

Barlow was hurrying up the driveway, O'Hara at his elbow. Inside the garage, Virgil pointed, wordlessly, and Barlow moved up to the pipe, peering at it, and then into it, and said, "There's something in there. I think we might have another bomb. Better get everybody out of here until we can have a tech look at it."

Virgil asked, "Is this the guy?"

"I'd be willing to bet that the pipe is right," Barlow said, as they backed away. "This kind of thing happens, too, especially with new guys. They don't really know what they're doing. They screw something up, and *boom.*"

O'Hara stepped away to take a cell phone call, and Barlow said, "The guy's got a lot of tools."

Virgil nodded. The garage was double-deep, three cars wide. The back half had been set up as a workshop, with storage cabinets in the corner and a long stretch of Peg-Board on the back wall. There were a half-dozen old Snap-on tool calendars on one wall—collector's items, now—photos of cars, an airplane propeller with one end broken off, a bunch of blocks of wood, most with oil on them, a half-dozen cases of empty beer bottles along one wall.

The back wall was taken up with mechanics and woodworking tools, the side wall with garden implements. Most of the tools still hung on the Peg-Board, though some had been knocked to the floor.

"The question is," Barlow said, "with this kind of setup, why'd he go to the college to cut that pipe? He could have cut it all right here."

"Good question," Virgil said. "But Jesus,

talk about looking a gift horse in the mouth."

"I hate gift horses," Barlow said. "Half the time, they wind up biting you on the ass."

O'Hara came back: "Erikson died. Never even got him on the operating table."

"Ah, man," Virgil said.

Then Barlow said, "Hey . . ." He stepped down the length of the garage and pointed to the floor. He was pointing at a thin silver cylinder a couple of inches long, with two wires coming out the bottom—it looked like a stick man with thin legs. "We got a blasting cap."

"Okay," Virgil said.

They looked at it for a moment and Barlow half-tiptoed around the rest of the garage, looking at the debris, and under it, and then Virgil asked, "How many bombers are married?"

"I don't know," Barlow said. "Some of them. Most of them, not—that's what I think, but I don't know for sure."

"I always had the idea that they were

like crazy loners, working in their basements."

"Not always."

"I really don't like this," Virgil said. "The guy's been so smart, and then he blows himself up?"

"You hardly ever meet any longtime bombers who aren't missing a few chunks, a couple fingers," Barlow said. "They fool around with the explosive. Sometimes they blow themselves up."

"With Pelex?"

"Not so much with Pelex," Barlow admitted. "Pelex is really pretty safe, you don't even have to be especially careful with it. But if you'd already rigged it as a bomb, with a sensitive switch . . ."

One of the ATF techs came up carrying a tool chest, and Barlow pointed him at the pipe. "Take a look in there with your flashlight. Don't touch it. But is it a bomb? Is it wired?"

The tech took a heavy LED flash from his box and stepped over to the pipe, bent over it, and shone the flash down the interior. Then he stepped away: "Better get Tim over here, with his gear."

"It's a bomb?" Virgil asked.

"It looks like it's stuffed with Pelex. I don't see any wiring, but I can't see in the bottom end—it could be booby-trapped."

Barlow moved everybody away from the garage, then asked Virgil, "Is Erikson's name on your list? In your survey?"

"No, he's not," Virgil said. "But I can't tell you what that means. Is he in your bomber database?"

"Give me two minutes on that," he said.

"I'll get to the NCIC," Virgil said. He walked to his truck, sat in the driver's seat, and called Davenport, told him what had happened. Davenport tracked down their researcher, who found Erikson's driver's license, and used the birth date to check his records with the National Crime Information Center.

Davenport came back and said, "She says he's clean."

"Goddamnit. This complicates things," Virgil said. "We've got two TV trucks here now, and they're going to start saying that we might have gotten the bomber. Maybe we did, but I don't believe it yet."

"What about your survey?" Davenport asked. "You started pushing the list yet?"

"Not yet. I'll do that now."

Barlow came back. "He's not in our database."

"Nothing with the NCIC," Virgil said.

Neighbors were starting to gather on the lawns adjacent to Erikson's house, and Virgil left Barlow and walked over to two women. "You guys friends with the Eriksons?"

"Is he really the bomber?" one woman asked.

"Well, a bomb went off, but we really don't know anything yet," Virgil said.

"Is he going to make it?" the second woman asked.

Virgil shook his head: "No."

"Oh, God, poor Sarah," the first woman said.

"That's his wife?"

"Yes. No children, thank God. I can't believe he's the bomber."

"Why not?" Virgil asked.

"Well, because . . . he's a car salesman kind of guy, he's always running around yelling and waving his arms, but he's a nice man. I can't believe he'd bomb people."

"Not exactly a loner, like you hear about," said the second one. "He was always talking to everybody, sort of bs-ing around the neighborhood. He'd fix lawn mowers—everybody's lawn mowers. Bring him a broken lawn mower, he'd get it running like new."

"Thanks." Virgil shook his head and walked back to Barlow and the tech, who were standing behind the wrecked car, looking at the backseat. Virgil asked them, "Did you guys see any other bomb-making stuff in the garage? More pipe, switches, blasting caps . . ."

"Just the pipe and the blasting cap," Barlow said.

The tech said, "But it's the same kind of blasting cap that was stolen from the quarry."

"Yeah? You're sure?"

"I'm sure."

They had a case, Virgil thought, as he watched the two ATF men prowl the perimeter of the explosion. Erikson apparently had the motive—the pollution of the trout stream—and he had the mechanical skills, judging from his garage workshop.

But it was all very pat. One bomb went off. One bomb remained in evidence, and one blasting cap. No more pipe, no more explosive, no more blasting caps. Just enough to hang him, without much diminishing the bomber's stockpile of explosive . . . if the bomber was indeed somebody else.

One thing I can check, Virgil thought. He found Ahlquist and said, "Where's the Chevy dealer?"

The Chevy dealer was five minutes away, on Highway 71: Virgil went that way, in a hurry, pulled into the lot and dumped the truck in a visitor's space. Inside, he showed his ID to the receptionist and asked to see the manager: "Is this about Henry?" she asked.

"Yes it is."

"Is he . . . all right?" She knew the answer to that: Virgil could see it in her eyes.

"No," he said.

"Ah, jeez," she said. "C'mon, let's find Ron, he was calling the hospital."

The manager saw them coming through the window in his office, hung up, looking at Virgil, said, "Are you with the police?"

"Yeah."

"Is Henry okay?"

Virgil shook his head. "No, he's not."

"Ah, boy. This is fuckin' nuts. No way—"

"I need to look at a calendar or a time card or something. I need to know if Henry was working two weeks ago Tuesday."

"He works Tuesdays through Saturdays, off Sundays and Mondays. He hasn't, hadn't, taken any extra days off lately. I can look at my schedule. . . ."

"Please look," Virgil said.

The manager turned to a computer screen and brought up a schedule, shook his head, and said, "I show him working eleven to seven on that Tuesday."

"And on Wednesday?"

"Same."

The bomb at the Pinnacle had gone off at nine A.M. on Wednesday, and the ATF didn't think it could have been planted any more than twenty-four hours earlier.

If that was true, Erikson couldn't have planted the bomb before work, because he wouldn't have had time to get back. He could have theoretically flown to Michigan after work . . . but then, how'd he get a bomb on the plane? Have to be a private plane. But a private plane would be obvious, there'd be lots of records, and a smart guy wouldn't do that.

No, it just didn't work. He'd have the researcher check, but it didn't work.

Erikson could, of course, have an accomplice in Grand Rapids, who planted the bomb on a Tuesday because that would give Erikson an alibi. . . .

But Virgil didn't like the feel of that, either.

The manager broke into his chain of thought. "Does Sarah know?"

Virgil went back to the bombed garage thinking that Erikson was more likely a victim than a bomber. If that were correct, then the obvious question was, Why?

Why Erikson, and not somebody else? There were at least two good reasons why *somebody* might be bombed.

First, the real bomber might be trying to hang a frame on somebody else, in preparing to end his own bombings. If he were ditching all of his Pelex, the blasting caps, the rest of the pipe, and so on, and if he did a complete and efficient cleanup of his workshop, then even if Virgil managed to identify him, a conviction would be tough: no physical evidence, plus another bomber candidate to point at.

Second, Erikson might have been killed because he knew something.

Which one?

Virgil stood outside the garage and watched the cops and the ATF people working. The ATF tech with bomb disposal experience had moved the pipe, from a distance, and nothing blew.

"How'd he do that?" Virgil asked.

"We've got all kinds of high-tech equipment with us, we just haven't had to bring it out yet."

"Like what? A robot?"

"A long string," Barlow said. "He dropped it over the end of the pipe, then we all cleared out, and he pulled it over.

So then we knew it wasn't booby-trapped, and when we got a close look at it, we saw that it'd been packed with Pelex, but he hadn't put in the blasting cap yet. We may be lucky: if it's got a good fingerprint, or a little DNA in the Pelex . . ."

"Isn't that a little weird, that he'd pack it without a blasting cap?" Virgil asked. "Wouldn't you have to take the Pelex back out before you put the blasting cap in?"

"No, not necessarily . . . I mean, we don't know if that's all the Pelex he was planning to put in there," Barlow said.

"Still seems weird to me," Virgil said.

"We don't know his working style yet, so we don't know if it's weird," Barlow said. He sounded, Virgil thought, like a guy who really wanted Erikson to be the Man.

Virgil stood and looked at the garage for a long time, and another thought occurred: if Erikson was not the bomber, then the bomber knew how to get into his garage, in the night, and where the workbench was.

Virgil went to Ahlquist, who was talking to another one of the neighbors. "I want to talk to Erikson's wife as soon as we find her," Virgil said. "Give me a call?"

Ahlquist nodded. "She's on the way, but she'll be another hour yet."

As Virgil was walking back to his truck, Pye showed up, with Marie Chapman. Virgil walked them across the police tape, and Pye asked, "Is this the guy? The bomber?"

"The ATF is leaning that way, and they could be right," Virgil said. "I have some doubts."

"Like what?"

"Like he couldn't have put the bomb in the Pinnacle. He would have needed an accomplice to plant it. I don't like the idea of two killers, linking up over that big of a space."

Pye peered at the garage, grunted, and said, "You know what? Neither do I. I'm not kissing your ass at this point."

Chapman wrote it all down, then said, "Mike Sullivan got out of the hospital. He's back at the AmericInn, but I think he's headed home to Wichita tomorrow morning, if you need to talk to him again."

Virgil shook his head. "I can't think of anything more. You guys gonna give up on the store?"

"Absolutely not," Pye said. "We've already replaced him, and we've got another guy coming up to take Kingsley's spot. Volunteers. I'm paying them triple time, forty hours a week. By the time the store's up, they'll have an extra year's pay in their pockets."

Barlow came over. "Mr. Pye. You want to take a look? This may be the guy. . . ."

Virgil left the scene, headed back to the county courthouse. He was halfway back when he saw the AmericInn, and that tripped off a thought about Sullivan, and that tripped off an entirely new thought, about the security cameras at the construction trailer.

He swerved into the AmericInn parking lot, parked, identified himself to the desk clerk, got Sullivan's room number. Sullivan's wife answered the door and said, "Virgil. We heard something happened."

"Another bomb."

She shivered and said, "I'm glad we're leaving. Was the man . . . ?"

"He was killed," Virgil said. "I need to talk to Mike, just for a second."

She stepped back and let him in. Sullivan was lying on the bed, half asleep. When his wife called him, he dragged open his eyelids, saw Virgil, and asked, "Everybody okay?"

"No." Virgil told the story again, then asked his question: "That recorder for the security camera at the trailer—how big was it?"

Sullivan held his hands eighteen inches apart. "I dunno . . . about like this. It looked like a stereo receiver, or a DVD player, I guess."

"Was the camera big or small?"

"Oh, you know, it was like the cameras you see in stores," Sullivan said. "Not very big. It was round, white, had some LEDs in it."

"Was it in a place where the guy would see it right away?" Virgil asked. "Or was it out of sight?"

"It was up in a corner over Gil's desk, where it could see the door. It didn't jump right out at you, but if you looked around, you wouldn't have any trouble finding it. . . . But after you found it, it'd take a while to find the recorder. That was in a cabinet on the floor, and it was locked shut."

"But he found it."

"I guess. The ATF guys say it wasn't there."

"I wonder if he'd been inside the trailer? You know, at some earlier date?" Virgil asked.

"Mm, there were guys in and out—city inspectors and stuff—but it wasn't really a place to hang out. It was too small. Mostly a place where you had some power, and you could get out of the dirt and noise and make phone calls and run your laptop."

"Is this going someplace?" Sullivan's wife asked.

"I don't know," Virgil said.

Sullivan said, "Well, if you want to look at the whole video setup, there's a new trailer on-site, brought up from one of our construction centers in Omaha. Donny Clark, he's my replacement, he'll be out there, he could show you."

"Don Clark . . . good luck to him, and God bless him," Sullivan's wife said.

Virgil drove out to the construction site and found Don Clark sitting in the new trailer, working on a laptop. A burly blond man with a curly blond mustache, he was as tall as Virgil but twice as wide. He took Virgil down the length of the new construction trailer and popped open a cabinet door. "There it is," he said. "They're all the same."

The server was an aluminum box with a couple of switches and an LCD panel. Virgil picked it up: four to six pounds, he thought. The camera was mostly plastic, and maybe weighed two pounds.

He left Clark and repeated his walk across the construction site and down through the brush and weeds to the river. The most obvious path came out at one of the pools where Peck had been fishing; nobody fishing at the moment. He got right down by the black water, startled a green heron out of a tangle of weeds, probably a nest. Couldn't see anything.

Thought about it.

Cameron Smith had said that there was a bridge to the west, and not too far. Virgil followed the riverside trail, a dusty rut off a gravel county road. There were two more pools between the first one he'd visited and the bridge. He stood on the bridge looking into the water, then got on his cell phone and called Ahlquist.

"You guys got divers for when somebody jumps in the lake and doesn't come up?"

"Not the department," Ahlquist said. "There's a bunch of divers out of Butternut Scuba, they've got kind of a rescue team. They help out if we need them."

"How do I get in touch?" Virgil asked.

"Go to Butternut Scuba—they're open every day. What're you up to?"

"Old BCA saying," Virgil said. "When in doubt, dredge."

"What?"

"Talk to you later," Virgil said.

17

Butternut Scuba was a storefront on the edge of downtown, around the corner from a bakery. Virgil stopped at the bakery and after some consultation with the baker, got a couple of poppy-seed kolaches. He stood on the corner and ate them out of a white paper bag, a little guilty that he should be feeling so relatively well fed, so shortly after that poor bastard had been blown to bits in his own car; and guiltily thankful that it hadn't been him.

When he was done with the pastry, he threw the bag in a trash can and walked around the corner to the scuba shop. A blond woman, thin as a steel railroad track and about as solid, was in the back room filling a scuba tank. When Virgil came through the front door, the overhead doorbell jingled and she yelled, "Hey, Frank—I'm back here."

Virgil clumped through the shop, with its displays of tanks and buoyancy control devices, masks, finds, and regulators, to the back, said, "I'm not Frank."

"That's for sure," she said, looking him over. She had a white smile and one-inch-long hair. A snake tattoo disappeared down the back of her neck, into her T-shirt. "Be with you in a minute."

Virgil went back into the shop and looked at a Cressi Travelight BCD for $460. He'd used a BC a few dozen times when he was on leave from the army, diving in the wine-dark Aegean; and he'd gone diving a bit back in the Midwest, with a DNR biologist who was researching the habits and habitats of large muskies. Virgil had gotten a nice *In-Fisherman* article out of that, but he hadn't had a tank on since the summer before.

"Can I get you one of those?" asked

the blonde, who wore a name tag that said *Gretchen*.

"Actually, I need some divers. I'm a cop and I'd like somebody to dive a couple of pools on the Butternut."

"You don't look entirely like a cop," she said, in a friendly way.

"Well, I am, Virgil Flowers with the Bureau of Criminal Apprehension."

"Okay, I've read about you," she said. "We do dives for the police. . . . Somebody drown?"

Virgil shook his head: "We're not looking for a body. We're looking for some electronic equipment."

"Uh, will we get paid?"

"We can work something out," Virgil said. "It's the state, so it might take a while to get the check."

A short, square, red-haired man with a red British RAF mustache came through the door, looked at Gretchen, then at Virgil, and Virgil said, "Hey, Frank."

The deal was done in five minutes, and Frank called a guy named Retrief and told him to bring his gear up to the PyeMart site, and make it quick. Thinking that he might rent some equipment and go in the water, Virgil dug out his certification card, and Frank asked him how many dives he had in. Virgil said, "Maybe a hundred . . . maybe. Haven't been down for a while."

Frank said, "We'd spend more time making sure you're okay, than it'd be worth. You get down there, and you can't see more than about two feet. Blind diving's a whole new thing. It's easy to get tangled up in shit."

That made sense to Virgil, since visibility was one of the reasons he quit diving in Minnesota; so he helped Gretchen and Frank load their gear in the back of Frank's truck, and they followed him out to the PyeMart site, and then back along the track to the river, Virgil plowing down the weeds in his government truck.

When they got to the river, Virgil found that a second truck had fallen in behind Frank's: Retrief, a balding man with tattoos on his neck, and an Australian accent. To Gretchen: "Workin' for the jacks now, izit?"

"They're paying us," she said.

"That makes for a change," he said. To Virgil: "Howya doin'?"

Virgil said, "You sound like you're from New Jersey."

They wanted to know more about the bombings, and about Erikson, and Frank said, "You get this guy, you oughta string him up by his balls."

"Right on that," Retrief said, and Gretchen said, "But what if Erikson did it?"

The water in the stream was cold, and the three divers pulled wet suits over swimming suits, doing a quick change in their trucks, then slung on tanks, masks, BCDs, and swim fins, and waded down the muddy banks to the end of the first pool.

While they were changing, Virgil dug his Nikon out of the truck, with a medium zoom, and started shooting. "How cold?" he called.

"Freezing," Retrief muttered.

"Not too bad," said Gretchen.

In waist-deep water, the divers popped in their mouthpieces and went down; Virgil could track them by watching for bubbles as they moved slowly upstream, turned, and then swept back downstream, and then up, back down, and up one more time. At the end of it, they popped up, and Frank called, "Nothing here. How far to the next one?"

"Hundred yards or so," Virgil called back.

"Best ride in the truck," Frank said. They all piled in the back of Frank's Chevy, and Virgil bumped through the weeds west along the bank to the next pool.

The second pool was longer and narrower than the first, and looked deeper and murky and even nasty. Virgil thought of snakes, which was another reason he didn't dive much in the Midwest; not that there were poisonous snakes, just that murky water made him think of them. The second pool went just like the first one, for ten minutes. On the first downward sweep, though, the bubbles stopped for a full minute, coalescing in one spot, then all three of them popped to the surface.

Gretchen pulled her mouthpiece and called, "Got them," and held up a camera, just like the one Virgil had seen in the second trailer; Virgil took three quick shots of her holding it up, and then shot the others, as the two men did one-armed sidestrokes to shore, towing a black metal box with wires dangling off the back.

And Virgil laughed out loud with the sheer pleasure of being right. He shouted down, "That's it, guys. Beer for everybody."

"You're a good man, Virgie," Retrief called back, and Frank said, "The paper's gonna eat this up. I love this shit."

"Better'n pulling out a body," Gretchen said. She climbed the bank, dripping river water, straining against the weight of her equipment, and handed the camera to Virgil.

They all drove back to the scuba shop, where the divers took turns taking showers and rinsing down their equipment, including the camera and the console. When they were done, they walked down the street to Mitchell's, a bar, carrying the recorder and camera. Virgil ordered beer, and when it came, called Barlow.

"Hey, I got that camera and the recorder from the first trailer," he said.

"You got what?"

"The camera and recorder from that first trailer, the one that was blown up."

After a moment of silence, Barlow asked, "Where'd you get them?"

Barlow got there in ten minutes, ordered a Coke, looked at the still-damp electronic gear. Virgil explained it all, and the grinning divers chipped in their bit, about finding the stuff in the murk—Frank had first found the recorder, and then a minute later, Gretchen found the camera—and finally Barlow asked Virgil, "How in the hell did you ever think of that?"

"I was just thinking about this guy stumbling around out there in the dark, carrying all this crap, and whatever tools he had to break into the trailer, and I thought, Why would he take them home? Why not just get rid of it? Where would he get rid of it? He was walking right by this river, and he was apparently familiar with the area, with these deep pools. . . ."

Barlow shook his head. "Dumb luck, that's what it was."

"Ever notice how dumb luck seems to follow smart people around?" Retrief asked.

"Where you're gonna need the luck is, the recorder," Gretchen said. "It's been underwater for days."

"It's a hard drive, and most of them are sealed units," Virgil said. "I think we're eighty percent for recovering the images. I'm more worried that he bashed it around than about the water. If he physically screwed up the disk, it'll be harder to get at the pictures." He looked at the case on the table. "It looks okay. He didn't hit it with a hammer or anything."

"How long before we know?" Barlow asked.

"I'll get it back to St. Paul today," Virgil said. "They'll pull the unit, and take a look. If it's not broken, we'll have images this afternoon. Or tonight."

"That's something," Barlow said. "That really is."

"What happened with Sarah Erikson?" Virgil asked Barlow.

"She's back," Barlow said. "She's pretty messed up, says her husband would never do anything like that. Wouldn't know a bomb from his elbow, is what she says. She says she'll come down and talk to us this afternoon. I'll call you."

"I gotta go talk to the paper," Frank said. "We oughta get a picture. I think they fired their only real photographer."

Gretchen demurred: "I don't think I want this bomb guy to know I was involved. I live alone."

Frank said, "Mmmm . . . you could move in with me."

"No, I couldn't," she said. She looked at Virgil and lowered her eyelids.

Retrief said, "Fuck 'im, if he can't take a joke. You gonna be in the picture, Frank?"

"I guess."

"Then it's you, me, and Virgie," Retrief said.

"I hope you know what you're doing," Barlow said to Virgil.

"I want him to know; I want him to feel me coming," Virgil said. "I want to shake him up. At the moment, I got nothing else."

Virgil, Frank, and Retrief posed with the recovered camera and recorder, and Gretchen pushed the button on Frank's cell phone and when he saw the photo, Frank said, "That's a thousand dollars in advertising, right here."

"Really? That calls for another round," Retrief said to him. "You're buyin'."

Virgil took the recorder and camera back to the county courthouse and put them in a box, and Ahlquist dispatched a deputy to take them to the BCA labs in St. Paul. "Man-oh-man, this could be the break we needed. If his face is on that video, we got him."

"Keep your fingers crossed," Virgil said. "Where do I go to see Sarah Erikson?"

"She's coming in here. So's Barlow. We figured we'd kill all the birds with one stone."

"We're birds?"

"You know what I mean."

"Bad metaphor, Earl," said Virgil.

"Tough titty. Go investigate your list."

"Which Erikson isn't on," Virgil said.

"Unfortunately," Ahlquist said.

Virgil pushed himself out of his chair. "I better get investigating."

"Somebody's got to do it," Ahlquist said. "Nice job on that camera, Virgil."

A few more letters had come back with lists of possible bombers. Virgil spent a half hour going through them, but nothing much had changed. Then Good Thunder called:

"We flipped Pat Shepard, and your guy from the BCA is here with the recording equipment. We're going to send Shepard to see Burt Block right away: we're starting to pile up people who know about this, and we need to move. We'd like you to come and help brief Shepard." Block was the second of the three city councilmen bribed by PyeMart through Geraldine Gore.

"When do you want me?" Virgil asked.

"How fast can you get here?"

The county attorney's office was upstairs. Virgil looked at his watch: "About twenty-two seconds, if I take the stairs."

"We'll leave the light on for you," Good Thunder said.

Pat Shepard was a middle-sized guy, tanned from the summer golf course, with a tight haircut; and he was pathetic and about the only person in the room who didn't feel sorry for him was the county attorney, a beefy man named Theodore Wills, who introduced himself as "Theodore." Wills was openly ecstatic about Shepard's confession, and scornful of the man himself.

Shepard, who'd been arrested, sat in his chair and wept, and Virgil had to look away. Good Thunder kept passing Shepard paper towels from a roll, which he pressed against his eyes. Shepard's public defender kept saying, "C'mon, Pat, it's gonna work out."

A BCA technician, who'd brought the sound equipment, sat in a corner and read a new copy of *Sail* magazine.

"Wife gone, job gone, gonna lose everything. My life is over," Shepard said.

"Can't do the time, don't do the crime," Wills said, and Good Thunder's eyes touched Virgil's with a slight disgusted roll.

Bill Check, the public defender, said, "Jesus, Theodore, you wanna take it easy? You're getting everything you wanted."

But, Virgil thought, as he watched Shepard, Wills was essentially correct. The guy had been entrusted to take care of the town, the best he could, and he'd sold his vote on a critical issue. His confession had been taken down by a court reporter, and had been signed and sealed. For his cooperation in bagging the rest of the gang, he'd get no jail time.

Wills said to Check, "No, I'm *not* getting everything I wanted. I wanted the sucker in jail for at least a year and Good Thunder talked me out of it. He's the last one that's getting a break like that. Everybody else goes down."

Virgil leaned across to Shepard and said, "You've got to pull yourself together. You need to tighten up. If you can't do this, if you blow this meeting with Burt Block, then the agreement won't hold, and you *will* do time."

"No, no," said Check, the public defender. "There are no guarantees that this is gonna work. . . ."

"But he has to make a good-faith effort, and if he goes in there fumbling around, and Block smells a rat, then the deal's off," Wills said.

Virgil reached over and patted Shepard on the shoulder. "Being upset is okay. If you show Block you're upset, that's fine, that's what he'd expect. Upset's okay, but you have to have your head under control. C'mon. Why don't you and I take a walk and we'll get you calmed down and talk about it."

"Good idea," Good Thunder said.

"I'm not so sure," Check said. "Leaving him alone with a police officer . . ."

"I'm not taking testimony," Virgil said. "I'm just trying to get him some fresh air."

So Virgil and Shepard took a walk around the courthouse. Shepard looked around, at the sky and the sidewalks and at some kids walking down the other side of a street toward a Dairy Queen, and said, "Everything looks just like it did when I went to work yesterday and I was a happy guy. Today, everything's gone."

"You know what? It's bad now, but three years from now, you'll have another job, probably in another town. You'll probably have a new wife, and it'll all start over," Virgil said. "I see this all the time. You're basically not a bad guy, but you made one big god-awful mistake. You'll pay for it, but then, you'll be done. If you can hold yourself together, you won't go to jail. That's huge. Not going to jail . . . that's a big deal. If you can hold together."

Shepard sniffed and said, "I can hold together."

"Well, you look like shit," Virgil said. He handed over a couple more towels. "Stop for a minute and press these on your eyeballs, and while you're doing that, stop crying. Let's get this over."

Shepard pressed the wads of paper into his eye sockets, and when he took the towels away, he asked, "You think I'll really get back?"

"Look. You're a smart guy," Virgil said. "You'll move to some place like Tucson, where they just really won't give a shit about your problem here, and you'll get a job. I'd bet you in three years you're making twice as much as a schoolteacher in Butternut Falls. I mean, that's what people make now—twice as much as teachers."

"Ah, man," Shepard said. But he didn't start crying again, and they walked back. "All my students are going to find out. I keep talking to them about good citizenship and all that . . . and look what I did. Now I'm going to drag everybody else down with me, just to save my ass. I'm such a fuck-up. I mean, even if I get another job, I can't stay here—I have to leave home. Leave my daughter, go someplace strange. I *like* it here."

Virgil asked, "Is this Burt guy an old friend?"

"No. I don't know him that well. I don't much like him, though." Then, thinking about what he was going to do, he said, "I'm such an asshole. I don't like him, but I don't like . . . dragging him down."

He'd calmed down by the time Virgil got him back to the county attorney's office, and they talked about his meeting with Block. "Don't lead him. Just refer to stuff that you've done," Virgil said. "You want to be a little shaky, a little remorseful. Tell him that sad story about Jeanne leaving you. He'll believe that. He'll try to pull you together, and when he does that, he'll give himself up."

They wired him up, and tested him for sound, and headed downtown, Virgil, the tech, Good Thunder, and Wills in one truck, with the sound equipment, Shepard on his own, in his Chevy.

Shepard was to meet Burt Block in Block's office—Block ran a temp service and employment agency in downtown Butternut. The tech, whose name was Jack Thompson, said, on the way over, "Wish we had a little more time to set this up. Be nice to have some video."

"I thought you hid cameras inside of briefcases and like that," Virgil said.

"Not so much. Tape recorders, we do."

"Yeah, I used one of those, once," Virgil said.

"Cameras would have been nice," Good Thunder said. "Juries like to see faces. I just hope the audio works through brick walls, or whatever."

"It'll be fine. This is state-of-the-art stuff," Thompson said. "Long as he doesn't fall in the lake."

Virgil told him about the recorder at the bottom of the Butternut, and Thompson said, "If he didn't punch a hole in the hard drive, you're good."

"Hope so," Virgil said.

The wire they'd put on Shepard was strictly one-way—they had no way to communicate with Shepard, except by cell phone. As Shepard pulled into a diagonal parking space in front of Block's office, Thompson started the recorder. Shepard sat in his car for a full minute— they could hear him breathing—then slowly got out. "I'm such an asshole," he muttered.

"C'mon, c'mon, move," Wills said, impatiently, from the backseat.

Shepard looked across the street at Virgil's truck, then turned, reluctantly, and said, "I'm going in," and went inside.

Inside, he said hello to a woman, who said, "Hi, Pat. Burt's in the back, go on in."

Dialogue:

   Block: "Hey, Pat. What's up?"

   Shepard: "Hey, Burt. Man . . . I gotta sit down. I'm really screwed up here, man. My wife bailed out on me last night. She found out I . . . I've been fooling around. She's so pissed, she knows about the PyeMart deal, she knows about the money."

   Block: "Whoa, whoa, whoa . . . She knows about me? She knows about all of us?"

   "Got him," Wills said, gleefully.

   Thompson said, "Shhh."

   Shepard: "She doesn't know exactly about you or Arnold, but she knows about Geraldine."

   Block: "But she doesn't know about me?"

   Shepard: "She *knows* . . . you know . . . but I never said your name or anything. But she knows."

   Block: "Ah, man, you gotta shut that bitch up. If she talks, we're toast."

Shepard: "I *can't* shut her up. She *left* me. She took what was left of the money, and she knows where it came from, so . . . maybe we're all right, but I don't know. I was thinkin' . . . I was lookin' for a way out."

Block: "Like what?"

Shepard: "If we got to . . . maybe we could buy her off? I mean, she's gonna need money. I only got twenty-five, I figured you guys got a lot more, you could help out—"

Block: "Whoa, whoa, whoa, that's *my* money. We all got exactly the same. You're gonna have to find some other way to shut her up."

Shepard's voice broke: "I wish I'd never seen any of you. Geraldine said it was no problem, but now, oh my God . . ." He began blubbering.

Block: "Jesus, man up, Pat. If we just find a way to shut her up . . . Maybe we go back to the PyeMart guy, tell them that we've got a problem, need to smooth it out."

Shepard: "That might work. Maybe. You think Geraldine only got twenty-five? I figured that you guys all did a lot better than that."

Block: "I don't know about Geraldine, but Arnold and I only got twenty-five. I mean, that's all there was. Maybe Geraldine clipped a little off our shares, she's crookeder than a bucket of cottonmouths. . . ."

They went on that way for a while, then Shepard asked, "So what do you think I oughta do? Talk to Geraldine? See if she'll talk to PyeMart? I'm not that tight with her."

Block: "I'll talk to her. But I'll tell you what. We'd all be better off if, you know, if Jeanne just went away."

There was a moment of silence in Block's office, but in the truck, Good Thunder blurted, "I don't believe he said that."

Shepard: "What? Went away?"

Block: "You, know, if she had some kind of accident. Then you wouldn't be getting a divorce, you wouldn't have this threat hanging over you."

Shepard: "Okay, that's fucking ridiculous."

Block: "I'm just sayin'."

Shepard: "I'm getting out of here. Nothing better happen to Jeanne. If it does . . ."

Block: "What? You're gonna talk to the cops? You're in just as deep as we are, you silly shit. Anyway, think about what I said. I'll talk to Geraldine, and we'll figure something out. Maybe if the PyeMart guy gets worried, we could sting him for a little more. Tell him we need a hundred to shut up your old lady, give her twenty, keep the rest. You know, we should have thought of this before."

Shepard: "I'm outa here."

Block: "Hey, Pat. Have a good day. Keep your fuckin' mouth shut."

Good Thunder said, "He is *so* implicated. We could talk conspiracy to commit murder."

Wills nodded: "We will. The thing is, if we agree to drop that charge, but leave jail time up in the air for the bribe . . . we could flip him, too, and get him talking to Geraldine. Man. We are looking . . . What's that asshole doing?"

"He's talking to himself," Thompson said.

Shepard was standing outside Block's office, looking through the window into the office, making an incoherent growling sound, like a nervous collie. Every once in a while, a word would pop out, but it didn't sound good.

Virgil said, "I'm gonna go reel him in," and he popped his truck door.

Good Thunder said, "Wait. He's moving."

Virgil stopped and looked over at Shepard. Shepard walked around to the back of his car, looked across the street at them, and lifted a hand.

"Got a flat tire?" Thompson suggested, as Shepard rummaged around in the trunk of his car.

"I don't . . ." Virgil began.

Then Shepard straightened, and in his hand he was holding a large-frame chrome revolver. A Smith, Virgil thought, vaguely, as Good Thunder said, "Oh, no," and Wills said, "Holy shit," and Thompson said, "Uh-oh, got a gun, Virgil?"

Virgil thought about his gun in the lockbox, turned to say something about it to Good Thunder, who was essentially sitting on it, but Good Thunder, still looking through the windshield said, "He's gonna . . ."

Virgil looked back in time to see Shepard turn the gun toward his own chest, and pull the trigger.

And Shepard went down.

18

Virgil got to him first.

Shepard was lying flat on his back, his eyes open and focused, and he was making the growling sound, his breaths short and harsh. His arms lay down his sides, and the gun was a few inches from his right hand. Virgil pushed it out of reach, heard Good Thunder shouting into a cell phone, calling for an ambulance. People were shouting on the street around him, and Wills was telling them to stand back, as Virgil pulled open Shepard's shirt, saw the wound just to the right of his breastbone, a small hole through which bright red, frothy blood was seeping.

Virgil looked around, for something soft and plastic, didn't see anything, shouted at Wills, "Keep them away," jogged back to his truck, got a trash bag out of a seat-back pocket, ran back to Shepard. Good Thunder was kneeling over him, saying, "Ambulance on the way, Pat. Ambulance is coming . . ." Virgil elbowed her aside, ripped a square of plastic out of the bag, and slapped it across the bullet hole and pressed it down.

The audio gear had been tucked under Shepard's belt line, and Virgil pulled it loose, and then ripped off the tape that held the microphone to his chest.

Shepard made another growling, coughing sound, and the first of the deputies arrived. Wills organized them to push back the rubberneckers. The ambulance was there a minute later, probably five or six minutes after the shooting, which was great time; the paramedics put oxygen on Shepard, moved him onto a gurney, and they were gone.

Virgil walked back to his truck and gave the audio gear to Thompson, got some Handi Wipes and washed the blood off his hands as he went back across the street. Good Thunder asked, "What do you think?"

Virgil shook his head. "Hard to tell with a gunshot. Depends on what it hit. If it hit a major artery, he'll die, and in the middle of your chest, that's easy to do. If he didn't, he could be walking around tomorrow. Bullet didn't go through . . ."

He went to the pistol and knelt next to it: the frame was big, long-barreled, a Smith & Wesson, as he'd thought, but in .22 caliber. A practice gun for the bigger calibers.

"I'll let the deputies pick that up," he said, getting to his feet. "It's a .22. He'd have to be fairly unlucky to die."

"I wonder if he wanted to?" Good Thunder said. "You'd think he would have shot himself in the head."

"I'm not a shrink, but a shrink once told me that suicidal people will sometimes try to kill themselves in a way which isn't disfiguring," Virgil said. "They want to look good."

Wills, the county attorney, was walking around in circles, talking into a cell phone. When he got off he came over and said, "I want to take Block as soon as we can get him alone. People are going to be talking about this all over town. We need to bust him, get him to the courthouse, get him with an attorney, and make a deal about Geraldine and the guy from PyeMart."

Good Thunder nodded. "I agree."

"I'll leave you guys to that," Virgil said. "That's attorney stuff."

Virgil was bummed: they'd taken an obviously distraught man, who'd said several times that his life was over, and they'd pushed him too hard.

Virgil hauled the others back to the courthouse, where they had a quick conference with Ahlquist, who agreed to send a couple of deputies to pick up Block. "He was looking out his office window, and saw me, so he might have figured out that something's going on," Wills said. "When the docs find that wire on

Shepard, the word's going to get out even faster."

"Nah, I took it off him," Virgil said. "But people were all over the place, some of them saw me take it off. I think we have to assume that Block will know something's up."

"Might make him more interested in a deal," Wills said. He said to the sheriff, "Earl, you gotta move now."

Ahlquist left to get the deputies moving, and Wills said, "Wasn't that just the damnedest thing? Damnedest thing I ever saw."

Virgil had thought Wills was a jerk; and he might still be, but at the moment, he was pretty human, and he'd been cool enough at the scene of the shooting. People, Virgil thought, were hardly ever just one thing: only a jerk, only a good guy.

As she left, Good Thunder asked Virgil what he was going to do.

"I've got to talk to Sarah Erikson— that's the main thing," he said. "There are a couple of questions we need answered in a hurry."

When Ahlquist came back, Virgil told him that he needed to talk to Sarah Erikson: "When are we going to do that?"

"We left it indefinite," he said.

"Do you know where she is?" Virgil asked.

"Last I heard, she was at her house. Want me to check?"

"If you could."

Ahlquist called one of the deputies still at the bombed house, who said that Sarah Erikson was in the house, along with her mother, a brother, and a couple of friends. Virgil said good-bye to Ahlquist, asked him to call when Block had been busted.

"No point in calling you," Ahlquist said. "Unless he ran for it, it's any minute."

A deputy came in, looking for Ahlquist, and said, "Hey, Sheriff, Randy called from the hospital, they're taking Shepard into the operating room, but the docs say he's likely to make it."

Virgil left for Erikson's, and on the way, took a call from Willard Pye.

"There's a rumor going around that

you're investigating my bidness," Pye said.

"Can't talk about rumors," Virgil said. "So, how're you doing, otherwise?"

"Cut the crap, Virgil," Pye said. "You think something was going on between my boy and this fella that shot himself?"

"Can't talk about stuff like that, Willard. I'm here basically to catch the bomber," Virgil said. "That's my number one priority, and I'm on the way to talk to Erikson's wife, right now."

"I'll take your evasions as a 'yes,' you are investigating PyeMart. Goddamnit, Virgil, we're clean as a spinster's skirt on this thing. I just talked to my boy who handled this whole issue—"

"Willard, I can't talk," Virgil said. "It's not proper, and anyway, I gotta go. I'm coming up on Erikson's." He clicked off.

Word, he thought, was getting around. If Block didn't crumble, they could have a problem getting to the mayor and Arnold Martin on Shepard's testimony alone. And if the mayor didn't crumble, they'd never get to the PyeMart expediter.

Virgil got on the phone to Ahlquist: "Could you get one of your smartest guys and put him in his private car and have him tag Willard Pye around? I'd be interested if he gets together with Geraldine Gore."

"I can do that," Ahlquist said. "I'll call Pye and give him some bullshit, find out where he's at."

"Thanks. Talk to you later, Earl."

The feds were taking the Erikson house apart. Virgil stopped to talk with Barlow, who said that things were just about where they were at when Virgil left. Barlow asked, "Were you around when this Shepard guy shot himself?"

"Across the street," Virgil said. "Everybody in town knows about it, huh?"

"Well, I know about it, and nobody talks to me, much," Barlow said.

Sarah Erikson was a brown-haired woman with a long nose and deep brown, almost black eyes, rimmed with red, where she'd been crying; she was dressed in a beige blouse and dark brown slacks and practical shoes, and sat alone in an easy chair, with her brother, her mother, and three female friends arrayed on the couch and a couple of chairs brought from the kitchen.

Her brother, whose name was Ron Mueller, told Virgil that his sister wasn't in very good shape to talk to the police.

"I know that, but I need to talk to her anyway. There are some seriously urgent questions that just won't wait."

"We already told the police and the sheriff how ridiculous this whole idea is, that Henry is the bomber. He's a good guy, he's always around home, he doesn't go sneaking off—"

"He's got that workshop, and there was a half-made bomb," Virgil said.

"The bomber *planted* it," Mueller said. "Plain as the nose on your face."

"I'm wiling to buy that—that's why I need to talk to Sarah," Virgil said. "Because if he's innocent, there are a whole bunch of other questions that come up, and we need to get them answered. So: I need to talk to her. Now."

"Be right back," Mueller said.

Virgil was just inside the door; Mueller went over to Sarah and spoke to her quietly, and nodded, and she nodded, and Mueller turned back to Virgil and waved him over. One of the women got up and gave Virgil her chair and said, "I'll get another one."

Virgil sat and said, "Mrs. Erikson, I know you're not in good shape to answer questions, but I do need some answers. You say your husband isn't the bomber? Okay—but then, who is? You know him, whether you know it or not."

That got her attention. She'd looked hazy-eyed when he sat down, but now her gaze sharpened up and she frowned.

"What?"

"If your husband is innocent, then the bomb was planted on him. It had to be planted by somebody who knew your husband had a workshop, knew which vehicle was his, knew he could get into your garage—or did you leave the door open last night? Could it have been random, the first open garage the guy saw?"

"No, no, the garage wasn't open last night. Henry had a lot of tools, he kept the door down."

"Then how'd the bomber get in?"

Erikson stared at him for a second, then looked over her shoulder, toward the kitchen, and said, "Well, uh, the garage door was down, but we mostly don't lock the access door on the side. That's behind the fence and so it's open, most of the time."

"Who'd know that?"

"Well . . . I guess maybe a lot of people would. I mean, we have backyard parties, barbeques, people coming and going. They'd know what was in the garage."

"Could they count on that door being unlocked?" Virgil asked.

"Sometimes it's locked," she said. "Most of the time, it isn't."

"You ever have a key go missing?"

"No, not that I know of," Erikson said. "But all our locks open with one key, and we've had a lot of those keys. I suppose somebody could have stolen one."

Virgil thought it over, and shook his head. "It can't just be the availability of a key. There has to be something . . . Is he involved in the PyeMart situation in any way?"

"No, except that he was against it," Erikson said. "He thought the Butternut was such a great resource. He grew up back there, his family had a farm. He used to float down it on rafts, and then he got a canoe—"

"So he didn't sell any of that land to PyeMart? Or his family?"

"No, they were way down to the south of there. They don't own the land anymore, anyway. His folks sold it years ago."

Virgil chewed that over for a moment, but couldn't see how it would go anywhere. Maybe the bomber had simply seen the size of the workshop, and chose him because it would make bomb production look more credible? Maybe.

Before he left the sheriff's office, he'd written down the names of the people who'd shown up more than once on his survey, plus the two who worked at the college. The kitchen was empty, and he said, "Mrs. Erikson, I'd like you to step into the kitchen with me for a moment. I want to show you something privately."

She looked around at her friends for a moment, then shrugged and stood and led the way into the kitchen. At the far end, at a breakfast nook, Virgil quietly explained his survey, then said, "I want you to look at this list. How many of the people do you know?"

She took the list, scanned it, blinked a couple of times, then stepped back to the kitchen counter and took a pencil out of a cup, put the list on a magazine and the magazine on the countertop, and started checking them off. "I'll put one check by the people I just know, and two checks by the ones who might know our house a little."

"There are some?"

She bent over the list. "Three. There are three."

"Do any of them seem to be the kind . . ."

She stared at the list for a long time, and then said, "I never liked Bill Barber. He's a jerk and he's angry, and I think he was once mixed up in some kind of assault."

"Doesn't have a record," Virgil said.

"His uncle was on the police force, before it became part of the sheriff's department. He might have hushed it up. Or maybe he was a juvenile or something. It was quite a while ago."

Virgil had brought an annotated master list with him, and checked Barber's name:

he'd been mentioned four times. Interesting. "Why would Barber have been here?"

"Because he lives down the block. He bought a couple of cars from Henry, though that's not a big deal: a lot of people have bought cars from Henry."

"Is his house like this one?"

"Mmm, a little. They were all built by the same contractor," she said.

"Okay. Okay . . . what about the other two?" Virgil asked.

"John Haden. I don't know why he'd be on your list, he's a nice enough man. I mean, Henry used to play guitar in a band. He was good. John used to build guitars, just as a hobby, electric guitars, and Henry got interested, and he started building some. They sort of got into it together. Henry was really good at the woodwork, and cutting the hollows in the back for the electronics, that kind of stuff. John did all the hand-finish work and the paint. They could sell the guitars for a thousand dollars each. They had a waiting list."

Virgil was interested: Haden was one of the two men who worked at Butternut Tech. "How many? In a year?"

"Ten, maybe? Sometimes a couple more or less."

"So Haden would have a reason to want to keep your husband alive, if anything."

"Oh, sure. They were friends."

"He works at the college, right?"

"Yeah. Math. I don't know why he'd be on your list, though. Maybe because he's a little odd. Kinda geeky, you know. Once you get to know him, he seems really nice. He likes cats, we've got cats."

"Nothing wrong with that," Virgil said. He liked cats himself. "When you say geeky, do you mean ineffectual? Or is he one of those, you know, more-manic geeks? Some of them have really strong beliefs."

"Oh, not like that. He has an off-the-wall sense of humor. Maybe you could ask one of his ex-wives."

"More than one?" Virgil asked. "He has trouble with relationships?"

"I think he's been married and divorced three times, hard as that is to believe," she said. "Who in their right mind would make that kind of mistake three times?

Anyway, Henry said that even though he's geeky, women like him. Heck, I guess I like him."

"Okay." He looked at the checks on her list. "What about this Gordon Wilson?"

"Gordy . . . he's another car salesman, he works over at the Ford dealer. He's been in and out of this house, off and on, sometimes he and Henry would be working deals. I don't know him that well, really. I don't know why he'd be on your list, either."

Virgil looked at the master list: Wilson had been named three times.

"You don't know this William Wyatt?" Wyatt was the other teacher.

"I've heard the name. It's a small town, in some ways."

"But you know Dick Gates? You gave him one check." Gates was another name with four checks after it, like Barber.

"I don't think he's ever been to the house, but we both know him, knew him. He's a police officer, you know, a wildlife officer. He patrols the lakes in the summer."

They went through the rest of the list; and when he asked her, she looked thoughtfully at the list and said, "I'm just guessing."

"That's all I'm asking," Virgil said. "I'll take it purely as a guess."

"And it makes me feel kind of crappy . . . but if I had to pick one, I guess I'd pick Dick Gates. Henry didn't like him, and he didn't like Henry. Henry liked to fish, and it seemed like every time he went out, and Gates was out, he would pull Henry over and check to see what he'd caught, and how many. After fifteen times, you'd think he'd know Henry was an ethical fisherman, who usually didn't keep anything." The tears started again, and she wiped them away with her fingertips. "But he just kept doing it. Because I think he liked the power. It got so, if Gates's boat wasn't at the dock, Henry'd just go up the Butternut and fish. Gates didn't go up the river. Too easy to get stuck, and then, nobody would help him out."

Virgil considered that. He knew lots of cops who liked the power—and that, he thought, was probably why Gates was on the list four times. If he didn't like the power, he might well have never been on it at all. Not that he was excusing him, just because he was a cop . . .

"Did Henry ever say anything to you about seeing something odd, up the river? Somebody who shouldn't have been there, or acted weird?"

She shook her head. "He had a lot of Butternut stories, but nothing like that. But, you know, if it was just a *little* odd, he might not have mentioned it."

They talked for a while longer, then Virgil thanked her and excused himself, and went out to the garage and watched the ATF crime-scene guys for a few minutes, and finally asked Barlow, "You still think he's the guy?"

"I'm saying sixty percent, and slowly dropping. We could be down to fifty-fifty by this evening. The thing is, we found all the bomb stuff at once—and then nothing else. It was right out in the open. And we don't find any of the small stuff you'd expect—more detonators, more batteries, a bunch of clocks or old thermostats. . . . Didn't find any rolls of wire. We did find some really odd-looking electronics, but we can't put them with any bomb-making techniques."

"He made electric guitars as a hobby," Virgil said.

"Okay. I'll mark that down," Barlow said. "The other thing is, I can think of good reasons he could be the bomber and at the same time, we'd only find one pipe, and one blasting cap."

"Yeah?"

"Yeah. Like, he was limiting his exposure. He was planning to do two more bombs, and he kept the other stuff off-site to limit the possibility of detection."

"Good thought, Jim," Virgil said, not believing it.

"So anyway, I haven't talked to Mrs. Erikson yet. I want to know exactly what to ask her, when I get to her," Barlow said. "I want her to have an attorney."

"Sure," Virgil said. "Keep digging. And call me."

The math professor interested him: not only because he'd been named on the list, but because he'd be a really bright guy, and he was a little odd, both of which the bomber apparently was, and because he might have some idea of how valid the survey might be.

Virgil looked at his watch, wondered how Shepard was doing—nothing he could do about that—wondered if Block had been arrested, then got on his phone and called the duty officer at the BCA and asked him to find out where John Haden lived, and what his phone number was.

He had the information in five minutes, called Haden, and was surprised when Haden promptly picked up: a good sign.

"I've got some questions for you," Virgil said, after introducing himself. "I wonder if I might stop by?"

"You think *I'm* the bomber?"

"I have no idea who the bomber is," Virgil said. "I mostly want to talk to you about a survey I took."

"Well, come on over. You can tell me about what happened with Henry."

19

John Haden was a tall, slender, pale man with glasses and a mop of brown hair; he wore a T-shirt with a hand-painted yoga warrior pose, simple black and white, which Virgil envied the moment he saw it, and jeans and flip-flops.

He lived in a modest brick house with a neatly kept yard, and pulled open the door and peered nearsightedly at Virgil, and said, "You look like a stoner."

"A flaw in your Vedic perception," Virgil said; his first wife had been a yoga practitioner. "I am, in fact, a cop."

Haden liked that and swung the door

back, and said, "Well, bring your cop ass inside. You want a beer?"

"Sure. But no more than two."

"We can sit out on the patio," Haden said. He got a couple of Dos Equis from the refrigerator, popped the tops, and handed one cold sweaty bottle to Virgil.

On the way out to the patio, he said, "So why do you think I'm the bomber?"

"I don't. Not *the* bomber, anyway. But, as Henry's business partner, you might have had reason to get rid of him. Either because the business was doing badly, or doing well. Either way. You might be copycatting the real bomber."

"Your theory's basically screwed—the business wasn't doing much of anything," Haden said. He took a webbed chair, pointed Virgil at another one, and said, "I don't want you to think I'm taking this thing lightly. I just don't really know what to say. Henry was a heck of a nice guy. Smart, happy, good marriage—he enjoyed his job. I freaked out when I heard. I was amazed. I went over there, but his wife was in the Cities."

"She's back now."

"She *was* in the Cities, anyway. So, I

canceled my summer school class, and I've just been wandering around the house wondering what the fuck? Why?"

"Found some bomb stuff in the garage," Virgil said. "The feds think he might be the bomber."

Haden waved the thought away: "That's absurd. If you knew Henry, you'd know how absurd it was. Somebody planted it there, which means, it has to be somebody who knows Henry." Then, "Oh, wait— that's why you're here. You're checking out his friends."

"That, too," Virgil said. He took a hit on the beer, which tasted good in the hot afternoon, looked around the small backyard, and said, "You're a marigold enthusiast."

"They keep moles out of your yard," Haden said.

"You got moles?" Virgil asked.

"No, because I plant marigolds."

"I didn't know about that," Virgil said. "I got moles."

Virgil said, "I was told you've been divorced three times."

"That's true," Haden said.

"Do you still think about the exes?"

"All the time. Especially when I'm not in a relationship," Haden said. "The thing about three exes is, there are always some good memories."

"True," Virgil said. He thought of Janey, and her ass.

"You'd know?" Haden asked.

"Yeah, I got three down myself," Virgil said. "I've given it up for the time being. I've got a girlfriend, but I think she's about to break it off with me."

"You want her to go?" Haden asked.

Virgil considered. He hadn't actually thought about it that way. Finally, he said, "Maybe."

"Ah. So you've maneuvered her into breaking it off with you, so you won't have to deal with the guilt," Haden said.

"That's a facile bit of pseudo-psychology," Virgil said.

"Facile. A subtle word for a cop. One bit of advice. If she breaks it off with you, don't sleep with her again for at least a year."

"A year?"

"Okay, six months."

"Is that your practice?"

"No, I won't sleep with them for at least three weeks, but then, I think I have a more resilient personality than you. You look like a kinder soul than I am."

They sat and bullshitted for a while, then Haden got a second beer for each of them, and Virgil passed over the list of names, and told him how he'd acquired it. He scanned the list and said, "There I am . . . Probably my department chairman. Somebody told him once that I smoke dope."

"He's a non-smoker?"

"Oh, yeah . . . Weird for a college professor, huh? So let me see if I get this right. You made this list with no real mathematical or statistical basis. It's a back-of-the-envelope guess by a bunch of hosers who are getting even with enemies, and may have a few good ideas as well."

Virgil considered again, then nodded: "I think that's fair."

Haden handed the list back, leaned back in his chair, and closed his eyes.

Thought about it. Then, "I'd say there's a better than even chance that he's on the list. You can probably strike several people off right away."

"We have."

Haden nodded. "From what I know about the bombs, I have no alibis, except that I couldn't have done the one in Michigan, if it was, in fact, a simple time bomb, as the newspaper said. I have a lady friend who'll tell you that, since I spent that night pounding her like a jackhammer. During the day, I was doing finals."

"I'll check, if I need to," Virgil said. "Give her my name. I'm not fooling around about this, John."

"I know that. I looked you up on the Net while you were on the way over," Haden said. Then he said, "I've been toying with the possibility that Henry was simply killed at random, but I don't think so. There's something in Henry's killing that's important to the bomber, and it's not just that Henry was somebody to frame. You gotta go pull Sarah apart. She must know what it is, even if she doesn't know that she knows."

"Mmmm." Virgil closed his eyes. "Nice out here. I need a patio."

"I'm serious. You know what Sherlock Holmes used to say."

"Sherlock Holmes actually didn't say anything," Virgil said. "He's a fictional character, invented by Theodore Roosevelt, or some other Boy Scout just like him."

"He said, and I quote, 'When you have eliminated the impossible, whatever remains, however improbable, must be the truth.'"

"I knew that," Virgil said. "I'm a professional detective."

"But you might be outsmarting yourself. Go back to the fundamentals of detecting. If there is such a thing. Another beer? I've only got two left, and it seems a shame just to leave them sitting there by themselves."

Go back to fundamentals, Virgil thought, when he finally left.

Shoe leather. Compile facts. Throw out whatever was impossible . . .

Whatever. Unfortunately, he didn't know

where to start walking, and while he had a lot of facts, they were mostly irrelevant. What about motive? The fundamentals would say that murder is committed because of greed and sex, to which Virgil added craziness, drug-induced or otherwise.

There was craziness here, but also a method: it wasn't the kind of compulsive, uncontrolled murder that's done by what psychiatrists referred to as nut jobs. This was craziness on a mission, and the mission probably involved greed or sex.

But not trout.

Virgil realized that he'd psychologically eliminated about half the people nominated for the bombings: the trout fishermen.

Trout fishermen, he thought, were notoriously goofy, right there with crappie fishermen, but it was a harmless kind of goofiness. A lot of trout fishermen wouldn't even hurt a trout, much less a human being, talking to the fish gently as they put them back in the water. He suspected a few of them had kissed their trout on the lips.

As a muskie fisherman, Virgil had to

laugh at the thought. Try to kiss a muskie on the lips, and you'd lose your fuckin' lips. They were all fishermen together, he supposed, but trout fishermen really were weird.

Anyhoo . . . the trout fishermen were out.

Which made him feel better.

Sex and greed.

He'd made some progress, fueled by three beers.

Back at the county courthouse, he told that to Ahlquist, who said, "Hold that thought, and let me tell you this: they've got Block upstairs, and they're squeezing him like an orange in a hydraulic juicer."

"Is he going to cave?" Virgil asked.

"Wills is starting to scare me," Ahlquist said. "This case has done something to him. He used to be this overweight frat boy. Now he looks like he's on cocaine, or something. His eyes are all big and he's got white circles under them, and he stood on the table and told Block that if he didn't cooperate, he was going for twenty years. *Twenty years.* You can *kill* somebody for half that. I saw Good Thunder coming out of the ladies' can, and she said he's serious. . . . So, I wanted you to know."

"Okay."

"Now what's this about greed and sex?" Ahlquist asked.

"The bomber's blowing stuff up because of greed or sex—I've eliminated trout—and I don't see how sex would fit into an attack on Pye," Virgil said. "So, it's greed, and there seems to be a load of money going around. The question is, how did the money lead to bombing? We need to talk to this expediter guy, the guy who bribed Geraldine. Is he being blackmailed? Did anybody ever try to blackmail him? Maybe we could get Wills to threaten him with twenty years, and see if he comes up with something."

"The guy isn't here," Ahlquist said. "He's long gone. Last I heard, he's down in Alabama, bribing somebody else."

"We need to get him back," Virgil said. "Subpoena him. Put the screws on Pye—maybe threaten to arrest Pye himself. Money is the root of this evil."

"Did somebody say that? The money thing?"

"Theodore Roosevelt, during the 1911 presidential campaign."

"Yeah? We gotta think about how to go about this. I'll get Wills as soon as he finishes breaking Block's balls."

Virgil decided he had to go somewhere and think, and he wound up in the chambers of a vacationing judge. Ahlquist said, "This is where I take my naps. You can lock the door from the inside."

Virgil went in and lay on the couch, his feet up on one arm. Lot of stuff going on. Had to think about it. After five minutes, he hadn't thought of anything, so he called Davenport and told him what was going on. Davenport summarized it: "So you cleaned up the town, but you don't have the bomber."

"Not yet."

"Well, let me know when you do. I gotta go."

"Why'd he try to kill me? That's what I want to know. If he'd killed me, he would have gotten a whole storm of cops in here."

"Maybe he was making a point of some

kind, about resistance," Davenport said. "Or maybe he wanted a whole storm of cops in there."

No help there.

He was still on the couch when the governor called. "Hey, Virgil, I talked to State Farm, and you're good to go. You haul the boat to the State Farm place up there, and they'll resell what they can—scrap, I guess—and you get a check for the boat and motor and a thousand in personal property."

"Ah, jeez, Governor. Thanks, I guess. There's nothing criminal in this, is there?"

"Criminal? This is the least criminal thing I've done this week," the governor said. "The second-least-criminal thing I've done is, I talked to an old buddy up at East Coast Marine in Stillwater. He's got a Ranger, there, a beauty, used, but not hard, owned by some rich guy who went out about once a year. . . . Anyway, your check exactly matches the asking price, including sales tax. You gotta go look at it."

"A Ranger?" Virgil's mouth started to water. "Jeez, Governor, I don't know—"

"Hey, don't worry about it," the governor said. "Everything's totally on the up-and-up. Well, as much on the up-and-up as these things get. Anyway, I gotta go violate somebody's civil rights. Talk to you later. It's Andy at East Coast Marine. He's making out the papers right now."

"Well . . . thanks," he said, but he was thinking, *Holy shit, a Ranger.* He had the urge to drop the entire bomb case and get the hell over to Stillwater before Andy died. . . .

"So Davenport said you'd been out to Michigan, to the Pinnacle. I didn't hear about that. What's going on there?"

Virgil explained the problem of planting the bomb, and his thoughts, and the governor said, "Any way he could climb it? Or come down? Parachute, maybe?"

Virgil thought back to the conversation he'd had with the guys at the Pye Pinnacle and said, "Someone would've seen a plane, or heard it at least. I thought maybe a helicopter, but you couldn't land one there without *someone* noticing. A hang glider, maybe, but the Pinnacle's the tallest thing out there. There'd be nowhere to launch it from."

The governor rang off, and Virgil closed his eyes and leaned back on the couch. The word "glider" floated through his mind, and he thought, *Hey, wait a minute. Did somebody say something about Peck flying a glider?* The guy at Butternut Tech. Huh. Could you land a glider on top of a building?

He didn't know anyone else who could answer that question, so he called Peck.

"Hey, George—could you land a glider on top of a building?"

After a moment of silence, Peck said, "A glider? Somebody told you I used to fly gliders?"

"Yeah, somebody did, but I'll be damned if I can remember who. So, could you?"

"Well, not me, personally, because I'd be too chicken. But I guess if you had a big enough roof, without any obstructions, you could."

"How big a roof?"

"Maybe . . . three hundred yards at the absolute minimum. But that would be scary as hell, even with perfect wind and good visibility. The problem is, you'd have to come in high enough to make sure you got on the roof—you don't want to crash into the side of the building. Then you'd have to stop before you got to the far parapet, because if you didn't, and hit it, you'd either get squashed like an eggshell hitting a wall, or if the parapet was low enough, it'd trip the glider and you'd go right over the edge and drop like a stone. Or both."

"You had me at three hundred yards," Virgil said. "The roof of the Pye Pinnacle is probably fifty yards across. Maybe less. It's got all kinds of pipes and chimneys and air-conditioning ducts up there."

"No way you're gonna land a glider on that. That's just not going to work."

And Virgil thought, *Hey, wait a minute. What'd Davenport just say? Maybe the bomber wanted a whole storm of cops to come in? Why would he want that?* Virgil closed his eyes and thought about it, and came up with exactly one answer: the bomber wanted a bigger, wider investigation. Why would he want that? Because a bigger, wider investigation would probably get into the question of whether the city council was bribed, and if it had been, then . . . PyeMart was gone.

So maybe there was a good reason to try to kill him—nothing personal, not anger or revenge or because Virgil was a threat, but an effort to get as many cops as possible into town.

The guy might be nuts, but there was a logic buried in his craziness.

So why did he go after Pye first? Why weren't there any warnings? Maybe because he was worried about heightened security around Pye, if he set the first one off in Butternut. So he went after Pye first—after the whole board of directors, but had failed. If he'd succeeded, what would he have done then?

Issued a warning, perhaps: quit building the PyeMart, or else.

But then, if the company didn't do it, what would he do next?

Virgil thought about it, and decided that there wouldn't have been a warning: he would have continued on to Butternut, and would have blown up the trailer even if he had been successful with the Pinnacle bomb.

The first bomb was an announcement

of his seriousness; the second bomb was the beginning of the actual campaign.

The third bomb, at the equipment yard, would slow down the construction process, and make it more expensive.

The fourth one, another attack on Pye . . . keeping the pressure on.

Then the attack on Virgil, maybe to bring more pressure into town.

And finally, the bomb at Erikson's.

He considered the list, and after a moment, focused on the bombing of the equipment yard. That one wasn't quite right: he took a big risk, to do nothing more than slow down the process. In fact, he wouldn't even slow down the construction or opening of the store— he'd just slow down the water and sewer connection by a couple of months. If done on schedule, the connection would have been made three or four months before the store was finished. Now, it'd only be two months.

So why would that have been important to him? Important enough to make a couple of dozen bombs, or however many it was?

Then, there was the bomb at Erikson's. If he was fully rational, he had a reason for picking Erikson as the fall guy. He wasn't just chosen at random. Why Erikson?

He thought about Kline, the pharmacist he'd visited on his second day in town. He knew everything and everybody. . . .

Virgil rolled off the couch and went out to his car and drove downtown. Ed Kline, said the girl behind the pharmacy cash register, was on break.

"Up on the roof?"

"You know about the roof? Let me call him."

She took out her cell phone, made the call, mentioned Virgil's name, then rang off and said, "Go on up. You know the way?"

"I do."

Kline was sitting in a recliner, looking out at the lake, his feet up on a round metal lawn table, blowing smoke at the sky.

"You find him?" he asked Virgil.

"No. But I can refine the list. The bomber, I think, is working through some kind of logic. I think it most likely has to do with money. There also has to be a link with Henry Erikson, but I can't see what it would be. And I think he's probably on my list."

"And . . ."

Virgil took the survey list out of his pocket. "So, I need you to look at my list and tell me who on the list would either make money, or save money, if PyeMart went down. I've already talked to a couple of the major possibilities, and sorta scratched them off. I really need an Erikson-money connection."

Kline worked his way through the cigarette as he studied the list, and finally shook his head and handed it back to Virgil. "I don't see it. I see the usual suspects, people who lose when PyeMart comes in. Nothing that involves Erikson."

"Did Erikson ever serve on the city council? I mean, was he ever in a spot where he could have affected what happened with PyeMart?"

Again, Kline shook his head. "No. Never ran for anything, far as I know."

"Sarah Erikson couldn't point out any tight ties between Henry and anybody on the list."

"I really didn't know him well enough to suggest any connections," Kline said.

They were sitting around, speculating, and Virgil took two calls, one after the other.

The first came from a BCA agent named Jenkins, who said, "Me'n Shrake are in town. We're busting the mayor, and then some guy named Arnold."

"God bless you," Virgil said. "Are you staying at the AmericInn?"

"We are. See you for dinner?"

"If it's not blown up."

A moment later, he took another call, this one originating at the BCA office itself.

"Virgil? Gabriel Moss here. We loaded up your disk drives, and we got images."

"How good?"

"The images are good enough, but you can't see a face. He's wearing a camo mask. We can tell you how tall he is, about what he weighs, and his shoe size, but there's no face."

"Can you send it to me?"

"Sure. I can e-mail it if you want. You'll have it in five minutes."

"And send me the numbers—height, weight, and all that."

Virgil rang off and asked Kline, "Could you think about this? How many ways are there to squeeze money out of PyeMart? Out of the situation? There's got to be something, and we're just not seeing it."

"I'll think about it," Kline said. "I think you're probably right, but I suspect I'll be awful damn surprised when you catch the guy. You might have to catch him before I can see where the money'd be coming from."

20

Virgil hooked into the sheriff's wi-fi and downloaded the video-clip file, watched it once—a murky series of black-and-white images of a man in camo moving around the inside of the trailer.

A note with the file said that the man was six feet, three and one-half inches tall, in his boots, the brand of which was unknown, but had approximately a one-and-one-half-inch heel; that the boots were size eleven, D width, one of the most common sizes for men; that he probably weighed between one hundred and seventy-five and one hundred and eighty-five—that is, was slender to average weight, but not fat or husky—and that the camo was Realtree. The man wore a mask commonly worn by bow hunters.

Virgil found Ahlquist talking to a couple deputies, and ran the video for them to see if they could pick out anything else. Ahlquist shook his head and said, "It's Realtree, all right, but hell, half the bow hunters in the state wear it."

"Yeah, I got some myself," Virgil said.

"So did Erikson, but Erikson was maybe five-eleven," Virgil said. "I asked when I found out the lab guys had saved the video."

"So it's definitely not him."

"I wouldn't say definitely," Virgil said. "The problem with labs, they come up with exact answers. Sometimes, they're wrong, and it really screws you up."

They all nodded.

He called Barlow and told him about the video, and about the size problem, and Barlow said, "So we're down to forty-sixty. I just don't have anybody else, Virgil. What are you doing?"

"Still talking to people," Virgil said. "Wandering around town."

He called Pye, who said he was at the store site. Virgil told him to stay there, he was coming out. "You get the guy?" Pye asked.

"Not yet," Virgil said. "But we're closing in on him."

Pye made a rude noise, and clicked off.

Pye was not particularly happy to see him. "I hear you're making more accusations," he said.

"It's gone beyond that, Willard," Virgil said. "We're taking down the city council— there are state investigators in town, right now, making arrests. We're probably going to bust your expediter guy, and I wouldn't doubt that when that happens, the prosecutors will try to work up the chain."

"There *is* no chain," Pye said. Over his shoulder, to Chapman, he added, "Keep taking it down. Put in there, 'Pye seemed unaffected by the rash accusations made by the hippie-looking cop.'"

"Whatever," Virgil said. "But that's not what I want to talk to you about. My focus is on this bomber. We got three dead now, and two hurt bad, and four or five scared shitless, who *could* be dead, except they got lucky. . . . Chapman says that you're a big goddamn financial and business expert. I need to know, how many ways are there to make or lose money when a PyeMart goes into a town?"

Pye stuck out his lower lip and said, "Everybody knows the ways—"

"No. *You* might, the rest of us don't," Virgil said. "We know that the oil-change place might go broke, and the pharmacy, and a bookstore and a clothing store. We know that some bricklayers are going to get some jobs, and somebody's going to pay the city to lay some pipe, and that means they've got to buy some pipe, and now they've got to buy a couple more pieces of heavy equipment . . . but I don't think anybody's going around blowing up Pye Pinnacle so they can sell another excavator. I've thought about the basic reasons people do this stuff, and I've come to the conclusion that it's probably money, in some way that I can't see. Since you're the money guy, I thought you could."

Pye took off his ball cap, scratched

his head, and said, "Chapman has done some research. Bombers are usually either plain nuts—they just want to bomb something—or they're political nuts. Like the Unabomber."

Virgil shook his head. "This seems to be too focused for a political bombing campaign. They hit the Pinnacle, they hit the city equipment yard, they hit you, me, then Erikson. . . . They didn't blow up the equipment yard, or Erikson, for some ideological reason. They're not Marxists or something."

"Barlow thinks Erikson might be the guy," Pye said. "Maybe."

"I don't believe he really thinks so," Virgil said. "He's grasping at straws. He's hoping. And I don't believe it. So: money."

Pye walked off a way, looking at the concrete pads that would hold up the new store—a store that Virgil now believed would never be built. Chapman said, quietly, "He's thinking."

"I can see the steam coming off his forehead," Virgil said.

A minute later, Pye wandered back. "I've got nothing specific for you, but I can give you some theory. Whether it'll help, I don't know."

"So give," Virgil said.

Pye said that there were three ways money would move in a situation like PyeMart. Some of it was quite direct and positive: people getting paid for building the store, people who would have jobs at the store, taxes that would come out of the store, profits made by the store.

There were direct and negative movements as well: money lost by people who couldn't compete with the stores. That money could be in the form of lost profits, or lost jobs.

"Or lost lives," Virgil said. "People who lose good jobs in towns like these don't get them back. Not in town," Virgil said. "They have to leave. Their whole life is changed."

"That, too," Pye conceded. "But it's just the way of the world."

"What's the third way?" Virgil asked.

"That's the hardest to see, and maybe that's where you should look, since you're not finding it in the obvious places,"

Pye said. "What it is, is lost opportunity. Somebody saw an opportunity out there, and was counting on it, and somehow the store upset that."

"Like what?" Virgil asked.

"Okay. Say a guy had an idea for a little computer store. Nothing like that in town. So he saves his money, and maybe starts trying to arrange a loan. Then he finds out a PyeMart's coming in, and he finds out that we have a pretty strong line of computers. All of a sudden, this guy's bidness plan makes no sense. He can't get the loan, either. This idea was going to make him rich, and in his head, he was already sailing a yacht on the ocean and hanging out with Tiger Woods. Then somebody took it away from him. Snatched it right away. No actual money moved—no currency, no dollar bills—but *potential* money moved."

"You can't see potential money," Virgil said.

"But it's real," Pye said, shaking a fat finger at him. "It's the thing that drives this whole country. People thinking about money, and how to get it. There are people out there who break their hearts over money. It happens every day. The shrinks talk about sex, and cops talk about drugs, and liberals talk about fundamentalist religion, and the right-wingers talk about creeping socialism, but what people think of, most of the time, is money. When I was the horniest I ever was, and I was a horny rascal, I didn't think about sex for more'n an hour a day, and I'd spend sixteen hours thinking about money."

"But that means that the motive might not have any . . . exterior . . . at all," Virgil said. "It's just something in some guy's head."

Pye shrugged: "That's true. But that doesn't make it unimportant."

"Not a hell of a lot of help, Willard," Virgil said.

"It might be, if you ever come up with a good suspect," Pye said. "Once you get a name, start analyzing his history, talking to his friends and neighbors, there's a good chance you'll find his . . . dream."

"Which you stepped on," Virgil said.

Pye shrugged again, waved his hand at the raw dirt and the concrete pads: "This is my dream. Why shouldn't I have my dream?"

Virgil had a few answers to that, but didn't feel like tangling with Pye right at the moment. So he said good-bye to Pye and Chapman, and headed back to his truck. Halfway into downtown, he took a call from Jenkins, the BCA investigator.

"All done. We're going over to a place called Bunson's. You know where it is?"

"I can find it," Virgil said, which he could, having eaten almost all of his meals there. "You get both Martin and Gore?"

"Yeah. Gore put up a fight, but we clubbed her to her knees, cuffed her. I don't know how she got those bruises on her face; probably a domestic squabble."

"You're joking," Virgil said.

"Of course I am," Jenkins said. "I only said that because you'd be worried that I wasn't."

"I'll see you at Bunson's," Virgil said.

Jenkins and Shrake were partners of long standing, both big men who dressed in sharp suits that looked like they might have fallen off a truck in Little Italy, and were referred to as "the thugs" around the BCA. They were often used for hard takedowns; they were fairly easygoing, when not actually involved in a fight.

Virgil found them talking over beers at Bunson's, took a chair, ordered a beer of his own, and asked how it had gone.

"Routine, but you know—you feel a little bad," Shrake said. "They were both crying and pleading. It's not like busting some asshole who knows the rules."

"I didn't feel that bad," Jenkins said.

"That's because you're cruel, and you enjoy the spectacle of other human beings in pain," Shrake said. "I'm not that way."

Jenkins said, "Mmm. This beer is kinda skunky."

Shrake said to Virgil, "So walk us through this case. Lucas said you'd flown in some private luxury jet over to Michigan."

Virgil took them through it, and when he was done, Shrake said, "So let me get this straight: you can't get anybody into this Pinnacle, but you think someone could have gotten down from the roof."

"But you can't get on the roof," Virgil

said. "I even found a guy who's a glider pilot, and he says you'd need at least three hundred yards to land a glider up there. . . . I asked about parachutes, but then you'd need a pilot who's an accomplice."

Shrake unwrapped his index finger from his beer bottle, pointed it at Virgil and said, "So I guess it's a safe bet that you never heard of motorized paragliders."

Virgil said, "Uh . . ."

Jenkins said to his partner, "No more beer."

Shrake said, "I saw a wi-fi label on the door, wonder if it's real." He groped around in his bag, pulled out a battered white MacBook, got online with Google, poked a few keys, called up a YouTube video, and turned the computer around so it faced Virgil.

YouTube was running a Cadillac ad, followed by a four-minute video in which a guy drove into a parking lot and un-packed what looked like a parachute, laying it on the concrete. He then pulled

on a backpack motor, with a small propeller in a metal cage, hooked himself to
the parachute, and fired up the motor.

The airstream from the propeller in-
flated the chute, and the guy took a few
steps across the concrete pad and was
in the air. He flew a few hundred feet in a
circle, did a short running landing, killed
the engine, put the backpack motor in
the back of his truck, folded up the chute,
packed it away, then threw it in his
truck . . . and did it all in four minutes and
ten seconds.

"Holy shit," Virgil said. "How did you
know about this?"

"I have wide interests," Shrake said.
"Also, insomnia."

Virgil spent another five minutes on
Google, looking up paragliders, then
gulped the rest of his beer and said,
"I gotta go," and he was gone. Outside,
he got on the phone to Barlow: "Are you
still at Erikson's?"

"Just left."

"Is Mrs. Erikson there?"

"Was two minutes ago."

"Head back there. Keep her there. I've

got a question," Virgil said. "You might want to be there when I ask it."

Barlow was standing on the front porch of the Erikson home, talking to Sarah Erikson, when Virgil arrived. Virgil said, "Mrs. Erikson, your husband has a propeller on the wall of his garage. What did that come from?"

Her forehead furrowed: "He used to fly, a kind of ultralight thing. But he did something stupid and went up when it was too windy for him and he crashed. He broke his ankle, and got some burns on his back, from the engine exhaust pipe, and was lucky to get away with that. The propeller broke and the engine was wrecked. He quit flying, and put the propeller on the wall to remind himself not to do it anymore."

"Was his glider . . . did it have solid wings, or was it one of those paraglider things, like a parachute?"

"He did both, ultralights and the paragliders," she said. "It was his paraglider that he crashed. Why are you asking all of this stuff?"

"Trying to work through some possibilities," Virgil said. "Did he fly out of an airport? Or just off the street? Or what?"

"Out of Jim Paulson's Soaring Center, out on 17," she said.

"Thanks," Virgil said. To Barlow: "Walk me back to my truck."

Barlow tagged along behind and asked, voice low, "What's that about? Paragliders?"

"Erikson flew paragliders. I just did some research on them. People have flown them to fifteen, sixteen thousand feet," Virgil said. "You can land on a spot a few feet across, and you could get one in the back of a station wagon, no problem. They're like a parachute with a motor, except they go up as well as down."

"Jesus Christ," Barlow said. "Why didn't we know about these things?"

"'Cause they're weird, and not a lot of people fly them," Virgil said. "But they're also cheap. You can get up in the air for a few thousand bucks, don't need a license."

Barlow looked back at the house: "So it *was* Erikson."

"I'm going out to this soaring center—try to nail it down," Virgil said.

———

Paulson's Soaring Center was almost invisible from the highway, down a gravel track past a cornfield, the track marked only by an unlit metal sign. Virgil found the track on his second pass, went four hundred yards in, and discovered a narrow tarmac airstrip that ran parallel to the highway.

A yellow metal building sat at one end of the strip, and a few yards down the landing strip, a phone pole held up a windsock. In the back, a long metal shed, open on one side, covered a half-dozen brightly colored gliders. Three men were hand-towing a brilliant red glider off the landing strip. They looked toward Virgil as he got out of the truck, and then continued on toward the shed.

Virgil saw somebody moving inside the yellow building, went to the door, which had a Welcome sign in the window, and went in. A gray-haired guy was sitting behind a counter and said, "Hey, what can I do for you?"

"I'm Virgil Flowers. I'm an agent with the BCA."

Virgil asked him—the guy was Paulson—about Erikson.

"Yeah, he used to fly out of here, he and some other guys had an ultralight, but one of them broke it up," Paulson said. "Then Henry started flying paragliders until he cracked *that* up."

Virgil got the story on Erikson and his gliding; was told that Erikson had been "okay" as a flier. "It ain't rocket science," Paulson said.

Virgil told him why he was asking: the possibility that Erikson was the bomber, and the possibility that he'd flown it onto the top of the Pye Pinnacle.

Paulson nodded. "Yeah, you could do that. In fact, there's a rich guy out in Los Angeles, he flies from his house out in Malibu into some hotel in Beverly Hills, lands on the roof, and walks from there to work. The neighbors are all pissed off about it, because of the engine noise."

He claimed that power paragliding was "safe as houses, if you know what you're doing."

"But that's what you *would* say, since you run a gliding center," Virgil said. "I mean, I know about two guys flying gliders: Erikson, who cracked up, and quit, and his former partner, who you just told me about, who cracked up and didn't quit."

"Neither one was hurt bad," Paulson said. "I'm not saying you can't kill yourself. You can. If you treat it with respect, it's safer than driving a car. . . . Well, maybe."

Virgil pulled out his survey list. "Look at this," he said. "Is there anybody else on this list who flies these things? The powered paraglider?"

Paulson bent over the counter, then took out a pencil, wet it with his tongue, and dragged it down the face of the list. "Oh, yeah," he said, after a moment. "Bill Wyatt."

He touched the wet tip of his pencil on the name, and made a dot. He went the rest of the way down the list and said, "He's about it."

Virgil felt a buzz way down in the testicles: Wyatt was the other teacher at Butternut Tech. "He flew a paraglider?"

"Still does. Not so much lately, haven't seen him for a couple of months, I guess. Good flier—way out of Henry's class.

He's got some balls. He was in Iraq One, back whenever that was, reign of King George the First."

"He teaches up at the college, right?"

"Yeah . . . history or something."

"Good guy?" Virgil asked.

Paulson said, with a grin, "I wouldn't go that far."

They talked about Wyatt for a couple of minutes. Paulson said he had no knowledge that Wyatt might be a bomber, or crazy, or anything in particular, but he was an angry, arrogant, self-centered prick. Most of the pilots around the place, Paulson said, didn't like him.

Virgil brought the conversation back to Erikson, and finally asked Paulson not to talk about the interview. "Could be a little dangerous. And unfair. We don't know that either of these guys has the least involvement. But if one of them does, then, and you ask about it, well, he's not a guy you want looking at you."

Paulson said, "We gotta be talking about Bill, right? Because Henry's dead as a doornail. And I'll tell you, I don't see any way that Henry's the bomber. No way at all."

"How about Wyatt?"

"Well . . ." Paulson looked out his narrow window, and shook his head. "You know, I got no truck with Saddam Hussein or terrorists or any of that, but I don't want to hear a guy bragging about killing them. About *smoking* them. I'm sorry, I just don't want to hear it. They're people, not paper targets."

"He does that?"

"If you know him for more than fifteen seconds, he does," Paulson said.

A guy who brags about killing. A guy who was in the army, and flew paragliders; a guy with some balls.

Virgil went out to the truck and called Barlow. "Got some pretty interesting stuff, dude. I got another suspect for you."

"Better than forty-sixty?"

"Oh, yeah," Virgil said. "I'm saying seventy-thirty."

"Gonna get your ass kissed?" Barlow suddenly sounded happy.

"Could happen," Virgil said. "Yes, it could."

21

Virgil and Barlow arranged to meet at the Starbucks. Virgil got a grande hot chocolate, no-fat milk, no foam, no whipped cream, and Barlow got a venti latte with an extra shot. As they took a corner table, Virgil said, "Remind me not to stand next to you if you're handling a bomb. That much caffeine, you gotta be shakin' like a hundred-dollar belly dancer."

"At least I'm not drinking like a little girl," Barlow said. "So tell me about this new guy."

Virgil told Barlow about what little he

had on Wyatt. He concluded by saying, "He makes me a lot happier than Erikson, at least, to start with. Erikson never looked quite right—you said so yourself. The *means* to get in the Pinnacle—that's the key thing."

"But Erikson had it, too."

"He had it once, but he didn't even have access to a paraglider anymore, as far as we know. And the last time out, he crashed: not a place you'd go back to, not without practice. Not to land on the top of a skyscraper in the middle of the night. Then, there's that whole thing about his work schedule."

Barlow held up his hands: "All right, all right. But I don't think we can entirely back off him. We have to nail down what we've got, just in case."

"I don't want you to back off," Virgil said. "I want you to keep pushing Erikson. I want a lot of cops around there. I want people talking."

"You want it to look like we got him. That's gonna be a little rough on Sarah Erikson," Barlow said.

"Yes. Cruel, but not unusual," Virgil

said. "I want the guy looking the other way. All I got is this slender thread. I need to do some background work on him. See if I can turn the thread into a noose."

"Into a moose?"

"A noose. NOOSE," Virgil said.

"So what you've got is, he can fly a paraglider, and he's a self-centered prick," Barlow said, summarizing.

"Who knew Erikson, and who I suspect knew Erikson's garage. They used to fly together."

"Okay," Barlow said.

"You sound like it's nothing," Virgil said.

"No, it's something all right. Last week, I'd have jumped all over it. But now . . ."

"The other thing," Virgil said, "is that Erikson doesn't look much like the guy in the video."

"Camo can be weird, it can hide a lot of stuff—that's why they call it camo," Barlow said. "But I'd be happy to hear that Wyatt looks *more* like the video. And whatever happened to your decision that PyeMart money is involved?"

"That comes next," Virgil said. "I gotta go see Pye."

He went to the AmericInn, and Chapman came out of Pye's room and said, "Willard's not sure he should talk to you. The state attorney has issued a warrant for one of our employees. Willard's a little worried about that, and really pissed off."

Virgil said, "Let me stick my head in. It's purely about the bomber."

"Wait one," she said, and went back into the room. A minute later, she reappeared and said, "All right. But he's not going to talk about anything that has to do with this warrant, or any supposed bribes, or anything like that."

"Deal," Virgil said.

Virgil went inside and found Pye sitting on the motel floor, doing an overhead arm stretch. Pye said, "What?"

Virgil: "You do yoga?"

"Of course not," Pye said. "I'm doing my stretches. Which I can do later." He got to his feet and said, "What do you want?"

"I got a guy that I'm looking at, for the bomber. I want to see if he has any connection with PyeMart. So I just want you to call up one of your people, and see if there's a William Wyatt connected to PyeMart in any way, shape, or form—or if your security people are aware of a William Wyatt."

"You're not saying we bribed him?"

"I'm not saying anything," Virgil said. "I just want to know if you ever had a relationship with him, of any kind, that ended badly, and that might incline him to bomb you."

"I can do that," Pye said. "What else?"

"That's it," Virgil said. "How long will it take?"

"A while—until tomorrow, probably, if I keep people looking all night. That's if you want 'any way, shape, or form.'"

"I'll take tomorrow morning," Virgil said. "Do not talk to anybody else about this. I'll call you."

"We did not bribe anybody, nohow, no way," Pye said.

"Glad to hear it," Virgil said. "But I'm pretty sure the grand jury will want to know where Arnold Martin's sailboat came from. And why two city councilmen tell a different story."

"You don't believe me?" Pye demanded.

Virgil scratched the back of his head and then said, "Well, Willard, personally, I like you all right. You got some color, and you're a smart guy. But I gotta say . . . no. I don't believe you. Have a nice day."

Chapman followed Virgil outside, the metal door banging closed behind them. "Is this store dead?"

"Yeah, I think it probably is," Virgil said. "Maybe you can donate those concrete pads to the city, as municipal tennis courts, or something. Take a tax write-off."

A wrinkle appeared on her forehead. "You know, that's not a bad idea. . . ."

Virgil looked at his watch as he left the motel: still broad daylight, but the sun was getting low. He'd have Wyatt on the brain overnight.

Thought about it for a minute, then thought about John Haden, the other professor he'd spoken to, that morning. He looked at his cell-phone record, punched up Haden's phone number, and got him.

"I need to talk to you."

"Well, I've got a friend over, we're just, uh, finishing talking. Give me fifteen minutes or a half hour? I got some black beans and pork chops I was gonna make for dinner, if you're hungry."

"See you then," Virgil said.

Virgil had nothing better to do, so he drove over to Haden's and parked down the block. An older Subaru was sitting in Haden's driveway, with the look of a visitor. Doorbellus interruptus, which he'd suffered on a number of occasions, just wasn't polite. He closed his eyes and thought about Wyatt's ride into the Pinnacle. It would have been thrilling, closing in on the building from above, those lights playing around the emerald glass. Wyatt would have had to find a place to dump his car, to take off, but given the Pinnacle's location, that wouldn't have been hard.

Finding the car again, in that sea of corn, might have been harder, but with a GPS . . .

Virgil got out his iPad, called up Google,

and looked at a satellite photo of the area around the Pinnacle. To the south, on the other side of the interstate, a gravel road cut deep into the countryside, with only a few farmhouses around. Plenty of room for a takeoff, he thought.

Haden's friend left his house a few minutes later, a friendly-looking blonde, but not exactly Virgil's image of a woman that Haden would be chasing. He gave him credit for more taste than Virgil had been expecting; that is, she was something more than tits and ass. She did a U-turn and drove back past Virgil. He went back to the Google map for a couple more minutes, trying to figure the best takeoff spot, calculating distances.

True, there weren't a lot of farmhouses, but if he'd taken off in the middle of the night, somebody should have heard him. On the YouTube videos he'd seen, the propellers were loud; louder than a lawn mower.

Of course, the sound might have been confused by trucks on the freeway. Huh.

He gave up—couldn't tell enough without being on the ground—and pulled up to Haden's house.

Haden was wearing sweatpants and a T-shirt, with flip-flops, his hair wet from a shower, and Virgil said, "I don't want to hear about it. I'm so horny the light socket ain't safe."

"So your friend is out in Hollywood with those producer guys . . ."

They talked about women for a while, then Haden drained a can of black beans through a colander, stuck the beans in a plastic bowl with some microwave rice, set it aside, got some pork chops out of the refrigerator and led the way to the patio, where he had a gas grill.

"So what's up?" Haden asked, as he fired up the grill.

"This is just between you and me," Virgil said.

"Yup."

"You know a guy named William Wyatt?"

"Yeah, Bill Wyatt," Haden said. "Is he the bomber?"

"I'm asking myself that. What do you think?"

The pork chops were beginning to sizzle, and Haden moved them around a bit, then said, "He could be. He's got a violent streak. He's a serious tae-kwon-do guy, which is fine in itself, but he had a reputation for hurting people, which you're not supposed to do."

"I talked to a guy today who said he was self-centered and mean," Virgil said.

"That'd be fair," Haden said. "But it's a big long step from there to blowing people up."

"Yes, it is. But he has a couple other skills that would be useful."

"Like what?"

"Like he flies powered paragliders," Virgil said. "We could never figure out how he could have gotten into the building, because the security is so tight. But it *is* possible to get down from the roof without anybody seeing you. If he'd come in at night, he could have pulled it off."

"Man, that's like a movie," Haden said. "I don't know—that sounds pretty extreme."

"Well, if you were going to pick out

somebody to do something so extreme it's scary, who else would you look at? At the college?"

Haden flipped the pork chops and then said, "Man, this is a little hard to get used to. I don't know . . . Bill Wyatt? The last time I saw him, it was at a staff meeting about reducing paper use."

Still, Virgil pressed, and Haden couldn't think of anybody more likely, except that "There are a lot of guys out there, women, too, who don't like PyeMart coming in. You know, rural lefties fighting the corporate culture, think globally, act locally, and all of that. I don't think Bill would care about that one way or another. I don't think it's political at all."

"I don't think it's about politics," Virgil said. "I think it's about money."

"Money? He doesn't have any money. He's about the brokest guy around. He got divorced, and his wife got the house and I heard that she got half his pension. He's renting some place."

"So he needs money?"

"Yeah, I guess so. I mean, who knows? Maybe he's got family money or something. But he doesn't look like it."

"I can get at that," Virgil said. "I can get to his tax records. Some of them, anyway, but it might take a while."

"I gotta say, I hope it's not him. I hope it's some shitkicker out in the countryside, worried about his trout," Haden said. "Bill's an asshole, but he's our asshole. Know what I mean?"

After dinner, Virgil drove back to the motel and lay in bed, thinking about Wyatt. He wished he could see him: thought about how he might make that happen. On the other hand, he didn't want to get caught at it, not before he made his move. The whole case was too tentative, too soft. His biggest fear was that the killing of Erikson was the bomber's sign-off, and that after that attack, he hauled all the remaining Pelex and blasting caps down to the Butternut and threw them in.

He was thinking about that, when Lee Coakley called from Hollywood, or wherever she was. They had a long and twisting conversation, some bits of which would pop back into his mind over the next couple of weeks, things like, "Things are getting more complicated," and "I think we have to calm things down for a while, give ourselves time to think."

Virgil had heard all those words before, and grew snappish, and she was offended, and they wound up snarling at each other, and signed off, angry on both sides.

Virgil thought: *Next time I see her . . . maybe it'll be okay if only I see her. Maybe I should take some time and fly out there. . . .*

His thoughts ping-ponged back and forth between Lee Coakley and the case against Wyatt. Before she called, he'd worried that Wyatt might be cleaning up after himself. If he did, Virgil could build only a weak case: that Wyatt *could* have flown into the Pinnacle, if he had balls the size of cantaloupes; he needed the money, so *maybe* he was going to get it *this* way. . . .

He really needed some piece of hard evidence—some piece of a bomb. Almost anything would do. Even then, a defense attorney would give him a hard time, by putting Erikson on trial. . . .

He woke up in the middle of the night, still worrying about it. He wanted to nail down the money angle: that's what he needed. And he thought of 1 Timothy 6:10: "For the love of money is the root of all evil."

When he got up in the morning, he was still tired. He called Davenport, got the okay to use Sandy the researcher, called her, and asked her to look at Wyatt's tax records. "I need to know what he's got, where his money comes from, and where it goes, if that shows up. I need to know what businesses he owns, if there are any, what stock he has. I need to know how far in hock he is: take a look at his credit records."

"Get back to you in half an hour," she said. "None of this is really a problem. You could probably do it yourself."

"Except that it would take me two weeks to figure out how to do it," Virgil said. "*Then* I could do it in half an hour."

"So you want a call, or e-mail?"

"Both. Call me, tell me about it, then send me the backup notes."

Virgil took twenty minutes cleaning up, got dressed, and headed down to Bunson's. Barlow was there, with two of his techs, and Virgil waved at them but took another table.

He'd been there for two minutes when Sandy called back.

"The guy is very boring," she said. "He and his wife have three regular sources of income—"

"I thought he was divorced," Virgil said.

"Filed a joint return two months ago," Sandy said. "He may be getting divorced, but it hasn't gone through. Nothing in the Kandiyohi court records about a divorce."

"Okay. So . . . three regular sources of income."

"Yeah. He gets paid sixty-six thousand dollars a year as a professor at a technical college there," she said.

"Butternut Technical College," Virgil said.

"Right. His wife is a real estate agent,

and last year she made a little over sixteen thousand."

"Hmm. Not a red-hot agent, in other words."

"Well, she's out in the countryside and the market was really crappy last year."

"All right. What's the third?" Virgil asked.

"He pays taxes on a small farm and rents it out. He gets eighty dollars an acre for a hundred sixty acres. That's a little less than thirteen grand. But then, he pays a couple thousand in property taxes. And, he owns a house, looks like there's still a mortgage, and that's another couple thousand in taxes. You want addresses?"

"That's it? That's all he's got?"

"That's pretty good for the town of Butternut. Probably puts him in the top five percent of family incomes."

"Shoot," Virgil said. "Where's the farm? It's not west of town, is it? Just outside of town, and just south of the highway?"

"No, it's pretty much south of town. I looked on a plat map—hang on, let me get it up again." She went away for a minute, then said, "Yeah, it's south of town."

"On the Butternut River?"

"No, no, he's a half mile from the Butternut. He *does* abut Highway 71, which has to be worth something."

"Yeah. Eighty dollars an acre," Virgil said. "So, e-mail me what you got."

"Two minutes," she said.

Barlow came over. "You're being stand-offish this morning?"

"Had some bureaucratic stuff to do," Virgil said. "I'm done now. You want company?"

"Sure. Come on over," Barlow said. "How're you doing with your alternate suspect?"

"Not as well as I'd hoped," Virgil said, following him back to his table. He nodded at the two technicians, and a minute later his French toast arrived.

"The thing that pisses me off is that I can't get a solid handle on anything," Virgil said.

"Welcome to the bomb squad," one of the techs said. "Half the time, we don't catch anybody. It took twenty years to catch the Unabomber, and he killed three people and injured twenty-three. And the

FBI didn't actually catch him—he was turned in by his family."

"Boy, I'm glad you said that," Virgil said. "That makes my morning."

The sheriff *did* make Virgil's morning. Virgil showed him the documents from Sandy, and Ahlquist said, "Come on down to the engineer's office."

Virgil followed him down to the county engineer, where they rolled out some plat maps and found Wyatt's property. Ahlquist tapped the map and said, "You know what? You'll have to check with the city, to make sure I'm right, but I *am* right."

"What?"

"The city development plan had the city growing south along Highway 71," Ahlquist said. "You can't put a development in without getting city approval—even outside the city limits. The idea is, the state and the county want orderly development, and they don't want a big sprawling development built on septic systems. They require sewer systems, with linkups to the city sewage treatment plants. So, the city was supposed to grow south. Toward Wyatt's land. Then PyeMart came in, and the city council changed the plan to push the water and sewer system out Highway 12, out west. With that line in, the next development would be west, instead of south."

"How much would that be worth?"

Ahlquist shrugged. "Maybe my old lady could tell me—but farmland is around three thousand an acre, the last I heard. I gotta think the land under a housing development is several times that much. If you'll excuse the language, when the city changed directions, old Wyatt took it in the ass."

"Oh, *yes*," Virgil said, a light in his eyes. "That feels so *good*."

22

Virgil drove down to city hall, found the city engineer, got a copy of the city plan, and worked through it. Wyatt's property was a quarter mile south of the last street served by city sewer and water. Under the plan, before it was revised to make room for the PyeMart, Wyatt's property would have been annexed within the next ten years, even under pessimistic growth-rate projections.

Next, Virgil figured out that a company called Xavier Homes had built the most recent subdivision in Butternut. Xavier

Homes was headquartered in Minnetonka, which was on the western edge of the Twin Cities metro area. Virgil got through to the company president, whose name was Mark Douka.

He told Douka that he was investigating the Butternut bombings, and said, "I need to know what you'd pay for untouched farmland with city water and sewer, outside of Butternut."

"There isn't any more of that, at the moment," Douka said. "Right now, I wouldn't pay nearly as much as five years ago."

"I'm trying to figure out what some land might be worth in, say, ten years."

"In ten years . . . assuming that the economy has recovered . . . well, you know, there are a lot of contingencies . . ."

"On average," Virgil said, his patience beginning to wear.

"I can tell you're getting impatient, but it's complicated. Everything depends on what we've got to do to the property, what the market is at the time, and, you know, what we can get it for. I can tell you this last subdivision out there, we paid about twenty-two thousand five hundred dollars an acre. I wouldn't pay that now. In ten years, I might pay twice that, but then, maybe not—it all depends."

"Just going on what you did last time, twenty-two-five," Virgil said.

"Yeah. But I don't want to hear that in court, because it's a kinda bullshit number," Douka said. "I'll tell you what, with what the Fed's doing right now, it's possible that ten years from now, I'd pay seventy-five thousand dollars an acre, and the Chinese will be using dollar bills for Kleenex."

"For Kleenex?"

"Or worse. They might be buying it on rolls."

"On rolls?"

"You know—toilet paper. Everything is up in the air," Douka said. "We paid twenty-two-five, but I got no idea what it'll be ten years from now. No idea."

"But whatever it is, it'd be worth more than raw farmland."

"I sure hope so," Douka said. "But with what the Fed's doing, we may need the corn. You know, to eat."

But Wyatt would have looked at that last subdivision, Virgil thought when he'd gotten off the phone, and most likely, he would have known that Xavier had paid $22,500. So a hundred and sixty acres, at that price, would be worth . . . three and a half million dollars? Could that be right? He found a piece of scrap paper, got a pencil out, and did the math: Three million six. As farmland, it was worth . . . more math . . . $480,000.

Virgil got on the phone to Barlow and told him about the subdivision. "When the city changed direction, Wyatt took a three-million-dollar haircut."

"Holy shit."

"Exactly. This is the first motive that feels real to me," Virgil said. "Without this, he's cold, stony broke. I've been told that his wife is taking him to the cleaners'."

"I'll tell you something else," Barlow said. "Think about the bombs out at the city equipment yard. We thought it was just another shot at trying to stop the PyeMart site. But it was more than that. If the city had even started to lay that pipeline, if they'd even put part of it in the ground, it wouldn't make any difference what happened with PyeMart. Even if PyeMart went down, the pipeline would still be there, and that's probably where the city would put the growth. They wouldn't rip up a brand-new pipeline and build another one south, just because PyeMart was gone."

"Jeez, Jim—you're smarter than you look," Virgil said.

"I keep telling people that, but they don't believe me," Barlow said. "So what's next?"

"I'm going to pile up as much as I can on Wyatt. Then, I'm thinking—what if you went to a federal judge and asked for a sneak-and-peek?"

"They don't like 'em, judges don't," Barlow said. "But in this case, I think we'd have a good chance. It's like drugs—if we raid him and miss, we won't have another chance."

"So let's think about that," Virgil said. "I'm gonna pile up as much stuff as I can, but we've got to move. Why don't you make a reservation to see a judge late this afternoon, and I'll give you whatever I've got."

Virgil went back to the courthouse, and with the help of the county clerk, who was sworn to secrecy, found that Wyatt had bought the property eight years before for $240,000 and taken out a mortgage for $180,000. So he'd only put $60,000 of his own money into it—and had been hoping to take out sixty times that much.

Virgil looked at Wyatt's property taxes and found references to two structures on the property. If he were living in an apartment, as Haden thought, he might very likely *not* be making the bombs there. Landlords sometimes sneak into apartments, to make sure everything is being taken care of; a smart guy like a professor would have thought of that.

He had to take a look at the property. He had the county clerk xerox the plat maps, and she added a copy of an aerial photo from the engineering department.

Before he left, he called Butternut Technical College and asked if it would be possible to reach Professor Wyatt's office. The woman who answered said she could try his extension, but he was scheduled to be in class at that hour.

Excellent.

On his way out of town, Virgil called the BCA researcher, asked her to check Wyatt against the National Crime Information Center and to check his driver's license. He didn't know where Wyatt lived, and asked her to see if she could figure that out; and to make that the priority.

Virgil made it out to Wyatt's property in ten minutes. To his eye, it seemed like good land, a rolling hillside rising slowly away from both the north-south highway and an east-west farm road. The field was covered with growing corn, not yet as high as an elephant's eye, but getting there. Virgil turned down the farm road and found an overgrown track leading up toward a crumbling old farmhouse.

He couldn't see anybody up at the

house, and since Wyatt was teaching, Virgil turned onto the track and took it up the hill to the house.

The house sat at the very crest of the hill, and was in the process of disintegrating. The windows had been covered with sheets of plywood, and the porch had been entirely ripped away. The front door, which stood three feet off the ground, was locked with a padlock on a new steel hasp. Next to the door was a large sign that said: DANGER: NO TRESPASSING. TRESPASSERS WILL BE PROSECUTED. Next to that, a hand-lettered sign said: *All metals have been removed from this property, and all collectibles. If you enter this property, you will be prosecuted for burglary.*

Virgil got out of the truck and walked around the house—the corn came to within ten feet of the sides of the house, and within twenty feet of the back. There was a hump in the backyard, the remnants of an old shed, or something, Virgil thought. The windows were boarded all the way around, but it would be easy enough to pull a board off. Virgil thought, Root cellar, but could find no sign of one. If there had been one, it was out in the field somewhere.

From the top of the hill, Virgil could see most of the hundred and sixty acres, which closed on the south side by a wood lot, with Highway 71 on the west, another cornfield on the east, and the farm road on the north. There wasn't a tree on the property, as far as he could tell: and he wondered if that was good or bad, for development.

Butternut Falls, the southernmost sub-division, was right *there*, a few hundred yards north of the road.

Wyatt must have been able to *taste* the money.

On the way out of the property, he called Sandy, the BCA researcher, and asked her if she'd come up with an address. "He shows two addresses, one for his home, but he also gets utility bills at four-twenty-one Grange Street, apartment A."

"Thank you."

Apartment A was not exactly an apartment—it was the end unit in a town house complex, three stories tall, a two-car garage on the bottom floor, and a door. Hoping that Wyatt was still teaching, he walked up and knocked on the door, and took a long look at the lock. It was solid, a Schlage. They'd need a landlord to open it, if they got the sneak-and-peek.

Barlow called. He'd made an appointment with a federal judge, Thomas Shaver, in Minneapolis, and with an assistant federal attorney, who'd handle the details of the warrant. Virgil gave Barlow all the information he had. "We don't have a lot of specific information on him, but we have two things: he is one of the few people who could have gotten into the Pinnacle, and he has more than enough motive," Virgil said. "He's been living here for years, so he also has the detailed background to plant these other bombs: the bomb on the limo had to be local work. And, if we get it, we need to get warrants for both places—his apartment, and the farmhouse out on his property."

Barlow nodded. "I think we'll get them. What are you going to do?"

"I want to see him. I've got a couple of guys in town, working the city council aspect of this thing. I'm gonna get them, and stake him out. See where he goes. I can provide a stakeout on him, when we go into his place."

"I should be back by six o'clock," Barlow said. "I don't think we'll have time to do it today."

"I agree. Tomorrow morning would be the first good shot at it," Virgil said. "When you get the warrant, call me—I'll track down his landlord, get a key for his place."

He found Jenkins and Shrake at the Holiday Inn, in separate rooms, reading separate golf magazines, got them together in the lounge. They said they'd been the front men on the three arrests, leading a group of sheriff's deputies. They'd seized all of the accused city councilmen's financial records, and their computers, and the same with the mayor.

"It looks like your pal—whoever it was—who suggested the deal would have something to do with golf carts was on the mark," Shrake said. "The first thing they found on Gore's computer was a sale of two hundred golf carts to a Sonocast Corp., which happens to be a supply subsidiary of PyeMart."

"Excellent. Is Gore still in jail?" Virgil asked. "Or out?"

"She's out. All of them are. They've got too much political clout to stay in. Gore paid cash, the other two put up their houses as bond."

"You gonna get the PyeMart guy?"

"Don't know," Jenkins said. "It looks like the way it worked, PyeMart bought the golf carts from Gore, who spread the profit around . . . keeping most of it for herself. That's what this Good Thunder told us. She took a quick look at the tax records, and she seems like a pretty smart chick."

"But there's no law against buying golf carts," Shrake said. "If Gore doesn't crack, and give us exactly the quid pro quo, we might not get him."

"That's bullshit," Virgil said. "You'd need a retarded jury not to convict."

"What's your point?" Jenkins asked.

Virgil told them about Wyatt, about how the paraglider revelation had worked out.

Shrake said, "So I solved two cases in one day."

"That'd be one interpretation," Virgil said. "But now, we actually got to work. We've got to keep an eye on this guy. I want to pick him up now, put him to bed, get him up tomorrow, take him to work."

"We can do that, if we can take along the golf magazines," Shrake said.

Wyatt, Virgil thought, should either be home, or arriving home soon. He gave the other two Wyatt's address, and they agreed to stay in touch by cell phone. Virgil let them cruise the house first: Shrake called back to say there were no lights in the windows. "We found a place we can park a block away, by a ball diamond, not too conspicuous, and still see his place. We'll sit for a bit. There's a game about to start."

Virgil took the break to stop at a McDonald's and get a cheeseburger and fries. He was still there, reading the paper, when Barlow called: "We got the warrant.

The judge thought we were a little weak on details, but he gave us six days. He says if we can't do better in six days, he won't give us an extension, and we'll have to give a copy to Wyatt."

"That's good. That should be plenty of time," Virgil said.

"You watching him?"

"Trying to. He hasn't shown up at home yet, but I've got two guys watching his place."

"Hope he hasn't flown the coop. You get a key?"

"No. I got sidetracked on this surveillance thing. Would you have time?"

Barlow agreed to run down the landlord and get a key. Virgil would call him in the morning, as soon as Wyatt was at the college, where he was scheduled to teach back-to-back classes.

Jenkins called five minutes later and said, "He's home."

"I'll be there in ten minutes—take your place," Virgil said. "Pull out when you see me coming."

He drove to Wyatt's—there was a car

in the driveway, an older Prius—and then continued up the block, and when Shrake pulled away from the curb at the ball diamond, Virgil took his place. There was a game going on, town ball, fast-pitch, and Virgil was looking down at the diamond from the parking place.

He half-watched the game, half-watched Wyatt's place, and at the same time, dug his camera out of the bag in the backseat. He used a Nikon D3, with a 70-200 lens and a 2x Nikon teleconverter. When put together, the rig was heavy and long, but also reasonably sharp, and good in low light.

He still had plenty of light, and he settled in to wait.

One of the ball teams, Robert's Bar and Grill, had a damn good pitcher; he was mowing down the other team, which was surviving less on pitching than on its fielding. In the two innings Virgil watched, Robert's had runners in both innings, while the other team never did get a man to first.

He was interested enough in the game that he almost missed Wyatt. He came out of the apartment carrying an oversized gym bag. A tall thin man, he was dressed in a T-shirt, jeans, and running shoes, and moved like an athlete. He looked like the figure in the construction-site trailer videos. Virgil propped the barrel of the camera on the edge of the passenger-side window, and ran off a half-dozen shots as he walked around the car, threw the bag inside, then got in.

Following him wasn't a problem: Wyatt drove out to the highway, turned toward downtown, pulled into a strip mall, got his gym bag, and walked into a tae-kwon-do studio. Virgil called Shrake and made arrangements to switch off.

The lesson had to last at least an hour, Virgil thought, so he took the time to load the photos into his laptop. When Shrake arrived, Virgil climbed into the backseat of Shrake's Cadillac and passed the laptop across the seat. "Portraits," he said.

The other two looked at the photos for a minute, then Shrake said, "Got him. Want us to stay with him overnight?"

"Ah . . . yeah."

"Shoot. Okay, are you in? Make it more tolerable," Jenkins said.

"I'm in. I'll take the middle shift." The

middle shift was the bad one—four hours in the middle of the night.

Shrake took the first watch, following Wyatt from the tae kwon do studio to a supermarket, and then back to his house. He waited there until midnight, when Virgil took it. Virgil sat for four hours, until four o'clock. Jenkins arrived right at four, and Virgil went back to the Holiday Inn and crashed. Shrake, who'd gotten a full night's sleep, took it at eight o'clock, and at nine-thirty, called Virgil and said, "It looks like he's getting ready to move."

Virgil brushed his teeth and called Barlow: "He's moving. Heading up to the college, we think."

"I talked to the landlord," Barlow said. "Got a key, and scared the shit out of him. He won't tell anyone."

"I'll be at your hotel in five minutes. We can ride over in my truck—we don't want a caravan."

Virgil picked up Barlow and one of his techs, whose name was Doug Mason, and they headed over to Wyatt's. "Doug knows computers," Barlow said.

"Excellent," Virgil said. They didn't have much to say on the way over, and half-way there, Shrake called to say that Wyatt had just walked into the college carrying his briefcase.

Wyatt lived on a working street, mostly younger families, and at ten-fifteen, the street was deserted. They climbed out, three men in jackets and slacks—Virgil was wearing a dress shirt and dark slacks, so he wouldn't hit a neighbor's inquiring eye quite so hard. Barlow had the key, and they walked up to the door and in. Just inside was a small square mudroom, with a stairway leading up, and a door to the left, leading into the garage.

They took the stairs, quickly, clearing the place: the second and third floors were probably eight hundred square feet each, and smelled of fresh-brewed coffee. The second floor had a small living room, a kitchen, a bathroom, and a bedroom that Wyatt was using as an office. The third floor had two larger bedrooms, a storage space with a low, slanted ceiling, a good-sized bathroom, and several closets. The place was cluttered with paper—books, magazines, newspapers. Virgil knew and recognized the symptoms: in the downdraft of a divorce, lonely guys often didn't have much to do, and so hung out in bookstores and newsstands, and acquired paper; and also hung out in bagel joints and movie matinees.

Mason went straight to the office and said, "I'm on the computer."

Barlow said, "I want to run down and look at the garage."

"I'll start upstairs," Virgil said.

He went through the bedroom in a hurry, but took care not to mess it up. He checked the closets, and a few boxes inside the closets, and found more symptoms of divorce. Wyatt had moved out of his house, but hadn't taken any junk with him. Hadn't taken his *stuff*. He'd simply packed up some clothes, a couple of spare tae kwon do uniforms—including a spare black belt—and had gotten out.

Virgil cleared the bedroom, bathroom, four closets, and the storage area in fifteen minutes. Back downstairs, he found Barlow in the office with Mason. Mason was sitting in the computer chair, his fingers laced over his stomach, watching a screen full of moving numbers. "Anything?"

"Not right off the top—but there's a lot of stuff in here, so I hooked up my own drive, and I'm mirroring his," Mason said. "I can look at it later."

"You know what the guy's got for tools?" Barlow asked. "A bicycle pump and a pair of needle-nose pliers. That's it."

"He's gotta have more than that—any normal guy does," Mason said.

"But he's getting a divorce. He might have a garage full of stuff at the other house," Virgil said. "Every time I got thrown out, my wives kept the tools. Women like to have tools around."

"Wives?" Mason asked.

"Or maybe there's something out at the farmhouse," Virgil said.

"Gotta be something, if he's our guy. He's not putting those things together with his bare fingers."

Barlow had been in the process of going through a file cabinet, and Virgil started working through the rest of the house.

Five minutes later, Barlow came out with a file in his hands. "The divorce is stalled out right now, over visiting rights with the children, and some money issues. The next court appointment is in August."

Five minutes after that, Virgil realized that they weren't going to find anything in the house: the house had been sterilized. Wyatt was smart: he'd anticipated the chance of a search. An hour later, he was proven right.

"The guy doesn't even look at porn," Mason grumbled. He'd been working through Wyatt's online history. "You hardly ever run into an asshole who doesn't even *look* at it."

They left empty-handed, as far as they knew—Mason still had to finish going through the computer files. Barlow said, "Doesn't prove anything. Guy would be an idiot to work in his own house, especially if he thinks he might bring somebody home with him. He's got a place where he does it, and he keeps it there."

"The farmhouse," Virgil said.

"Somewhere," Barlow said.

It was another quiet day out in the corn-field, nothing moving but a couple of crows that flapped overhead as they were arriving. Virgil had told them how the house was laid out, and Barlow had brought along a crowbar. They checked all four sides of the house, picked out the window with the shabbiest-looking ply-wood covering, and pried the board loose. Virgil backed his truck up next to the wall, took a flashlight with him, and climbed through the window from the trunk's bumper.

The interior of the house was dim and smelled like dried weeds, or corn leaves. The floors were wood, and creaked un-derfoot. A stairway led up; two of the stair treads were broken, and there was a pa-tina of dust on the others.

He went through a doorway into the back, getting a face full of spiderweb as he went through the door.

Barlow called, "Anything?"

Virgil was standing in a bathroom, in thin light seeping through the cracks around the doors and window openings.

All the faucets and handles were missing from a sink basin and toilet, and there was nothing but a hole in the floor where a tub had once been. He stooped and shone his light into the hole, then up toward the ceiling. He called back, "Come in here a minute."

He heard Barlow clamber through the window, and called, "Back here."

Barlow stepped up beside him and looked in the door. "What am I looking at?"

"Nothing," Virgil said.

"Nothing?"

"Yeah. Look at the holes in the ceiling. Shouldn't there be some kind of pipe feeding down to the toilet?"

Barlow scratched his head and said, "Yeah. Should be. Probably feeding off a pump at the well, through here, and then to another bathroom upstairs. With a branch off to the tub down here."

"Nothing feeding the tub. I looked."

"Huh," Barlow said. "The mystery of the missing pipe. I'll tell you, those holes are about the right size."

"But where's he working it?" Virgil asked. "There's nothing here."

"Been down the basement?"

"Not yet. I'm not sure there is one."

They found a basement door, but there were no steps going down. "No steps, no power," Barlow said. "That's not a work-shop, that's a hole in the ground."

"What the hell is the guy doing?" Virgil asked. He was lying on the floor, shining the flash down into the basement. He could see nothing but rock wall and dirt and more spiderwebs.

Going back through the rotten old house, Barlow borrowed the flash and carefully climbed a few steps toward the second floor, but stopped short when one of the steps started to give. "Nothing up here but dust and bat shit," he said.

Outside again, they pounded the plywood window back in place. "I don't know," Vir-gil said. "That pipe was probably the right size . . . but you can get that pipe any-where, just about. Any old house. They may have taken it out to sell it."

"Yeah. But it'd be a coincidence."

"I gotta think about it," Virgil said, as they bounced back down the hill in the truck. "I can keep my two BCA guys, at least for a couple of days. If I can find a way to push Wyatt into going out to his workshop."

"Push him?"

"Yeah. Give him a reason to worry about us. Get him out to where he works, to close it down, or bury it or whatever. Gotta think about it."

23

Virgil did his best thinking in two places: in the shower, and in a boat. His boat, unfortunately, had been blown up, and he'd already had a shower. He wound up driving over to the PyeMart site, drove across it to the far side, got out his fly-fishing gear, including a pair of chest waders, and carried it through the brush down to the Butternut.

He spent an hour working down through the river's shallows, casting down into the deeper pools from the upstream side, teasing the banks with a dry fly. He got a hit in the first two minutes, missed the fish.

And that was about it. The trout weren't in the mood, but that really didn't make a difference—it was the activity that counted, feeling his way down the cool, quiet stream. Forty-five minutes out, he came to a conclusion, sat on the bank and dug out his cell phone. He found John Haden's phone number in his cell phone's history, and called him.

Haden picked up on the fourth ring: "Virgil?"

"Yeah, it's me. I need to talk to you about something . . . something I want you to do, that you might not want to do. But, it's necessary. So, where you at?"

"You don't need the 'at' at the end of that sentence," Haden said. "If you'd asked, 'Where are you?' that would have been fine."

"I'm colloquial," Virgil said. "Can we get together? Now?"

"I've got a class in . . . forty-eight minutes. I sometimes run down to Starbucks about now, for a shot of caffeine."

"Have you ever seen Wyatt there?"

"No, I never have," Haden said.

"I'll see you in fifteen minutes," Virgil said.

He made another call on his way out—he called Shrake and said, "Don't leave Wyatt. I got something working"—and made it to Starbucks in exactly fifteen minutes. Haden wasn't there, and Virgil got his hot chocolate, got a table, opened his laptop and signed on. He found a note from Lee Coakley in his in-box; it said: *I guess we're done. I'm really sorry about that. I was thinking about it before I went to bed and all morning. I don't think I want to talk to you again for a while. I mean, quite a while.—Lee*

He thought, *Well, shit.* He had seen it coming, but hadn't wanted it . . . although a voice in the back of his head added, *Not yet.* He needed time, he thought, to revise his entire philosophical approach to women. . . .

Damnit: bummed him out.

"You look like somebody ran over your pet skunk."

Virgil looked up and saw Deputy O'Hara peering down at him, a cup of coffee in her hand. He said, "What, no doughnut?"

"The doughnuts here suck," she said. "If you want a good doughnut, you gotta go down to Bernie Anderson's."

"Yeah, well, I'll write that on a piece of paper, when I get one," he said.

"My, my," she said, "you really are in an uproar. Well, if there's anything I can do for you, hesitate to call."

"I will," he said, and she left. He watched her go past the window. Left in something of a huff, he thought. What, she maybe thought he was going to buy her that doughnut? Goddamn women.

He was almost finished with his hot chocolate, wondering if he'd been stood up, when Haden came through the door, in a hurry. "I'm running late," he said, dropping his briefcase by Virgil's foot. "Watch this, will you?"

He was back in four minutes with what Virgil thought might be a venti, if that was the extra-large. He pulled out a chair and sat down, asked, "All right: you want me to betray my old pal Bill Wyatt, in some way, is that right?"

"That's not the word I would have chosen, but yeah," Virgil said. "I don't really want you to betray him, I want you to give him a little push so that if he's the bomber, he'll betray himself."

Haden regarded him over the top of his coffee, for just a moment, and then said, "Huh. That sounds like a nice little piece of sophistry, but I'm listening."

"I've found some things that make me think Wyatt is my guy. But: I need to get him to wherever he keeps his bomb-making stuff. I need to lay a hint on him that we're coming. That we've got something."

"Like what?"

"I'd like you to bump into him, and ask him if he knows about my list. Tell him that you're on it, and that he's on it, too. That somebody named both of you. Ask him if he knows who," Virgil said. "Tell him that I came over and talked to you, but I backed off, and something I said suggested that I was going for a search warrant for somebody. That I knew something. Ask him if I'd talked to him yet."

"I could bump into him, but I don't know exactly how I could bring all that up, without sounding . . . phony," Haden said.

"Sorta like I said it. Tell him that I came over, was impatient with you, then said I was wasting my time anyway. Say that I apologized, and confessed that some-body else was first on the list. That we had a tip, and we might know where the bomb stuff was."

"Man, that sounds . . ."

"Well, hell, I don't know. Make some-thing up," Virgil said. "You're the big brain. But that's the idea I want to get across. That we've got something. Not that he's a target, just that he was on the list, and that we've got something."

Haden took a gulp of coffee, swallowed, looked at his watch, and said, "I gotta run. I'll think of something. I'll call you when I've done it."

When he was gone, Virgil called Shrake: "Still sitting there? Any movement?"

"Not a thing," Shrake said. "On the

other hand, I have learned that I'm probably turning my hips too soon, in my drive, which is why I slice. I need to shift my weight to my left before I start turning my hips. That gives me a natural inside-to-outside swing, which I've always needed."

"I'm pleased you've had this learning experience," Virgil said. "Listen, we're going round-the-clock on Wyatt. I'm giving him a push. And I want two guys on him, so I'm going to try to borrow a guy from the sheriff. You guys do what you have to, then get some sleep. I'll pick him up in a few minutes. I'll want you guys around midnight, to do the overnight."

When he'd worked a timetable with Shrake, he called Ahlquist: "I need one of your guys to sit with me. I'm staking out Wyatt."

"Starting when?"

"Right now. You know my truck, and I know Wyatt's car. I'm going to spot it in the parking lot up at the college and I'll be at the other end of the lot."

"Get somebody there soon as I can," Ahlquist said. "You need any sandwiches or anything? Coffee?"

"I'll get some Diet Coke on the way

over, but a couple of sandwiches would be great."

Virgil picked up a half-dozen Diet Cokes, stuck them with some ice in his cooler, and drove out to the college. He spotted Wyatt's Prius, and took up a spot as far away as he could get and still see the front entrance and Wyatt's car.

A half hour after he'd settled in, there was a knock on the passenger-side door, and he saw Deputy O'Hara looking in at him. She was carrying a white paper bag.

"Ah, for Christ's sakes," he muttered. Ahlquist's idea of a joke. He popped the door, and she climbed in, handed him the bag, and said, "Here's your sandwich, sir. Anything else I can possibly get you?"

"I'm good," Virgil said. "Where's your uniform?"

She was wearing a pale blue blouse and khaki slacks. "I thought this would be less obvious. But I brought my gun."

"That's good. Don't shoot anybody unless I tell you to," Virgil said.

"Yes, sir," she said.

"No sarcasm, either." She said nothing,

but smiled, and Virgil dug into the bag and said, "You got me an anchovy sandwich, right?"

She shuddered. "I never heard of such a thing. They're chicken salad on caraway rye. There are two of them."

His eyebrows went up. "Deputy O'Hara: that's one of my favorite sandwiches in the United States."

"I'm happy for you. You owe me seven dollars."

He paid her, unwrapped a sandwich—damn good sandwich, too—and said, around a mouthful of chicken salad, "All right. Here's what we're trying to do."

He spent a couple minutes explaining, and she said, "So if he takes the bait, we might follow him right out to where he's got, like, twenty pounds of high explosive, right?"

"Yeah."

"And he's already killed three people, attacked a cop and one of the richest people in the world, and injured or scared the crap out of a bunch of other people. Right?"

"Yeah."

"So, I don't want to seem obstreperous, or anything, but . . . you do have a gun?"

"Yes."

"Could you get it out? And check it? Where I can see you do it? I don't mind going in on something like this, but I don't want to have to look after your ass, as well as mine."

Virgil said, "Let me finish the sandwich. I've got a gun. Really."

He got a call from Haden: "I feel like Judas, but I did it. He was interested."

Virgil said, "Thank you," and hung up.

Deputy O'Hara asked, "You gonna eat that other sandwich?"

"You can have it, for three-fifty," Virgil said.

"I only want a half."

"Then one-seventy-five."

Deputy O'Hara, it turned out, was an art freak, and on her weekends off, worked as a docent at the Minneapolis Institute of Arts. She also worked an off-duty second job at the local mall, an hour before and after closing time. "Those are the high shoplift times; and then, I make sure everybody gets out of the place with their money."

"Are you doing this because you really need the money? Or is it simple greed?" Virgil said.

"Every penny of my off-duty work, except what I need for taxes, goes in my travel fund," she said. "Then every fall, I take off for Europe. I go to museums."

Virgil said, "Hmm."

"What? You're against culture?"

"No. I was thinking that's a great way to go through life," Virgil said.

She looked at him suspiciously: "But not something you'd do."

"Not exactly," he said. "But I could probably be talked into it."

Shrake called: "Anything?"

"We're watching his car, but haven't seen him yet," Virgil said. "You okay for midnight?"

"Yeah, I talked to Jenkins. We're all set. You by yourself?"

"I got a deputy with me," Virgil said.

"See you at midnight."

O'Hara said, "I gotta call my night job, tell them I can't make it."

"If he goes back home, I could probably drop you," Virgil said.

"No, I'd rather have the overtime. Earl said overtime is okay, as long as it's not *too* much."

"Good of him," Virgil said.

Wyatt finally walked out of the college building an hour after his last class ended. Virgil worried a bit that he'd snuck out some other exit, and walked somewhere, but there was nothing to do about that.

Wyatt stood blinking in the sunlight for a moment, looking around the lot, then spotted his car and walked over to it, jingling his keys. He was carrying a big leather academic briefcase, which he put on the passenger seat, then walked back around the car to get in the driver's side.

"He was being pretty careful with that suitcase," O'Hara said.

Virgil said, "Huh," and when Wyatt was moving, pulled out behind him.

They took him to a supermarket, took him home, took him to tae kwon do, took him to a movie, alone. Virgil followed him in, at a distance, and caught him as he was settling in for *Pirates of the Caribbean*. Virgil watched the movie from the back row, occasionally texting O'Hara to keep her current. He left ten minutes before the end, no longer caring what happened.

"Like it?" O'Hara asked. "The movie?"

"No," Virgil said.

Wyatt came back out ten minutes later, drove to the Applebee's, spent an hour there, sitting at the bar, talking with people. He looked like a regular. They took him home at ten o'clock; he put the car in the garage.

He hadn't moved at midnight, when Jenkins and Shrake took it.

O'Hara lived in a modest clapboard house not unlike Virgil's: "I will pick you up at fifteen minutes to eight tomorrow,"

Virgil said, when he dropped her. "Be ready."

"Yes, sir," she said, and saluted.

And Virgil thought, as he drove away, that Lee Coakley hadn't called. She must've meant what she said: didn't want to talk.

Thor was working in the office as he went through, and called, "Hey . . . looks like Mr. Shepard is going away, huh?"

"I wouldn't count on it," Virgil said.

"Everybody's heard that he was arrested, and that he ratted out everybody else," Thor said.

"Yeah, but first he's got to recover, and then there'll be negotiations," Virgil said. "So . . . how's everything going with the hot Mrs. Shepard?"

Thor's eyelids lowered a quarter inch. "She took the pizza," he said.

Virgil went straight to bed, with both his alarms set, and a wake-up call. He lay awake for a while, thinking about how

God played with people's lives, and thinking that Coakley might call yet. It was still not past eleven o'clock on the West Coast. He was still waiting when he went to sleep.

He woke at seven-fifteen, cleaned up in a hurry, got O'Hara, who was standing in her front yard, waiting, and made it to a McDonald's drive-through, got Egg McMuffins with sausage for both of them, a coffee for her and a Diet Coke for himself, and made it to Wyatt's at exactly eight o'clock. Working in a town where almost nowhere was more than a mile from anywhere else, and there was almost no real traffic, had its benefits.

Shrake and Jenkins had nothing to report.

"We'll do this one more night, if we have to, and then you guys can go back to the Cities tomorrow morning."

"We won't be going to bed until this afternoon, so if anything comes up, call us," Jenkins said.

Virgil said he would, and he and O'Hara settled in with their McDonald's bag, to watch.

Virgil was reading a Michael Connelly

novel on his iPad when O'Hara poked him and said, "Garage door."

Virgil shut down the iPad and watched as Wyatt backed his Prius out of the garage. He drove to the same McDonald's where Virgil and O'Hara had gone, rolled through the same drive-through, then headed south through town. "He's going out to his farm," Virgil said.

But he didn't. He went to Home Depot. O'Hara said that as far as she knew, Wyatt didn't know her, so Virgil sent her inside to see what he was doing. She came back out ten minutes later and said, "He's in the checkout line. I couldn't get close enough to see what he was getting, but it was in the 'fasteners' section. Window latches, or something."

"Wonder if you could use them in a bomb, you know, to detonate one?"

"Don't know," she said. And, "Speaking of bombs, I can still taste that Egg McMuffin. Wish I hadn't got the sausage."

Wyatt came out a minute later, and again, turned south. "Toward the farm," Virgil said again.

This time, he *was* going to the farm, taking the turn on the county road toward the track up the hill. Virgil pulled over onto the side of the highway, past the county road, and said, "I'm going."

"I'm coming."

"Gotta run," he said. "There's nothing in the house, so he's probably got the stuff ditched outside."

They ran across the highway, across the roadside ditch, climbed a barbed-wire fence, and jogged into the cornfield. They were coming at the house from the side, and couldn't see anything below the exterior windowsills . . . which meant that Wyatt couldn't see them, at least until they got higher on the slope. Halfway up, Virgil could see the top of Wyatt's car, and said, "We gotta get lower."

They continued running, bent over, up the hill; another hundred yards and Virgil waved O'Hara down, and to a stop. Standing slowly, he looked over the top of the corn, and immediately saw Wyatt walking up to the front of the old farmhouse. He appeared to be empty-handed. Virgil said, quietly, "He's going inside. We couldn't find anything in there. . . ."

"If we get right under the house, we could hear what he's doing," O'Hara said.

"Let's get a little closer, anyway," Virgil said. Now they were virtually crawling, as fast as they could. Another fifty yards, and they stopped, and both popped up their heads. Wyatt had unlocked the front door. There was no porch, so he had to boost himself inside.

Virgil sat down and got his cell phone and called Shrake: "We might have something going. You guys head south on 71. About six blocks out of town . . ."

He pushed to his knees, watching the house, as he gave directions to Shrake, O'Hara beside him.

The shock wave, when the house exploded, nearly knocked them down.

24

When the house went, it wasn't at all like watching a slow-mo, where the building bulges, and then flies apart, or sags, and falls into a heap. The house went like an oversized firecracker: *BOOM!* And it was gone.

Virgil pushed O'Hara flat, covered his head with his hands, and covered her head with his right arm and elbow. She tried to push away so she could look up and he shouted, "No, no, cover your head, cover your head."

She looked at him like he was crazy,

and then the first chunk of plank landed a few feet away, and then the heavy thunk of masonry, maybe a piece of the old brick chimney, and then all kinds of trash, small pieces of wood and dirt and stone and shingles and concrete, some of it no bigger across than a little fingernail, but some of it the size of a bathtub.

She caught on and curled up, covering her head, and the debris kept coming down for what seemed like a full minute, and may have been. Virgil heard several large pieces land, stuff that could have killed them.

Then it all went silent, and O'Hara stirred and did a push-up, and said, "Oh my God," just like a Valley girl.

They both got to their knees. Other than the foundation, there was no sign of the house from where they were. The superstructure had vanished. Wyatt's champagne-colored Prius was still sitting there, but it had no windows.

Virgil stood up and walked toward the house, while O'Hara started screaming into her cell phone. A minute later, Virgil's cell phone rang, and he absently took it out of his pocket, said, "Yeah?"

"This is Shrake. There's been a hell of an explosion. That wasn't you, was it?"

"Yeah. Wyatt just left for the moon," Virgil said. "Where are you?"

"Five minutes away. Jenkins says he can see the dust cloud. We're coming."

Virgil clicked off, heard O'Hara talking to Ahlquist, and then she clicked off and caught up with him. They passed the car, which had been turned probably thirty degrees sideways. The near side had been torn to pieces by shrapnel from the house. Where the house had been, there was nothing but a hole in the ground.

Virgil thought, almost idly, *No more spiderwebs . . .*

"Was it an accident?" O'Hara asked. "Or did he do it on purpose? Maybe he figured you had him. . . ."

There were sirens everywhere and the first patrol car blew past the subdivision at the bottom of the hill, coming fast. Virgil was aware that the car looked hazy—that everything looked hazy—and he realized that he was walking through an enormous cloud of dust, which was still raining down on them. O'Hara's red hair was turning gray with the dirt, and he was sure his was, too.

He took her by the elbow and said, "Come on, we've got to get out of the dust."

She resisted. "What about Wyatt?"

"Elvis has left the building," Virgil said. "Or maybe, the building has left Elvis. And we're breathing in all kinds of bad shit, maybe including little pieces of asbestos, or glass fibers, if the place had insulation. We've got to get out of the cloud. Cover your mouth and nose with your shirt."

Using their shirts as masks, they walked down the track to the county road; the patrol car turned into the track, and Virgil waved them off. The car stopped, and they walked down to it, and Virgil said, "Pop the back door, let us in. Keep your window up."

They got in the back, and Virgil told the deputy about the dust, and then about Wyatt.

The deputy asked O'Hara, "So you guys think he's dead?"

"I think he was vaporized," O'Hara

said. "I think he somehow touched off everything he had left. It was like . . . it was like the movies they showed us in Iraq. It was like an IED."

Virgil asked the deputy to take him back to his truck. As they rode over, he called Shrake and said, "Wait a bit before you try to go up the hill. That dust cloud may be toxic. I'm parked on the highway. I'll meet you there."

Shrake and Jenkins arrived two minutes later, and more patrol cars came along, and were waved off, and then a fire truck. Rubberneckers were piling up on the highway, and Virgil sent a couple of the cops to keep them moving. Then Ahlquist came in, and a moment later, Barlow. They stood on the shoulder of the road, watching the dissipating dust cloud, and Barlow said, "If it took out a whole house, that was probably the rest of it."

"That's what I said," O'Hara told him.

Ahlquist asked, "No chance that he got out? That he set off a timer thing, then went out the far side and ran out through the corn to the other side?"

Virgil said, "No."

Shrake said, "You sound pretty sure of that."

"I am," Virgil said.

"Suicide by cop," Barlow said. "He knew you were coming, and took the easy way out."

"I think we can go up there," Virgil said. The cloud was thinning, under a light westerly breeze.

They drove up the hill in a long caravan, with the fire truck trailing behind. They found a hole, but no sign of Wyatt.

"If it killed him, his head should be around here somewhere," Barlow said, and Virgil remembered what the deputy had said the first night he was in town. O'Hara remembered it, too, and looked at Virgil and nodded.

"Then we need to get some people together to walk the field," Virgil said. "We had bricks coming down eighty yards out, so if we . . . you know, his head shouldn't have gone much further than that."

Barlow looked at him, but nodded.

Ahlquist pointed at a deputy and told him to get some cops and start walking the field. Barlow walked over and looked in the hole, the former cellar. He shook his head. "Damn good thing we didn't go down that basement. The thing must have been unstable—or maybe it was set to blow if anyone found it."

Virgil: "You think the bomb was in the basement?"

Barlow nodded. "I know it was. If it had been upstairs, the floor would have been blown into the basement. But the explosion was below the floor, and everything went straight up. That's why the basement's so clean. The whole building, including the floor, went *out*."

He added, "You two were lucky. You were down below the shrapnel line and partly sheltered by that foundation. About nine thousand pounds of shrapnel blew right over your heads."

"And you think that was the whole stash of Pelex," Ahlquist said.

"Just about had to be, to do this kind of damage," Barlow said. He looked around and shook his head. "I need to get pictures of this. This is something we don't see very often."

The cops were walking the field, slowly, looking behind every cornstalk. Virgil got his Nikon and a short zoom, and walked around the blast zone, documenting the effects of the explosion at Barlow's direction—and Barlow wanted three shots of everything, at slightly different exposures.

They'd been at it for fifteen minutes when the cops found a piece of a human body, what looked like a hip joint. Virgil took a couple shots of it, and then, a minute later, the ragged remains of a foot.

"No question now," Shrake said, his face grim.

"Never was a question," O'Hara said. She'd been tagging Virgil and Barlow around the field. "He walked through that door and it was about a count of one . . . two . . . and *boom.* He didn't have time to walk halfway through the house."

Virgil was tired of taking photos of body parts, but there wasn't anyone else to do it, and for what it might somehow be worth, he kept at it, as more and more body parts were found. Wyatt's head was eventually found, only seventy feet from the house, under a piece of the roof. There were no features remaining: nothing but a bloody skull.

Virgil thought, *F8 and be there,* and took the shot.

"Must've gone straight up," Jenkins said. "Like a baseball."

"Another cop said like a basketball," Virgil said. He turned away from the mess, sick at heart. "Doesn't look like any kind of sport, at all."

A patrol car arrived, in a two-car set with a civilian car, a Toyota Corolla, and a woman got out of the Corolla and looked up the hill.

Ahlquist said, "Mrs. Wyatt. It's Jennifer, I think. I better get down there to meet her." He turned to a deputy: "I want tarps or something over all the body remains. There's nothing for her to identify, and I don't want her to see the scraps." When the deputy seemed to hesitate, Ahlquist snapped, "Get going! *Get going!*"

Barlow came up and said, "We'll have to do DNA. Just to make sure."

O'Hara was getting testy: "I told you: he didn't have time to get out."

Barlow shook his head. "Time is strange, after something like that. You think it was two seconds, but you were almost killed. Things speed up under those conditions. If it were ten seconds—"

"Then where did the body come from?" O'Hara demanded.

"That's something we'd have to determine," Barlow said. O'Hara said, "Oh, bullshit," and Barlow put up his hands. "I think it's ninety-nine percent you're right. But, we check."

Virgil walked around with his camera, shaking his head, and O'Hara asked, "Are you all right?"

"No," he said.

Ahlquist and jennifer Wyatt walked around the house, talking, and Wyatt began to cry, and Ahlquist put an arm around her shoulders. Virgil watched. Barlow came up and said, "Her house and his apartment are both crime scenes. I'm talking to my ADA to make sure we don't need search warrants, and if we do, to get them. We're going down and taking her house apart."

"I'll come along, too," O'Hara said.

"Ah, you can go on home," Virgil said. "Get cleaned up. You're sorta a mess."

"Nope. I'm going," she said. "Either I ride with you or I'll ride with somebody else."

"Better go with somebody else," he said. She stalked off and Virgil looked at the weeping Mrs. Wyatt, and told Shrake and Jenkins, "You guys hang tight. I gotta get out of here and get something to eat."

"To eat," Shrake said, doubtfully.

"Yeah. Food," Virgil said.

He told Barlow that he was going, and that he would e-mail all the photos that evening; and he walked down to his truck.

Bunson's was almost empty. He got the French toast—it was still more or less morning—and told the waitress to keep bringing the Diet Cokes, and he sat and worked it through.

One thing didn't fit, and he couldn't make it fit. He closed his eyes and took himself back to the Pye Pinnacle visit. Thought about all the explanations, about the dead and wounded, about the board-room explosion, about the ludicrous sight of the birthday pies smeared all over the ceiling. . . .

He thought about how Pye had a "sanctum sanctorum" where he worked out his problems, and where not even the cleaning lady was welcome. Not that the cleaning lady would have been there, early on a Monday morning.

So here was a question: Why didn't the bomber, coming down from above, put the bomb in Pye's office? If he'd used some kind of mousetrap trigger, and stuck the bomb in the desk leg hole, he would have gotten Pye. Why would he do something so uncertain as to stick the bomb in the credenza? In the credenza, any number of things could have led to its discovery.

He thought about it, and thought about it, and eventually came up with an answer, in the best tradition of Sherlock Holmes. Once you've eliminated all the other possibilities, whatever was left had to be the answer.

What was left was simple enough, Virgil thought. It should, he thought, have been apparent to anyone with half a brain.

Even with half a brain, Virgil thought he was probably correct.

He made a phone call to St. Paul, to Sandy, the researcher, told her what he wanted, and asked her to make some phone calls.

He finished the French toast, and the waitress came over, a young girl with dark hair and big black eyes, and smiled at him and said, "You're Virgil Flowers.'"

"Yes."

"Your two friends said I should ask you why you're called 'that fuckin' Flowers.'"

"They said you should ask because they're assholes," Virgil said.

She was taken aback, a stricken look on her face, and Virgil touched her arm as she turned away and said, "Wait, look . . . I'm sorry. I was up at that bomb this morning, and I'm still a little shook up. That's why I'm sitting here stuffing my face."

She put her hand to her face and said, "Oh, jeez . . ." and, "You've got stuff all in your hair, is that from . . ."

"Yeah, it is. And really, I'm sorry. I didn't mean to sound like a jerk," he said. "They call me that because . . . well, because I'm so good with women."

Now she ventured a tiny smile, and said, "That's what I thought," and she left him.

Virgil got an address for Wyatt's house from the sheriff's dispatcher, went that way, and found Barlow's truck outside, and a couple sheriff's cars. Barlow was inside, with O'Hara and two other deputies. He'd found some bow-hunting equipment and some camo, and showed it to Virgil.

"Not Realtree," Virgil said.

"But he had some, and he could have had some more, someplace else."

"Could have, but probably didn't," Virgil said.

"How do you know that?" O'Hara asked.

"Because he wasn't the bomber. He was murdered."

Barlow said, "Aw, man, don't start this shit again. First Erikson, now Wyatt . . ."

"Erikson led to Wyatt," Virgil said. "The bomber led us down the garden path. He wanted us to look hard at the first setup, so we'd buy the second one."

O'Hara was curious. "You know who it is?"

"Yeah, but I need another piece of the puzzle. I should get it this afternoon. I want you both to get down on your hands and knees, praying that the call comes through."

"Well, who is it?"

"I don't want to slander anyone," Virgil said. "Wait until the call comes through."

They all got pissed at him, so he slouched out to his truck, drove out to the PyeMart site, intending to do some fishing. When he got there, he found Pye looking at the footings; Chapman was looking over his shoulder.

Pye saw him getting out of the truck and said, "Well, you fucked me. And, I still gotta kiss your ass, for nailing down this Wyatt guy."

"Wyatt's not the guy," Virgil said.

Pye took a step back. "So, you fucked me, and then you fucked me again?"

"I didn't think you used that kind of language, Willard," Virgil said.

"I don't, unless somebody really fucks me," Pye said.

"I'll get the guy this afternoon. Or maybe tomorrow, depending."

"Depending on what?"

"I'll let you know about that," Virgil said. "In the meantime, keep your mouth shut about this. I only told you, because he tried to kill you."

Pye bobbed his head, and Chapman nodded.

Virgil said, "So, you're pulling the store out?"

"Sounds like it. I been all over Ahlquist, and what he says is, three city councilmen and the mayor have been suspended, and under state law, the governor is going to appoint replacements until there can be an election. The first order of bidness is gonna be to reverse the zoning changes on grounds that the former council was bribed. I don't believe it, I still gotta talk to my boy."

"Tell you what, Willard: just between you and I and Marie's potential two million readers, you bribed their asses. You know it, I know it, and Marie's two million readers know it. There's gonna be a trial, and it's all gonna come rolling out."

"Well, there will be if there's a trial—but who knows what might happen, between now and then?" Pye said, showing the slightest crinkle of a smile. "Anyway, it's time for me to get the crap outa town."

"You're not gonna stay for the ass-kissing ceremony?"

Pye looked at his watch, then asked, "When you gonna get him again?"

"Today or tomorrow. Tomorrow at the latest."

"And you won't tell me who it is?"

"Not yet," Virgil said.

"Can you tell me how you knocked it down?" Pye asked.

"Two things. You almost had a birthday party, and I was in the right place at the right time. I'll tell you the rest of it tomorrow."

Virgil was getting his fly rod out of the truck when he took a phone call from Sandy the researcher. "You were right," she said. "We've got a receipt, but they've got no video."

"Goddamnit. I don't suppose he signed his own name," Virgil said.

Sandy said, "Not unless his real name is Mick E. Maus."

25

Virgil put the fly rod away and called Ahlquist from his truck, and said, "I'm coming over. I can tell you who the bomber is, but we have to talk about how to catch him. Probably ought to have Good Thunder there, if you can get her. Somebody from the county attorney's office, anyway. Anybody you think should know. I'll call Barlow, get him in, and my two guys from the BCA."

"Fifteen minutes?" Ahlquist asked.

"Yeah, that's good. I'll see you there."

He called Jenkins and told him to bring Shrake, and Barlow. "I got my call. I think

I can tell you how it happened, and who did it."

Virgil pulled into the parking lot outside the county courthouse, left his car in a slot near the door. Shrake and Jenkins went by in Shrake's Cadillac, Jenkins lifting a hand to Virgil, and found a spot farther down the lot. Preoccupied with his thoughts about the bomber, Virgil didn't see Geraldine Gore come through the courthouse door until she shouted at him, "You dirty sonofabitch."

She was accompanied by a man in a gray suit, white shirt, and pink tie; he might as well have had an ID patch on his back that said, "Lawyer." He said, "Geraldine, Geraldine," and tried to catch her arm, but she twisted away and came steaming toward Virgil. She was carrying a big leather purse and Virgil had the feeling that she was going to swing it at his head.

She did. He stepped outside the swing, and said, "Take it easy, Mayor, for Christ's sakes."

She said, "You motherfucker," and came

back in, angrier and angrier, swung again and missed. Shrake and Jenkins came up and Shrake said, "I bet she takes him."

Jenkins said, "You're on for five. That fuckin' Flowers has got the reach on her and twenty pounds. Okay, three pounds."

Her attorney was on her by then, shouting, "Geraldine, Geraldine, stop it, stop it!" He wrestled her away, then turned to Virgil and said, "I hope you're not offended."

Jenkins jumped in: "Offended? You mean, because she committed aggravated assault, assault on an officer of the law, extortion of a witness, obstruction of justice? And those are just the felonies."

Gore screamed, "Shut up, you asshole."

Virgil said, "I forgot you guys had been introduced."

Shrake said, "Oh yeah, the three of us go way back."

The attorney: "Agent Flowers . . ."

Virgil said, "Just don't let her shoot me, when I turn my back, okay? I'm going inside."

"So we're okay?" the lawyer asked.

"Yeah, except now I need an aspirin," Virgil said.

Gore shouted, "You're gonna need more than an aspirin, you shit, you shit, you shithead, you peckerhead, you . . ."

The lawyer hauled her away, sputtering and screaming.

Shrake watched them go, then said to Virgil, "You find the most interesting crooks."

"You got an aspirin?"

They gathered in a courtroom, Virgil, Ahlquist, Barlow, Good Thunder, Shrake, Jenkins, O'Hara, and a tall fat deputy that Virgil didn't know, but who turned out to be the chief deputy, and whose name was Jeneret.

"So who is it?" Ahlquist asked. They were sitting in the court pews, with Virgil on a chair in front of them.

Virgil held up a finger. "We thought, when we started, that we could figure out who did it if we could only figure out how he got the bomb in the Pye Pinnacle. If it was an accomplice, finding the name would give us a human tie. If he placed it himself, he had to have some special skill."

"Like flying in with a motorized paraglider," Barlow said.

"Exactly," said Virgil. "A brilliant way to get in there. There was only one big problem with it."

Ahlquist: "What was that?"

"That we'd figure it out sooner or later, and it'd take us straight to the bomber. And we *would* figure it out. We looked right at a clue at Erikson's house: a garage with a pipe, Pelex, and some detonators, plus, it had a broken propeller hanging right there on the wall. A propeller from a motorized paraglider, right in front of our eyes. That, all by itself, would hang it on Erikson, except for one thing—the real bomber couldn't know where Erikson was the day before the Pye Pinnacle bombing. And he couldn't ask, because then somebody would wonder why he asked. But, it would point us at the idea of a motorized paraglider. Shrake, here, mentioned the paragliders to me, and I jumped in my truck and hauled ass out to the soaring center. One minute later, we had Erikson, and one minute after that, Wyatt."

"What about Wyatt's motive? All that money?" Barlow asked.

"Great motive, the best motive of all," Virgil said. "And hard to see. But, once we had Wyatt's name, we'd go scouting around, and we'd *find* the motive. Just a matter of time. See, the thing is, we were supposed to see that Erikson was a setup. Because that would take us to Wyatt, and nobody would believe that there were two setups."

"So who is it?" Ahlquist asked again.

Virgil held up his finger again. "So we've got means and motive. A paraglider, and land that would be worth a fortune, if PyeMart went away. Wyatt was known to be something of an asshole and something of an adrenaline junkie, somebody who could fly a glider onto the Pinnacle. I bought it. I did. But then, we searched his house, and we searched the old farmhouse out at the farm, and we found nothing at all. Nothing.

"So we send John Haden to Wyatt, with a tip that we were looking at him, hoping he'd move. We followed him around the clock, and the day after John tipped him off, Wyatt goes out to the old farmhouse, and . . . *boom*.

"I can tell you several things about that

boom," Virgil continued. "First, the bomber had no idea that Jim and I had been inside the farmhouse. Second, Wyatt went in there empty-handed. Third, the bomb was in the basement—Jim says it was, anyway."

"It was," Barlow said. "Easy to read, if you know what you're looking for."

"I believe you," Virgil said. "And Wyatt had no time to get to the basement. O'Hara knows it, and I know it. He wasn't in there more than two or three seconds, tops, when the place blew. And there were no basement steps. Getting down in that hole would have been tricky. Also, when we went in the house, I lay down on that floor and looked down the basement, and there were all kinds of spiderwebs down there. Nobody had been in the basement for a long time.

"What I think is, the bomber went down there, rigged his bomb, and then set some kind of trap that blew when you stepped on a board, or hit a trigger string, or something. There's an item here: Wyatt's head was found right in the backyard, under a piece of the roof. So, it went almost straight up. He was standing on top of the bomb when it blew."

Barlow nodded: "I'm buying that. I should have seen it."

"So who is it?" Ahlquist asked.

"John Haden," O'Hara blurted.

Ahlquist said, "Haden?"

Virgil nodded. "Yeah. John Haden."

"How'd he get in the Pinnacle?" Barlow asked.

"He didn't," Virgil said. "He went to a FedEx in Grand Rapids and sent the bomb to Pye's personal secretary. He sent it First Overnight, which means, delivery before eight-thirty A.M. And he sent it from Grand Rapids, which means there'd be no mistake." Virgil turned to Barlow. "Remember that birthday pie splattered all over the place?"

Barlow said, "I do."

"I suspect what happened is that Haden sent Pye's secretary a birthday gift, maybe even wrapped in birthday paper, with a note from somebody like a board member. The note would have said something like: *Stick this in the credenza, out of sight, so we can get it when the time comes. It's a surprise. Be sure you don't tell Willard.*

"She did that," Virgil said. "She would even have told us about it, except that she was killed."

"How'd he know about the credenza, if he'd never been in there?" Ahlquist asked.

"How do you know about anything anymore?" Virgil asked. "The Internet. There's a corporate report from last year, showing Pye and the board of directors gathered around the table in the boardroom, and the credenza is right there."

"You've got a couple long stretches in there," Good Thunder said. "It's not evidence—it's speculation. Can't really go to trial with speculation."

"It *was* speculation, but not anymore," Virgil said. "We got the receipt from FedEx. He brought the package in Tuesday night, to the FedEx store in Grand Rapids, with early guaranteed delivery to Angela Brown. We have exact measurements—it was a little bigger than a standard shoe box— and we have the weight, about eight pounds. A hefty little thing. Probably felt valuable, to Brown."

"You figured this out just on the basis of the birthday cake?" Barlow asked.

Virgil shook his head. "I'm not that smart. I figured out who did it, and then I started figuring out how he must have done it. He couldn't get the box in himself, so how would he get it in? How would he get it placed right there?"

"How did you figure out it was Haden?"

"Because Haden steered us. Looking back, I can see it, but I couldn't feel it at the time, because he's smart. I wouldn't have been able to see it later, either, just looking back. Except . . . a couple of nights ago, I called him up and said I wanted to come over and talk to him. He told me to hold off awhile, he wanted to get his girlfriend out of the house. Well, I was right there, so I parked in the street and waited for her to leave. She did and I went and talked to Haden."

"The girlfriend's important?" O'Hara asked.

"Yeah, she is," Virgil said. "Because I saw her again, this morning. She came up to the farmhouse, to see where her husband got blown up. She's Wyatt's wife."

"Son of a gun," Ahlquist said.

Virgil ticked it off on his fingers: "Haden has exactly the same problem as Wyatt, and maybe worse. He's been divorced three times, he's living in a little teeny house because his ex-wives have carved him up, he's got no money, and he's a bit of a Romeo. He knew about the land, either from Wyatt or his wife, and figured out how valuable it would be. He also knew Mrs. Wyatt would inherit, if Bill Wyatt got killed before the divorce went through. He's already nailing her—"

"That's an offensive phrase," O'Hara said.

"I kinda don't think what he was doing was love," Virgil said. "He was nailin' her."

O'Hara said, "So he tipped off Wyatt that we might be watching him, or searching him . . ."

"Just like I asked him to. He probably told him that he'd seen us out at the farmhouse, or some such thing. We won't find out now," Virgil said.

"And then he goes out there and sets the bomb," Barlow said.

"Not knowing we'd already been through the place and didn't find a bomb,"

Virgil said. "He didn't know that we were watching Wyatt around the clock—that we'd know that Wyatt couldn't have placed it himself."

Virgil held up his hand again, ticking off his fingers: "Haden had motive, he figured out a way to get a bomb inside the Pinnacle, he knew the inside of the Erikson garage, he knew that if he could keep Mrs. Wyatt rolling, she'd inherit."

Good Thunder said, "I wonder if he plans to kill Mrs. Wyatt?"

"Why not?" Virgil said. "He'd get to keep it all, if he did that."

"Totally fuckin' psycho," O'Hara said.

Ahlquist said, "You know what I've told you about that language . . ."

"Sorry, Sheriff." O'Hara hitched up her gun belt. "He almost blew me up. I'm gonna bust his ass."

Virgil said, "Not yet. There was no video at FedEx. We're sending a photo over for the night clerk to look at—we do have her signature—and maybe she'll recognize him. I kinda think not, though. I doubt that he'd go in without some kind of disguise.

A beard and glasses, whatever. He couldn't have counted on Brown getting killed, so he had to believe she'd be around to tell us about the birthday package."

They all mulled that over, and then Ahlquist said, "I expect you got a plan."

"I do," Virgil said. "It's not the brightest one in the land, so I'm looking for suggestions."

Good Thunder said, "I got a trivial question, if you don't mind. How'd you know he sent it FedEx?"

Virgil shrugged: "Would you trust a bomb to a company called 'Oops'?"

Virgil had said his plan was half-assed, and they all agreed it was: another sneak-and-peek federal warrant.

"I'm worried about it," Barlow said. "I can get the warrant, but if this guy is so smart . . . he may see us coming. There's no perfect way to get in and out of a place, if the guy's set up some telltales."

"What's that?" O'Hara asked.

Barlow said, "Little things that get disturbed. Stick hairs across your dresser drawers, with a little spit. If they're gone, somebody was there. Not something you'd notice, just searching the place."

"I got nothing else right now," Virgil said.

"We could think about it some more, but I agree with Virgil that we ought to get a warrant going," Ahlquist said. "We don't have to use it, if we think of something better. If we don't, we can at least get a look around. How about one of those bomb-sniffer things. Don't you have some sniffer things that tell you if explosive has been around?"

"Yeah, but it can be defeated. It's possible—and if he's that smart, probably likely—that he worked with the explosive somewhere besides his house," Barlow said. "Of course, if he didn't wash his clothes after he worked with it . . . we could have a shot."

"So let's get the warrant going," Ahlquist said.

"I'd like to get somebody to make an announcement that we've confirmed that Wyatt was the bomber. Make a show over at his house," Virgil said. He looked at the sheriff. "Earl?"

"Then announce tomorrow that I was lying?"

"That you were deliberately setting up the real bomber," Virgil said.

"I do like TV," Ahlquist said.

O'Hara said, "You know, with all due respect to Virgil, I've got a better idea about how to get Haden than a bullshit sneak-and-peek warrant."

She explained, and when she finished, Virgil said, "Okay. That's Plan B."

26

Haden had seen Virgil's truck too many times, so Virgil and O'Hara squeezed into O'Hara's Mini Cooper and parked it outside a house that had a For Sale sign in the front yard, a full block over from Haden's house. Virgil brought along a pair of Canon image-stabilized binoculars, and they took turns watching Haden's house; and watched a woman across the street and two houses down who wore little in the way of clothing as she vacuumed the carpeting on the other side of her living room picture window; and watched a small spotted dog that walked up and down a gutter, apparently lost.

"I gotta do something about that dog, if we don't do anything else," O'Hara said.

Virgil said, "I think I can see a collar and probably a tag . . . maybe it's just an outside dog. It's not big enough to bite anybody."

"I see you're watching Miz White Trash again," O'Hara said after a moment.

"I'm trying to figure out whether she's breaking any laws. I mean, she's apparently in her own home."

"I read about a case like this—it apparently depends on her intent. If her intent is to distract an officer of the law, or anybody else, by deliberately displaying her flesh, then she is breaking the law against indecent exposure. If she has no intent to expose herself, but the exposure is inadvertent, sporadic, or unintended, then she is not breaking the law."

"Gonna have to do more observation to determine intent," Virgil said. But he was joking; the woman actually didn't have that much going for her, in his opinion, and O'Hara knew it.

Haden first appeared outside his home

a few minutes before ten o'clock. He looked in his mailbox, then up and down the street, as if expecting the mailman, then went back inside.

"So he's up," O'Hara said.

Ten minutes later, the mailman showed up, delivering Haden's street. Haden met him at the door, took the mail, went back inside. Three or four minutes later, his garage door went up, and Haden backed into the street.

Virgil went to his cell phone: "He's out, and he's headed your way."

"We're set," Shrake said. "Hold on . . ." Then: "Okay, he just went past. Looks like he's going downtown. We're on him."

Virgil called Barlow: "He's moving. Headed downtown."

"We're still hovering out here. . . ."

Shrake called: "He's at the Wells Fargo drive-through. Jenkins will take him from here, I'm going to fall off."

O'Hara said to Virgil, "That was probably his paycheck in the mail."

"He's going to be late for class, if he doesn't hurry," Virgil said.

Shrake called again. "Jenkins is on him, he looks like he's headed over to the school."

Jenkins, a few minutes later: "He's inside the school. He was hurrying."

Virgil called Barlow: "He's at the school. Let's go."

Virgil and O'Hara arrived first. As had been the case with the other divorced suspect, William Wyatt, Haden was a renter. Virgil had gotten a key from the home's owner, and had silenced the owner with threats of life imprisonment ("accessory after the fact to four murders") if he talked to anyone about it.

They parked in the street, walked up to Haden's door, and went inside. Once in, Virgil walked around to the garage and opened the door. Barlow and two techs arrived a minute later, drove into the garage, and Virgil dropped the door again.

They did a quick walk-through, found a small shop in the basement, with the bodies of three gorgeous electric guitars hanging from the rafters.

"That's great work," one of the techs said. "This guy knows what he's doing, guitar-wise."

"He's got everything he needs to make the bombs," the other tech said. "If he's the guy, this is where he made the bombs."

They had a wheeled cart full of electronic equipment, which they'd brought into the kitchen from the garage. Now, they went back up the steps, picked it up, and carried it down the stairs. "Tell you something in five minutes," Barlow said.

While the techs ran some preliminary tests, Virgil and O'Hara cruised the main floor. Haden was a neat man. Virgil pointed out that he'd vacuumed two of the rugs in a way that left the short nap standing upright, "So that when we walk on it, we leave footprints."

"We'll re-vacuum before we leave," she said. "Of course, we'll be clothed."

They took ten minutes working from his bedroom outward, and found nothing that would point to him as a bomber; not that it was all uninteresting. They found a box that once contained a gross of ribbed, lubricated condoms, with maybe thirty left; and two vibrators, including one with a wicked hook on it. In a storage closet, they found a PSE X-Force Vendetta bow with a five-pin sight and a Ripcord fall-away arrow rest, and a batch of high-end carbon-fiber arrows, five of them set up with Slick Trick magnum four-bladed arrowheads.

In a backpack hanging in the same storage closet as the bow, they found a range of deer-hunting gear. Two bottles of scent-killing detergent sat on a shelf.

"Now," Virgil said, in his best pedantic tone, "what's wrong with this whole scene?"

"I dunno," O'Hara said. "I woulda got a Solocam, myself, but that PSE's a pretty good bow."

"What's wrong, my red-haired friend, is that he's got all this scent killer, but where's the camo he's gonna spray it on, or wash it with?"

"There is no camo," she said.

"Because he got rid of it, because he read in the paper that we found that video recorder," Virgil said. "There are no bow hunters without camo. Most of them wear it when it's anything less than ninety degrees, just to prove that they're bow hunters. His mistake was, instead of just throwing away the old stuff, he should have also bought some new camo pattern that wasn't Realtree, run it through the washer a few times, then hung it up here. That would counter what was seen on the video."

"I believe you," O'Hara said. "I also believe that if you made that argument in court, the judge would hit you on the head with her gavel."

They heard Barlow running up the stairs. They stepped out to look, and Barlow said, "Okay. He's the guy. We've got molecules of Pelex in the basement. But . . ."

"I hate that. I hate when people say 'but,'" Virgil said.

Barlow ran on: "But . . . what he did

was he scrubbed up the whole basement with some kind of strong chemical cleaners. You can still see the marks on the floor. We don't have anything physical except our test, which is good, but a defense chemist could make the argument that all we're picking up is some chemical signature of something used in the cleaners."

"Is that possible?" Virgil asked.

"Unfortunately, yes," Barlow said. "I don't believe it, in this case, but we don't know what cleaners he used. We need to check that now."

"Do we have enough to bust him?"

Barlow stroked his mustache a few times and then said, "It'd be marginal. Just the fact that he scrubbed up the basement in a rental house would tell you something. We did get that Pelex signature. If we had an aggressive prosecutor . . . and then, whatever Mrs. Wyatt could tell us, if she'd tell us anything."

"All right. We're about done up here and we didn't find much to help. Just another negative," Virgil said. He told Barlow about the missing camo.

"What does it all mean?" O'Hara asked.

"It means we may have to go to my Plan B," Virgil said.

"*Your* plan B?" Hands on her hips. "Wait a minute, buster . . ."

27

John Haden found himself in something of a trap. Not a legal trap, but a relationship trap. Sally Wyatt had come over and had thrown her . . . psyche . . . at him, after she'd come back from the scene of her husband's death. She'd been overcome with remorse, both at his death and about her relationship with Haden.

She still loved him, she said, but this death changed everything: she needed space to think, she needed time to grieve, she needed to be alone with her children. She needed help. He calmed her down, as much as he could, he let her weep, he gave her the name a grief counselor he'd heard about from another instructor whose wife had died.

"She's supposed to be really good, and as I understand it, she really did help Jeremy get through his wife's death," he'd told her, sitting beside her on the couch, one hand on her shoulder. "You think you have to go through it on your own, but you don't. It helps to have somebody who understands the fault lines of family tragedy."

As soon as she was out the door, he said aloud, "Jesus Christ, this is gonna be a pain in the ass."

The trap part of the relationship was . . . he needed to keep her close, but he wouldn't want Flowers to see them together. Actually, he didn't want anyone to see them together, at least for a while, and that wasn't easy, in a small city like Butternut Falls. So he needed her close for strategic reasons—their potential marriage—but at the same time, for tactical reasons, he now needed a little distance. At least until Flowers got out of town.

He got Flowers's cell phone number off his own cell phone and called him.

"Virg: you never called to tell me what happened out there," he complained. "Was Bill the guy? We're hearing that up at the school."

"We're about ninety-eight percent and climbing," Flowers said. "The thing we don't know is, was it an accident, or was it on purpose? There's no question that most of the remaining Pelex must've been touched off. There're pieces of that farmhouse in fuckin' Farmington. And probably far-off Faribault."

"To say nothing of freakin' Fairmont," Haden said. "Well, you know what? I'm still not sure. So when you get to a hundred percent, let me know."

"I'll do that," Flowers said. "You could buy me another beer or two."

"You're on," Haden said.

When he got off the phone, Haden got a half-full bottle of red wine from the fridge, popped the vacuum cork, and carried the bottle over to the couch, where he could think.

This whole thing would have to be carefully handled. He'd made Sally fall in love with him—that wasn't difficult. She'd needed somebody, in the biggest emotional crisis of her life, and there he was. He'd been funny, and sensitive, and sexy, had listened thoughtfully to her complaints about Wyatt, and to her intellectual and political positions.

Had argued with her, from time to time, had confessed that as a mathematician, he was sometimes pulled toward the arguments made by the Republicans about the economy. He'd only done that, though, after hearing that her father had been a longtime Republican county chairman, and figuring out that her father was a major force in her life. The old man was, thankfully, dead, so at least Haden wouldn't have to deal with that.

But.

The big But.

When their relationship came out in the open, there'd be talk. There was always talk, especially in the academic community. He could handle that, as long as it was off in the future . . . when the bomber had faded, at least a bit, from people's concerns.

He took another long pull at the wine.

Almost done, now.

Then . . . well, he knew she was going to be a pain in the ass. He'd finished the bottle of wine, and then had driven to the grocery store and stocked up on Smart Dogs and Greek yogurt, had gotten a pre-made black-bean salad and a baguette and a six-pack of Dos Equis, stopped at the coffee shop for a cappuccino. He'd had a quiet dinner, took to the couch again, to digest it, then spent ninety minutes at the Awareness Center, his yoga school.

He was in the parking lot, throwing his yoga bag back in the car, when his cell phone rang. He looked at the LCD: Sally Wyatt.

"Sally? Everything okay?" he asked. He let concern seep into his voice.

"Oh, God, that man was here. That agent. He thinks . . . I don't know what he thinks. I'm worried about . . . things."

"You want me to come over?"

"Better not. The neighbors are having a barbeque, there are people all over the street. I really don't need any . . . questions."

He mentally sighed in relief.

"Could I come over to your house?" she asked. Nearly a whimper. She was falling apart. "I sent the kids to my mom's, until I could get the funeral stuff taken care of."

"I didn't think . . . Never mind. Come over, please." He got off the phone and groaned, and then half-laughed. He'd almost said, "I didn't think there was enough left to bury." Christ, that would have been sticking his foot into it. He had to be more careful. Thinking about it, he started laughing again.

Boom!

She was there in ten minutes. When she came through the door, he went for a little squeeze, a little hug, a quick kiss on the neck, but she fended him off and perched on his easy chair. She said, "John, my God, what am I going to do? I've got no money, I've got nothing, the funeral expenses . . . and now, maybe I need a lawyer. This Flowers, he kept asking about what I thought about PyeMart and if I'd noticed anything going on in Bill's workshop. He thinks I was involved."

"I've talked to him," Haden said. "He thinks he's a pretty smart guy, but he's not as smart as he thinks he is. What you do is, you're just honest. You don't know anything about anything. If they make an actual accusation, tell them you need a public defender. But, I really don't think it'll come to that. Bill was obviously unbalanced. It's not something that two people would do."

"I can't believe . . . I lived with Bill fourteen years. He could be a jerk, but I don't see this. I'm, I'm . . ."

"Well, you know . . . the prospect of that money," Haden said.

She looked away from him. "That's something else that Flowers said. Virgil said. He tells me to call him Virgil, like he's a friend of mine, but I can tell he isn't. I can tell he's up to something. . . ." She trailed off, put her face in her hands for a moment.

He was sitting on the couch opposite her, and asked, "What was the other thing he said?"

"He said that if the town development went back the way it was, I'd be rich," she said. She wiped her eyes with the heels of her hands, one after the other. "He thought that might be a motive. He thought that was Bill's motive, and he thought it might be mine."

"What'd you say?" Haden asked.

"I told him that Bill didn't care that much about money," she said. "When the town changed direction, he just laughed it off. Said he didn't need the money for another thirty years, and by then, it'd be even more valuable."

"And what'd he say?"

"He said that was interesting," she said.

Haden looked at her for a moment, and then asked, "When did you send the kids away?"

"Right after the bomb . . . right away. Oh my God, they're going to be so messed up. Bill would come over every other day, take them out. He really was a good father. Good as he could be, anyway, you know . . . He never even said good-bye to them."

"Okay." Haden got up. "You want a beer? Or a glass of wine?"

"No . . . but I need to ask you something."

"Yeah?"

"I just remembered, you asked a lot of questions about the farm," she said. She twisted her hands together. "You know, that first night I came over. I just, I mean, you seem really interested. . . ."

He frowned. "Sally, where are you going with this?"

"Well, I don't know." Her hands flopped in her lap. "It just seemed you were always more interested in the money than Bill was, and you started talking about maybe us getting married, and I started to think . . . I mean, oh, God . . ."

He laughed. "You think *I'm* the bomber?" *This wasn't good.*

"No. No, of course not. It's just that you came on so hard with me. Nobody ever did that before. You're so good-looking and the other women, you know, are always looking at you. I wondered why you . . . I mean, I know what I look like, I'm pretty average . . . I'm not that smart . . ."

"Sally, for Christ's sakes." *That ol' sinking feeling.*

"And then . . ."

There was more? "What, what?"

"I remember last week, you were telling me how we'd slept together the night before that bomb went off at Pye's building . . . but we didn't. The bomb was on a Wednesday, and Billie has her dance line on Tuesday evening, and then her cello lesson, and we're never home before ten o'clock. It was on *Monday* we slept together. And on the way over here, I wondered why you'd even bring it up—that we'd slept together the night before the Pye building thing, when we didn't, and I thought . . . I don't know what I thought."

"That I was building an alibi?"

"I'm sorry," she said. "I'm so sorry."

"Did you tell any of this to Flowers?" Haden asked. "I really don't want him jumping down my throat."

"I didn't tell it to anyone. Nobody knows about us, not even the kids. It's so embarrassing. Bill leaves the house, and three days later I'm in bed with a friend of his. I mean . . . I'd be ruined, if my friends found out."

"Sally, people don't get ruined anymore," Haden said. "They only get ruined in Victorian novels."

"And small towns," she said. "Anyway, you didn't do it. I mean, Flowers asked if I'd been seeing anyone, and I lied and said no, and that's when all this silly stuff started going through my head. And then I started thinking, I just lied to a police officer. I think I could really be in trouble, I think I might have to go back and tell him that I was seeing somebody. I think that would be best."

Oh, shit. The whole plan goes up in smoke.

He thought, Nobody knows where she's at. Nobody knows that we've been sleeping together. If Flowers finds out, finds out I mentioned marriage . . . that would be inconvenient. If Flowers kept coming, if he ever stumbled over that FedEx store in Grand Rapids . . . and who knows what would happen if they took too close a look at that videotape? Would there be some way they could tell it wasn't Wyatt?

He felt a surge of anger, ran his hands through his hair. Hated to give it up. Hated it.

But the anger was running so hot, and the frustration. He'd been one inch away. . . .

Wyatt stood up and stepped toward him. "John," she said. "They won't care. I mean, I won't tell them, you know . . ."

He slapped her, hard, and she fell on the floor. "You bitch!" he shouted. "You're taking it right out of my pocket."

She was weeping, and trying to turn and crawl away from him. He straddled her, and dropped his weight on her hips, pinning her facedown. She cried, "You did it."

"You silly bitch. All my work. All my planning."

"I won't tell anyone," she screamed. "I won't tell anyone."

"Yes, you will. You'll tell everybody," he

said. He swatted her on the side of the face with an open hand. "Now, I want you to tell me something, and I want you to be honest about it, because if you're not honest about it, I'll catch that little bitch of a daughter of yours, and I'll spend two days raping her virgin ass, then I'll strangle her and throw her body in a ditch so the animals can eat her. You hear me? You hear me?"

He hit her again, and she sobbed, "Yes."

"Who did you tell about us?"

"No one," she sobbed. "Honest, no one, and I never will tell anyone. Just let me go, let me go, I'll never tell anyone."

"You're fuckin' lying." He hit her yet again, and her head rocked with the blow.

"Why . . . why did you kill that car man? Why?" She tried to push herself up against him, but he pinned her. "I know why you killed Bill, but why . . . that car man . . ."

"Because I needed him to lead Flowers to Bill," he said. "Now, listen, Sally, I'm really sorry about this, but I'm going to have to choke you a little—"

"Please don't do this, please don't . . ."

She thrashed against him, and he felt the hard knob in her back, and cocked his head, and frowned and she shouted, "Safety."

Haden said, "What?"

Virgil stuck his head in the door and said, "Get off her, John."

Haden, stunned, looked down at Wyatt, then back up at Virgil, his mouth open. He said, "Virgil . . ."

Virgil said, "Get off her, John."

Haden stood up and said, "She accused me—"

Virgil said, "Too late, John."

Haden took a quick step toward Virgil, as if to push him out of the way. Virgil's response was instantaneous: the punch came from somewhere behind his waistline. As it passed his shoulder, his fist was already traveling at the speed of sound— well, almost—and when it collided with Haden's beaked nose, there was an immensely satisfying crunch, at that perfect distance where your hand and knuckles don't feel it too much, and your shoulder takes up some of the recoil, and the nose guy's head rockets off your knuckles like a tennis ball flying off a racket.

Haden stumbled over Wyatt's legs and smashed into the wall, and went to his butt. O'Hara pushed past Virgil and said, "That's what happens when you resist." Jenkins was right behind her, and said, "Good punch."

Wyatt wailed, "He was on top of me, he had me by the throat, he was choking—"

At that moment, Haden, who'd rolled up on one leg, as though he were just coming to his feet, suddenly fired off the floor, like a runner coming out of the blocks. He was headed toward the patio door. . . .

Which was closed.

He hit the glass headfirst, full tilt, went through in an explosion of splintered crystal, crashed into the lawn furniture, and went down again.

Virgil and Jenkins and O'Hara were on top of him before he could recover again. O'Hara put the cuffs on.

Ahlquist had come through the front door in time to see the sprint.

Haden looked up at him, his face a mass of blood, and said, "I think . . . I think I'm really hurt."

Ahlquist bent down, looked at him for a moment, then said, "Tough titty."

28

O'Hara and five other cops, in three sheriff's cars, lights all flashing and sirens screaming, drove Haden through town to the hospital, leaving no doubt in the mind of anyone who heard them, or saw them, that the bomber had been caught.

At the hospital the docs propped up Haden's nose and sewed shut a few cuts from when he'd gone through the glass door, and then O'Hara and the escort cops drove him with sirens screaming and lights flashing through town to the jail, and locked him up.

When all that was done—it took three

hours—Virgil and Ahlquist, O'Hara, Barlow, Theodore Wills, the county attorney, Good Thunder, Pye, and Chapman took part in an hour-long press conference jammed with TV, newspaper, and online reporters, and the one public radio reporter with his recorder and microphone. Ahlquist wore a silky pale blue suit from Nordstrom and served as master of ceremonies, giving broad credit to Virgil, Barlow, and O'Hara for cracking the case.

When they were all done, Ahlquist took the stage back from Wills, who was the final speaker, to shout, "We're all headed down to Bunson's, folks. You're all invited."

They all trekked down to Bunson's and Pye stood on a table to announce that it was all on PyeMart, and got half-and-half boos and cheers, and one fat guy who shouted he'd never drink Pye's beer. The fat guy was wrestled out of sight by the Aussie scuba diver, whose name Virgil couldn't remember.

He did remember the name of the short-haired scuba blonde with the snake tattoo down her neck—Gretchen—and he said, "Hey, Gretchen: How'd you find us?"

"Retrief can smell free beer from miles away," she said. "I was going to call you up. I'd like to hear about your muskie research project. . . ."

They talked about that for a while, and Virgil found her to be intelligent, well informed, and stacked. She touched his chest: "Slobberbone—I haven't seen one of their shirts since UNT. They're one of my favorite bands."

George Peck showed up, and patted Virgil on the back and said, "Told you."

Virgil said, "George, I'm gonna have somebody contact you about this whole market research thing. We need to write something about it for the FBI or somebody."

"I would be flattered," Peck said. Peck was wearing a gray banker's chalk-striped suit, a blue shirt, and a bright yellow necktie. He was on his third Rusty Nail and muttered, "I don't think Pye saw the sign outside of town."

"What sign?"

"The one that says, 'Butternut Falls—a Little Drinking Town with a Nasty Fishing Habit.' This free booze thing will cost him a fortune. I'm soaking up as much as I can, before he calls it off."

Somebody put Willie Nelson's *Stardust* album on the Bunson's sound system, and people started dancing on the lakeside patio to "Georgia on My Mind."

Virgil danced with Gretchen, the snake girl, and then O'Hara, and then took Good Thunder and Chapman around the floor, scuffling along in his cowboy boots, thinking only rarely of Lee Coakley.

Barlow stuck strictly to beer, and was mostly sober when he got Virgil in a corner and asked, "You think we got him? You know, enough for a trial?"

Virgil nodded. "There's enough circumstantial evidence, backing up our recording. If they got the tapes thrown out for some reason, we'd have a problem, but everything was on the up-and-up, so I don't see how they can do that."

"I talked to Charlie—one of the techs—and he says Haden's computer history was wiped, but he forgot about the cookies. He was looking at bomb sites—"

Virgil interrupted: "But he could always say that he got interested when the bombings started in Butternut, and did some research."

Barlow shook his head and continued: ". . . and some of the cookies go back before the Pye Pinnacle."

"That's large," Virgil said. "That's very large."

A part of the crowd began running and screaming and they looked that way, and then somebody came back and said, "George Peck fell in the lake. He's okay. Just drunk."

Jeanne Shepard came ghosting through the crowd. She looked tired, but relaxed, wore a sheer white blouse and turquoise Capri pants and sandals, and looked, as Thor the desk clerk once told Virgil, like the second-hottest woman in town. She nodded at Virgil, and then came over and said, "I hope you don't mind if I'm here. I heard about John Haden, and you know . . . I wanted to hear more."

"Hey, you're more than welcome," Virgil said. "Join right in. Let me get you a drink."

He got her a Bloody Mary and a thoroughly soaked George Peck lurched over and said to her, "Jeanne, nice to see you. With Jesus Christ as my witness, I say to you, I am seriously fucked up."

"Why, George," she said, "I've never heard such language." To Virgil: "George and I once dated."

They turned away, talking about old times, and Virgil drifted off; a few seconds later, Thor the desk clerk idled into the room, wearing cargo shorts and a Third Eye Blind T-shirt. When Virgil saw it, he said, "God bless me: I will give you one hundred dollars for that T-shirt."

"I could get three times that on eBay," Thor said. He had a toothpick in one corner of his mouth, and a drink in his hand.

Virgil looked at it and asked, "How old are you again?"

"Eighteen. But I'm a jock, so it's okay," Thor said. "I'm just keeping an eye on that little heifer." He was watching Jeanne Shepard.

"I don't want to hear about it," Virgil said.

"Well, if you heard about it, you'd probably change your mind and say you were glad you heard about it," Thor said.

Virgil began, "Listen, Thor—"

"I don't need a lecture," the kid said. "We're running really hot right now. I figure it'll last for most of the summer, then she'll go back to teaching school and I'll go off to college and that'll be it. But I sure don't need any sermonizing. I mean, it's just too good."

"I was gonna tell you, don't drink too much—I once had a few beers and ran my old man's car into a ditch and missed a big old cottonwood by about six inches. I was very lucky I didn't kill myself," Virgil said. "Scratched the hell out of the passenger-side door."

"Semper fi," Thor said. "Jeez, you know, Jeanne's got an ass like . . ." He stopped, his voice trailing away, then he whispered, "Jesus God: Who's the chick with the snake on her neck?"

Late in the evening, Ahlquist hooked Virgil's arm and dragged him into a room behind the bar, saying, "You gotta take a minute."

When they got back there, they found Chapman and Pye, Barlow and Peck and O'Hara, and Pye said, "It's an ugly thing to have to do, but I'm a man of my word and I'm willing to pay up."

At that point, Virgil took part in an unusual ceremony, wildly applauded by the spectators. Pye muttered, "Now I really need a drink," and O'Hara said to Virgil, "You gotta nice ass there, surfer boy."

Chapman wrote it all down.

The party went on for a while, but at some point after midnight, Virgil found himself sitting on his motel bed, talking to Davenport, a night owl, who'd seen cuts from the press conference on the late news.

"Get that cleaned up as fast as you can—we've got some trouble down in Wabasha," Davenport said.

"Somebody's dead?"

"Well, since they only found the feet,

they're not sure. But, that's what they suspect," Davenport said.

"Ah, man, how old?"

"Six, eight weeks. The newest two, anyway," Davenport said.

"The newest two?"

"Yeah, they found three feet. People down there are talking cannibals."

"Ah, boy . . ."

Davenport said, "I can hear a shower running . . . so . . . I guess I'll hang up now. But call me tomorrow, as soon as you're clear of the Haden thing. You gotta get down to Wabasha."

"All right . . . tomorrow, I'll let you know."

Virgil sat on his bed, naked, a bottle of Leinie's on the nightstand, a white towel over his thighs. Listened to the shower, and thought, So damn many good women in the world. Chapman and Gretchen the snake woman, Good Thunder and even O'Hara. Lee Coakley, for sure.

He sighed, and stood up, headed for the bathroom. The fact was, Davenport had called just as he was adjusting the temperature control. There was nobody else in the shower.

Nobody but Virgil, a little drunk, looking up at a showerhead at the Holiday Inn, on a starry night in beautiful downtown Butternut Falls, Minnesota.